GHOST

Peter Barsocchini

GHOST

E. P. DUTTON NEW YORK

Published in the United States by E. P. Dutton,
a division of NAL Penguin Inc.,
2 Park Avenue, New York, N.Y. 10016.

Published simultaneously in Canada by
Fitzhenry and Whiteside, Limited, Toronto.

Library of Congress Cataloging-in-Publication Data

Barsocchini, Peter, 1952–
Ghost / Peter Barsocchini. — 1st ed.
p.   cm.
ISBN 0-525-24739-4
I. Title.
PS3552.A745G47 1989
813'.54—dc19   88-25638
CIP

Designed by Steven N. Stathakis

1 3 5 7 9 10 8 6 4 2

First Edition

To my mother and my father.
For everything.

ACKNOWLEDGMENTS

Helpful comments on early drafts came from Sara Davidson, John Dodds, and Adam Linter. Thanks to Virginia Barber for support and good literary guidance that extends beyond the duties of an agent. Special thanks to Dick Marek, for belief and expertise, and his willingness to share them in great quantities.

PART

1

He was a small figure against the night, invisible to the cars driving past the wood and stucco church. The fumes from the plastic gasoline containers he carried made him feel nauseated. But he worked quickly. Earlier in the day, he had surveyed the old church, studying it in a way he had never done on any Sunday. Its sanctuary was supported by a web of exposed wooden beams. He planned to ignite them from outside and let the beams burn through to the sanctuary within.

The boy climbed up the rear wall of the church, carrying one of the containers with him. He soaked two of the beams with gasoline, then climbed down for the other container. At the base of each beam he built small pyres of gasoline-soaked cloth and kindling. He used his T-shirt to clean his hands. Then he dropped a match on the first pile. It flashed into flame, and the flame traveled up the beam, turning it into a strip of fire. He lit the other rag piles, then dropped to the ground and ran to the curb. The flames were climbing the beams, which started to crackle. He stood for several seconds, staring at the fire, surprised by its sudden success. Then he darted toward a dark corner building across the street and watched traffic on Lankershim Boulevard in North Hollywood coagulate at the sight of fire. Motorists slowed their cars for a better view, others sped away on a side street. One elderly Mexican man drove his truck right up on the sidewalk, jumped out, and grabbed the pay telephone in front of the building.

The fire had passed the reach of the gasoline, spreading to

the wooden trim that surrounded the dome over the sanctuary. The growing crowd of spectators watched the crown of flames illuminate the summer night sky. The sound of this fire, a dull, rolling roar, surprised the onlookers as flames were sucked into the sky, matter changing into heat and smoke then disappearing in the night. You could see the primal fear evoked by fire in the spectators' eyes. It was a church, after all, a church was burning. Sirens, at first a distant whine, began closing in.

The stained-glass window behind the altar started glowing. The boy saw the glow and knew then that the fire had spread within, enfolding the sanctuary in flames; pieces of burning wood fell into the empty church, igniting prayer books and hymnals that were stacked in the pews. He walked to the corner and away from the church. Fire trucks passed him, sirens wailing and red lights spinning. He did not turn around to look after them.

2

Thomas "Ghost" Galvin—he picked up the nickname in high school, the only white player on the basketball team—stood alone at the bay window in the second-floor library of his Beverly Hills estate. He had turned out the light so that his guests, who were filling up the backyard terrace below, could not see him. The party sprawled throughout the first floor of the house, spilling guests onto the terrace and the patio by the pool. Waiters and waitresses, clad entirely in white, carried trays of canapés and bottles of champagne. A string quartet filled the summer evening with Mozart and Schubert. Out in the tented tennis court the rock-and-roll band Fast Magic waited its turn to play. Ghost glanced at the pink message form, delivered to him minutes before by his secretary, Miss Dupree. He looked at it as if he expected to see more than simply a name and number because of who it was from; he was certain there was a specific message to go with it. Then he slipped it into his pocket and continued watching his guests.

"Have you seen him?" one of the waitresses asked another, pausing at the terrace bar.

"No," the other answered. "I've seen everyone else, though. Can you believe who's here?"

"I want to meet Ghost. I've seen the rest of them."

"You just want to *meet* him?"

Looking down at the terrace, it was easy for Ghost to pick out his special guests, his teammates from the Los Angeles Lakers of the National Basketball Association. The shortest of them was Ghost, at six feet four inches; the others ranged in height from six feet five to over seven feet. The Lakers were this year's world champions, and Ghost their leading scorer.

The limousine carrying James Hardin, owner of the Lakers, and his guest, Rebecca Blesser, arrived at the gates of the estate. The estate was hidden from the street by eucalyptus and elm trees, and by an ivy-covered iron fence. It was a three-story Georgian mansion, surrounded by lawns and gardens. Night-blooming jasmine and bougainvillea hung from the balconies like tired ballerinas.

A butler waited on the portico to greet guests. Recognizing Hardin, he sent for Miss Dupree.

"I'm sure I'll be the only person here who doesn't have a tan," Rebecca said, as the limousine rolled up the long driveway.

"Not everyone in Los Angeles is tan," Hardin said.

"Yes they are."

Valets opened the doors of the limousine, and the butler walked down the steps.

"Madame, Mr. Hardin," he said, "welcome to Mr. Galvin's home."

A maid took Rebecca's linen jacket, worn over a cream-colored silk dress.

Miss Dupree was waiting for them in the foyer. She was in her early fifties, crisply dressed in a dark gray Chanel suit; her eyes were dark like the suit, and her short, dark hair stood out against her pale skin.

"Let me introduce you to Rebecca Blesser," Hardin said, greeting Miss Dupree. "Miss Dupree is Ghost's assistant," he said to Rebecca.

Miss Dupree stood at arm's length, offering a slight nod of her head, rather than shaking hands, and looked at Rebecca as if she were a delivery that Miss Dupree was not prepared to accept.

"We spoke on the telephone, I believe," Miss Dupree said to Rebecca. "Unfortunately, I wasn't able to accommodate your request for an interview with Mr. Galvin."

"I still hope to arrange that."

"I'll let Mr. Galvin know that you're here, Mr. Hardin," Dupree said. She walked away, heels clicking on the glossy parquet floor.

"That was a frosty greeting," Rebecca said, walking with Hardin toward the terrace.

"Maybe she doesn't like attractive young women," Hardin said. "I'm used to her. Anyway, when you deal with Ghost Galvin, first you deal with Miss Dupree."

They were handed glasses of champagne, and drank a toast to the evening.

"You know, I read that article you did on adoption," Hardin said. "I had my secretary look it up after we met. She tells me you were awarded a prize for it."

"That came as a surprise."

"A well-deserved one."

The cover story, published in *Time*, was entitled "Finding Out: Adoption in America," and it used Rebecca's unsuccessful search for her birth parents as a model for the difficulties faced by many adoptees who wish to investigate their origins.

"I've been asked to turn it into a book," Rebecca said.

"I would have thought the article might have brought your parents forward."

"That hasn't happened."

"The other night at the Forum you mentioned a new article," Hardin said.

"I'm including Senator Galvin in a piece that I'm working on," she said.

Rebecca had met Hardin in the press lounge during one of the Lakers' play-off games; at fifty, Hardin was one of the city's prominent bachelors.

"It's nearly ten years now since the senator died," Rebecca added.

Hardin seemed surprised, and wary.

"Why him?"

"*Life* is doing a special issue on prominent Americans whose careers were cut short. Senator Galvin was well on his way to becoming vice-president when he died."

"He had a heart attack, I believe," Hardin said.

"Does his son ever talk about it?" she asked.

Hardin took a sip of champagne and looked carefully at Rebecca. "If this is an interview, no comment."

6

Her face softened. "No, it's not. I'm sorry."

"You should have told me you called Ghost for an interview," Hardin said to her.

A waiter arrived with more champagne.

As she took a glass from the tray, Rebecca could see the small, rigid figure of Miss Dupree watching her from inside the house.

3

The two waitresses went looking for Ghost. One carried champagne, the other a tray of raw vegetables. They worked through the first floor, then took a service stairway to the second.

"If Mr. Sommers finds us," the one girl said, "we're dead." She was tall, with ebony skin and hair done in tight cornrows.

"He won't find us," the other girl said; this one was blonde, with a compact surfer's figure, all bounce and tone and teeth. "If Sommers finds us, we'll just say someone told us to bring champagne and snacks up here."

All the doors on the floor were closed, except the one to the library. The blonde girl pushed it open.

Ghost turned at the sound.

"I'm sorry, Mr. Galvin. We were told to bring these trays up here. We'll get out of your way."

"Come on in," he said, reaching for a light switch.

"You have an absolutely incredible house," the blonde girl continued, setting her tray on a coffee table. "My name is Ivy and this is Julie."

"How do you do, girls," he said. "Why don't you have a glass of champagne with me?"

"We're not allowed," Julie said.

"I'm paying the bills," Ghost said. "You're allowed."

He popped the cork, filled three glasses, then plopped into an overstuffed leather chair in the center of the room. "Here's one of my best toys," he said, opening a box on the coffee table. It contained a bank of control buttons. He pushed the first; two bookcases slid apart, revealing a small electronics room. Another button activated a tape machine, and Blondie's "Dreaming" began blasting from hidden wall-mounted speakers. Ghost turned a dial in the box, dimming the room's lights; another button closed then opened the curtains over the bay window; he felt like he could do that for hours, push the buttons and listen to the music, rather than call the number on the message form in his pocket—the judge wouldn't call him at night with any kind of good news.

Julie refilled their glasses with champagne.

"I'd love to see you girls dance," Ghost said. "I'll bet you two can really dance."

"Julie's a good dancer," Ivy said.

"I knew it."

"Actually, we're both actresses."

"Why not," Ghost said. "But who wants to talk when you can dance?"

"Will you dance *with* us?" Julie asked.

"I'll do it," he said.

Blondie's album moved into "One Way or Another." The girls kicked off their shoes and started dancing. Ghost emptied the bottle into their glasses, then opened another.

"I knew you girls were dancers," he said, standing to join them. "I knew it."

Dancing on the library's thick carpet wasn't easy, but the music and champagne made it seem so. Ghost danced around the room, pausing for champagne whenever he passed the coffee table. The girls, mesmerized by his supple movement, followed him, like satellites. They moved closer so they could touch him. The song changed to "Darling"; the girls embraced Ghost from either side, swaying to Deborah Harry's smoky voice. He picked the bottle of champagne from the table and took a swig, then handed it to the girls. Ivy slid a hand across Ghost's chest, Julie lifted the shirt tails from his trousers and ran a hand over his muscular back. "That's good," Ghost said, unable to remember the girls' names, "that's very good."

Downstairs, guests flowed through the house to the terrace, out to the pool and the tented court. Ghost recognized many of them: the agents and actors, producers and executives. His teammates were there, too, most with their families joining them to share in the celebration of the championship. Moving to the music, Ghost closed his eyes, while the girls removed his clothes and their own. Dancing brought a sheen of sweat to their bodies; the girls felt smooth and warm against Ghost. He allowed them

8

to surround him, suspend thought by the press of their flesh. Bracing herself against the window seat, Ivy guided Ghost into her; Julie held him from behind, trickling champagne onto his back and spreading it with her lips. Ghost hummed the "Darling" melody. The girls moved with the beat of the song, switching positions after a while. Ivy found another bottle of champagne in the room's refrigerator. Ghost took a long pull from it, holding Julie with a powerful arm. "Room with a View" blasted from the speakers. Ghost rocked his head back and closed his eyes, moving with his unseen partner, until finally he slumped forward on the window seat, the girls formed around him like sculpture. Sounds from the party outside reentered his brain, and he realized that the Blondie album had finished playing. With the sounds of scattered voices, memory of the message form folded in his coat pocket returned to Ghost, and the lightness he'd felt with the girls disappeared.

Ghost saw James Hardin standing by the bar on the terrace. Rebecca Blesser stood next to him. She looked up at the house. Ghost knew she could not see him, yet he felt the intensity of her dark eyes, and sensed a familiarity in her eyes and in her face, though he knew he had not met her.

Still clinging to Ghost, Ivy and Julie saw who he was looking at.

"Is she someone famous?" Ivy asked.

"I don't know her," Ghost answered.

"She can't see us, can she?"

"No."

He stood and started dressing, feeling the residue of Rebecca's gaze upon him.

"I suppose I better get down to my party," he said.

"Don't forget," Ivy said, "I'm Ivy and that's Julie."

"You should come over and use the pool sometime," Ghost said absently.

"That would be great."

"Just call and come on over."

"Okay, I'll just say it's Ivy and Julie," she said.

Ghost nodded, though he hadn't heard what she said, as he was on his way out of the room.

The girls went into the bathroom to dress.

Miss Dupree appeared in the doorway.

"I think it's time for you to return to work," she said to them, and waited in the library until the girls went downstairs.

4

For thirty-five years Judge Davis Ely kept the same key to the Galvin home, in the resort community of Nippersink, Wisconsin. People never changed locks in this region of lush farmlands, dairy pastures, and rolling properties with white fences that looked like part of the land. The judge lived on the shores of Lake Geneva, several miles from Nippersink, but knew the resort well, with its Tudor-style lodge and guest bungalows, and its dark little Lake Tombeau, where guests fished for bass and bluegill; the resort's original owners had given the lake its name in memory of their son, who had drowned in it.

The private homes within Nippersink's boundaries were old and solid and owned for many years by families from Chicago, who used them weekends and summers. At the lodge, the same guests checked in year after year and knew many of the home-owners and locals.

When Judge Ely went to see Marie Galvin, Ghost's grandmother, this humid and hot June evening, he knocked on the door, then, without waiting for a response, used his key to open it. He found Marie sitting on the couch in the living room. The television was on but she wasn't watching it. In her lap were some old letters that she had been reading.

"You look like you're cold, Marie," Judge Ely said to her.

At first, she didn't recognize him. She turned her failing liquid blue eyes toward his approaching figure.

"It's Davis," he said gently.

"Judge," she replied, awareness returning to her face, "I hated to bother you."

"Bother me, honey? Don't be silly."

Her familiar chest pains were worse than usual this evening, prompting her to call the judge.

"I couldn't get out of this chair," she said to him. Then she pointed to the telephone on the table in front of her, and added, "That's as far as I could go. I couldn't get out of the chair to take my medicine."

"You know you can call me anytime day or night, rain or shine," he said. "You *know* that."

"Well, I hate this," she answered. "I hate not being able to get out of this chair."

He sat down on the couch. "Remember," he said, "how we all used to love sitting here on nights like this? Just sitting here with gin-and-tonics and lots of ice, all the windows open, crickets going a mile a minute and the lightning bugs. We'd hear Thommy bouncing his basketball out on the porch in the dark. Remember how he used to practice his dribbling out there in the dark just so he'd get the feel of the ball?"

"That was a long time ago," she said testily.

"Can't you just picture it, though?" the Judge said, patting one of her bony thighs. "I see it like yesterday, right in front of my eyes. You know, I like thinking about it because I miss senator Thom every day of my life, just the way you do. Every day of my life. And the hell with people who say you shouldn't spend time talking about the past. When I was young I swore, like everyone else, that I wouldn't get old and think about the past. But there's an awful lot about the past that's better than the present, isn't there? When you're young, you don't appreciate that fact. The past's just not important to you then because you don't have one. But later on, later on . . ."

"I can't fix you a drink," Marie Galvin said, "because I can't get myself up. But you can fix yourself one."

He walked over to the bar in the open dining room and poured himself a gin-and-tonic in a tall glass. The judge looked back at Marie and thought how tiny and frail she looked, sitting in that chair. It's awful, he thought, the way nothing good happens to old people at night. They sit and watch television, play cards, read, but nothing much good happens to them. You're old, he thought, when you stop looking forward to night.

Marie waited until she heard the sounds of the judge cracking open the ice tray, then she gathered together the letters from her lap, bound them with a rubber band, and slipped them into the drawer of the lamp table next to the couch. She had been rereading some letters written to her by the senator during the final months of his life, but she did not want to talk to the judge about that right now.

"Thommy is having a party tonight," Marie said, when the judge returned.

"Yes, he sent me an invitation," the judge said, "it's nice of him to do that."

"He told me he'd fly me out there. I'm still scared to death of airplanes. He knows I won't fly."

"Well, it's just nice to know he was thinking of us."

Judge Ely lifted his drink from the table. He was looking through the screened-in porch, and could see the outline of the

11

willow tree at the top of the yard. He said, "So, how have the card games been? Sheriff Baines hasn't closed you down yet?"

"We're still playing. I haven't lost the house yet."

"That's good. I know you love those games."

"It gives me a chance to visit with the girls."

Judge Ely nodded. "And how have you been feeling? In general, I mean."

"I get so tired," Marie said. "That's what I hate. I'm always tired."

She played canasta on Tuesdays with three lady friends. The judge knew all of them. Mary Boylen had called and told him that Marie was now falling asleep at times during the games, that it was hard for her to keep a train of thought, and lately she'd been talking about the senator. Since the senator's death, Marie Galvin had said little about him, at least until recently; she had never been one to reminisce.

But Mary Boylen had told the judge that Marie was now talking about the senator, and not remembering having done it. He would have let that go, too, except for the fact that he'd gotten a call from Rebecca Blesser. Of course he declined the interview request, but then Marie got a call. She referred the call to the judge, who did not hear again from Miss Blesser. But then he learned that Miss Blesser had turned up in Nippersink, and had met with Marie Galvin. So he visited Marie and asked her about Miss Blesser. But Marie could hardly remember meeting her, and remembered nothing of what they'd discussed.

Judge Ely finished his gin-and-tonic.

"Let's get you to bed," he said, gently guiding Marie out of the chair. Her slippers scraped across the wooden floor, a dirgelike sound that went on and on and on. He walked her to her bedroom, and helped her off with her robe and into bed.

"Tomorrow you'll feel better."

"I'm supposed to take two pills from each bottle," she said to him. "They're in the kitchen on the counter."

"I know."

"Oh, yes. You do take me to the doctor every week, don't you? Too bad they don't have pills for memory. Well, I guess you don't have to have a good memory as long as you've got friends who do."

She patted him on the arm.

"I'll tell you, Judge, when my son was alive we had more friends than I could count. But now I can count them."

12

"Friendships don't end when people die. That's when they get tested. You've got all the friends you need. The right kind of friends, I'm talking about. Now get yourself comfortable."

He went to the kitchen, drew a glass of water, then took a small plate from the cabinet. There were several bottles of pills on the counter, all of which he was familiar with, having sat with Marie when the doctor explained what to take at what time. It was the judge, in fact, who insisted Marie make the weekly trips to see her doctor, and whenever the judge visited he checked the pill bottles to make sure she was taking the heart medication. Now, he looked at the small plastic cylinders of pills, but did not open them. Removing a plastic bag from his pocket, the judge dropped four sleeping pills onto the plate. He thought about the thousands of criminals who had stood before him in court, awaiting sentencing for crimes that ranged from shoplifting to multiple murders; he had listened to all the stories and all the reasons and explanations that people had for killing other people. There were thousands of reasons people killed. For profit, for their country, self-defense, by accident, pure anger—thousands of reasons. Dozens of laws against killing existed, but people killed for thousands of reasons. It was left to the juries and judges to sort them all out. Certain of the reasons people killed were complex and fantastic, others brutal and simple. As a society we tended to protect, he knew, the kind of killers we silently and secretly envisioned ourselves as being: killers for revenge, passion, of mercy, killers for right reasons. The judge had spent enough years on the bench to know that, regardless of written laws, most people possess private codes of morality when it comes to killing. By now Judge Ely could look in a defendant's eyes and know which side of right they were on, regardless of the verdict, regardless of the law.

The judge brought the pills and a glass of water to the bedroom. Marie swallowed them one at a time, then put her head down on the pillow.

"Thank you," she said. "My lady friends are in bed by eight. I'd be in trouble if I had to rely on them. Now go home and tell Eleanor we're not having an affair."

"Oh, I like to keep her on her toes."

"It's kind of silly going to bed this early, isn't it?"

"You're tired."

"No wonder I can't make it to my grandson's party. I'm in bed as soon as it gets dark outside, and he stays up all night. It

13

would be better for him to just settle down. He gets that from his father, never settled."

"A United States senator doesn't get much chance to settle, does he?"

"That's not what I mean."

He looked at her and felt sad; she had never talked like this.

"Good night's sleep will do us all good," he said.

"Good night," she said. "Thank you again for helping out."

"God bless."

The Judge looked at the Galvin family photographs that were under the glass of Marie's vanity table. He saw the senator and the senator's wife, Nicole, and there were pictures of Ghost and Marie, and even a few of himself. All good memories, he thought, preserved in captured light, a record of the past to be cared for amidst a world that attacks things of value, a world empty of respect for permanance. Some of the photographs were old and fading, like the last light from a dead star, light that travels through space waiting for absorption to give it purpose. The judge had read about a process that seals photographs from oxidation, and he now made a mental note to look into that further.

He turned out the light and walked quietly out of the room. He fixed himself another gin-and-tonic, then sat in the living room, listening to the crickets and the natural noises of the old house.

"God bless," he said, again, settling down in the chair, knowing that Marie had loved her son, the senator, deeply, and would want nothing to wound the memory of him, would abhor the idea of anything picking away at the senator's reputation and accomplishments; in that sense, he felt he was protecting her wishes by causing her death. The judge was certain Marie would rather die than unknowingly say something irretrievable to Ghost about the senator. So this did not seem like killing to him; this was preserving, giving, keeping.

By now, the pills had dropped Marie into a dreamless sleep. Her body didn't stir when the judge returned to the bedroom, put a pillow over her face, and held it there while the life went out of her. He wept at the simplicity of the act, and its rightness.

5

At Miss Dupree's cue, the string ensemble delivered a hasty crescendo. The estate's lights dimmed, and from out on the tennis court the rock band kicked into a bright medley of reggae music. Platoons of waiters fanned through the crowd with magnums of champagne and, while the drinks were being dispensed, the band built the tempo of the music. A spotlight hit the terrace doorway, and Ghost made his first appearance of the night. Raising a fluted glass, he faced James Hardin. The music stopped.

"A toast to our guest of honor who built this team, made it a winner, and made all of this possible," Ghost said, speaking in the steady tones of one used to being listened to. He waved toward the tent, cueing the band into a rocked-up version of "Proud Mary," while a line of exotic dancers, wearing teddies designed like Laker uniforms, snaked out of the guest house, parading past the pool, through the cheering guests, and up the stone steps, until they flanked Hardin. Two other dancers wheeled out a cake made in the shape of the NBA championship trophy. The music stopped to allow Hardin to make his own toast.

"Those were kind words, Ghost, and as usual it's a hell of a party you've got going here. All the guys on the team made this season possible, and I'm proud of each and every one of them. I pay them too much money, but I love them anyway. I think we *all* are in agreement that there are great players, and then there is Ghost Galvin, who is something else altogether. Cheers!"

The band started in while Hardin cut the cake. Purple and gold skyrockets exploded over the house, and the dancers ringed the pool. A single spotlight focused on Ghost, who now held a basketball. Winding up, he threw it in a high, long arc, and when it splashed down in the center of the pool, another volley of skyrockets exploded, and the dancers dove as one into the water.

When the lights came up, Hardin shook Ghost's hand and said, "Holy bejesus, you've outdone yourself, kid. Now I want you to meet my date." He turned to Rebecca. "This is Rebecca Blesser. Rebecca, Ghost Galvin."

"How do you do," she said, extending her hand, eyes mapping his face.

"It's a pleasure." The scrutiny of her eyes made him feel uncomfortable.

"I've been admiring your home and the grounds," she said.

"Thank you. I can't take much credit for it. My secretary handles the house. I just sign the checks. Have a look around, if you like. Have you been inside?"

"Just the entry."

"Miss Dupree will show you around, if you're interested."

"I'd like that."

He summoned a waiter and sent for Miss Dupree.

Ghost asked her, "Will you show Miss Blesser the house? She admires what you've done with it."

"Much of it is closed for the party," Miss Dupree said.

"That's all right," Ghost replied, surprised and irritated by Miss Dupree's reluctance. "Give her the cook's tour anyway."

When the women walked away, Hardin said to Ghost, "What's Miss Dupree got a bug up her ass about?"

"I don't know. Who's Rebecca?"

"She was at a couple of the play-off games. I met her in the Forum Club. Big New York writer."

"Sports?"

"No."

"Attractive."

"Not one of my usual bombshells, you mean," Hardin laughed.

"Exactly."

"I hope I'm not being hustled. She's writing something about your father," Hardin said.

"I don't understand."

"*Life* magazine is doing something about important Americans who died young. She's writing about your father."

"He died ten years ago," Ghost said. "What's to write about now? She's my age, what would she know about my father's life?"

Hardin shook his head.

"I don't like it," Ghost said.

"Listen, I had no idea this was what she was up to. I don't like it either. She seemed kind of nice."

"She looked at me like we'd met before," Ghost said.

"Don't all women look at you that way?"

Ghost smiled.

Hardin said, "I'll get rid of her."

"She's probably got Miss Dupree tied up in a closet and she's rifling the house," Ghost said.

"I think that idea excites you."
They both laughed.

6

"Some furniture has been moved to accommodate the party," Miss Dupree said, escorting Rebecca into the living room. The floor was herringbone patterned oak, bleached white with Chinese rugs throughout.

"I like that painting," Rebecca said, cutting through the crowded room. The painting hung above the fireplace. It was an Impressionist work of a cornfield, green-gold stalks reaching to a cerulean sky.

"Is the artist well known?" Rebecca asked Dupree.

"I wouldn't think so," Miss Dupree replied. "No."

"Is this something Mr. Galvin found himself?"

"Yes." She turned to lead Rebecca out of the room.

"Who's the artist?" Rebecca asked, catching up with Miss Dupree.

"A gentleman from Wisconsin, a local artist."

"From Nippersink?" Rebecca asked.

Miss Dupree slowed but did not turn around. "I really don't know," she said. The word *Nippersink* had hit her.

"Have you been there?" Rebecca asked.

"Wisconsin?"

"Nippersink."

"No, I haven't."

"It's a lovely area. I was there on a story recently. I can see why Mr. Galvin would select that painting. Out in the farm country near Nippersink everywhere you look you see cornfields."

"I'm told it's lovely."

Miss Dupree led Rebecca through a sun room that jutted into the rose garden. They toured the billiards room, downstairs library, dining room, and kitchen, then took the service stairway up to the third floor to look at the guest suites and warming kitchen. Miss Dupree kept a measured distance between herself and Rebecca, as if she did not want the least risk of physical contact.

"Have you been with Mr. Galvin a long time?" Rebecca asked.

"It isn't necessary to discuss my employment."

"He seems to rely on you for almost everything."

"I try and do my job satisfactorily. We'll go down to the second floor now. And, Miss Blesser, I really do not want to discuss myself or my employer. I'm sure you understand that such a thing is not well thought of. Nor do I think well of a journalist arranging an invitation to a party in lieu of an interview."

She started down the stairway, Rebecca following.

"I don't mean to confuse curiosity with my job," Rebecca said.

"I see."

"It's just that after spending the past two months researching the life of Senator Galvin, I have some curiosity about his son. The senator was quite an extraordinary man. Do you know much about him?"

"No. These are Mr. Galvin's living quarters. His library is in there, bedroom down here, the dressing area connects through there." She waited in the hallway while Rebecca walked through the rooms; Rebecca felt the force of Miss Dupree's eyes following her from room to room.

"Mr. Hardin will be waiting for you," Miss Dupree said when Rebecca walked out of the library.

She escorted Rebecca down to the terrace, then went to the downstairs library and locked the door. Miss Dupree sat in a chair facing the massive wooden desk in a corner of the room. It was the only piece of furniture that had been in Ghost's family. The desk was from the senator's office in Washington, and bore a brass plate affixed to the front of it bearing the seal of the state of Illinois.

Miss Dupree stared at the desk for a couple of minutes, then picked up the phone, punched in the private line, and dialed the operator, placing a long distance, person-to-person call, charged to another number. She placed the call to Judge Davis Ely. Judge Ely, however, was not at home.

7

Rebecca did not see Hardin or Ghost on the terrace. She wandered out past the pool, to the estate's guest house, and let herself in. The living room was filled with clothes and carry bags belonging to the dancers, who were still out in the pool. Floorboards creaked as Rebecca walked down the hall. The first room she came to appeared to be Miss Dupree's office, with its gunmetal gray filing cabinets and matching desk. Hanging on the wall behind the desk was a framed poster of Ghost in his Laker uniform. Built into a cabinet against one wall were half a dozen small video monitors, all turned off, which Rebecca assumed were part of the security system. Across the hall from the office was a large bathroom, loaded with the dancers' makeup kits. Next to the bathroom was a bedroom. All of the rooms had lights on and doors open, but at the end of the hall was another door that was closed. Rebecca glanced over her shoulder, then opened it, stepped inside, and closed it behind her. There was space in the room for a rolltop desk, coffee table, and two leather recliners. Sports and business magazines were piled on the coffee table. Letters and papers were sorted into groups on top of the desk. There was a framed photograph on the wall above the desk. The imposing figure of Senator Galvin, wearing a trench coat and holding a thin leather valise, was immediately recognizable. He looked distracted, as if he were late for a plane. On his left was his mother, Marie, arms folded, expression unrevealing. Nicole Galvin, the senator's wife, stood to the right of her husband, in back of young Ghost, her hands on his broad shoulders. Nicole's eyes fell just off center of the lens, her lips parted in a remote smile, as though her thoughts had taken her to a private place. Ghost, standing there with his simple, boyish smile, looked out of place amid the others. Under one arm he held a basketball, and with his other hand he kept his collie on a leash.

Rebecca had recently spent two weeks at the University of Chicago, where the senator's papers were kept, sifting through his correspondence and memos. There were letters to colleagues, companies, and constituents, but little of a personal nature. It was correspondence written during the final months of the senator's life that interested Rebecca, and she had been unable to find anything other than official business written during this period. Judge Ely was trustee for the collection, and he had directed the librarian to inform Rebecca that no additional correspondence existed.

Rebecca slid open Ghost's file drawer. There was barely enough light coming through the French doors to see inside the drawer. The papers did not appear to be organized. There were letters and brokerage statements and handwritten notes.

The floorboards in the hallway started creaking, then stopped. Rebecca froze. The sound started again. She hurried out the French doors, which opened to a garden behind the tennis court.

8

Ghost's party raged past midnight. He made the circuit inside the house and throughout the grounds, saying hello to all of his guests, stopping to shake hands and exchange a few words.

He went off to his guest house for a respite. The dancers were in there, changing out of their costumes. One girl had a Polaroid camera, so Ghost spent a few minutes posing for pictures and autographing underclothes. Then he went down the hall, past Miss Dupree's office, to the small office he used when working with Miss Dupree in the guest house. Ghost detected a faint veil of perfume in the room.

He pulled from his pocket the pink message form that he'd been carrying all evening, and read the name: Judge Ely. There was a notation on the message that requested Ghost call no matter what time. Usually, he spoke with the judge every couple of months; Ghost would talk about pro basketball, and the judge would catch Ghost up on the events at Nippersink and tell him how Marie was doing. Ghost knew that a call tonight, at this hour, would not bring good news.

Ghost knew the number, and dialed it. The judge answered on the second ring.

"It's the middle of the night back there," Ghost said.

"Thommy?"

"How are you?"

"Well, I've been better. I'm afraid I wasn't calling tonight with good news. We lost your grandmother this evening."

"I see."

Ghost looked down the hall and could see two of the girls

in the living room sharing a large chair. One was combing out the other's blonde hair. Their dancers' bodies were lean and athletic. He thought about lying perfectly still between them, feeling their warmth pressing against his skin. He would lie still and sleep in the complete darkness of his room.

Ghost knew the judge was waiting for him to respond, but he sat there in silence, watching the girls. It was his habit upon hearing bad news to pretend at first that he hadn't heard, that the news hadn't penetrated, and he would grip the few seconds between hearing the news and acknowledging it as if searching for a way to hold onto the past and prevent the future.

When they told him that his father had died, Ghost reacted this way. He had just returned to Stanford University for his junior year. A university administrator found him in a registration line and brought him to the dean's office. On the way to the office the man had said to Ghost, "There's been an accident in your family. A Mr. Laundier, who I understand is a friend of your family, is in with the dean, and I believe they have your mother on the phone." He had finished speaking and had opened the dean's door for Ghost, who entered the office to see Jay Laundier and the dean looking uncomfortable and grim, as though they had a confession to make. "Thommy," Jay said, "your father's had a heart attack." Ghost had looked at him and said, "Is he all right?" "It was bad," Jay said, lowering his head. "Where is he?" Ghost replied urgently, feeling the eyes of the three men pressing into him; he had felt the power of their knowledge as they gradually released it to him. "He's dead. I'm sorry." "I'm very sorry," the dean said. "We have a line open to your family's home." He pointed to the blinking button. "Your mother is waiting to speak with you," Jay added. At that moment Ghost had felt himself retreat from the men and what they were saying. He hadn't wanted to pick up the phone. Then it would have become real. He recalled looking out the window at the eucalyptus trees and trying to lose himself in them. Then the dean had handed Ghost the telephone.

A few days later, at the funeral, Jay Laundier took Ghost aside to tell how impressed he'd been at the calm and courage Ghost had displayed when he'd taken the news. And Ghost acknowledged him, but remembered thinking at the time that, in fact, he hadn't taken the news at all.

Now Ghost stared down the hall at the dancers, suspending himself in that vision, until the judge's voice brought him back.

"You know, with Marie's heart," the judge said, "the clock was running out on her. What a goddamned thing it is to get old. There wasn't any suffering, though. She was asleep when it happened."

"Well, I guess we knew it was going to happen," Ghost said.

"When you've got to go, that's the way to do it. And look what she had to be proud of in life, with a son like your dad, and you as a grandson."

"I'm glad you brought her into town when I was back last time."

"Oh, I kept my eye on her. She was a busy lady right up to today. Just don't get old, Thommy, it's not worth it. You get old by remembering too much, and then you can't remember anything the way you should. It's a hell of a business."

"What arrangements need to be made?" Ghost asked. "My secretary . . ."

"I've taken care of everything. She never wanted a funeral. You don't worry about anything."

"She didn't want a funeral?"

"You know your grandmother. She told me exactly what she wanted. She didn't want any more funerals in her family. I've taken care of it," Judge Ely said.

"Thank you."

"Well, you let me know what your plans are, son, and don't worry. I hear a lot of music out there."

The band was playing a Rolling Stones medley. Girls were dancing in the living room of the cottage.

"It's the party I'm having for Hardin and the team."

"Right, well, hell, Thommy," the Judge said, "raise a glass to Marie. She had a long and good life and a hell of a lot to be proud of. That's the way we want to remember her. Just like that. And that's what's important, how we remember her. Getting older, you learn that."

"All right, Judge, I'll drink a toast."

"That's what to do, drink a toast to her memory. That's exactly what she'd want from us."

"Okay."

"I'm sorry this had to be tonight, but I didn't want to go through the night without calling you. Your party should be a celebration. You've won the world championship, Thommy, and that's not something many men could say. I can see your father looking down and being proud. You should be pleased. It's not a night to be sad."

"Well, good night," Ghost said.

"Good night, son."

Ghost replaced the phone on its cradle, and looked above the desk at the photograph of his family, knowing that he was the only one of them still living. He opened the French doors to air the scent of perfume out of the room.

9

"Are you coming back to bed?" Judge Ely's wife, Eleanor, said in a hoarse whisper of half sleep.

"Soon, sweet," he answered, dropping his sterling silver cigar cutter into the pocket of his robe. The old robe had the shiny look of worn upholstery.

Each step was deliberately chosen as he descended the stairs, aware of what a fall at his age could mean. The floorboards creaked beneath the carpet, sounds of comfort to the judge. He knew each stair and how it sounded in the same way he knew his favorite fishing holes in Lake Geneva.

Opry, the Elys' housekeeper, was awakened by the sound of the judge picking his way downstairs. Her quarters were on the first floor at the south end of the house. She had expected the judge to be rising in the night, after what had happened with Marie Galvin. Opry had already set out his bottle of cognac and a snifter on a tray in the gaezbo. He knew it would be there. First he stopped in his den and opened the cherry-wood humidor given to him one Christmas by the senator, and selected a Monte Cristo cigar, which he took with him outside.

His was the largest estate on the lake. Neatly tended lawns swept down from the main house to the shore, where a dock and boathouse jutted into the water. In the sudden silence created by his movement, Judge Ely's leather slippers scraped across the flagstone steps leading to the gazebo. Once the screen door slapped shut behind him, and the judge settled into his rattan chair, the sounds of crickets and bull frogs returned to the night.

"Well," he said to no one, "it's cooler out here." On these humid nights it was always cooler down by the lake. The long cedar match hissed into flame, illuminating the tabletop next to the judge's chair; there he kept his ashtray and his telephone. Twenty years ago it had been necessary for the telephone company to run special underground lines in order to put a phone in the gazebo, but they were willing to make the exception for the judge. He lit the cigar and gently blew on the burning end until it returned an orange glow. Then he dipped the butt into his cognac, and summoned a long, smooth draw. Cigar smoke floated around him like ground fog.

He'd kept a watchful eye on Marie Galvin in the years since the senator's death, visiting often, arranging for the kitchen at the Nippersink lodge to deliver hot meals daily to her; and he and Eleanor invited Marie over to the house for supper every Sunday. Four months ago he began noticing the changes in Marie: her eyes would go out of focus and she'd become suddenly quiet, as if she were listening to a powerful voice in her head. Then the reports from the canasta ladies that Marie was absently jabbering about the senator. And the arrival in Nippersink of Rebecca Blesser. For weeks he'd known something would have to be done.

Knowledge is the burden of being a judge, he thought, puffing on his cigar and taking a sip of cognac. For years he sat in his courtroom, gazing down at those people who couldn't believe what was happening to them, listening as they denied things they couldn't possibly have done. And it had so little to do with the truth, because, he believed, the truth became what a judge allowed to be entered into the record.

He knew what the record would show for Marie Galvin: she died of heart failure, having had heart problems the last five years of her life. Marie's doctor, and the judge's friend, Dr. Boylen, had arrived at the hospital just when the paramedics had pulled in with Marie's body. They reported that Marie had been dead when they found her. The judge had followed the paramedics to the hospital and had spoken briefly with Dr. Boylen.

"We all have our time," Dr. Boylen had said to the judge. "The human heart can only take so much, then it stops. And that's that." Marie was old, her death expected, natural; there were no questions; there would be no autopsy. Her death was right and good because it was her time, and because the past must be protected. The record would show it. This thought elated the judge.

It is a judge's sworn duty to be a protector of the past, he felt, and it was the weight of this duty that brought Judge Ely out to his gazebo many nights, and this night especially, to smoke his cigar, look at the dark expanse of the lake, and wonder what was at the bottom of it.

10

Hardin found Ghost surrounded by dancers in the guest house. "I'm picking a hell of a time to leave," Hardin said to him.

"You don't have to," Ghost said.

"My generation is leaving the party. Yours is just getting started."

"Hell, send your friend Rebecca home with the chauffeur. Stay awhile. Her type likes chauffeurs. It's a thrill for them."

"My heart can't take this many pretty girls in one room," Hardin said. "That's your department. It was a great party, thanks. Don't walk me to the door."

He shook Ghost's hand and left the cottage.

Ghost caught up with him on the terrace.

"I want to say good night to your friend."

Rebecca was waiting in the foyer. As Hardin and Ghost approached, Hardin said, "I rescued him from the grips of ten exotic dancers, and he may never forgive me. I'll go send for the car."

"It was a lovely party," Rebecca said to Ghost.

"You enjoyed your tour of the house?"

"Yes, I did."

"Did Miss Dupree show you my little cottage out back?"

"We didn't get that far," she said.

Ghost let a moment of silence hang between them, then leaned over and kissed her on the cheek, smelling her perfume before she could step back.

"So you did that on your own," he said.

"You had me followed? What an original idea."

"I didn't have you followed, Miss Blesser," he replied, "but the perfume smells familiar. What are you writing about my father?"

"I wouldn't think I would have to explain Senator Galvin's fame to you."

"Remember something. When you're talking to me about Senator Galvin you're not talking about some goddamned figure from the news, you're talking about my father, and you'd better be—"

"Careful?" she said quietly. "Why?"

He looked hard at her. "Miss Blesser, I don't know what you're up to, but stay away from me."

Ghost walked away, leaving Rebecca standing alone in the foyer.

Miss Dupree appeared from out front to tell her that Mr. Hardin was waiting in the limousine.

11

Back in her room at the Chateau Marmont, Rebecca started the water in the bathtub and poured herself a vodka rocks. She opened the Lakers press kit and shuffled through a stack of publicity photos until she found Ghost's. She adjusted the flow of water, stepped into the tub, and settled into its encircling warmth. She sipped the vodka and looked at Ghost's picture, holding it at arm's length. His features were finer than those of his father, she decided, but the strong outline of his father's face was unmistakable. The dark eyes and high cheekbones were there, as was the same unrevealing gaze into the camera, so different from the childhood picture of Ghost she'd seen back at the house. The eyes in that picture had been open; what they had seen of life had been good. She set the picture on the commode, and slid deeper into the water until it touched her chin. She looked at her own image in the retractable mirror connected to the tub. She looked at her eyes and cheekbones and lips and ears and forehead. Rebecca reached again for Ghost's glossy, but there was too much steam in the bathroom and the photo was beginning to wilt. She drained the tumbler of vodka and closed her eyes, weightless in the water.

The party drove into the night. The families had left long ago. The socialites, executives, politicians, and working actors were gone, too. What remained was that struggling platoon of people you see at the end of parties in Los Angeles, those who feel pressured by dawn's approach, and crave something to take into the new day: a deal, a number, a person, or simply the satisfaction of having outlasted the night. Ghost walked among them without stopping to talk.

The previous month, when the Lakers won the world championship, the pictures of Ghost in the papers didn't show the usual champagne-soaked joy of a celebration. A photograph that had since become famous showed Ghost sitting alone in front of his locker, a Lakers publicity man shielding him from the press, trying to explain that Ghost was exhausted and didn't want to be interviewed. Now, as he walked heavily up the stone terrace steps of his mansion, his expression was much the same as in that photograph.

The bar on the terrace was still open. Ghost ordered a grapefruit juice with ice.

"Some party, Mr. Galvin," the Cuban bartender said, handing Ghost the drink.

"Was it good?" Ghost asked absently.

"They don't want to go home, these people."

"I'll bet you do, though."

"I take a nap before coming to work. I know I'm going to be up late."

"Make sure to take a bottle of champagne home to your wife so she won't be mad at you for being so late."

"Okay," the bartender said. "Thank you, Mr. Galvin."

"You should go home to your wife."

"Pretty soon now."

"I think it's time to close down the bar. You go home."

"Okay, Mr. Galvin."

Ghost felt reluctant to go inside. He thought about Rebecca walking through the house. There was nothing for her to touch or take in there, but thinking about her left him uncomfortable, the way he felt when he made eye contact with someone, and later wished he hadn't. He thought about her visit to his office, and wondered what could possibly interest her there.

Miss Dupree, her dark gray Chanel suit uncreased, found Ghost at the terrace bar.

"You're still here," Ghost said, surprised.

It was four-thirty in the morning.

"The cleanup crew arrives at seven. Magda will look after them. I've asked them to keep the noise at a minimum."

"I just told the bartender to close the bar. I think I'm going to bed, now."

"I'll see everyone out," Miss Dupree said.

Ghost went upstairs and lay down on his bed. As soon as he closed his eyes, he pictured his grandmother. She had been a short, rigid woman who liked people to keep their distance; her business was her business. Only when Ghost's father was around did she have much to say. They used to walk in the fields at Nippersink and talk. In fact, Ghost found himself jealous of those memories, the long talks between his grandmother and his father, because his father tended to be quiet when visiting Nippersink; he liked to smoke his cigars and watch Ghost shoot hoops, or go with Ghost down to the lake for bass fishing, but little was said on those occasions. Now, there was no family. There were distant relatives from his mother's side who lived in France, but Ghost had never met them and had no plans to. This was an odd feeling; he felt both stranded and liberated. His family was now only what he remembered them to be.

Once everyone was out and the last car had pulled through the iron gates, Miss Dupree, trailed by a security guard, dutifully toured the house and grounds. She was glad that Ghost gave large parties infrequently; it was such an invasion to have this mob of people who felt free to roam the house and stay so late. It had required all of her patience to allow the guests to stay this late, but when she learned of the death of Ghost's grandmother, she knew that Ghost would be up late and would want some guests around. But now he had gone to bed. Miss Dupree looked up at his bedroom window and saw that his lights were out and the shades drawn. She finally left when the hazy light of morning cut away the night.

2

Ghost was awakened at one-thirty in the afternoon by a call from Miss Dupree, reminding him of a three o'clock appointment with his attorney, Norman Jamison. He went to his bedroom window and pulled open the drapes to see that the sky had clouded over and a light rain was falling. Workmen had disassembled the tent and the bandstand; the caterer's bars and tables were gone, too. The yard looked large and empty.

A cleaning crew was downstairs doing the floors. Ghost hurried past them to the safety of the kitchen, where Magda, his housekeeper, was straightening up the remnants of the party. The newspapers were laid out on the breakfast table. Magda had eggs, coffee, juice, and toast ready in a couple of minutes.

"Where did this rain come from?" Ghost said, sitting down to his breakfast.

"Clouded over about ten. Just a little rain."

"It's not supposed to be raining," he said, scanning the *Los Angeles Times.*

She shrugged, "We can use a little rain, after all the heat."

"I guess so," he said. "Why not?"

On the second page of the sports section there was a small item about Ghost's grandmother below a picture of Ghost.

Magda placed half a grapefruit in front of him. "I was sorry to hear the news," she said.

He didn't look up from the paper. "She lived a good life."

"I say a prayer for her."

"Thank you. She wasn't well for a long time. But she wanted to stay in that house. You know, after my father died . . ."

"That's the hardest thing on a woman," Magda said, wiping the kitchen counter, "to have her son die."

Ghost pushed his plate away and looked out the window. "How many grandchildren do you have?"

"Five. They probably be very happy to see me go, because I won't leave them alone." She cleared Ghost's plate. "I'm sorry, Mr. Thomas, that was nothing for me to say to you this morning."

"It's all right," he said. He was thinking of the house at Nippersink, where his grandmother lived up to the end; if he had family left, he thought, it was that house, because that's where his memories were.

Ghost looked out the window to the tennis court, where there was also a basketball hoop. He watched the fine rain form into droplets on the net, then drip steadily to the ground.

2

The yellow-and-white striped awnings of Giorgio in Beverly Hills looked bright against the dark sky. A doorman greeted customers as they came in off the street. Gentlemen who were shopping with their wives were invited to enjoy an aperitif at the mahogany bar in the middle of the store. Gowns and dresses were swept off the racks to be matched with shoes, belts, hats, and jewelry. Over in the men's department, suits, ties, shirts, and casual clothes were sold in a less theatrical fashion. The store's owner, Fred Hayman, moved quietly amid the customers, greeting friends, directing his staff, offering opinions on the purchases. Hayman greeted Ghost warmly; he was a regular customer and his presence in the store always generated excitement among the out-of-towners.

There was a seating area with large leather couches and a working fireplace separating the men's and women's sections of the store. The walls around the couches were covered with signed photographs of Giorgio's celebrity clients.

Norman Jamison was sitting on one of the couches, waiting for Ghost.

"You don't look any worse for the wear," Ghost said as the lawyer stood up to greet him.

"How are you today, Ghost? That was a hell of a party."

"I don't have to ask you if you had a good time. I saw the girl you left with."

"Listen, I'm not ready to turn in the spurs yet," Jamison said.

A waiter arrived with espressos for Ghost and Jamison.

"I read the papers this morning," Jamsion said. "My condolences."

"Thank you."

"If there's anything I can handle for you, arrangements of any kind . . ."

"Judge Ely's back there."

"Of course."

"So," Ghost said, "you spoke with Hardin last night?"

"Yes. We talked last night and he called this morning. He wants the new contract drafted and signed. So what do you say, do we make it easy on him or are you going to hold out for the moon?"

"I'm sure he made a healthy number this year," Ghost said.

"No question about it. He's got plenty to spend."

Ghost looked at Jamison. "Norman, I'm not sure I want to play anymore."

"That doesn't leave me a lot of negotiating room." Jamison smiled.

"I'm serious."

"I know we've made some very good investments over the years. But right now we're talking about one of the largest contracts the sport has ever seen. I can tell Hardin we have to leave it for later. With your grandmother having passed away, he'll understand."

"I don't want to make a game of it with him."

"If we tell him you're not playing at all, he'll think for certain we're screwing with him."

Jamison shifted around on the couch. "Is this something you've been thinking about for a while, Ghost? I've never heard you mention retirement. You're only twenty-nine. . . ."

"I haven't been thinking about it. I just thought about it this morning when I woke up. When I walked off the court the other night after we won the finals, and the place was going crazy, people grabbing me and I couldn't see with all the flashbulbs in the face, I felt calm. I can't remember ever feeling that calm. I sat down in front of my locker and the press was yelling at me. I sat there thinking about something that happened the year my father died. Remember when I was at Stanford and I sat out that year? The year I didn't play?"

Jamison nodded.

"My father and I hardly spoke that year because he didn't understand what I was doing. He was busy with primaries. But I remember one Sunday when the Lakers and Celtics were playing on television for the championship and it was the last game. We were at Nippersink for the weekend; I had flown in for my mother's birthday. My father couldn't understand that I didn't want to watch the game with him. Even though I wasn't playing that year, he thought at least I'd want to watch the championship game of the pros. I happened to walk in during the last couple of minutes of the game, and when it ended and there was all that craziness on the screen, I looked over at my father and saw tears in his eyes. I'd never seen him cry before. Ever. He didn't look at me or say anything. He just kept staring at the screen."

Jamison reached for his espresso.

"And I hadn't thought about it in ten years, until after we won the game the other night, with all the craziness afterward. I sat there in the locker room thinking about that afternoon when my father was watching the game on television. I wanted to know what he was thinking that day that made him cry. I figured he was watching the Celtics win the championship and I guess all he wanted in life was to see me up there doing it. I'd told him that morning that I wasn't going back to the team in the fall, either. But I suppose I should have just asked him why he was crying. I never did. He never said anything about it. In fact, we hardly spoke the rest of that summer."

Jamison leaned forward. "You know I deal with a lot of athletes, professionals. Now, few of them are in your class as an athlete, but they all need a break after a season like the one you've had. They just go stale on the game."

"It's not the game," Ghost said. "It's just that after we won the other night, I felt stone empty. I should have been ecstatic, right? I should have felt something."

"Well," Jamison said, "I can't say I know what to make of all this. But I'm here to do what you want."

"I don't want to sign a contract for next season."

An electronic flash popped in the middle of their silence.

32

"Do you mind?" a woman asked, holding a camera out in front of herself.

"It's all right," Ghost said reflexively.

"You're my first star," the woman said. "We're staying down the street at the Beverly Hilton. We're from Minnesota."

Ghost smiled and the woman snapped another photograph. The flash attracted other tourists in the store, carrying cameras of their own. He posed with those tourists, and with several more who came in off the street to see what was going on.

"I think it's time for me to leave," Ghost said.

"I'm going to do nothing until I hear from you." Jamison walked out of the store with Ghost.

While they stood on the corner waiting for their cars, Ghost asked, "Did you get a call from a journalist? She was at the party last night with Hardin. Rebecca Blesser."

"I was introduced last night. I remember her. She called the office a couple of days ago. But I get a lot of press calls for you. I give them all the same answer."

"Did she say what her angle was?"

"Evidently a story on your father."

"You see, I don't get that. I know my father was famous, but he wasn't the goddamn president of the United States. He's been dead for ten years. I don't see any point in *Life* doing a story on him now."

"Maybe it's her way of getting a story on you."

"She's not getting a story from me."

"Then I wouldn't be too worried about it. I know you like your privacy, but you can't shut off the press. Not possible."

"I just don't like the idea of reading about him in a magazine right at this point in my life. How do they know what's true and what isn't? They're usually not even close."

"Hey, maybe she's a first-class writer and you'll be happy with the story."

"When you met her, what did you think?"

"I just said hello; that was about it."

"But what did you think of her?"

"Good-looking, if that's what you mean."

"I wasn't thinking that."

"She *was* good-looking, though."

"In a way."

"You're spoiled, Ghost. That was a good-looking woman."

"I don't know what she wanted," Ghost said.

"Her story. What else?"

"I don't know."

When the valet brought Ghost's car around, Ghost handed him five dollars.

"Would you call the magazine?" he asked Jamison. "See what you can find out about her. That she's legit and all."

3

The clerk in the lobby of the Chateau Marmont summoned Rebecca to take a telephone call. She had been sitting with two colleagues from the magazine's Los Angeles bureau.

She lifted the receiver. "Yes."

"I want you to meet me tonight," Ghost said, speaking from the telephone in his car.

Rebecca didn't recognize the voice.

"James?" she asked.

"No, it's me."

"Who?"

"What were you looking for in my office last night?" Ghost asked.

Rebecca paused. "Mr. Galvin?"

"Yes."

The line was crackling with electronic interference.

"I'm having a hard time hearing you," she said.

"Then let me say it again. What were you doing in my office?"

"Nothing. I got turned around."

"You hustled Jim Hardin just to have a look around my place. That's not a nice thing to do. Especially for a big-time writer. I want an explanation. I'm sending a car for you at eight. And then you can do all the talking."

"Don't send a car because I can't see you. I have guests."

"I'm sending the car at eight."

"I'll call you and try to arrange an interview," she said. "But I don't think I'll have much luck getting past your Miss Dupree."

"Look, I don't want to give any goddamned interview. I just want to know what the hell you were doing at my house."

He hung up.

At eight o'clock the limousine Ghost rented arrived at the Chateau Marmont. The concierge rang Rebecca's room, but there was no answer. When the driver called for further instructions, Ghost told him to wait fifteen minutes and try again. The driver waited, but there was still no response, so Ghost told the driver to leave.

4

The hallways of the hotel were quiet and empty after midnight as Rebecca walked to her room. For safety, she had left on the TV and put the Do Not Disturb sign on the door. She heard Johnny Carson interviewing someone as she entered the one-bedroom suite. Rebecca bolted the door, then went directly into her dressing room, where she hung up her linen dress and packed away her shoes. She started the bath and washed her face.

After bathing, she wrapped herself in a thick terry robe and walked into the living room–kitchenette to fix a cup of tea. It was then that she saw Ghost sitting in a chair by the door. He was wearing Levi's, black high-top sneakers, and a black leather jacket. His eyes were bloodshot. He stared at her.

Rebecca felt her skin go cold.

"I asked you on the phone today what you were doing in my office," Ghost said. "You haven't given me an answer."

Rebecca snatched the telephone receiver from its cradle.

"Don't waste your time," Ghost said. "They know me downstairs. Answer my question."

"Get out of this room."

"I've been sitting here an hour. I'm starting to get used to it."

"Get out!"

Ghost stood and closed the bedroom door.

"I want to talk with you," he said.

She dropped the phone and grabbed a knife from the kitchenette counter top.

He sighed impatiently.

"I'll talk with you tomorrow," she said. "You're drunk and I want you out of here."

"I walked into my office and the desk drawer was open and the outside door was open and I smelled your perfume. You make a terrible spy. What do you want?"

"You told me it was all right to have a look around your house. So I did. I was surprised not to see any photographs, pictures of your family. None. I thought I might find some in the guest house. And that's all I saw. Just the one picture."

"And it's not really your goddamned business, is it?" Ghost said.

"I thought it odd."

"I leave the decorating up to my assistant," he said. "And you can put the knife down; it wouldn't cut through a piece of toast. Tell me what you want with my father?"

"You don't break into people's hotel rooms and scare them just because you suddenly feel like talking."

"I'm here, so we might as well talk. Then I'll leave."

"There's this network of silence among the people who knew your father. I'm surprised you aren't more curious."

"What am I supposed to be curious about? He's dead."

"He died of a heart attack at forty-nine," Rebecca said. "Yet there was no heart disease in the family."

"My grandmother—" Ghost began.

"Was eighty-seven," Rebecca said. "But your father was a healthy man."

"So healthy he had a heart attack."

"He was fishing, wasn't he?"

Ghost stared at her. "What's your story about?"

"Your father's career. His accomplishments. What he might have done, had he lived. That's where it begins. I just find these loose ends when I come to the part about his death."

"Who else is the article about?"

"A cross section of people—politicians, writers, entertainers, scientists—all of whom died just before their prime. . . ."

"What's the fact that my father was fishing when he died have to do with anything?"

Rebecca continued. "He was fishing the morning he died. But he went fishing dressed in a business suit. That was in the coroner's report and in the police pictures."

"I never looked at them. What's your point?"

"It was an odd discovery, I thought. In fact, it seemed ridiculous. Why would Senator Galvin go fishing in a suit? I asked some people. They thought I was making it up. And the people I thought might know something about it didn't seem to want to talk with me."

"Why should they?" Ghost asked.

"They don't have to. I only intended to include your father as one part of the piece the magazine is doing. But it was strange. I looked through the file of photographs our researchers gathered, I put them in chronological order, and I kept looking through them because it jumped out at me that your father, who was a handsome man, changed more in the last year of his life than he'd done in the previous twenty. It was remarkable. I was shocked by the way he aged. That's what I thought I might find in your house—a string of photographs, some family pictures to give me a clue about what was going on in his life, because obviously something was wrong. In all the photographs I looked at from that last year there were almost none taken with his family. Which was unusual for a vice-presidential candidate. Candidates love being photographed with their families. I thought maybe you'd talk to me about it."

"What I'd like is for you to leave my family alone. I don't need you to tell me about my father," Ghost said. "You must be upset that my grandmother died. You've kind of run out of family to annoy."

A silence settled between them. He felt she was lying about something, either about what she knew or her purpose for being here at all. And Rebecca could see that Ghost was holding on to a thought like it was the one thing he wanted kept from a thief.

"Why are you afraid to talk to me?" Rebecca asked.

"I want to know what it is you want," Ghost said, staring at her "You can't be here just to dig up graves. My grandmother is being cremated, so you're out of luck there."

"I met your grandmother. She seemed like a nice woman."

"You're proud of trying to pick off an old lady?"

Rebecca watched him shifting in the chair, and realized that he was scared, too, being in the room, talking about this. There was strain in his voice.

"Your father was well known for writing letters. I asked your grandmother about that. If she had saved any of them. We've got all the official correspondence. I'm interested in something more personal, a window into the man. That's all I was talking about with your grandmother."

"I don't believe you. And I don't like you," Ghost said.

"I want the story," she said to him.

"For that you feel free to trash around my life? It's a wonderful job you have, Miss Blesser. Or is it the other thing? Are you one of those reporters who likes nosing around stars and celebrities? Like the women who hang around our hotels when we're on the road, sitting in the lobbies and bars, asking us these important questions they got out of a magazine article? A little screw and they leave you alone. How about that? Make it easy and say it." Ghost walked over to the dresser and picked up the black-and-white publicity photo of him that was resting on top of some Laker press releases. He was familiar with the picture, having autographed thousands of them. He didn't even think of the person in the picture as himself, that person was "Ghost Galvin," basketball star. But now he looked at the photograph and it made him uneasy that Rebecca had it in her room, as if she could look at it and know that the person in the picture was not the person standing a few feet from her.

He dropped it on the carpet.

Then he left.

5

When a person leads a public life, people tell him things. About himself, his life, his past. They'll stop him in restaurants, airports, on the street, almost anywhere, just for a few moments of contact, as if an encounter with someone famous is a chance to live outside the bounds of daily reality, a brief spray of immortality. And if that famous person in some way disappoints the fan, perhaps by being too small or taciturn or distant, then the fan can quickly turn mean, feeling cheated. Ghost was constantly approached by fans, most of whom felt obliged to say something intimate, trying their best to prove they were not just another fan. They would tell him about moves he had made in a game six years before, or they would describe clothing he had worn after a game in Cleveland. They would ask about a girl they'd read he was dating, and would inquire about the pleasures of wealth. Often, usually on a road trip, Ghost was approached by someone who'd seen him play as a kid, in high school and even in grammar school. And in almost every city he traveled to someone approached him and said, "I was a friend of your father's." It seemed that everyone who had ever voted for the senator considered himself his friend, and wanted to shake Ghost's hand, to tell him what a good man his father had been. Ghost had heard things from so many thousands of people that he had gradually created a picture of his father to fit and deflect comments from the public. Ghost would nod and shake the person's hand, telling them that, yes, the senator had cared deeply about this issue or that; yes, their city actually was the senator's favorite and, yes, the senator would have made a good vice-president—or even president. The constant comments had chiseled an image of the senator in Ghost's brain; there was "the senator," and there was his father, and it was "the senator" that the public knew, not his father. "The senator" was simpler for Ghost to think about than his father, because the senator was like a character from a story still being written, changed and shaped by whoever was talking about him at the moment. But his father was a person Ghost was never going to see again, and if there were things he would like to reshape, to change, it would not be possible.

The morning after visiting Rebecca's room, Ghost awoke troubled by his conversation with her. He felt foolish and exposed for having shown up there, and for talking with her at all. And in some way he felt as if she were watching him now, as he rose from bed; she knew things about him, he thought, and he found that disturbing. When the public or press stopped him with something to say about his father, invariably the person they were talking about was that chiseled image, that composite man whom Ghost kept at a distance, "the senator." But Rebecca's words had cut straight into Ghost, as if what she knew was as important to her as she thought it should be to him. She was not talking to him, he sensed, simply to get a reaction. What she said had come at him too quickly, this information about his father having gone fishing in a suit, the question of letters and coroner's reports, police photographs. When she was talking about these things she was talking about his father, not "the senator." She had been saying things that Ghost wanted to grab from the air and stuff back into a box, contain. It was like that blinking light on the telephone in the dean's office at Stanford, when Ghost had been brought there to be told of his father's death. All those men sitting around looking at a little blinking light. Ghost hadn't wanted to pick it up and talk with his mother. He had wanted to stare out the window at the eucalyptus trees, stare at them forever.

Ghost stood at the window of his bedroom and looked down at the grounds of his estate; he looked at the empty basketball court and thought about the photograph of himself that he'd dropped on the carpet in Rebecca's room.

6

Ghost walked through the kitchen, past the table where Magda had set out breakfast, and went directly to the garage. He fired up his Porsche and drove to a rental agency called Rent-a-Wreck, which rented only vintage Detroit heaps: Ford Falcons, Chevy Impalas, Oldsmobile 88s. Most of their customers were celebrities in search of privacy, there being no surer path to anonymity in Los Angeles than driving a lousy car.

Ghost chose a chiffon yellow 1965 Ford Galaxy convertible, with torn black vinyl bucket seats and a top that would not fully close. "And the radio only gets one station," the clerk said.

"It'll be fine," Ghost said, presenting his credit card.

"How long would you like it for, Mr. Galvin?"

"I have no idea."

"I'll leave the return open, then," the clerk said, typing up the form.

"Can you have it delivered to my house?"

"Right away."

"Good. Call this number," he said, writing on a scrap of paper, "and ask for Miss Dupree. She'll arrange everything."

He drove to City National Bank, cashed a check for six thousand, and by the time he returned home the Galaxy was waiting for him.

Magda was looking it over when Ghost arrived.

"I like your other cars better," she said.

"I won't have to worry about this one."

"I don't think so."

"Can you help me pack some things?"

"Take out what you want and I'll pack it up."

"I just want to get away for a while."

Miss Dupree was waiting in the kitchen.

"Mr. Hardin called this morning," she said, "and offered his jet in regards to your grandmother."

"I won't need it," Ghost said.

"I understand there are to be no services."

Ghost looked up from the notepad he was jotting a list on.

"Judge Ely called, as well," Miss Dupree said in her steady, even tone. "Evidently, that was your grandmother's desire, not to have a service."

"Right," Ghost said.

"You have some other messages this morning."

"Anything important?"

Miss Dupree opened her black leather notebook and silently scanned the list of names: Judge Ely, James Hardin, Norman Jamison, Ivy and Julie from the party, Tony Grant from the Lakers publicity office, Christiane Burnap from his agent's office, Rebecca Blesser.

"You met with Mr. Jamison yesterday, and I told you about Mr. Hardin and the judge. I believe the rest can wait."

"Okay," he said. "Will you call Caesar's Palace and book a couple of nights for me?"

Ghost outfitted the Galaxy with a tape player and a box of cassettes, a suitcase, carry bag, and an athletic bag. Out of habit he threw a basketball into the trunk. Magda hastily packed a cooler with sandwiches, fruit, and cold drinks, and Ghost fit the cooler on the floor in front of the passenger seat.

"That's it," he said to Miss Dupree and Magda, who stood in the doorway. "I'm gone."

"So what do you think of that?" Magda said.

Miss Dupree watched the iron gates open and close, and saw the yellow Galaxy disappear behind the trees.

"He didn't say how long he planned to be away," Miss Dupree said.

"He didn't say one thing," she answered. "You saw him, he was in and out of here like a storm. You ever see such a car?"

"He likes to have a schedule, an itinerary," Miss Dupree said. "Things function smoothly that way. I should think he would know that by now."

3

The previous day's rain had cleared the air in Southern California, and when Ghost reached the Mulholland pass, overlooking the San Fernando Valley, he could see the hills encircling the valley and beyond them to mountains he knew were there but had never seen through the smog.

It was still unseasonably cool. The sky was free of clouds and Ghost knew that once he passed through the mountains and into the desert, the sun would be intense. He slipped a Marvin Gaye tape into the machine and pumped the volume way up, easing the accelerator toward the floor. The old engine introduced a rhythmic rattle that steadied out at sixty miles an hour, and Ghost let the sound slide into the beat of the music.

He passed through Barstow early in the afternoon, stopping at a service station for gas and to purchase a Dodgers cap for protection from the sun. *Otis Redding's Greatest Hits* blasted from his tape machine; having spent most of life playing basketball with black teammates, Ghost's selection of cassettes was almost entirely rhythm and blues. He popped open a can of iced tea, provided to him by the case since the company that manufactured it paid him a substantial sum to appear in their ads, and alternated it with bites of Magda's tuna salad sandwich. He kept singing, even though he had a mouthful of tuna. The Galaxy churned along at a steady sixty, although the speedometer read eighty-five; Ghost took it up to ninety-five once, but the chassis started rattling and the convertible top shot up in the air like a reentry parachute, so he took it back down to cruising speed.

Ghost felt good in the open desert, a couple of sandwiches

in him, the warm air and the music swirling around his head. He felt best when no other cars were in sight—just the open road and the music and the hot air and the predictable chunking of the engine. He tilted his head back and sang straight into the wind, like a lone figure wading into surf. Louder and louder he sang, trying not to think, simply to drive and sing and feel the wind slashing across his face. But his thoughts were rolling just the same, back over the past two days, the party, his grandmother's death, his meeting with Jamison, Rebecca. Pressing his foot down on the accelerator, Ghost squeezed a few extra rpms out of the engine; he wanted to get to Vegas, away from Los Angeles. But he began thinking it was not so much Los Angeles he wanted to get away from as it was Rebecca, and having to think about his father. Thinking about his father had dominated the moment when the Lakers won the world championship, and while the other players celebrated, Ghost had sat quietly by his locker, angry that he felt empty, and knowing he felt so because his father wasn't there to watch the game. He had believed that winning that game would give him a feeling of completion, of reaching the end of a path that began when his father put a basketball in his hands when Ghost was four years old. He knew exactly how he would have felt at the end of the game if his father had been there; they would have exchanged glances and the world would have belonged to the two of them. But he hadn't seen that look from his father in a long time, because during the last year and a half of the senator's life Ghost didn't play basketball. He was at Stanford, the most celebrated player ever to attend what was not considered a basketball school, and during his sophomore year Ghost decided he wanted time away from the game he'd played every day for thirteen straight years. It was during that year and a half that Ghost and his father rarely spoke, and it was at the end of that time that the senator died. That was the year of the senator's life Rebecca wanted to know about. What bothered Ghost was the fact that he knew almost nothing about his father's life that year. In fact, he'd felt an impulse to ask Rebecca about it that night in her room. But he hadn't.

Fuck it. It was better just to get the hell out of L.A.

2

The parking valet at Caesar's Palace in Las Vegas looked disdainfully at the Galaxy when it came rolling up to the front entrance of the hotel. But he recognized Ghost, and jumped into action.

"Ghost Galvin, man," he said. "Ghost Galvin."

"How's it going," Ghost said, opening the trunk.

"Hey, you lose a bet, man? Never seen you here in a thing like this."

"It rolls right along."

"Okay," the valet said. "okay, all right, I like it."

The assistant manager arrived to greet Ghost, while a bellman took the bags.

"It's always a pleasure to welcome you back to Caesar's Palace," the man said.

"Been a while, Andy."

Andy escorted Ghost to a two-story, two-bedroom suite in the hotel's Fantasy Tower, with a view facing the Vegas strip. The living room had floor-to-ceiling windows, and a Jacuzzi large enough to handle eight people. Room service delivered a platter of cheese and fruit and a bottle of Dom Perignon. "The operators will locate me if there's anything at all you need," the assistant manager said, moving toward the door. "Do you know how long you'll be with us?"

"I'm not sure," Ghost said.

"As long as you like," Andy said.

"Thank you."

Ghost put his clothes in the bedroom and turned on the shower. The telephone started ringing. He let it go seven or eight times then picked it up.

"Hey, guy, it's Carol," the woman at the other end said, her voice quiet and knowing.

"Chrissakes," Ghost said, "you have radar."

"Word travels."

"Fast."

"Fast. You in for a while?"

"Don't know."

"What about tonight?"

"I just walked in the door."

"Town's busy."

"Yeah, looks it."

"You up the Tower?"

"Same suite."

"You need company."

"You think so?"

"I hear it in your voice, honey."

"I need not to think."

"That's usually when you turn up here."

"I'm here."

"Vicky might be free, too. Why don't you invite us over and we can all not think."

"Yeah, come on over. Bring Vicky."

"See you, honey."

"Yeah," Ghost said, setting the phone down.

Ghost showered, dressed, then walked over to the two-story semicircular picture window. The Jacuzzi was raised on a platform in front of the massive windows, with a railing surrounding it that Ghost leaned against. The neon lights of the strip were glowing, lighting the dome of sky. Standing there was like being in the nose of a spaceship, stuck in a galaxy of gaudy stars. There was nothing for Ghost to look at but neon lights.

"Hey, guy," Carol said, sliding a hand across Ghost's chest when he opened the door of his suite. Tall and blonde, she was attractive. But looking at her hard you knew she wouldn't photograph well. Vicky, who was also tall, followed Carol into the suite; she had red hair and spoke with a Southern accent.

"I was about to shave," Ghost said, escorting the girls to the living room. "How about a drink, a little champagne?"

He poured three glasses of Dom Perignon.

"We watched the play-offs on television," Vicky said. "I kept saying to Carol, 'I can't believe we know that guy.' So here's to the champ."

"Here's to something," Ghost said, touching his glass to theirs. "I'll go put a tie on. Change the music if you like." He paused again by the picture window, facing the thousands of lights illuminating the strip. "It's almost pretty here, isn't it?"

"At night," Carol answered. "Almost."

Ghost shaved and dressed, then guided the girls through a maze of second floor hallways and cut through a service area that left them at the Palace Court restaurant. The maître d' suggested that rather than order from the menu, it would be the chef's pleasure to prepare a special meal for Mr. Galvin and his guests. Champagne arrived at the table. Carol sipped the champagne, just enough to be polite, but Vicky felt like drinking, and kept pace with Ghost during the meal of asparagus, wild mushrooms, rack of lamb, and fresh vegetables.

"Honey," Carol said to Ghost, as a platter of fresh fruit was served for dessert, "I read in the paper about your grandmother. I'm sorry."

"She was getting up there," Ghost said.

"It said she lived in Wisconsin. I've got a sister there. You on your way back?"

"I just felt like getting out of L.A.," he said, "I guess I'm on the way back there." He hadn't thought about driving all the way to Nippersink. For what? So he was surprised to hear himself say the words.

"Still have family there?"

"No, no family. Some friends."

"You're like me," Vicky said. "No family, just friends."

Carol flashed an irritated expression at Vicky, but Vicky wasn't looking at her. She was enjoying the champagne.

"I thought all Southern girls had big families," Ghost said, picking at the fruit.

"Not this Southern girl. Well, maybe I do, I just don't know who they are."

She laughed.

"Hell," Ghost said, "maybe that's good. Maybe they're the Rockefellers."

"Yeah," Carol said, "I'm sure that's the case."

"I'll just have to ask my daddy that," Vicky said. "I'll have to ask him if he's one of the Rockefellers. First, I have to meet him. Then I'll have to sober him up long enough to ask him." She laughed again, her red hair falling forward across her face.

The waiter brought another bottle of champagne.

Carol said to Vicky, "Honey, easy on the loudmouth soup."

"Send it out to the floor," Ghost said to the waiter. "I think we'll play the tables a bit."

Word had spread through the hotel that Ghost Galvin was dining in the Palace Court, so when he and the girls emerged, they were met by a crowd of fans. He signed autographs and posed for pictures, gradually working his way to the casino floor, where a manager rescued him from the crowd. The casino manager cordoned off a blackjack table for Ghost and the girls. Four security guards were stationed by the stanchions and velvet ropes. Plainclothesmen worked themselves into the crowd. Two

46

hundred onlookers, waving and calling Ghost's name, gathered to watch. Ghost remained focused on the game. He signed a marker for three thousand dollars and gave a thousand to each of the girls. Champagne was brought to the table. The usual casino noise, combined with the shouting around Ghost's table, created a chaotic atmosphere in the gaming area. The crowd was shouting instructions and encouragement to Ghost and the girls, especially since the first hand was a bust for the house. Ghost found it easy to concentrate amid the chaos; in fact, he liked the noise and liked hearing his name cut through the laughter and shouting. Energy and adulation poured down on him like the desert sun, creating a cocoon of attention around Ghost that he absorbed and used to free himself of other thoughts. Drive back to Nippersink? For what? The dealer moved the game along at whatever pace Ghost indicated, while the crowd waited and watched to see what he would do. It was similar to how crowds behaved in basketball arenas, when Ghost stood on the free throw line with the fans shouting, waiting for him to put up the shot; they were controlled by his movements, their emotions held in his hands like a beating heart; as an athlete he learned to use the emotions of the crowd to protect himself from his own, because under pressure he could not allow himself to become too elated with success or too disappointed at failure; both conditions, his father had taught him, were imposters that affected one's performance.

Ghost pushed out two thousand dollars, won, let it ride, and won again. He looked at the stacks of black hundred-dollar chips and let them ride again. He was dealt seventeen and the dealer showed fourteen; the dealer pulled an eight and busted. Word flashed across the floor that Ghost was starting to lay down good money. The news swelled the crowd, causing the casino manager to summon more security. Carol had won seven hundred dollars and pulled her chips off the table. But Vicky was winning and still playing. Sitting to Ghost's right, she'd upped her stake to two thousand. Pit bosses flanked the table and monitored the action, joking with Ghost between hands. They pulled the five-thousand-dollar-maximum sign off the table. Looking at sixteen thousand in chips, Ghost contemplated his next move, while the crowd called for him to let it ride. He left a thousand in the betting circle, while Vicky let two thousand ride. Carol closed her eyes. The house dealt Ghost fifteen, Vicky nineteen. Dealer showed five, pulled a three and a jack, and paid Vicky, while collecting from Ghost. Vicky put up three thousand and won again. She was drunk by now, and Carol kept nudging her to take her money off the table. Instead, Vicky pushed out six thousand and was dealt blackjack. She had fifteen thousand in the betting circle, and the attention of the crowd had shifted to her seat. "Keep it down, baby, you're rolling!" someone shouted. "Let it play, let it play," yelled another. She bet five thousand and watched the dealer bust.

"Honey," Carol said, "take this good thing right out of here."

Vicky ignored her, bet another five thousand, lost, then won it back. The crowd moved to improve their view of Vicky's action. Two aces. She split them. The dealer placed a card, face down, atop each ace. The crowd noise sounded like ringside at a championship fight. Vicky had ten thousand riding on each ace. The dealer revealed his hole card, a six, to go with his five showing. Carol closed her eyes as the dealer pulled a new card. Eight, for a total of nineteen. He flipped Vicky's first card, nine, for twenty; second card, ten, for twenty-one. Twenty-thousand-dollar payoff, pushing Vicky's winnings to fifty thousand.

With a sharp clap of his hands, the pit boss summoned a cocktail waitress, who was dispatched for more champagne. The dealer helped stack Vicky's black chips into piles of tens, and then brought out the thousand-dollar chips. Ghost sat back on his stool, rigid and silent, barely looking up when the waitress returned with the champagne. On the first deal from the new shoe, Ghost bet five thousand, lost, bet another five thousand, won, let it ride, dropped ten thousand, and in a quick succession of five hands, dropped another ten thousand. Vicky was placing small bets. The crowd was yelling for her to up the action. Every head in the casino was focused on Vicky's fingers, as she moved her bets forward. Next to her, Ghost felt weak and empty as he sat back in his chair. "Let's go have some real dessert," Carol said, taking Ghost's arm, "something gooey and fattening." He arose without resistance, guided by Carol; the crowd could no longer buoy him, they were with Vicky. The dealer loaded Vicky's chips on a tray. A phalanx of security guards escorted the trio to the cashier's window. Flashbulbs began popping, and the guards were saying, "No cameras in the casino, no cameras." Gamblers reached through the wedge of guards, trying to touch Vicky's arm. "Just look at me, honey," a man called after her. "Just look at my eyes." Vicky was laughing, wobbling along, too drunk to know how much she'd won. At the cashier's counter, Carol kept an eye on the chips as they were stacked and counted, then paid out in a cashier's check and ten thousand in cash.

"Let's just have one drink," Vicky said.

"Up in the suite," Carol said. "Let's go up to the suite. How about it, Ghost?"

He nodded. Carol led both of them, Vicky light and laughing, Ghost silent and yielding, to the elevators and back up to the suite.

Vicky flicked on the stereo and jammed rock-and-roll through the four wall-mounted speakers; Carol went to the kitchen to make a pot of coffee.

When Carol walked back into the living room, she looked at Ghost and said, "Honey, you need some cheering up." She pushed the button that started the huge Jacuzzi. She helped Ghost undress. Vicky had already thrown off her dress and was in the water.

"I'm going to bring in some coffee," Carol said, as Ghost stepped into the bubbling water.

"Sweetie baby, you were right," Vicky said, sliding over to Ghost. "You were right. I've never *seen* so much cash. You were right. I'm the Rockefellers." She laughed and rested her head on the Jacuzzi's fiberglass rim. The neon lights shining through the window rainbowed across her white skin. "I'm sure my daddy never had a penny of what I've got. I've never seen so much cash. And it's thanks to you, Ghost, honey."

He was drunk and hearing half of what she was saying.

She swung herself around in the water and floated into Ghost's lap. "You're a real sweetie baby and I want you to have a good one. We're going to give you the best, we always give you the best, don't we, sweetie? How about a little more of that champagne, just a little more and that'll be it."

"I don't think I can drink any more of it," Ghost said, resting his head back, looking at the lights.

"Sweetie, I want to be so drunk I won't know what's happening tomorrow morning. I want the hangover of death." She laughed. "I was stupid to get knocked up like a jerk. You'd think I'd know better, you really would. Carol's taking me to the doctor in the morning. He'll suck it right out of there. So I'm as safe as a saint right now, sweetie, and I want you right there. You're my good luck charm. Bet you never screwed a Rockefeller before, right? You want to wait for Carol and make it family night?"

Her head fell back against Ghost's chest, then her body went limp in his lap. Ghost lifted her out of the water and laid her out on the tile by the Jacuzzi, wrapping her in one of the robes left there by the maid.

Carol walked into the room carrying a tray of cups and a pot of coffee.

"Jesus," she said.

"She's out," Ghost said.

"I've never seen her drink like that. I'm sorry, Ghost, honey."

"She had plenty."

"I couldn't get her to stop. She's not a drinker. You ever seen her take more than a drink or two?"

She put down the tray and poured Ghost a cupful, with just a splash of cream.

"I've had plenty myself," he said.

"Well, honey, I'm feeling fine. You just relax and let mama do the work."

"I think I need to get some sleep."

"Not alone, you don't," Carol said.

"Just some sleep."

She brought the cup and saucer over to him. Ghost was sitting on the edge of the Jacuzzi, dangling his legs in the water.

"She told me about tomorrow," he said to Carol.

"What's that, honey?"

"Vicky told me you're taking her to the doctor tomorrow."

Carol sat down on a chair near Ghost.

"That girl shouldn't drink."

"You're taking her to the doctor in the morning?"

"You shouldn't have to hear about that crap, honey. She shouldn't be talking about that. Rattling on about her daddy and all that. She shouldn't drink. Not when she's out. Listen, honey, let's forget about it. Mama's got what you like . . ." Carol walked over to Ghost and began stroking his hair.

He felt deeply weary.

"I've got to go use the bathroom," he said, walking into the bedroom.

Carol propped Vicky up and forced her to take a few sips of the coffee, then helped her to her feet and led her to the other bathroom. "You're going to hate me now, but you'll like me better tomorrow," she said, pushing Vicky into the shower; Carol turned the water on to cold and braced herself against the door. Vicky screamed but Carol held firm. After a couple of minutes she let her out and toweled her down. Vicky sat on the bed drinking coffee.

"We're going to get the fuck out of this hotel," Carol said.

"Let's stay and play with Ghost. He's good luck."

"I think he went to sleep."

"Let's wake him up."

"Not tonight, honey. We're getting out of this hotel. We've got too much cash. You have no idea. We want out of here."

Ghost was lying on his bed looking at the mirror that was set in the ceiling directly above him. He had dozed off but Vicky's yelling in the shower awakened him. The sounds of the casinos rattled around in his head, like after a game when he could still hear the crowd chanting his name long after he'd left the arena. After certain games, when Ghost had played particularly well, making a game-winning shot in the final seconds, the home crowd often stayed in their seats, chanting "GHOST, GHOST, GHOST," until he would come out of the locker room and wave. And still sometimes he'd hear the chant as fans filed out of the arena and into the parking lots.

"You stunk," his father had said to him after watching one of Ghost's high school games. The game had been won, Ghost had scored thirty-three points, and the crowd had surged around Ghost after the game, chanting his name. "You were forcing shots. Tonight they happened to go in. But they were not good shots," the senator had said. And Ghost had known he was right.

He heard Carol and Vicky talking in the living room. Ghost pictured Vicky in the doctor's office, her legs spread in the metal stirrups. There would be a sheet over her so she could not see what the doctor was doing. And the doctor would go in there with that little vacuum and suck the life right out of her womb. He could just see it, this little pellet of protoplasm, *whoosh!*, pulled out of her like a dark hand plunging out of the mirror above Ghost's bed, grabbing him and pulling him up and into the night.

"Jesus," Ghost whispered, sitting up in bed. "Jesus."

He was half dreaming, half imagining. He rolled out of bed and walked around the room, his heart pounding.

Flicking on a light, he reached for the telephone and dialed the Chateau Marmont in Los Angeles.

"Rebecca Blesser," he said, when the clerk answered the ring.

He was put on hold for a moment, then told that Miss Blesser was still registered, but there was a "Do Not Disturb" on her line until seven-thirty in the morning.

Ghost fell back on his pillows and turned out the light.

It was just as well. He really had nothing planned to say to her.

4

In the morning the suite at Caesar's Palace was quiet and dark and smelled of the night with that singular blend of money and booze that circulates in the hotel's air-conditioning system. Ghost rolled out of bed and walked to the shower, calling room service from the phone in the bathroom to order juice and coffee. After showering, he called the front desk and asked that his bill be sent to his office in Los Angeles. Ghost didn't bother shaving, and dressed himself in jeans, sweatshirt, running shoes, and the Dodgers cap pulled low over his black sunglasses. The bellman arrived for luggage; Ghost sent him off with ten dollars and asked to have the car brought out front. He checked the room. On the bar in the living room he found a white envelope with his name written across it. Inside was a note and twenty one-hundred-dollar bills. The note read: "Honey, you're an angel. Here's our stake. The girls." He pocketed the money and left the suite without closing the door. He knew someone would be along soon enough to clean it.

Nudging the Galaxy into the early morning strip traffic, Ghost turned right on Dunes Boulevard and followed it to the freeway. He stopped at a red light and shoved a Percy Sledge tape into his machine. There was a decision to make: a right turn meant west, Los Angeles; left, east. He thought of no compelling reason to return to L.A. and, in fact, felt drawn east, sensing more promise in not having a destination than in having one. When the light changed, he cut across two lanes and took the on-ramp heading east. Halfway up the grade, he saw a thin boy with a backpack slung over one shoulder and a Walkman in his right hand. Ghost slowed down and the boy stuck out a thumb.

"What the hell are you doing?" Ghost said hoarsely, stopping his car by the boy. "You shouldn't be hitchhiking here, kid."

"I need a ride," the boy said, his eyes darting toward the interchange below the overpass.

"This ain't a great spot to be hitchhiking," Ghost said. The kid looked to be eleven or twelve, with shaggy brown hair and pale skin. He wore a tan nylon windbreaker and blue jeans that needed washing; his black high-top sneakers were laced three-quarters to the top.

The boy tossed his pack into the backseat of Ghost's car and reached for the door handle.

"Wait a second, cowboy," Ghost said. "You take a bus. Here," he reached into his pocket and peeled off a twenty.

"I really need a ride, mister."

"Where to?"

The boy narrowed his eyes but didn't answer.

Ghost said, "Where do you need a ride *to?*"

"Just a few miles. I'm kind of late."

"For what?"

"School."

"In June?"

"I missed the bus this morning. If I'm late, I'm going to get into a lot of trouble." The boy's eyes kept returning to the road below the overpass.

Ghost looked away from the boy, up toward the freeway. The boy jumped over the side of the car and into the backseat.

"Yeah, okay," Ghost said, turning around, "since you're so polite, I'll drop you off. Why not?"

Easing the Galaxy up the road and into the stream of traffic, he pulled his Dodgers cap down to keep it from blowing off in the breeze, and hoped the boy wouldn't recognize him.

"What off-ramp you want?" Ghost asked.

Listening to the Walkman, the boy stared blankly ahead.

Ghost reached back and tapped his knee. "Where do I leave you off?"

"Just a few miles."

"And how do I know when that is?"

"I'll show you."

Ghost brought the Galaxy up to cruising speed. When he checked the rearview mirror, he knew the boy was paying no attention to where they were going. Ghost reached the outskirts

54

of Las Vegas in ten minutes and turned to the boy.

"This is the end of the line, my friend."

But the boy was asleep, or feigning sleep, holding his pack like a shield in front of his chest. Perfect, Ghost thought, perfect. He took the next exit and pulled into the parking lot of the Sunburst roadside diner. The boy awoke when the car stopped.

"End of the line," Ghost said. "Good luck to you."

The boy gathered his pack and slung it over his shoulder.

He was skinny and needed cleaning up; his small jaw was thrust forward.

"Have you had breakfast?," Ghost asked.

"No."

"You look like you could use it. Come on, I'll spot you some eggs. What's your name?"

The boy followed Ghost into the diner without answering the question.

"You know," Ghost said, as they sat in a booth, "if you took those headphones out of your ears for a few seconds you might hear what I'm saying."

A young waitress arrived with coffee and menus. Ghost did the ordering, and included half the items on the menu. When the food started arriving, he said, "Just pick out what you want." He went out front to buy a newspaper. He returned to find the boy stuffing himself with sausages, eggs, and pancakes, using both hands to shove in the food.

"Easy," Ghost said, sitting down. "Easy. No one's taking this stuff until we finish it. So, what's your name?"

"It's Radio," the boy answered, his mouth full.

"That's your name?"

He nodded.

"You're not on your way to school, Radio," Ghost said, "so where are you going?"

"Past here."

"Do you live here?"

"No."

"Then what the hell are you doing hitchhiking in Las Vegas?"

"I just came here," Radio said, still eating, not looking up. "I'm going to meet my father." The word *father* came out of the boy's mouth like a promise.

"Where is he?"

"He's in Michigan."

"The *state?*"

The boy nodded.

"Then you've got a ways to go, my friend."

The boy was busy with an egg yolk and a piece of wheat toast.

"So, are you running *to* home or away from home?"

Radio shifted around on the bench, taking an occasional glance at the door and the parking lot.

"Maybe after you eat," Ghost said, "you'll be a little more chatty."

A police patrol car rolled into the lot and parked next to Ghost's Galaxy. The officers got out, stretched, and strolled toward the diner's door.

Without a word, Radio slid out of the booth and hurried across the restaurant into the rest room.

The officers entered and exchanged greetings with the waitress and the cook, then seated themselves at the counter.

Ghost finished his coffee and scrambled eggs and waited for Radio. Finally, leaving a twenty on the table, he walked to the men's rest room. It was empty. The small window over the sink was open.

Ghost went to his car and glanced in the back. Radio was curled up on the floor with the backpack covering him. Ghost stood for a few seconds by the car, looking at the distant, hazy skyline of Las Vegas.

Then he walked back into the diner.

Ghost waited at the counter while the waitress packed a brown bag with sandwiches and two apples. Customers chatted away all around him. The two police officers were talking about power boating on Lake Mead; someone else was complaining about management of the Grand Hotel. Ghost listened to them talk about the streams of their daily lives. He stood there, waiting, unrecognized. Usually, his presence changed people's rhythms, turned their attention away from their lives and onto his. And now, without that, he felt awkward, like last night when the crowd was screaming for Vicky, unsure if what he was feeling was freedom or simply a strange pocket of privacy. He felt challenged by the anonymity.

"Five eleven," the waitress said, for the second time.

"Oh," Ghost said, looking down at her, "here." He handed her a ten dollar bill. "I don't need the change."

"Geeze," she said, "generous and cute to boot. Thanks."

He walked outside, oddly aware of the motions of his body, like hearing his heartbeat in the middle of the night.

Tossing the bag of food on the front seat, he felt both relief and disappointment to see that the boy was gone. He looked back into the diner to see if anyone was watching. No one was. Ghost backed his Galaxy out of the lot and rounded the corner heading to the freeway.

Halfway up the on-ramp he stopped the car. Ghost looked at the bag of food he'd bought for the boy, then turned toward the shrubbery that bordered the road.

"Hurry up and get in," he said, "before I change my mind."

Radio peered through the dense shrubbery at the bottom of the on-ramp and then, deciding all was clear, burst through the bush and made a run for Ghost's car, tossing his pack in the back and hopping in after it.

"Now," Ghost said, still parked, "you can tell me what you're doing."

"Is it okay if we go now, mister?" Radio said, lying low in the backseat.

Ghost checked the mirrors and eased the Galaxy back onto the freeway.

The boy said, "Thanks."

"Where are you from?" Ghost asked.

"Los Angeles."

"And you're planning to go to Michigan?"

The boy nodded.

Ghost said, "Why is your father there and you here?"

"That's where he is," Radio said. "He's in jail there. I'm pretty sure."

"What if you get yourself to Michigan and your father is in jail, then what happens?"

"We're going to live at this place."

Ghost rolled his eyes.

"What makes you think you're going to be able to get your father out of jail?"

"I'm just going there," Radio said, as if the journey itself was its own purpose.

"And does this place where you're going to live have a *name?* Is there something you don't like about saying *names?*"

Radio reached into his pack and produced several soiled and

wrinkled pages from a *National Geographic* magazine. He leaned over the front seat, holding the worn pages tightly.

"See," he said.

Ghost glanced at a couple of the photographs and recognized the Lodge at Sun Valley, Idaho.

"I think I've seen that before," he said. "It's in Idaho, right? Sun Valley."

Surprised, Radio looked at Ghost suspiciously.

"Yeah," Ghost continued, "I've been there, actually. It's very beautiful. I was there in the summer, once. For trout fishing. Some of the best trout fishing in the country."

Radio had removed the pages from the magazine at his school's library, just two weeks before. He'd been looking at them for months, however. Again and again, during study period, he had sat in the library, studying the photographs. The layout showed Sun Valley both in winter and summer, depicting the ski runs on Bald Mountain and the streams traveled by trout. People in the pictures were active and smiling, skiing, hiking, white-water rafting, hunting, fishing. The colors were vivid. Radio had never seen colors like that, nor had he seen snow, steep clean white slopes with people floating down them as if riding clouds. There was a picture of a house on the Wood River; a man and his two boys were fishing from its back porch. Right from the porch.

"You were there?" Radio asked.

"I stayed at the lodge that's in the picture there."

Radio, certain Ghost was lying, stowed his pictures.

"Where are you going, mister?" Radio asked, after a while.

"I'm not absolutely sure, since you're asking. Michigan wasn't on the list."

Pointing to the Caesar's Palace tag on Ghost's tote bag, Radio said, "I was there."

"High roller?"

The boy looked at him blankly.

"You must be a big gambler. That's where the big players stay. Caesar's Palace."

"Two army guys made some bets for me."

"Bets?"

"They won and I got the money," Radio said. "So I can pay for gas."

"What do you mean, two army guys?"

"I waited out front of that hotel and I saw these two army guys and asked them if they would make a bet for me and at first they wouldn't do it but, finally, they said they would. And I got the money because they won."

"For christ's sake, Radio. You're damn lucky you're in one piece. Listen, you didn't quite finish your breakfast. Eat this." He handed him the brown bag from the diner. "That's what I went back inside for."

They rolled along beneath the increasing heat of the desert sun. Radio ate the sandwiches and Ghost knocked off a couple of cold drinks, put into the cooler by Caesar's room service. He listened to Raashan Roland Kirk, while Radio was once again hooked into his Walkman.

"So you think your father is going to get paroled," Ghost said. "Is that the deal?"

"I guess so."

"But you don't know if he's going to be paroled or not?"

"No."

"You just can't sit around Michigan waiting for him to get out."

"I'm just going there."

"You told me that. You ever been in an airplane?"

"No."

"That's what I think you should do. Get on an airplane in Salt Lake City. I've been thinking about it. We'll drive to Salt Lake and you can fly back to Los Angeles. I'll arrange the whole thing. Give me the number of your family at home and I'll have somebody pick them up and take them to the airport to meet you. Right to your doorstep."

"I don't want to go there."

"Unfortunately, pal, that's where you should go. What you're doing now is a lot of bull. You know that, don't you?"

"Mister, I'll just get out."

"We're in the middle of the goddamned desert."

"I'm still thirsty," Radio said, "I'll buy one of those drinks from you."

"You don't have to buy it. Here," Ghost said, taking one of the soft drinks from the cooler. "How old are you?"

"Sixteen."

"Right."

"I am."

"Bullshit," Ghost said, jamming the car over the side of the road, raising a shower of dust. "We'll just sit here and bake until you tell me how old you are."

"I can get out," Radio said.

"I know you can. You'll cook like an egg."

They sat in silence in the heat.

Ghost felt perspiration rolling down his neck. The heat of the sun began penetrating the protection of his cap.

Finally, Ghost said, "You're eleven," and started up the car. "That's right," Ghost continued, easing the car back onto the road, "isn't it? You're eleven."

"Yeah," Radio said.

"Okay."

"I'm kind of tired," Radio said.

"Then take a nap. Now that I know how old you are."

Radio lay down on the backseat and put his pack over his head to shield himself from the sun. Ghost could hear the tinny music from the boy's radio.

2

The hot desert wind sawed at their faces as they cut through the northwest corner of Arizona and crossed into Utah. Radio slept for a couple of hours while Ghost went through his Roland Kirk tapes and moved into *The Best of Jimmy Cliff*. They stopped for gas in St. George, Utah.

He said, "Bet you never thought in your lifetime you'd make it to where we are right now. Do you know where Utah is?"

"No."

"A long way from Los Angeles, pal, and a longer way from Michigan. I think I'm ready for a sandwich or something. I couldn't eat that other tuna sandwich from the diner. It got too hot. You don't want hot tuna. How about you? Hungry again?" Ghost found a small grocery-delicatessen, half a block from the town's park. He stopped the car and got out to stretch. Radio looked around cautiously.

"I'll go get the food," Ghost said. He opened the trunk and took out the basketball. "Why don't you go shoot some baskets?

Get some exercise. Want to lock your pack in the trunk?"

"I'm keeping it."

"Suit yourself."

Ghost went into the store and ordered turkey sandwiches, cole slaw, oranges, brownies, and juice. Waiting for the food, he picked up a copy of the Salt Lake newspaper and glanced at the sports section. There was an Associated Press story out of Los Angeles at the bottom of the page headlined:

GHOST DOES DISAPPEARING ACT

Los Angeles Laker superstar Ghost Galvin has reportedly declined to open contract negotiations with the Lakers, according to sources close to the team. Laker owner James Hardin refused comment, as did Galvin's attorney. It is also rumored that Galvin canceled his contract to appear in the new motion picture *The Hunt Club,* scheduled to begin shooting in Oregon in two weeks. Galvin's agent also declined comment.

Ghost paid for the food and returned to the park, where Radio was sitting in the shade atop a grassy knoll. He was watching two kids playing a game of horse twenty yards away on the basketball court.

"Where'd you get this ball, mister?" Radio said to Ghost, attempting to spin it on one finger.

"Call me Thom, and stop with the mister stuff. The ball was given to me. I don't even remember by whom."

"It's an NBA ball."

"Is that what it is?"

"Yes."

"I've never seen one," Radio said, turning the leather ball over in his hands.

"You play ball?" Ghost asked.

"Yeah."

"Here's the food," Ghost said.

"I'm not that hungry."

"Eat the orange, anyway."

"I ate the apple when we were in the car."

"Well, this is an orange. You should always eat a lot of fruit."

"I'll buy it from you, if you want," Radio said, "then I don't have to eat it."

"You should eat it."

"This is the kind of ball they use on television in the games," Radio said.

"I guess so. I don't know."

Ghost peeled the orange and gave a couple of wedges to Radio.

The afternoon was warm, not hot as it had been in the desert. The two boys were now playing one-on-one on the asphalt court, and the sound of the ball rebounding off the rim traveled languidly through the air.

"So who's in L.A.," Ghost asked, "if your father is in Michigan?"

"Nobody."

"Where's your mother?"

Radio thought about the question, while spinning the ball like a globe on his finger.

Finally, he said, "She died."

"How long ago?"

"I don't know."

"One year, ten years?"

"I don't know, a couple of weeks ago."

"Jesus, Radio, I'm sorry."

Radio watched the spinning ball.

Ghost said, "So you lived in L.A. with your mom?"

"Yeah."

"Who did you live with when she died?"

"This lady, Karen. She's a friend of my mom's. They worked together at this bar."

"So you ran away from Karen's house, then?"

Radio nodded.

"Was she mean to you?"

"No."

"Are you telling me the truth about all this?"

"Yeah."

"You just decided to run away. Did you get yourself in some trouble?" Ghost asked.

"I'm going to meet my father. I said that."

"People are going to be looking for you. You're not going to be able to just disappear. They won't let you. I think you should go back to L.A. That's the best thing you can do right now. They won't let you just wander across the country."

"Who?" Radio said.

"The authorities. They have lots of laws about kids, minors."

Radio stopped spinning the ball, and looked it over intently. Its seams were wider and deeper than on any ball he'd ever seen. He shrugged. "I just got on a bus and left."

"I ran away once," Ghost said.

Radio looked at him.

"What for?"

"Well, I didn't get too far. Certainly not as far as you've gotten. But it was that thing about making up your mind to run away. I think I was like eight or nine. My father used to travel a lot, all the time, really. It was because he was in politics. I remember we were out at the place in Wisconsin where we used to live during the summer and my father had come out for the weekend. He had to go back to Washington and I didn't want him to go. I figured if I ran away they'd have to come looking for me and he wouldn't be able to go. He had to leave, but my mom found me out in the cornfields and I got into a lot of trouble. That was the big adventure."

A smile crossed Radio's lips.

"Keep the ball," Ghost said. "Maybe it'll be good luck for you."

Radio turned the ball over in his hands. The leather surface was tacky for easy gripping, the ball felt balanced, as if it could spin toward the basket on its own; all he had to do was throw it up in the air. "That's pretty cool," the boy said, still looking at the ball. Then he looked up at Ghost.

"Are you a queer?"

"Am I a queer?"

"A faggot," Radio said.

"No, I'm not."

" 'Cause if you are, I'll just leave."

"Right. Well, you can relax about that."

"Thanks for the ball."

Ghost collected the scraps of food and stuffed them into the brown sack. He said, "Why don't you break it in? I'm going over to the store to make a couple of calls."

"Are you going to call the police?"

"No."

The boy shouldered his pack, took the ball, and went over to the court.

Ghost found a phone booth on the corner near the deli. He placed a call to Norman Jamison.

"You sound like you're in Alaska," Jamison said.

"St. George, Utah."

"Where?"

"I left Vegas this morning. Now I'm in Utah."

"Going where?"

"I've just been driving."

"Clearing the head?"

"Yeah. I think I'm going to drive on to Nippersink."

"That will give you some time."

"Have you seen the papers?" Ghost asked him.

"Right, it was in the *Times.*"

"I made the *St. George Courier.*"

"I don't know who leaked the story," Jamison said. "No one in this office. I'm the only one who knows here."

"Maybe Hardin's pissed off and he leaked it to make me look like a jerk."

"It's conceivable. But I doubt it."

"You know what? I don't give a goddamn. Listen," Ghost said, "I've got a problem. I picked up this kid hitchhiking out of Vegas. I mean a *kid.* He's eleven. He was on the damn freeway and I was half asleep and I just pulled over. We went to this diner for breakfast and he took off when two cops showed up. Anyway, I've still got him."

"Get rid of him," Jamison said. "It's trouble."

"I don't want to do that."

"Then go to the police and make it their problem. Go to the police. That's step number one."

"Norman, I don't want to get involved with the police. Can you see me trying to explain what I'm doing *here* driving around in this old heap I rented? And I don't think he's a bad kid. He's kind of ballsy. I don't want to just leave him at a police station."

"He's obviously in trouble, Ghost. It's for the authorities to handle."

"I thought maybe I could get him to Salt Lake and put him on a plane; he's from Los Angeles. Then I thought you could help. I'll call you from Salt Lake. Hey, listen, did you find out anything more about that reporter Hardin brought to the party?"

"I made some calls, and about all I can tell you is that she's legit. They tell me she writes serious stuff, stays completely away from the fluff. Well thought of at the magazine, a comer."

"Okay. I'll be in touch."

Ghost dropped the phone back on its hook, feeling a faint

sense of disappointment at Jamison's report about Rebecca. If it had come back to him that Rebecca was an ambitious personality writer hiding behind the credibility of *Life* magazine, then he could stop thinking about her. But he had picked up the phone last night and tried reaching her, to ask her to send him whatever she had about his father, so that he could read it and decide if he wanted to pursue it any further. He knew, however, it wasn't going to be that easy. Not leaving a message for her to return the call had given him a momentary feeling that what happened next with her was up to him. But Ghost knew they would be talking. Just like he knew earlier, when leaving the Sunburst diner, that the boy would be waiting at the next on-ramp. The only decision had been whether or not to stop. And he wanted to believe that that decision, at least, had been his own.

3

When he saw Ghost approaching, Radio waved him over to the court. Ghost saw the two other players and stopped at the grassy knoll. "Come on," Radio called to him.

Ghost sat down.

"Wait here," Radio said to the two players, then ran to Ghost.

"Can you play, mister? You had that ball in your trunk. . . ."

"No, I don't play. You play. I'll watch."

"You're tall," Radio said. "You don't have to be good. You can just stand there and get rebounds and we can beat those guys."

"What guys?"

"The guys standing right there. You can just rebound. I can shoot."

"Can you?"

"Yeah."

"Then go shoot."

"Let's play a game with them."

"No, thanks," Ghost said.

"Then why do you have the ball?"

"It was in my trunk. I told you, someone gave it to me. I don't feel like playing, Radio. I want to get to Salt Lake. So let's go."

"They've got my ten dollars."

"How'd that happen?"

"I lost it."

"How?"

"One-on-one. First I played the tall guy, then the other guy. I'm a better shooter, but they're too tall."

"Well, sounds like you're out ten bucks."

Ghost looked at the two players. They were fifteen or so, probably high school players. "You shouldn't have played those guys. No way."

"They've got the ball," he said.

Ghost looked at him.

"I played the tall guy again. Double or nothing."

"Shit, Radio."

Radio was looking at his opponents. "Now they've got your ball."

"*Your* ball. . . ."

"Mister, let's just play them one game."

"I don't know where you got the idea you were going to beat them. They've both got a foot on you."

"They're just tall. They're not that good. That's why if you can get the rebounds, I can shoot."

"All right," Ghost said. "Let's see if we can get the ball back. Shit."

"Okay. Thanks, mister. Just rebound and I'll shoot."

"I hope you can shoot," Ghost said.

They walked over to the court, and one of the kids looked at Ghost and said, "That guy's too tall."

"I told you I'd get a guy and this is the guy," Radio said. "He's not a player, anyway. He's just tall. So let's play."

"Okay, Bobby," the kid, whose name was Jake, said to his friend. "Let's take it out and beat these guys."

Radio stole the inbound pass and tossed it to Ghost, who was standing unguarded under the basket. But he threw it right back to Radio and let him do the ball handling. Radio worked his way around Bobby and popped a fifteen footer that fell short on the front rim and kicked off to Jake, who nailed a twenty foot set shot. These were good high school players, and in a few minutes they built a ten-to-nothing lead. Twenty was game. Radio was having trouble getting a shot off over Bobby, who stood a foot taller than he.

"Back that guy in or something," Radio said. "You can shoot right over him. And guard him closer. He keeps getting right by you."

Ghost let the score run to sixteen-two, then subtly began taking control of the game, blocking shots, banking off-balance turn-around shots that appeared to be lucky when they dropped in. The change in the game's momentum fired up Radio who, using Ghost's picks, contributed four quick baskets. At eighteen-sixteen Radio stole the ball from Bobby and knifed down the lane for a game tying lay-in. Then he missed a shot from ten for a win, but Ghost snatched the rebound out of the air and tossed what everyone, including Radio, thought was a terrible shot, but actually was a pass that hit Radio in the hands and left Bobby and Jake looking in the wrong direction. Radio put it in for an easy basket and the win. He collected his ten dollars and took the ball.

Bobby said to him, "You're a lucky little shit. You probably didn't have the hundred if you lost. You probably didn't have another five bucks."

Walking away, Ghost said, "You bet him a hundred against the ball and the ten?"

Radio shrugged.

"Do you even have a hundred?"

Radio didn't answer.

"You know," Ghost said, "that's a lot of pressure to put on yourself, playing for that kind of money. Any way you slice it, you didn't make a good bet."

The boy walked alongside Ghost, turning the ball over in his hands.

Performing well under pressure was Ghost's signature as a player, according to the sportwriters; Ghost Galvin *owned* the final ten minutes of the big games. That was one kind of pressure. Another kind was playing two kids for a hundred bucks if you have only fifty in your pocket. Or being fourteen years old and having your father fly in from Washington just to watch a game, the plane waiting to take him back minutes after the final buzzer. It was annoying to Ghost to be dragged into this pickup game, yet he found it exhilarating to watch the intensity in Radio's eyes; it's the look a player gets when he's playing for someone else, or for something else. No one likes to have to defend against that kind of player. Ghost knew the look.

"You're saving up this money to get to Michigan, then Idaho with your father?" Ghost asked. "Is that what the deal is?"

They had reached the car.

Radio said, "I'll split the ten with you, mister. I'll give you your cut."

"Keep the money," Ghost said. "Stop calling me mister."

4

They reached Salt Lake City at eleven o'clock that night. Ghost drove through the downtown area until he found a Hilton Hotel. He paid cash for two rooms then returned to the car and awakened Radio.

"We made it to Salt Lake," he said. "It's late, we'll get some sleep and organize ourselves in the morning."

"How much does it cost?"

"I'm taking care of the rooms. Let's just get some sleep."

"Are you rich?"

"I'm not broke."

Ghost located the adjoining rooms and said, "Knock on my door if you need anything. In the morning we'll work on things for you. And I'm not going to do anything you don't want me to do. You got that? So stay put. Take a shower or bath or something; you don't smell great."

Radio locked himself in his room. He emptied the contents of his backpack on the king-size bed. There was a sweatshirt, a pair of socks and underwear, and one pair of jeans. Also, two packs of matches, the radio, pocket knife, wallet, an oilskin in which he kept his *National Geographic* pages, a map of the United States with Michigan outlined in red. Paper-clipped to the map was a black-and-white photograph of a man, surely his father. The photo was faded and smudged, and the man looked unhappy about having his picture taken, as though the photographer had caught him off guard.

Radio had run away from Karen's house four days before, at dawn, when Karen was in her soundest sleep. Like Radio's mother, Karen never returned from work until the cocktail lounge closed at two A.M. Even then she wasn't able to fall asleep until three-thirty or four. On the way to the bus depot, Radio had stopped by the shack where he and his mother had lived. It was behind an old house on Acama Street in North Hollywood. An alley abutted the back of the shack. Radio climbed the fence and looked into the bedroom window. From there he could see a bedroom, bathroom, and combination living room and kitchen. Peering through the window, Radio saw the home as he'd left it. Rent was paid to the end of the month, and the man who lived in the main house felt superstitious about putting in a new tenant until then.

The beds were unmade, two dresses were draped over his mother's chair, and on the nightstand sat an alarm clock, a few coins, a picture of Radio, and a half-filled glass of water. The sewing basket sat at the foot of the bed, its usual place, with mending spilling out of it. On the wall above Radio's bed hung the old Mickey Mouse in a spaceship clock that Radio liked; his mother had bought it for him once when they went to Disneyland; the clock was noisy at night but he liked it. In the kitchen, salt and pepper shakers were on the chipped Formica-topped table; there was a bowl on the table with flecks of Rice Krispies in it. The pillows on the couch in the living room were bunched up the way Radio's mother liked them for watching television. He could see into the bathroom where a hand towel was draped on the doorknob; there were still stains from his hands upon it. It was always something he and his mother did before meals; she'd inspect his hands to make sure he'd cleaned the dirt out from underneath the nails. Radio would surrender his hands to her and she would really look at them, and it was always good to feel her hands surrounding his. When he sat there on the fence looking into the shack, he did not feel like his mother had died. Instead, he felt invisible; everything in his world was still in place, waiting for him, but it could no longer see him.

He didn't want to go back to Karen's house, because he didn't really know her. His mother talked to her on the telephone and Karen visited their home sometimes at night, but Radio was always asleep. He told Karen and he had told the old priest from the church that he was going to see his father because he knew him, and of course Karen and the priest had never heard of Radio's father—Radio's mother never talked about him—so they just looked at him and didn't say anything. Then the priest wanted them all to pray. The Lord's Prayer was carved in wood and framed on the outside of the church, directly in back of the altar. That's the prayer the priest wanted to say. "Our Father which art in heaven, Hallowed be thy name. Thy Kingdom come.

Thy will be done in earth, as it is in heaven. . . ." They were always talking about your Father in church, your protector, and your salvation. "Honey, I don't think you know your father," Karen had said, looking to the priest for some help, when Radio started talking about finding his father in Michigan. "I don't think you've met him. Your mother never said . . ." Radio looked away and tuned them out. He had the photograph and he had the map—that was better than they had in church—and he knew where he wanted to be with his father. That was something to go on. In church you just knelt and prayed, and the priest looked at you like he knew things that you didn't. "I want you to say the Our Father every day," the priest told Radio. His mother used to say that prayer, too. Radio heard her sometimes at night. She'd say the first few words out loud, then whisper the rest. People were always doing that in church. They'd say "Our Father which art in heaven," out loud, and mumble or whisper the rest, like it was a secret, or like they were afraid. He hated that about going to church with his mother; it made her afraid and sad.

Later that night, after listening to the priest and Karen talk about his mother, Radio had spread kerosene and ignited the deserted church. He was surprised by how quickly and easily the flames wrapped around the rear of the building, climbed the wooden support beams, and washed over the carved wooden plaque of the Our Father. The building was imposing, rising above him in the night like a dark ship, but the fire skipped up its side and soared, a power all its own. And he had used that power to put himself on the bus.

5

In the other room, Ghost rested in the darkness. He felt it was even money as to whether the boy would still be there in the morning. It was also questionable, he felt, whether Radio had a father in Michigan or that his mother was, in fact, dead. The simplicity with which the boy discussed these things made Ghost suspicious.

Ghost began thinking about that Friday in September ten years before when he last saw his own father. His mother and grandmother had packed up the summer things and had driven back to Chicago, leaving the men behind to close the Nippersink house. Later that day, Ghost was catching a flight for San Francisco, to resume school at Stanford, and the senator was planning to spend one more night at Nippersink, writing speeches, before rejoining the campaign.

It had been the hardest summer of Ghost's life, that being the year he hadn't played for Stanford. The senator was baffled and hurt by Ghost's decision. Ghost had been All American his freshman year at Stanford, an accomplishment made greater by the fact that Stanford had never been known as a basketball school. But he sat out his sophomore year, and made no plans to play his junior year. The subject had come up again that last Friday morning at Nippersink.

"You've got a God-given gift," the senator said, "and you've worked hard all your life to improve it. I don't see the point now in not using it."

At first, Ghost had planned only to skip usual summer league training following his freshman year at Stanford. That decision had upset the senator; then when Ghost decided not to play at all his sophomore year, the conversations between them had dwindled to exasperated telephone calls. Ghost had watched his father become increasingly withdrawn and reticent during the year. Not to the public, of course. The speeches still flowed with power and wit. That was "the senator," however. But Ghost could see that it was more performance than passion. He was certain that when the convention came, bringing with it the expected vice-presidential nomination, his father's spirits would lift, that Ghost's not playing ball would fade in the activity and euphoria of a successful campaign. The convention came, as did the nomination, but Ghost continued to find his father distant and disturbed. In the past, basketball had been what got their conversations started.

That second summer passed, bringing the Friday in September, and the last time Ghost saw his father. To Ghost, his father seemed that morning unusually edgy, constantly looking away from Ghost, out toward the fields.

"What is it that you want from me, son?" the senator had said. "Is there something you want me to do in order for you to play ball?"

Ghost didn't know what to say to his father. In fact, he wished his father would answer his own question, because Ghost wasn't sure how to answer it. To say he simply didn't feel like playing seemed inadequate; it just wasn't something he wanted to say to his father.

"Watching you play ball is what I enjoy most," the senator had said. "Not giving speeches. That's business, giving speeches. Watching you play is when I feel"—the senator had looked out the window, as though the words he wanted were floating over the cornfields in the distance—"pure. It's the one time in my life I feel absolutely pure. You're a little young, I imagine, to know what the hell I'm talking about. But you bounce around enough in life, take chances, and do things, some right, some wrong, and by then there aren't many things that feel . . . pure. It's hard to deal with the rest without that, isn't it?" He hung the question with a nod on the clouds over the cornfields, and didn't turn around to face Ghost.

It isn't like my father, Ghost had thought at the time, to stand and stare.

The next morning Senator Galvin died.

Ghost was back in California when he received the news. A military plane brought him to Chicago, and he met his mother at their town house. Judge Ely had been there with her.

All his mother had told Ghost was that it had been a heart attack and that it had happened at Nippersink. When someone dies suddenly and unexpectedly one's mind races with questions rather than grief; one grasps for an explanation. But during the flight from Moffit Field near Palo Alto to Chicago there was no one whom Ghost could ask where his father had died, when he had died, what happened just before, had he made it to the hospital and died there? When he landed at the airport, a government car had taken him home. While stopped in traffic downtown, Ghost had seen a newsstand, and all the papers had had banner headlines about his father's death. He had wanted to jump out and grab one, but had resisted doing so, not wanting to be recognized. It had been awful, watching people reading the papers at the stands, feeling that they knew more about his father's death than he did. Everyone on the street had seemed to be looking at him in the car. They knew about his father's death, and somehow they seemed to know that Ghost knew nothing about it. He had hated the feeling and had turned away from them and implored the driver to speed through the traffic and get him home.

"What happened?" were Ghost's first words to Judge Ely.

"Sit down, Thommy," Judge Ely had answered.

But Ghost hadn't wanted to sit down. People were always telling him to sit down when they had bad news, as if to control him.

"Go ahead and sit down," Judge Ely had repeated quietly. And when Ghost did, the judge had continued. "His heart just gave out on us. It should have been me. It should have somebody other than your dad. But that's it. Thommy, it's the worst thing that will ever happen to you in your life. There's nothing else that can happen anymore. Your life will only get better. You'll have a wonderful life. Your father was a great, great man. I know you know that, but it helps me to say it. He was a great, great man."

"When did he die?" Ghost had asked.

"Early this morning."

"What was he doing?"

"Fishing. He was just trying to relax a little before heading into town and the campaign. I was going to take the helicopter in with him. He didn't suffer. He had a heart attack and died on the spot. He didn't suffer at all."

"We drove by the newsstand on the way in."

"Don't read the papers, Thommy. Don't watch the news. They're sons-of-bitches."

That was a familiar refrain from the judge. Ghost had heard it from him dozens of times. "You have to watch the press," he'd told Ghost. "They're sons of bitches. You can never let them know that we know that. But we know that. They're only interested in selling advertising space." The judge had stood up. "Your mother's in her room. You better go to her."

And Ghost had not read the papers or watched the news during that time. He had started to a couple of times, but as soon as he saw a photograph of his father he couldn't proceed.

Ghost flew back to Chicago for Thanksgiving Day that year. Judge Ely and his wife had Ghost and Nicole Galvin and a few friends over. After dinner, the judge sat with Ghost in the study of the apartment, and they talked about the fact that Ghost had resumed playing basketball for Stanford, and that his game hadn't suffered from the layoff.

"Not when you've got what you've got do you lose it," the judge had said.

There had been a lull in their conversation and Ghost had

asked, "Did you talk to my father that morning? When he died?"

"We talked the night before. We were going to meet the following afternoon before he left for the campaign."

"Did he say anything about me?"

"We talked about the campaign. You know we spent plenty of time talking about you, but not that evening."

"He was very upset with me," Ghost had said, trying to drop a weight off himself. Put it at the feet of the judge for . . . what? . . . forgiveness?

"He'd be very proud of you right now. Your father was very proud of you, son. He loved you."

"I don't understand why he died," Ghost had said, unable to ask the question he'd been thinking about at night: Had his father killed himself?

"It was a tragedy that he died," the judge had answered. "The world hasn't figured out a way to stop tragedies. You'll have to be content knowing your father loved you. I'm too old to tell you anything else. He just died."

Ghost had looked at the judge and felt that he knew things about the senator's death that Ghost did not. But it seemed pointless to ask questions when he didn't want the answers. It was better to move on. The season was starting. There would be practice and travel and games every day until spring.

The judge had not looked away from Ghost's gaze. He had said simply, "Just know your father loved you."

5

Rebecca awoke from a dream, the images pursuing her into waking the way music resonates following the final notes of a symphony. The dream was familiar to her; its framework had changed little over the years: There was a woman standing by a large window in the living room of an old house; she wore a full dress with high collar, like a figure from a Victorian cameo; the view from the window was unseen in the dream. This woman did not resemble anyone Rebecca knew, yet Rebecca believed her to be her birth mother. There was no evidence supporting this, just a feeling. She'd felt it from the first time she'd had the dream, which was when she was sixteen, a year after her parents explained to her that she was adopted. The dream recurred a couple of times a year until Rebecca was in college. It was then that she began seriously researching her background. By that time she was having the dream a few times a month, if only for a matter of seconds. And since then it had become not so much a dream as a part of her life, as constant as sleep itself.

After her parents told her about the adoption, Rebecca let the knowledge settle for a year. She didn't tell her friends or discuss it with anyone, because she didn't want to be different. Rebecca loved her parents and liked her life and didn't want anything about it to change. But as the dream continued, it made Rebecca curious. There were questions she couldn't ask anyone. Who was this woman? Why did she give me away? Where is she now? Does she know who I am? During her first year at Brown, Rebecca began making inquiries, feeling that her curiosity—and at the time it felt like only that, curiosity—had to be satisfied. Quickly she learned that the discovery process was not simple. Each state had its own laws about adoption, and the information available to the adoptee was slight. Mr. and Mrs. Blesser had arranged for the adoption through an attorney who dealt with adoption agencies in several states, and the Blessers' only requirement had been a white infant from healthy parents; they hadn't wanted to know anything else.

Rebecca contacted the attorney, who attempted to dissuade her from pursuing the issue. He was kind to Rebecca but persistent in his views.

"Why don't you think about it for another year or two?" he asked. "Because, first of all, I don't have all that much information. Second, it puts a lot of strain on your parents, whether you know it or not. They begin wondering if they didn't do all they should; they feel inadequate. Third, what people often find when they chase these things is that they wish they hadn't."

He put Rebecca off with conversations like this until she was nineteen. The attorney then reluctantly revealed the name of the agency that handled the relinquishment and adoption. There, Rebecca hit a complete block. The agency, located just outside of Chicago, allowed Rebecca to look at the adoption papers, but its policy was to black out all "identifying" information. She also found out that her birth certificate, like those for almost all adopted children, had been altered, that the original was sealed and could be obtained only by court order. The court order was nearly impossible to obtain without the complete cooperation of the birth parent. The names on the birth certificate, the adoption officer explained, were rarely useful, because under state law the birth parent could name the child almost anything. In Rebecca's case, her given name was "baby girl." As each lead took her nowhere, Rebecca became outraged that there was information filed away about her that was simply not available to her. The curiosity became an obsession.

Friends advised Rebecca to keep her search in perspective, that discovery of the past wasn't essential to a good future. But these people didn't have questions come in the night like dark messengers. Rebecca saw the woman in the dream and wanted to ask her if there was something in the seed that sent her to the hospital to arrange adoption. Had she been too young, too old, too poor? From too good a family, or too bad? Did I have the wrong father for you to keep me, or was I the wrong child? Who made the decision? Was it you, was it my father, or was it the two of you together? Perhaps it was not your decision at all.

The first time Rebecca made love a scream escaped from her when the boy released himself inside of her; she grabbed the back of his head and held his face against her shoulder, to keep him from seeing the tears on her face. The scream had escaped when she flashed on what was happening, the possibility of conception, desire entangled with the part of her capable of doing what her birth mother had done. The image of the altered birth certificate had popped into her mind. Mother: blacked out. Father: unknown. Child: Baby girl. It was an infuriating sensation to know that under the blackout was a woman's name, Rebecca's natural mother, yet for Rebecca there was no access to that name. And there was no lead to the father without first tracking down the mother. The adoption agency explained that fathers were often impossible to find, because frequently the father's correct name and whereabouts were unknown to the mother.

Rebecca graduated from Brown and was hired as a researcher by *Time* magazine. She began compiling a massive file on adoption in America. She advanced to a writer's position, and the adoption article was her first major piece for the magazine. The auspices of the magazine opened corridors of information to her, but it was simple deception that provided the first major break in her own case. Rebecca employed an old but useful technique. She arranged for a meeting and interview with the director of the agency that handled her adoption, and asked that her own file be used as a model for the interview. One of the reporters at *Time* taught her the practical journalistic technique of reading upside down. When the agency director had enough documents out on his desk, including certain ones containing "identifying" information (and therefore not available to Rebecca) she was able to read the name of a hospital in Virginia. With that information she took her birthdate and time of birth and contacted the hospital. The hospital was a private institution supported in large part by endowments. Again, the available information was minimal, since the original birth certificate was sealed, and the mother's name on the altered certificate was blacked out. Rebecca did, however, make friends with a secretary in the administration department. She took the young woman to lunch and called her a few times. And it was this girl who then researched the birth records at the hospital and found that a "baby girl" was born on Rebecca's birthday and time to an Elizabeth Folger; age, Social Security number, address, etc., not available. The secretary told Rebecca that, in fact, the lack of information on Elizabeth Folger was unique, even for a birth parent. Also unusual, the secretary told Rebecca, was that the forms were signed and dated three days after the birth, instead of the day itself. The secretary didn't have access to any further information, however.

A year of dead ends followed that break. Rebecca obtained telephone books for many cities in Virginia and for the suburbs of Chicago near the adoption agency. She and several assistants called every Folger in these books and in doing so turned up several Elizabeths, but none that had anything to do with her possible birth parent. The article ran in *Time,* and she wrote another piece for *Life* that went into detail about the process of her personal search, revealing the name Elizabeth Folger. The stories attracted wide discussion on television and radio talk shows, and Rebecca received thousands of letters from adoptees searching for birth parents, and from birth parents who wondered what had happened to the children they surrendered. Among those letters were dozens from people who knew an Elizabeth Folger. Many of the letters were responses to letters that Rebecca and her assistants had sent. Of course, most of these letters came back unopened or with a note from someone saying she'd found the wrong Folger. Rebecca utilized hundreds of computerized magazine mailing lists, and sent letters to those Folgers as well. She followed up on all the responses that held any shade of promise. One letter came in from a woman in Chicago who said she'd lived in the same building with an Elizabeth Folger for many years, and Elizabeth Folger's age at the time described by the woman corresponded with the chronology Rebecca had published in her article.

"You know, I'm eighty-three now," Mrs. Towsley told Rebecca, who had flown immediately to Chicago to see her. "And I'm not that good with numbers, but I think it was twenty-three, twenty-five years ago that Elizabeth moved from across the hall. And she'd lived there for a good four years. I've lived here almost forty years."

The building was on Lake Shore Drive, facing Lake Michigan.

"Now," Mrs. Towsley continued, "Elizabeth was about

78

twenty-two when she moved here. I remember her telling me that when a number of gifts were delivered to her on her birthday one year. And she seemed such a mature young woman, so her age stuck in my head. Her apartment was the one just across the hall, on the view side of the building. Being here so long I always get first choice of the view apartments, but I never take them because I don't want all the rent. I'm comfortable right where I am, don't you know." Mrs. Towsley sipped 7-Up during the interview, and clutched a handkerchief in her left hand. She said the 7-Up helped settle her stomach.

"Elizabeth must have been paying quite a bit of rent," Rebecca said to her.

"Oh, she was, she was. Certainly. It wouldn't sound like a lot now, but back then she was paying top dollar."

"Did she have a job?"

"She didn't talk about it. Didn't seem to keep regular hours, don't you know, and traveled all the time. I know that because I looked after her mail and things. She gave me a key to her apartment and I'd put the mail on the kitchen table, and I'd water her plants. She always had a lot of fresh flowers in the apartment. The florist was constantly delivering something for her. I don't know if they were from gentlemen friends, or one gentleman, or what, but there were plenty of flowers."

"So you must have known her fairly well?"

"Dear, I can't say *well* and be honest with you, because I don't think anybody in the building knew her *well*. Kept very much to herself, Elizabeth did. Pleasant, but not one to be dropping in on the neighbors. Kind of aloof. Not haughty, just kept to herself. I'll bet I was the only one she had more than one or two words for. And she didn't have a lot of visitors. I don't think I ever remember her having visitors. Unless they were very quiet. Just the delivery boy from the florist."

"Did you pay any attention to the mail you picked up for her, Mrs. Towsley? I don't mean reading it, just noticing what was there?"

"Gosh, I don't think so. Just the newspapers. She must have read a lot. I knew she was very bright, Elizabeth. You could see that in her eyes. She got the Chicago papers and the New York paper and the Washington paper. A whole stack of them in the mail every day. And the magazines. She got plenty of those. Not ladies' magazines. Elizabeth got the news magazines and business magazines. Lots of them. Whenever she returned from a trip I had a stack of newspapers and magazines waiting for her. I would make a comment here and there, like 'when do you find time for all this reading.' She told me that she liked to keep up on the news and the politics. She clipped articles. We'd have coffee and she would be clipping articles and photos about politics."

"Did you ever see her out of the building?"

"Only in the lobby or out front. I don't drive, you see, and I'd be out waiting for my cab, and there'd be Elizabeth arriving in the biggest Cadillac limousine you've ever seen, a big black car and a driver who wore a cap. I suppose he was bringing her back from one of her trips, or sometimes from shopping, because she'd have packages."

"No one else in the car?"

"Just the driver. What I do remember," Mrs. Towsley continued, "was that when she'd return from one of her trips, she didn't have a lot of luggage. Just a makeup case and small bag. That's all."

"You wouldn't happen to have any photographs of her, would you?"

"No, no I don't. I don't believe that Elizabeth liked being in photographs much. Which was very interesting to me, because she enjoyed taking pictures. She kept a camera on her windowsill. More than once I saw her taking pictures out her window. I imagine she photographed the lake and the boats. It's quite colorful when they have the boat races. But I never saw the photographs she took. She was shy about that. I never saw one.

"She was a handsome young woman, Rebecca, she certainly was. Always dressed neat as a pin, always. Morning, noon, or night. Whenever I saw Elizabeth, she was fresh as a daisy. Never anything flashy, like some young people like to wear. Always neat and elegant, just so. Sitting here looking at you, I see Elizabeth in your eyes. That sort of mysterious quality you both have. You have your mother's dark eyes, right as rain."

"Why did she move out?"

"I don't know for certain. Even though I was curious, I never pried with Elizabeth. I knew something had to be going on, not that anyone else in the building would have noticed a change. Elizabeth was quiet and serious and always had a look in her eyes like she was busy thinking about things. Not daydreaming, but thinking. That was Elizabeth. Mind you, she always had time for a little conversation with me. Just pleasantries. She was always bringing me little gifts for taking care of her plants and the mail. Toward the time she moved out, though, there was something in her eyes. I don't know for the life of me what it was. But whatever it was she was thinking about it all the time. I knew that much. Elizabeth wasn't traveling then. She hadn't gone away for a few months. But I hardly saw her. I'd hear her go down the hall and drop things in the garbage chute. I'd hear that door open and close a few times, because Elizabeth had all those newspapers and magazines. Piles of them. I was in the hall with her, doing the same old thing with my garbage, and I watched her toss newspapers down the chute, but I could see that they had been clipped, you know, with scissors. I suppose if I'd been nosier I could have found out more, but I'm not that way. And I'm sure that's why Elizabeth and I got along.

"One day she knocked on my door, and there she was, neat and nice as usual, and she told me she was moving out the next day. I asked where she was moving to, and she said she had business in the east, and that she would send me a card with her new address. Of course, she never did, or I would have sent her a Christmas card every year, don't you know. Last time I saw her was the next day. The men were in there packing boxes and moving things, and I saw Elizabeth standing by the window looking out at the lake. I said hello and she turned and smiled and said good morning, then went right back to looking out the window. Like she was already gone from the building. The men moved everything right out and down the service elevator. All that was left in there was Elizabeth, her purse, and two boxes she wouldn't let them take. They were not small boxes, but I watched her tie strings around them like handles and insist on carrying them downstairs herself. They were full of her clippings. Those were the last things to go, and she carried them herself."

2

After the visit with Mrs. Towsley, Rebecca had thought about her description of Elizabeth Folger. This woman could be her birth parent, and she might not be. The possibility existed, however slim. But did she want this woman to be her natural mother? That was also hard to know. She decided, though, that not knowing had to be worse than whatever she might find. "In the best interests of the adoptee" was the reason given for sealing adoption records. Rebecca had come across the phrase constantly in her search. But whose decision was that? Whose judgment? Her natural mother had decided years ago that Rebecca should not know her. And then the system that provides for adoption formalizes that decision. But what about *my* choice, Rebecca thought. When do I get to decide whether or not I want to know this person? The questions never left, with the dream of the woman incessantly reminding her of them. Because of the dream, Rebecca at times dreaded sleep, reading long into the night to avoid seeing this woman, avoiding the power the image and its secrets held over her. Other nights, Rebecca sought sleep in search of the dream, basking in the aura of the woman, sensing a kept promise by the woman's presence, a part of herself waiting to be discovered, completed.

Rebecca had spread among her colleagues what information she'd received about Elizabeth Folger. Then the preceding March a senior editor at *Time* stuck his head in Rebecca's office to ask if she had a picture of this Elizabeth Folger. She told him no and asked why. He had worked for the *Chicago Tribune* for ten years, the Associated Press for five, and *Time* for ten, most of those years in Chicago and Washington. Plenty of that time had been spent covering Senator Thomas Galvin. There was a woman he used to spend some time with in Washington, and even for a short while in Chicago, who would have been the right age and somewhat close to the description Mrs. Towsley provided. The woman's first name was Elizabeth.

"Were they having an affair?" Rebecca had asked her older colleague.

"That was the rumor. I think she was in and out of his life more than once. Rumor was that she was someone he met in Chicago and she moved to Washington to be around him."

He had no idea what Elizabeth's last name was, because the affair went on in the days when the press didn't pay serious attention to that sort of information. The editor told Rebecca that *Life* was planning to include Galvin in a series on prominent Americans whose lives were cut short. Rebecca volunteered to loan herself out to the magazine to work on the piece.

Now, stirring in her bed at the Chateau Marmont in Los Angeles, Rebecca opened her eyes, letting the residue of the dream drain from her mind. The room was in blackness, except for the pulsating red message light on the telephone. She pushed herself up and opened the heavy green curtains to let in the light. It was a hot, hazy morning. From her window she could see homes built into the side of a hill. They were ugly one-story, flat-roofed houses, built in the late fifties, that now cost $400,000 because they faced city lights. She wished she was facing the gray silent stone of St. Patrick's Cathedral in Manhattan; that was the view from her two-bedroom apartment on East Fifty-first, in an old building a few doors down from the Olympic Towers, kept alive only by rent control. Rebecca at times stopped in at St. Patrick's on her way to the office, to watch sunlight illuminate the stained glass and cast columns of color on the great arches. She'd wander past the chapels and alcoves where the pilgrims and tourists light prayer candles in front of the statue of Jesus of the Sacred Heart. Though not a Catholic, Rebecca did once light a prayer candle there; she did so not to see the flame, but to burn something. It was an envelope Mrs. Towsley had given her that contained a note from Elizabeth Folger. Rebecca saved the note inside to have the handwriting sample. Then—prior to her colleague suggesting a link between an Elizabeth from Chicago and Senator Galvin— Rebecca stopped in at St. Patrick's Cathedral one evening in February and stood in the cavernous quiet, looking at the prayer candles. On impulse she took the envelope out of her purse, removed the brief note, and placed the envelope upon two candles; as the envelope unfolded in flame, a narrow plume of smoke floated up, past the statue and into the darkness above, like a sacrificial offering. The envelope curled up into scraps of ash that were as black as the blacked-out portions of Rebecca's birth certificate. Pilgrims come here to pray, she thought at the time, asking God to keep and protect their souls. Her offering was not to God but to Elizabeth Folger, that she return the part of Rebecca's soul that she withheld by concealing herself. What is withheld, she thought, becomes sometimes more important than what we share. Would the crowds pour into St. Patrick's, she wondered, if eternal salvation were given freely, rather than withheld?

Rebecca let the curtain in her suite at the Chateau Marmont fall closed, and the room became dark again. The telephone rang.

4

Ghost arose early and went for a run. The morning was clear and warm and a fresh breeze floated down from the mountains. Running through the quiet Salt Lake streets, Ghost felt solitary, free. It was the freedom of motion, as in a basketball game, where the years of practice allowed his movements to be instinctive. He felt the push of his shoes on the pavement but seemed to float along over it, his legs propelling him forward. Only thoughts of Radio and Rebecca distracted him.

After showering, Ghost called the Chateau Marmont and asked for Rebecca. She answered on the third ring.

"This is Ghost Galvin," he said.

"Yes."

"I thought you were going back to New York."

"I've got some other business."

"I want you to help me," he said.

"In what way?"

"First of all, I made a mistake the other night. I shouldn't have just showed up in your room. Let's forget about it."

"That's not entirely up to you."

"I'd like you to use your resources to get me information about a runaway kid from Los Angeles. Help me on this and I'll read over your story about my father and correct facts. We'll call it even."

"That really isn't enough, Mr. Galvin. But you can help me right now," she said.

"How?"

"Do you know Alan Webster?"

"I haven't seen him since my father's funeral. I was a kid when he worked for my father. I can't say I know him all that well."

"Your father trusted him?"

"He was the top aide. God, he worked for my father for almost twenty years."

"He's living in Los Angeles now."

"I didn't know that." Ghost was truly surprised.

"I'm interviewing him this evening. Can I believe what he tells me?"

"He was very loyal to my father. My father trusted him."

"Which means he'll probably tell me nothing," she said.

"Are you going to help me with this kid, or not?" Ghost asked.

"I'll talk to Alan Webster and see how it goes. Maybe you should call and ask him to cooperate."

Ghost dropped the phone on its cradle.

"For christ's sake," he said.

He looked out through the sliding doors of the room's balcony. It was still early. The streets were empty. There was one street that stretched straight out from the hotel, and for as far as Ghost could see it was empty of cars, just a succession of traffic lights. In the distance the mountains caught the early morning light, looking brown and golden. He had thought last night and again during his run that maybe it was time to go back and read all the newspaper articles about his father's heart attack that he'd never read. He'd been thinking that perhaps Rebecca could take him straight to the center of everything. Purge him. But her attitude, Jesus—she'd had an edge in her voice that made him uncomfortable, that made him think her help would come at a price. Now all he felt like doing was driving. Being alone and driving. Ghost threw his toiletries into his carry bag, then went out into the hallway. He stood outside Radio's door and thought for a few seconds. What the hell was he going to do towing an eleven-year-old runaway with him? It would be better if he left the kid plane fare. Why disappoint him, Ghost thought, if I decide halfway to nowhere that I want to go someplace else? I might want to fly to Tahiti, drink some beers, and get laid. Find Marlon Brando. Fuck this shit. Ghost reached into his pocket and peeled off four one-hundred-dollar bills and slid them underneath the door.

He hurried down the stairway to the rear parking lot. From ten feet away he tossed his carry bag into the Galaxy's backseat.

Radio yelled and stuck his head up.

Ghost stopped by the front fender.

Radio had a blanket wrapped around himself. His eyes were wild.

"What are you doing?" Ghost said.

"Why did you throw that at me?"

"I didn't know you were there." Ghost walked around and opened the driver's door. "How long have you been there?"

"I don't know."

"When did you come out here?"

"It was still night," Radio said.

Ghost crossed his arms and leaned against the car, looking away.

"Jesus, Radio," he said, "I was just going to get breakfast. What the hell are you doing out here?"

"Sleeping."

"Where's the rest of your stuff?"

"I've got my stuff," Radio said. "I left the ball in the trunk."

"I was just going for breakfast. You should be asleep. Jesus. Now we can both get breakfast. Let's get the hell out of Salt Lake. Let's just drive."

"How come you're mad?"

"I'm not mad. You startled me."

"You're mad, mister."

"Just tell me why you're sleeping in the car?"

" 'Cause I left the ball in the trunk."

"So what?"

"I like that ball, and I thought you might leave."

"Did I say I was going to leave?"

"No."

"Then why did you think I was going to leave?" Ghost opened the door and dropped into the front seat. He felt transparent, the way he'd felt when Rebecca was talking about his father the other night in her hotel suite.

"I just thought if you left I wanted to have the ball. You gave it to me, remember?"

"I remember."

"How come you're mad?"

"I'm *not* mad." Ghost buckled himself in and started the car.

"I've got their blanket," Radio said.

"Never mind," Ghost said, backing the car out of the lot, "the maid isn't going to say anything. Believe me, she's going to think you're the greatest eleven-year-old person on the planet. Forget about the blanket, and forget about me going anywhere with the basketball. It's your ball now and I'm not taking it, all right?"

5

Rebecca turned off Sunset Boulevard and onto Stone Canyon Road in Bel Air. She drove a quarter mile, past mansions concealed from the street by shrubbery and gates, to the Bel Air Hotel, with its Spanish arches, private bungalows, and parklike grounds. Swans floated in the creek that separated the parking lot from the hotel's entry.

The doorman helped Rebecca from her rental car, and she walked across the small bridge that led to the courtyard entrance of the hotel.

She had been calling Alan Webster for two months. The calls were neither taken nor returned. Two days ago she arrived at the offices of the law firm where Webster had recently become a partner and waited in the reception area until three P.M. when he returned from lunch. Webster had looked Rebecca over and, clearly, her presence made him uneasy. He avoided direct eye contact, but kept sneaking peeks at her, the way people look at the handicapped.

"I'll keep coming here until you agree to speak with me," Rebecca told him.

Webster finally agreed to meet her for cocktails.

"Good evening, Miss Blesser," Webster said, his deep voice cutting across the cocktail-hour chatter in the dark bar.

She stood in the entryway, allowing her eyes to adjust to the darkness.

Webster shook her hand and guided her to his table.

In his gray suit, pale pink shirt, and black silk tie, Webster was a handsome man, perhaps sixty years old, or a weary fifty-five.

"Please call me Rebecca," she said to him.

"Rebecca," he said, "I'm Alan."

"Thank you for seeing me."

Webster summoned a waiter. "Usual," Webster said.

"I'll have a bloody Mary," Rebecca said.

"Two bloody Marys," the waiter said.

"Do you ever miss the Hill," Rebecca said to Webster, "now that you're out here with the sunshine and movie stars?"

"I live out at Malibu now. Wake up every morning looking at the ocean. I don't think I miss Washington all that much. Oh, sometimes when things heat up back there I think about being in the thick of it. I miss knowing what's *really* going on. But you get spoiled out here, don't you? The ocean and the warm weather. It lulls one into a sort of sense of well-being. Isn't that what it's supposed to do?"

He would only look directly at her for a few seconds at a time. She watched his eyes bounce around the room, focus briefly on her, then flick away. Rebecca felt Webster was looking at her with a combination of fascination and fear.

"I know it's disconcerting to have the press calling," she said.

"Hell, after fifteen years on the Hill and twenty in politics, I'm used to it. Besides, I was expecting to hear from you again."

"I don't understand."

"Word was out on the story," he said quietly, as though sharing a small secret and expecting a reward for doing so.

"What 'word' was that, Mr. Webster?"

"Some of us still talk now and then. I knew you were in town. I got a call."

"From whom?"

"Doesn't matter, does it? I figured you'd get around to me."

"I see."

Webster finished his bloody Mary. "Would you like another cocktail? Freshen that one up?" He motioned for the waiter. "I like this hotel, don't you? A lot of locals don't even know where it is, tucked up in here. I like it quite a bit. The senator was fond of it, too, though he didn't get out here much."

"You were with the senator for a long time," she said.

"Ah, the interview, right." He leaned forward, his tan showing up in the candlelight. "If you had come to my office in the first place, instead of just calling all the time, I might have done an interview right from the word *go*. I don't remember too many journalists being this pretty." He reached across the table and patted Rebecca's hand. "I'd been living in London for the past nine years, and you see nothing but scandal sheets over there. I almost stopped reading the papers."

The waiter placed two fresh bloody Marys on the table.

"Why did you stay with the senator all those years?" Rebecca asked.

"He was a good man and a hard worker. I have tremendous respect for what he did as a politician and public servant. Not too dramatic an answer, is it? A driver, ambitious, but with the right intentions. I admired him. Up at five-thirty every day, read all the newspapers by six-thirty, briefing papers by seven-thirty, then usually a breakfast meeting. In the office by eight-thirty and put

88

in a full day. He'd help you get your own job done, but was too busy to wait around and hear thank you."

"How about his family?"

Webster looked at her warily.

"Ghost, Nicole, and Marie. And I suppose you could call the judge and his wife family."

"His wife and son didn't live with him in Washington. I find that odd."

"The senator didn't want his boy growing up there. Ghost was doing so well in Chicago with his basketball practically from the day he learned how to walk. And Nicole wasn't crazy about Washington."

"Then why did she marry a politican?"

"She didn't. She married a soldier. Oh, she came to town for all the important functions. And he was on a plane for home every weekend. Remember, Nicole was French. French women don't cling to their husbands like American women do."

"So you feel he was devoted to his family?"

"He worshiped that boy," Webster said. He drained his drink and the waiter brought another.

Webster sat back in his chair, seeming pleased, relieved. Rebecca leaned forward, waiting for Webster to look at her. When he did, she said, "Tell me about Elizabeth Folger."

His eyes bounced away. Webster peered down at his drink.

To Rebecca, he looked sad, and there was a new heaviness in his voice when he spoke.

"What do you want from me?" he asked, still staring at his drink.

"I want to know about Elizabeth Folger."

"It's a name. The senator knew a lot of people."

Webster's face was beginning to resemble an apology.

Rebecca felt a burning in her stomach, the way she'd felt sitting opposite the director of the adoption agency, or sitting opposite the administrator of the hospital where she was born; they held information that belonged to her, laws empowered them to control that information "in the best interests of the adoptee. . . ." She'd found that when speaking with people about adoption it was always better to appear not to care, to be unemotional, as if she were researching the title to a piece of land. Emotions scared people when talking about adoption. If she was emotional they would look at her as if she were about to explode, as if she were something dangerous and volatile, uncontrollable.

Or they would be embarrassed by her, sometimes secretly repelled, as if as an adopted person she was carrying some genetically inherited disease of which she was unaware because she did not know her roots. She saw those emotions in Webster—a kind of collective guilt that ran from his eyes to his drink.

He lifted the glass and took a swallow.

"He knew a lot of people," Rebecca said quietly, "but he seemed to know that person very well."

It had been a guess, a long shot, that Webster would react. She watched his eyes and knew that he was churning inside.

"He may have known her," Webster said. "What difference? That was in another lifetime."

Whose? she wanted to ask.

"Was she his mistress?"

"This interview is over," Webster answered, starting to rise.

She grabbed his wrist and pulled him back to his chair.

"Look, this doesn't have to go into the article. I just want to know what happened."

"There were always camp followers," Webster replied.

He looked trapped.

"That's just the way it is," he went on. "Until recently, no one's ever thought it was too important to write about them." He finished his drink and the waiter quickly brought him another. Webster waved his hands, then dropped them into his lap. "It's always better when this much time has passed to leave things alone. That much I think I know."

He kept looking at the doorway, picking out his path. Rebecca knew he was ready to bolt, and decided to back away from Elizabeth Folger. She reached into her small valise and pulled out a file. Webster looked at it as if it were a weapon.

"Tell me something about that last year," Rebecca said. "Something happened. The senator changed."

"It was a campaign year. You want to know about stress? Try getting into a campaign."

"Senator Galvin was a career politician. He thrived on it. He'd been through ten campaigns. But look at these."

Webster flinched when Rebecca opened the file. He seemed relieved to see that the contents were photographs of the senator.

"These were taken chronologically during the last six months of Senator Galvin's life," Rebecca said. "His looks changed. He aged."

"He was a man about to die," Webster said, lifting his drink to emphasize his point. "Do you think he's going to look like he's back from a month at a health spa?"

"There was something wrong during the end of his life. And there was something wrong in the way he died."

Webster had finished half the new drink. He put it down on the table and looked with unfeigned surprise at Rebecca.

"What do you mean by that?"

"The entire situation surrounding Senator Galvin's death is cloudy. There was something wrong."

She could see that Webster was confused, suspicious.

"I don't know what you're getting at, but I have to say I think you're a little off your rocker." Webster signed the check, drained his drink, and stood up.

Rebecca dropped the file of photographs back into her valise and went after Webster, who was moving with the self-concious gait of a drunk.

"Tell me who to talk to," Rebecca said, catching up to him.

"Oh, you can call old Judge Ely, but it'd be a waste of time. If you do call him, don't mention you talked to me, will you?"

"Why?"

"Because he's the one who told me you'd be calling, and he preferred I didn't talk to you."

"So why did you talk to me?"

"I guess I miss the senator. And, look, I have no beef with you or anyone else. That was another lifetime. Whatever happened then happened then, and we all have to get on with now."

"Why won't you tell me what else you know?"

He wobbled ahead and wouldn't look at Rebecca.

"I want to call you again," Rebecca said.

"I don't think I have anything else to add."

He seemed deeply sad, repentant.

"Mr. Webster, I'm going to need your hel . . . assistance."

The valet brought his car around.

He stepped in without answering. His thoughts had gone elsewhere.

She approached his car.

"I don't think you should be driving."

He laughed. "This is the first time a journalist has ever worried about a lawyer."

"Perhaps you should take a cab. Or I'd be happy to drop you..."

"I'll be fine. I'm a lawyer. What's somebody going to do? Sue me?"

Webster drove his Mercedes out of the lot.

Rebecca stood on the bridge that crossed the creek. Below her, a pair of swans floated with the current, looking like small moons in the dusky light. She searched her purse for the valet's ticket and a tip, and was not aware of the pale green Olds Cutlass that followed Webster's car out of the lot.

6

Ghost cut a straight shot toward Cheyenne, stopping along the way only for gas and food. When they reached Cheyenne, he booked a room at a Holiday Inn and bought Radio a bathing suit. "Go have a swim while I make some calls," Ghost told him.

The first call was to Miss Dupree. He had tried calling her from a couple of gas stations along the way, but without success. This time she answered.

"I'm calling you from Cheyenne," Ghost said. "You probably haven't been there lately."

"No, I haven't." She sounded relieved to hear his voice.

"There are quite a few messages, Mr. Galvin," she continued (Ghost had tried persuading her to call him Thomas or Ghost, but she insisted on Mr. Galvin), "but most of them are matters I can handle for you."

"Good."

"Everything at the house is fine. We installed the new drainage system around the tennis court, and the patio furniture arrived this morning. I think you're going to be pleased with it."

"I'm sure I will."

"Aren't there some arrangements I can make for your travels, Mr. Galvin? I feel as though I'm not being helpful."

"There's nothing to do at the moment," he said. "I've just been burning up a little highway is all."

"I see."

"I'll keep in touch."

"Is there any particular location where I can reach you if something important comes up?"

"I'm on the float," Ghost said, "so I'll have to call you."

Next he called Norman Jamison.

"I thought you'd still be in Salt Lake," Jamison said.

"I felt like getting out this morning," Ghost said. "The kid is still with me."

"What you suggested yesterday is the proper course of action. Put the boy on a plane and let me handle it at this end."

"Yeah, well, Norman, I'm still thinking about it. I'll be in touch."

He hung up. Someone was knocking sharply on the door. Ghost opened it and found three housekeepers standing there, paper and pens in hand. One had a camera.

"You're Ghost Galvin, aren't you?" the woman with the camera said.

Ghost didn't respond.

"I told you he was," the woman said to the others, then turned to Ghost. "What are you doing *here?*"

"Just on a little vacation with my nephew," Ghost said, signing the autographs, "showing him the country."

The room was on the second story facing the front of the hotel. Ghost could see two people standing in front of the office, looking up at him.

Radio came trotting through the parking lot, dribbling the basketball. He stopped when he saw the commotion around Ghost.

"Okay, ladies," Ghost said, seeing Radio, "time for me to go." He called over to Radio, "It's time to hit the road, pal."

Ghost retreated into the room and Radio followed. "How come that lady took your picture?" he asked Ghost.

"They've never seen a Dodgers cap here. Get your stuff."

"We're leaving right now?"

"Yes."

"Can we stop at this place?"

"What place is that?" Ghost asked.

"At this school near here. It's just a block away."

"I thought you were swimming."

"I saw this place when we were driving in here. I went over to shoot some baskets."

"You shot some hoops," Ghost said, "so let's go. It's time to get out of here."

"Are we in trouble?"

"No. I just want to leave."

"There's a pretty good game over at that school," Radio said.

Ghost finished packing. "We went through that yesterday, Radio."

"You know what," Radio said, "I think we can make fifteen bucks."

"Yeah, well, I don't want to make fifteen bucks."

"I do."

"Well, you had your chance. Did you make it?"

"We need a game to make it. There's these guys."

"I don't feel like playing basketball," Ghost said. "And I don't like being included in other people's bets."

"Just drop me off there," Radio said.

"Let's get out of this motel."

They hurried down to the car and drove out of the lot. Radio didn't notice the people waving from the office.

"Turn left. It's just down the street, across from there," Radio said, standing on the front seat, holding on to the top of the windshield as if he were navigating a ship.

"How many guys did you bet?"

"I think there'll be a game there. . . ."

"Don't bullshit me. You made a bet. How many guys did you bet?"

"Three."

"Hey, you're playing three guys," Ghost said, "and good luck to you."

At Radio's direction, Ghost parked the Galaxy adjacent to a football field that was surrounded by a ten-foot chain link fence. The basketball courts were in back of the bleachers on the far side of the field.

"Where do you get in?" Ghost asked.

"That gate over there. It's locked, so you have to climb over it."

"If I don't like the looks of things, I'm taking a hike."

"We just have to play one stupid game."

"It's not my game. You're on your own with this one. And it's *your* fifteen bucks."

Radio scrambled up and over the fence. Ghost climbed after him. He followed Radio across the field and could see through the bleachers cement courts shiny with wear, rusted rims, and frayed nets. He heard the sounds of a pickup game. Ghost thought about the thousands of fences he'd jumped, the janitors he'd bribed, locked gates squeezed through, all in search of a hoop to use on a summer evening. That was when a rusted rim and torn net could become the parquet floor of the Boston Garden. Back then he'd play from the late afternoon into the soft darkness of summer nights, playing until the worn spot on the soles of his sneakers became a hole, and the hole went through the sock, leaving bloodstains on the court.

He paused and looked at the playground.

Ghost couldn't walk onto a playground without thinking of his father. The massive arenas, like those in Detroit and Seattle, seating upward of thirty thousand fans, created a different feeling in Ghost from the playgrounds and gyms that reeked of forty years of accumulated sweat and hot breath; the old gyms smelled like the inside of a kid's sneaker at the end of vacation; the new arenas were like stages, theater, and the professional game was as much show as it was sport. The senator had never seen his son play the professional game, and so to Ghost it was almost another sport from the one he had played when his father was watching. Yesterday had been the first time in years Ghost had entered a playground, and it was as if the ten years since the senator's death had vanished, and Ghost had felt that surge in his stomach he'd felt the first time he'd stepped onto a court after the funeral. That night, after the friends and dignitaries had left the house, Ghost had slipped away to a high school gym and shot hoops. Hundreds of them, until his arms were tired and he thought he might sleep. But every shot that night felt like a shove in the stomach.

Now, standing on this playground was like being in a room with his father where they could see each other but were unable to speak. The image came to Ghost's mind of Rebecca standing in his office looking at the only family picture to be found on the four-acre estate. He could hear her voice and it was as if she, the interloper, could speak with Ghost's father, and Ghost felt drawn to her voice and at the same time feared it, because she seemed to know that there was "the senator" and there was his father, and it was his father that she wanted to talk about. Driving to the gym that night after the funeral he'd passed a newsstand, and had known that the late editions carried pictures from the morning's funeral and follow-up stories about the senator. He remembered seeing Judge Ely walking up the steps of their town home, stopping to pick up the newspapers and discard them, as if he could change the past just by dropping the papers in the trash. "You don't need the newspapers to tell you about your father," the judge had said.

When Ghost's father came to Nippersink in summer, usually arriving in the evening after dinner, he'd look for Ghost at the courts, listening for the bouncing ball and scraping sneakers. Often he'd find Ghost in darkness shooting free throws. The distance from the free throw line never changed from court to court. You didn't need light to practice that shot, only feel. The senator could discern the sound of Ghost's shots going through the net as they fell so cleanly, the ball swishing sweetly and falling softly to the ground. And he'd call Ghost's name, once, clearly and firmly, like an arrow hitting a target, and wait while Ghost stopped practicing and looked out in the night for the direction of the voice. At times, Ghost would go right to the sound, or follow the scent of his father's cigar; then they would meet and laugh and go home together. Other times, he'd play right through the sound. And there were times Ghost heard his name called, and he'd stop and look around, but his father was not there. He'd go on practicing.

The fall following his father's death, Ghost ended his layoff from the game, and rejoined Stanford's team. And he practiced harder than his teammates, making use of Maples Pavilion, which was kept open nights for Ghost's use. The team's formal practice ended at seven, but Ghost always stayed for another hour, sometimes two or three, shooting a hundred free throws, practicing each of his shots in ever widening circles from the basket. In the empty pavilion the ball exploded off the wooden floor, and whipped through the net with a clean sound. Once, two teammates of Ghost's planned a joke using a sound effects tape concealed in the second deck of the arena. But when they were setting up the machine one of the players kicked a cup and the sound echoed through the arena. Startled, Ghost stopped his practice, looking around at the empty stands. The expression on Ghost's face changed the minds of his teammates about playing the trick; they snuck out of the pavilion and never mentioned to anyone what had happened.

Now, disguised in Hawaiian shorts, sweatshirt, Dodgers cap, sunglasses, and a three-day beard, Ghost walked with Radio to the courts at this high school in Cheyenne.

"You didn't say you were bringing a college guy," one of the three players at a basket said to Radio. "No way."

Ghost liked the way Radio glided past the kid without answering.

Another kid said to his friend, "Big deal, let's play them."

"You spot us ten points," the first kid said to Radio, " 'cause you got the tall guy."

"That's not the bet," Radio said. "Anyway, he's got a bad left arm and he never takes his hand out of his pocket because he can't use it."

Ghost was standing a few feet from Radio, listening to the conversation. He kept his hand in his pocket.

Another of the kids approached Radio. "Where's your money?"

Radio pulled a twenty halfway out of his pocket, then stuffed it back in. "Where's yours?"

The boy showed him three fives.

"Forty by ones," the boy said.

"Yeah, forty by ones is okay," Radio said.

The third boy was standing at a distance from his friends. He was looking at Ghost.

"Shoot for outs," Radio said.

Ghost walked to the center of the court and said, "Name's Thommy, that's Radio."

"I'm Frank," the leader of the others said, "he's Warren and he's Bill. Let's play."

Bill shot a twenty footer for outs and missed, so Radio inbounded the ball to Ghost and the game was on.

Frank and Bill double teamed Ghost, while Warren stuck with Radio. As Radio dribbled past, Ghost said, "Just keep moving and use my picks."

"Why don't you just announce it to everybody?" Radio said.

Ghost's picks were too strong for the young defenders to fight through, enabling Radio to shake free for a series of short shots that found their mark more than half the time; when they missed, Ghost followed with a tip-in. They were up nine to nothing in a hurry. Pleased with the progress of the game, Radio started showboating around the court, dribbling awkwardly behind his back, forcing shots that he knew didn't have much chance of going in, assured that Ghost would be there to follow the miss. But Ghost backed off, allowing Warren and Bill to get rolling. They reeled off seventeen unanswered points, and pushed the score a few minutes later to twenty-six to fourteen. In another ten minutes, they rolled it up to thirty-eight to eighteen. Radio grabbed a rebound and called for a time-out.

"No time-outs," Frank said.

"We're *taking* a time-out," Radio said, walking over to the drinking fountain. Ghost, left hand still in pocket, followed.

"What's going on, man?" Radio said. "If you're going to play, *play*. We're getting our butts kicked."

"What's going on, you little shithead, is that you started out playing like you halfway knew the game, then we get a little lead, and you start playing like a jerk."

"*You're* playing like a jerk." Radio, red in the face, added, "You haven't made a basket since we had eleven."

Frank was watching the argument from a distance and yelled to them, "How about double or nothing?"

"Asshole," Radio said under his breath.

"Who's the asshole who made a stupid bet you couldn't back up, then played like a jerk when you thought you actually might win?" Ghost stared at Radio, until Radio finally looked back at him. Then Ghost said, "If you stop throwing up those ridiculous shots you have no idea how to make, I'll show you something out there. That's if you're ready to play smart."

"Don't boss me."

"Two points to game," Frank called over.

Ghost said to Radio, "Now, there's *another* little asshole."

Warren was still carefully eyeballing Ghost, and said to Frank, "Just shut up and let's win."

Radio inbounded the ball to Ghost.

"Two points to game, big guy," Frank said to Ghost. Ghost palmed the ball, pulled straight up in the air, lifting himself well over the heads of his surprised defenders, and floated in a twenty-five-foot jump shot that snapped the bottom of the metal net. The players and Radio stood paralyzed by the unexpected one-handed shot. It was as if rain had fallen from the clear sky.

"Thirty-eight nineteen," Ghost said, taking another inbound pass from Radio, pulling up from thirty, and putting it in with all net. Radio came over to him and said, "Mister . . ."

"Set some picks for me," Ghost said.

Radio obeyed, speeding around the court to set screens, while Ghost dropped in eleven consecutive shots; when he missed the twelfth, he followed it in with a tip of the fingers.

Thirty-eight to thirty-one.

"What the hell is that guy doing?" Frank asked Warren.

"I don't know," Warren said to Frank. "I knew I didn't like something. He's got huge hands. I don't know."

Radio worked hard setting the picks for Ghost, and the others were roughing up Radio pretty good, trying to distract Ghost.

Though the jump shots were falling, Ghost was operating at about fifty percent of his abilities. He liked the way Radio was digging it out with the other guys, so he started raising his own game another level. He fired a twenty-foot fall-away that missed. Frank snatched the rebound, but Radio knifed between Warren and Bill and stripped the ball from Frank; it skidded toward the free throw line, Radio dove on the cement, knocking the ball in Ghost's direction. Ghost picked it up, whirled in midair, and slammed through a reverse dunk that left the backboard shaking on its metal pole.

"Let's wrap it up," he said to Radio, whose knee was bleeding from the dive.

Ghost danced a couple of moves on Frank and Bill, leaving them flatfooted and looking in the wrong direction.

Thirty-eight all.

Ghost pumped home another jumper. On game point he screened for Radio, who popped a ten footer that missed. But Ghost slashed across the key and into the air as if walking up invisible stairs, and slammed home the rebound in a one-handed dunk.

Game.

7

"Who are you, mister?" Radio said to Ghost, jumping into the Galaxy's backseat. "You play like a pro."

"Because I am," Ghost said, looking for the Interstate.

Radio held on to the headrest and pulled himself forward. "No, you're not."

"Okay, I'm not."

"How come you didn't want to play, then?"

"I've played enough pickup games."

"You didn't even want to shoot around, though."

"Hey, I played, we won, remember?"

"What's your name?"

"Thom Galvin."

"You're not Ghost," Radio said, really looking at him.

Then Radio flopped back down in the seat.

Ghost checked the mirror. He dropped a Temptations tape into the machine, found the on-ramp, and rolled into cruising speed.

After fifteen minutes passed, Ghost took out his wallet and held up his driver's license.

Radio looked at it but didn't say anything. Ghost kept driving.

"Then how come you're driving this crummy car?" Radio said finally.

"I have other cars," Ghost said. "I rented it. I like this car."

Radio shifted around in the backseat, fooling with the reception of his Walkman. "I saw a picture of you in a magazine one time and you were standing there by a red sports car," he said.

"That's possible. I think it was an ad."

"How come you're not driving that car?"

"People notice me when I'm driving that kind of car. I'm driving this car and nobody pays attention to it. Most people already have lousy cars, so they're not interested in somebody else's lousy car."

"How come you don't want anybody to see you?"

"Because I felt like being alone. I'm going to Wisconsin to settle some personal business. That's where my family used to live. There and in Chicago."

Radio pulled out his map and looked for Wisconsin.

"The place is called Nippersink," Ghost said. "It won't be on your map, believe me."

"Is that where your mother and father live?"

"Where they used to live," Ghost said. "They're not alive. My grandmother was living there. She died a few days ago, so I have some things to settle."

"Do you have to go the funeral?"

"There isn't one. She didn't want a funeral."

Radio put his map away. "What do they do if they don't have a funeral?"

"Some kind of memorial ceremony. I think her friends already had it. They get together in church and say some prayers and that's that."

Radio was leaning forward, holding on to the passenger seat headrest. "I went to the funeral for my mother. They had it at the place where they buried her. They don't let you see them put the coffin in the grave. They have these sheets around it and you have to leave. I kind of wanted to see, but they don't let you."

"Maybe it's not so bad that they don't let you watch that."

"This priest from the church came to Karen's house, and they thought I was asleep, but I wasn't, and I heard them talking about it. He was wrong. I don't like him. There's another priest at the church who is really nice, but he wasn't the priest who was there. This was his boss, the old guy, and I don't like him."

"Why not?" Ghost asked.

"Because he's a liar."

"About what?"

"My mother."

"What did he say?"

"That my mother killed herself. I could hear him talking about that with Karen when they thought I was asleep. But she didn't, because Karen told me she didn't. She was in an accident."

"What was the priest saying to Karen?"

"They were having this big argument because Karen wanted them to bury my mother at this one place, and the priest was saying something like my mother killed herself and if you kill yourself you can't be buried at this place, if that happens you have to be buried at another place. He was a liar. My mother made me go to that church sometimes, but I didn't like to go. I don't like that liar. Karen told me that, too. That he was a liar."

Radio leaned back and braced his feet against the front seat. He was thinking about the church, its white walls and the stained glass that lit up in the morning. There was the large stained glass over the altar showing an old man who was supposed to be God. He had a white beard flowing down past his waist, and he wore layers of robes. His eyes were flashing and his finger pointed down like the tip of an arrow. The other stained-glass windows were on the sides of the church. Angels. They were tall and thin and their faces looked peaceful, as though the things they knew were good. Radio's mother had told him that the angels were God's messengers for good works on earth, tall and gentle and happy, able to fly silently without being seen. When his mother took him to church she told Radio to pray, but Radio always prayed to the angels, because the man in the stained glass over the altar frightened him.

Radio drifted into a nap, while Ghost watched for a restaurant or a store.

They drove on toward Nebraska, smelling the fertile earth.

The warm evening air felt good blowing against their faces. There was a Welcome to God's Country sign by the road as they crossed the state line.

8

Ghost found a diner called the MisSteak House that had three items on the menu: steak, corn, potato. The owner was dressed in jeans and a work shirt and stood behind the counter smoking a cigarette. He did the cooking; his wife waited on the eight tables.

"Can we fry something up for you?" she said to Ghost.

"Couple of steaks sounds good."

"Corn on the side?"

"Corn on the side," Ghost said. "How about some milk?"

"We got that," she said, taking the order over to her husband.

"How about washing your hands before we eat," Ghost said to Radio.

"They're pretty clean."

"No, they're not. They're dirty from playing ball. I've got to wash mine." He stood and went to the rest room. When he returned, he caught Radio's eyes and motioned to the rest room. "Clean 'em up," he said.

Radio looked at his hands. He looked at them as if they belonged to someone else. Ghost could see on Radio's face the look of suspicion and distance he first saw in Las Vegas.

Radio got up and walked toward the rest room.

The waitress returned with two glasses of cold milk.

Ghost sipped the milk and waited, tapping his fork on the Formica tabletop. When a few minutes had passed, he stood and went to the rest room. He opened the door, looked around the small room, and thought it was empty.

"Radio?"

"What," the boy answered in a flat voice.

Ghost let the door close. Radio was standing in the corner next to the hinges. His eyes were red from crying. Ghost took him by the shoulders and held him. The boy's rigid shoulders relaxed and he started to cry again.

"I don't want to wash my hands," Radio said. He looked at his dirty fingernails, and thought about the towel hanging in the bathroom of the shack where he had lived.

"Washing your hands is not the end of the world."

"I don't want to."

"Hey, it was a suggestion. I'm not here to tell you what to do."

The boy went over to the sink and leaned against it, his back to Ghost.

They stood there for a few minutes, until the waitress banged on the door and told them the steaks were up. Radio cleaned his hands, then he followed Ghost back to the table.

9

Ghost drove until his eyelids started to drop, then he found a Motel 6, where he and Radio spent the night. They hit the Interstate just after dawn the next day and except for gas, didn't make a stop until noon.

"I'm planning to go back to New York today," Rebecca said to Ghost from her room at the Chateau Marmont. He was calling from a phone booth at another gas station.

"Look," Ghost said. "I need help tracking down this kid's father and finding out what the story is with his family in L.A., if he's got any. You'll be able to do that five times faster than my attorney or my secretary, and my name in the middle of it will only make it more complicated."

"I can help you. But are you prepared to help me? Open doors."

The blinking light, he thought, looking out the window.

"What doors?"

"Like Judge Ely. Dr. Thomas Wyndham. Friends of—"

"Wyndham?"

"Yes."

"I don't think he was close to my father."

"He's the Cook County coroner. He was involved in your father's case. I want to talk to him, and he's another one who doesn't want to talk to me."

The blinking light.

"I don't know what I can do. We can talk about it. But I'd like you to sit down and talk with this kid. We'll make Des Moines tonight. I could have my secretary book a reservation, arrange for your ticket, and we could meet in the morning."

"I'll handle my arrangements."

"Then you're coming?"

"If you'll help me."

"We'll be at the Holiday Inn by the airport. Call me back and let me know when you'll be in."

"Okay."

10

In the United Airlines terminal at Los Angeles International, Rebecca looked at people's faces. This was habit. She observed their eyes, the angle of the forehead and the lines of the cheekbones, how a person carried himself, his mannerisms. In others she looked for signs of familiarity, signs of herself, as though she might instantly recognize her mother. All the aspects would be right. There would be a knowing, an unmistakable recognition in the eyes that cut across years and lives lived in different places and different ways. That was how Rebecca imagined it, that the eyes would tell of continuity and connection with a life that came before hers and carried forward with hers, like the fine mystery of several generations of family standing together, bloodlines to buffet feelings of absolute solitariness Rebecca sometimes sensed within herself. She felt too guilty to tell anyone, especially her parents, that being loved was not sufficient for her to feel complete; she was certain there was a secret in the origins of blood that she desperately needed to know.

At the counter she purchased her ticket, checked the gate assignment, then turned and looked for the direction signs. A man's stare cut through the crowd at the ticket counter and locked into Rebecca's eyes. He was a short man, with a build like a washing machine; his eyes appeared emotionless, weary. As Rebecca started for the concourse, the man walked calmly toward her, as if they had a long-standing appointment. Rebecca was good at reading faces, but had no sense of what this man wanted, and she felt a knot of fear that centered itself in between her stomach and her spine.

Rebecca continued walking toward the concourse, but the man intercepted her. "Miss Blesser," he said, with a voice that sounded like it came from a sore throat; from the way he said her name, it was clear that he knew exactly who she was.

"Yes."

"I'm Detective Ross from the Santa Monica Police Department."

He produced a wallet that displayed a badge and a laminated I.D. card.

Ross was wearing gray slacks, a blue jacket, and a pale orange tie; his white button-down shirt seemed to be two sizes too small for him, squeezing his neck to the point where his eyes appeared to bulge out.

"What can I do for you?" Rebecca asked, her voice businesslike. Inside, she felt foreboding, and sensed that Ghost Galvin was somehow involved in whatever the detective was about to say.

"I didn't mean to startle you," he said, "but when you left for the airport we thought we'd better catch up with you."

"I don't understand."

"There's been an accident. We wanted to ask you about it."

"Involving who?"

"A gentleman named Alan Webster was in a serious automobile accident yesterday evening on PCH—that's the Pacific Coast Highway. He's in intensive care, and we won't be able to speak with him for at least a couple of days, if at all."

Her first impulse was to say that it wasn't an accident; she recalled the look of remorse and melancholy on Webster's face as he wobbled toward his car. And she felt disquieted by the thought that Webster was the first person close to the senator, in fact, the only person, who had talked of him in a personal way. "My god," she said, quietly, in recognition of what the detective had just told her. "I'm very sorry."

"They found a high alcohol count in his blood, very high. The guy was pretty well pickled. His secretary told us he'd left the office about five for an appointment"—the detective said, pulling a small notebook from his breast pocket and looking at it—"at the Bel Air Hotel. I take it that was with you."

The detective stared at Rebecca without blinking, as if waiting for her to tell him something specific. She'd interviewed plenty of cops. They liked to do that: just stand and stare, bore their eyes right into the center of someone's conscience, because people, finally, *like* unburdening themselves.

"Yes, we met in the cocktail lounge at the Bel Air."

"He must have been hitting the sauce pretty good."

"He did have too much to drink," Rebecca answered, her thoughts racing ahead to try to understand why the detective was talking to her, what he was going for. She felt guilty about Webster, that perhaps their conversation had edged him into having more drinks than he should have, that in talking about Elizabeth Folger she had pushed him into an area that was painful . . . but why painful for him? "I think he had been drinking before I even got there. I suggested that he not drive. In fact, I offered to get him a cab or give him a lift."

"He should have listened to you."

"Was anyone else hurt in the accident?"

"No. He jerked his car right off the road, took it through a guardrail and down a hill. The whole reason I went down there to have a look was that the officers on the scene reported the skid pattern to be unusual. Very sudden. He really jerked the car hard, either to avoid another vehicle, kill himself, or maybe miss a dog. People don't watch their dogs out there at the beach. They should."

Rebecca was certain he knew something else. And he was tossing out a bit at a time to see what she might suddenly come up with; she was familiar with what he was doing because she used the same technique when interviewing people.

"Did he say where he was going when he left the hotel?" the detective asked.

"No. He did tell me he lived out at Malibu. I'm a journalist; I was interviewing him for a story. Detective, I'm not clear on what I can tell you that might help."

"Nothing, if there is nothing. We did find these other skid marks at the scene, and they were fresh. The problem is this: There are cars skidding around there all the time, every day, so those other skid marks could have happened an hour before or whatever. But they were at an odd angle. Forcing him to swerve on that turn would be about the only explanation. When you spoke with Mr. Webster, was he upset about anything?"

"I don't think he was upset," Rebecca answered, wanting the detective to tell her more, trying to draw him out.

"When a citizen is involved in an accident, and he is as intoxicated as Mr. Webster was, it's very difficult to piece things together. So this is all fairly routine. I'm not trying to alarm you. We just want to close the books on the thing."

"Detective, if it's routine, you wouldn't be involved with the case, and you wouldn't be waiting for me at the airport. You would have picked up the telephone and called me."

"We're not holding you responsible for any of this. I don't want to give you that impression. The only reason I'm here is that perhaps you can tell me something useful to help us close the books. It's probably just a guy who drank too much and managed to get himself in a wreck. This happens about fifty times a day in Los Angeles. But with those other skid marks and the angle of the accident, we just want to make certain."

Ross glanced around the concourse, taking several seconds to look for someone. Then he turned his attention back to Rebecca.

"I can tell you that I did have a man check you out last night. Actually, check out your rental car. Just to check the tires. Since you were the last person to see him, as far as we know, and there were these other skid marks, it was just a routine thing for us to do. We know you had nothing to do with the accident. Those certainly weren't skid marks from your car out there on PCH. But I do have to ask you another question. It's become sort of an item of curiosity with us."

Ross let her stand there a few moments. They like to do that, she thought, let you stand, shift back and forth on your feet, feel your weight, see what comes bubbling up. Rebecca had seen detectives interview criminals when the criminals' heads seemed visibly to get heavier and heavier until they nearly toppled over.

Ross said, "Are you aware that you've been followed the past couple of days?"

There was no surprise or particular concern in Ross's voice. He said everything in the same tone, revealing little of what importance he placed on one statement over another. Rebecca returned his stare, wondering if this was the game he wanted to play for a moment, Indian poker. If it was, he was winning, because she felt her stomach turn over. Years had gone by in the search for her parents, with only pockets of momentary success along the way. But with Ghost and Webster and this detective all coming into her life, Rebecca felt that she was not propelling the search as much as it was beginning to propel her.

"I don't understand," she said to Ross.

"You're being followed."

"By whom?"

"I'm hoping to have more of answer in a minute or two. One of my partners is here working on that. We already know 'who' it is following you. I thought maybe you'd fill in the 'why' of it."

"Tell me who it is."

"So you're aware that you've been followed?"

"No." Rebecca began not liking this detective, not liking the way he poked at her with information, as if she were an animal he was probing for sensitive spots. It made her angry, in the same way she felt when she talked with hospital administrators, adoption agency workers, or anyone connected with Senator Galvin; they answered her questions with questions and looked at her as if she were an interloper. If Ghost was having her followed, which was what came to mind, then she wanted to know it before she stepped on the plane to meet with him in Iowa.

"Detective, I know you're doing your job, but I'd like you to tell me what's going on here, because I have no idea, and I'm sure I have a right to know."

"I'm only checking on this because of the Webster case, which may be total coincidence and probably is. You know what it's like." He scratched around for his notebook. "Normally, it's none of our business if someone's following someone else, as long as they're not harassing them or breaking the law. There's not much we can do about someone following someone else. We really don't have time to worry about it. But when the detective went to check your tires last night, I guess you were just leaving the hotel to go out to dinner, so he followed you. But it turned out that he also followed someone who followed you. The man followed you to"—the detective checked his notebook again—"Chianti restaurant on Melrose . . ."

"I met a colleague for a late dinner," Rebecca said, then regretted her defensive tone.

"Whatever. . . . Then you returned to your hotel. The guy was still on your tail, and he stayed there all day today."

"You know who it is?"

"Sure. We checked him. He's a private investigator. He came right here to the airport behind you. He's a legitimate guy in town. My partner is here somewhere having a word with him.

My only interest in this is the Webster situation, otherwise it's none of our business if someone wants to have you followed. It's usually for an insurance case or a divorce." He said the words *insurance* and *divorce* as if they were two of the most annoying terms in the English language. "Are you involved in something like that? You don't have to tell me if you don't want to."

"No," Rebecca said. "I'm not involved in something like that." The name *Elizabeth Folger* had evoked a strong reaction in Webster's eyes, but she hadn't mentioned the name to Ghost. For a moment, she considered the possibility that it was Elizabeth who was having her followed, a thought that made Rebecca feel that her search was on course, but then she realized that if Elizabeth was behind the private investigator, it would be to keep Rebecca from getting too close. If Elizabeth knew about Rebecca and wanted to see her, she could simply walk up to her and introduce herself. Rebecca considered the bitter possibility, as she'd done in the past, that she was looking for someone who did not want to know her.

"Detective Ross, I'd like you to tell me who is following me because I want to talk to him myself."

"Now that's a touchy area, legal-wise. If it's got nothing to do with our case, we're obliged to keep our nose out of it. Do you think it has something to do with our case?"

The monotone. The stare.

"I can't imagine how," she said.

"You're a journalist, you said?"

"I work for *Time* and *Life*."

"Read 'em both. Maybe somebody wants to know what you're writing about. We'll have a word with him, and if there's anything to come of it we'll call you. Otherwise, we'll have to stay out of it. Where can I reach you the next day or two?"

"I'm traveling on a story. But I'll be in touch with my office every day. My assistant's name is Mary Lee."

Ross continued staring at her with his unblinking eyes.

"That'll be fine," he said, finally.

He extended his hand, which she shook.

"I'm sorry we couldn't do this on the phone," Ross said. "It's just that I've always found it better to speak with people in person. I'm sorry we had to speak with you at all. It's just all these loose ends."

"Yes."

Ross stood, arms at his side, and waited for Rebecca to go

through the metal-detection checkpoint. He watched her walk down the corridor toward her boarding gate, knowing that if he did not, she would follow him, and he didn't like being followed.

Once aboard the airplane, Rebecca settled back in her seat and closed her eyes. On the way to the gate Rebecca thought about changing her ticket again, going back to New York, and letting whatever she had set in motion in Los Angeles by seeing Ghost and Webster come to a halt. But a stronger feeling pushed her on board the flight to Iowa. She was tired of empowering Elizabeth's unseen presence to change the course of her life, to leave doubt in her mind. But if it was the search for Elizabeth that was causing someone to have Rebecca followed, or resulted in Webster's landing in the hospital, then it meant she must be moving toward answers. And she had to keep moving, even if that meant walking directly into the danger, physical or emotional. Knowing that she was adopted but being unable to learn enough about it was like being taunted by an unseen presence whispering threats on the other side of a high wall. At a certain point it was less fearful to climb over the wall and confront whatever was there than to live with the disquieting whispers. If the unseen voice she heard belonged to Elizabeth, Rebecca at least wanted to see the face.

PART II

6

The telephone rang in staccato bursts. Rebecca reached for the receiver, muscles stiff from sleeping on the uncomfortable mattress. She grabbed the phone with one hand, and pushed open the curtains with the other; a blast of white light blinded her, and she fell back down upon the mattress.

"What time is it?" she said.

"Ten," Ghost said. "I've already been for a run."

"You're the athlete."

"Sleep all right?"

"I don't know yet."

"I've ordered breakfast," he said, "unless you want to try and get more sleep."

"I'm up now."

Rebecca's flight had arrived in Des Moines at ten-thirty the previous night. Ghost had been there to meet her and bring her to the hotel. She had arrived feeling unsettled from her encounter with the detective, but chose to get a night's sleep before confronting Ghost about anything.

"Radio's still sleeping."

"Radio?"

"The kid I mentioned to you last night. That's his nickname. He's got a Walkman in his ear all the time. He's in the next room sleeping. I'll explain it all over breakfast. I'm in four-sixteen. I ordered room service. I mean, they don't have room service here, but they've agreed to send the food up for me."

"Let's eat in the restaurant," she said.

"I've already ordered. I'm just down the hall from you. I

want to talk with you about Radio before you meet him."

Rebecca showered then dressed in jeans and a blue cotton blouse. She took a notebook and pen and went to Ghost's room.

He answered the door and extended his hand to Rebecca. She let him stand there a few seconds before taking it, and then he wasn't sure if she was looking at him with anger or fear. Her handshake was a quick squeeze, then she dropped his hand, and he glanced down as she rubbed her fingers together, as if she was checking the feel of his flesh upon hers.

"We keep meeting in hotel rooms," Ghost said.

"Not by my choice."

"Come on in."

Hesitating in the doorway, she poked her head forward and looked around his room.

"I'm alone. The kid's next door. Expecting someone else?"

"I'm still a little groggy," she answered. She was still thinking of Detective Ross and of Webster's accident.

"For starters, it'll make things easier if you start calling me Ghost. I assume you don't mind being called Rebecca."

"I prefer that," she answered, walking to the table and chairs by the balcony at the far end of the room.

She sat down, placing her notebook on the tabletop.

"I forgot to tell you last night that I appreciate you flying out here, making the effort and all."

"It's part of my job, isn't it?"

Her coolness irritated him. Because of her he'd been thinking of his father the past few days, and having her here was causing all of the thoughts to return, and he wanted to ask her what she knew, but he didn't want talking about his father to be somebody's job.

The waiter from the restaurant downstairs arrived with a cart of food.

"Keep the omelet in the warming box," Ghost said, "but serve the rest of it, please."

The waiter set the table and uncovered the fruit and eggs and hot cereal that Ghost had ordered. Ghost tipped him and said to Rebecca, "Help yourself." Then he got down to his knees and checked the metal warming box, making certain Radio's omelet was properly covered.

"Who besides yourself knows I'm here?" Rebecca asked, as Ghost sat down opposite her.

She was tapping her pen on her notebook and the sound was

annoying Ghost. He felt there was something coiled inside of her.

"Nobody. Why?"

"That's what I want."

"Does it make a difference?"

"I thought I'd ask you that."

"I don't understand."

"You had me followed in Los Angeles."

He looked at her steadily, wondering if this was some kind of a game that reporters play when they ask something they know is wrong in the hopes they'll be corrected with a fact they didn't know about. If it was a game, he decided not to play it.

"I didn't have you followed."

"Then your attorney, perhaps? I understand his office checked up on me."

"They checked up on you because I asked them to. But he didn't have you followed. He wouldn't do that without asking me, and nobody asked me. Shall we call him?"

"It's not necessary."

"Why the hell would I have you followed?"

"That's something I was going to ask you."

"When you turned up at my party asking about my father I wasn't thrilled, because I like my personal life left alone. But that's the end of it. I have no idea what you've been doing in Los Angeles."

"I met with Alan Webster," she said to Ghost, searching his face for a reaction.

There was none. "Haven't seen him since the funeral. Like I told you on the telephone."

"He's based in L.A. now," she said.

"So you told me."

"He was in an auto accident after leaving the interview."

Ghost looked surprised and concerned.

"He's in critical condition. He had a lot to drink during the interview, and before, I think."

"I'm sorry to hear it."

"The police contacted me. They're checking out hit-and-run."

"Hit-and-run?"

She gave him Ross's stare. "They're really not sure what happened."

Ghost pushed himself back from the table. "So why the hell are you looking at me with an accusation on your face? Do you think I flew back to L.A. and ran Webster off the road for talking to you?"

Rebecca blushed and looked away. She composed herself and faced Ghost. "I'm trying to get some straight information, and I have to tell you that this hasn't been simple. Your father was in a lot of trouble before he died, Ghost. I don't know if it was political trouble or personal trouble. I've looked at photographs of him taken during the last year of his life, and it's a record of a man in decline. And nobody wants to talk about it. Not you, not Alan Webster, not your grandmother, and not this great friend of your father's, Judge Ely. Now your grandmother has passed away and Webster is in the hospital, and they were the only people who talked with me at all, and that wasn't much."

"So talk to me and forget about everybody else. Because if my father had a problem in the last year of his life it didn't have anything to do with anybody but me." Ghost stood and opened the sliding glass door to the balcony. It was a release to tell somebody.

"I don't know if you can understand this, but it was killing my father that I wasn't playing ball during that last year. That meant everything to him, and I didn't feel like playing. It worked away at him. That was his problem. Me." The words spilled out. "If you want to write about it, go ahead. But I really want you to help me with the kid, Radio. He's something you can help me with. Write about the other thing if you want to."

Rebecca wasn't prepared for his candor, and wondered if she should push him. She wanted to ask about Elizabeth Folger, and see what his reaction was. Either he was a great actor, or he believed what he was saying was true. There was something Ghost was holding back, she could see that. Maybe the name Elizabeth Folger would unlock something else, and secrets would be dropped. But what if I'm wrong, she thought. What if I give him the name and tell him that it is possible his father and Elizabeth Folger were lovers, and at one point Elizabeth Folger had a child, and I want to know if the senator is my father? What if I tell him all this and I'm wrong, or I simply cannot prove it one way or another? She wondered if it was right to plant in Ghost the seed of suspicion and doubt she'd lived with during these years. Once she told him the name his life would change, as hers had changed. It would change the way he saw his father and the way he looked at himself. She would hand him a past he didn't

116

know belonged to him, and all she could provide was a birth certificate with *Mother:* Elizabeth Folger and *Father:* Unknown. Because that was all Elizabeth had left her. It would have been better if there had been nothing at all.

"Maybe it's not that simple about your father," she said.

"It's that simple."

"What are you holding back?" she asked in a tone that was almost tender. Let him bring it up.

He turned from the balcony and faced her.

She saw in his face that he was hurting from what they were talking about, but she protected herself thinking What about *my* pain; what about *me?*

"Do you want to dig him up and ask him how he died?"

"Do you?" she asked.

"No."

Ghost walked out on the balcony and leaned against the railing. One thing he wouldn't say to Rebecca, or to anyone else, was that sometimes he hated his father for dying. Hated him because you can only answer people who die, never question them. You can do the things they had asked of you in life, whether it was playing basketball or running a farm, and you can do the things they asked of you in death, such as bury them in the family plot in the shade of a willow tree. But you can't question the things they had asked of you, unless you are prepared to forge your own answers. The answers his father wanted seemed clear to Ghost—to play ball—and his father would live on in that. Answers are so goddamned easy, Ghost thought, looking out at the morning; people run around looking for answers, but that means nothing; it's the questions you can't ask that age you.

Rebecca and Ghost didn't speak for a couple of minutes. She was sketching wavy lines in her notebook, but not writing anything down. Rebecca decided to leave the subject of the senator for a while.

"You told me how old this boy is," she said, "but I've forgotten." It was as though they both were exhausted by his outburst. And Rebecca decided it was not the time to ask about Elizabeth Folger. She had expected the arrogant, evasive man who had broken into her hotel room, but that wasn't who she was seeing this morning.

"Eleven or twelve. I never know when he's exactly telling the truth. Radio says his father's up in Michigan in jail. And he thinks he's going to get him out and live happily ever after."

"Does he know who you are?"

"Now he does. The first couple of days he was just hitching a ride. Little hustler talked me into a couple of basketball games. That's his way of raising money, hustling basketball games. He had it figured we sucker bet our way right to Michigan. Now I'm not sure what he thinks. But I know if I go to the authorities, the kid'll get slammed one way or another, or he'll just run away. You've got the kind of contacts to get information. Find out about his family in L.A. He told me his mother died a few weeks ago and that's why he ran away. He thinks it's his father in this prison, but who knows?"

"I can try," she said. "But don't you think a social agency experienced with this kind of thing . . ."

"Please don't give me the same crap my attorney started giving me. Do you want to sit there while this kid explains to some social worker he wants to get his father out of jail and set up housekeeping in Sun Valley? The kid really believes he can do something about this."

"You're not doing him any favors by letting him think he can."

"We can find out a few things before throwing him to the wolves. We can do that much. You want to spend all this time on people who are dead, let's spend some—"

"Hey," she said, cutting him off, "I'll talk to him."

"Maybe you'll get more out of him than I get. I've gotten his name and the address where he says he lived in L.A. That's about it."

There was a knock at the door.

Rebecca looked at Ghost, who was still on the balcony; he gestured toward the door.

"That'll be Radio," Ghost said. "You might as well meet him. Go on and open it."

Rebecca opened the door. Radio was standing back from it, as if he wasn't sure he was at the right room. He could see Ghost leaning against the railing of the balcony. Then he looked quickly at Rebecca, and bolted down the hallway.

Ghost called after him, but Radio kept going, running down the stairwell, through the hotel's delivery entrance, and across the employee parking lot.

"Did he have his pack with him?" Ghost asked Rebecca, who was standing in the hallway. "I couldn't see."

"He had a knapsack."

"Shit."

"I thought you told him I was going to be here?"

"I did."

"I suppose he thinks I'm the police."

"Who knows," Ghost said, going back into the room for his keys, wallet, and sunglasses. "It's not like I've been fooling him."

"Now what?"

"We get in the car and start driving. If he wants to be found he'll go to a schoolyard or a park. If not, I don't know what the hell he'll do."

Ghost cruised the area surrounding the Holiday Inn, several blocks of businesses, motels, and fast-food restaurants. They stopped at McDonald's and Denny's and Burger King, and checked two 7-Elevens. Ghost asked the clerks if they'd seen a boy with a knapsack, but no one had.

Then they came to a neighborhood, about a mile from the Holiday Inn, where the homes were small, with large yards and mature trees. Ghost asked two kids playing catch in the street if there was a school around, and they directed him to Church of All Saints. They found the white wooden church and the school a block away. He stopped the car in a shady spot across from the church and schoolyard, and said to Rebecca, "Let me take a walk around here. Maybe it's better if you wait in the car in case he's watching us."

Ghost opened the trunk and took the basketball with him.

He walked past the elementary school's rows of classrooms, and looked through the windows. The desks and chairs looked impossibly small. The chalkboards had been scrubbed clean for summer. He walked from classroom to classroom, from kindergarten to seventh grade. The furniture seemed to swell in size as the grades ascended; the globes grew larger and more detailed, and there were books, maps, and models of the solar system. Ghost recalled the feeling of returning to grammar school each year, when the added details of a new classroom affirmed the fact that something had changed from June to September.

He turned and followed the walkway as it led past the cafeteria to a small recreation hall and around to the back of the church.

Radio was sitting in a gravel garden, resting against a tree that shaded the minister's entrance to the church. He was listening to his Walkman and did not seem to hear Ghost approach.

"You're going to go broke without this," Ghost said, dropping the basketball in the gravel next to Radio.

The boy spun around.

Ghost followed Radio's gaze to the convertible in the distance, Rebecca sitting in its front seat.

"She's not a cop," he said, "and she's not here to take you back to Los Angeles. She's a journalist, a writer, and she's going to help get some information on your father. I can't guarantee how much information she can gather, but she's going to try."

"She looks like the lady in Las Vegas at the police station," Radio said.

"You haven't told me about that."

"There was this lady cop but I got away."

"They picked you up there?"

He nodded.

"Well," Ghost said, "it's not the same lady."

The boy's gaze continued across the playground, resting on Rebecca.

"She's a friend of yours?"

"Well, I know her," Ghost answered, "and I think she's all right. I think she might be able to help."

Radio's map and pictures were spread on the gravel next to his pack. He had been looking at the pictures of his father and of his mother and him. In the picture she was wearing black slacks and a white sweater; her arm was around Radio. As he helped Radio gather the materials, Ghost realized that Radio's mother looked somewhat like Rebecca.

"Look how far I can throw this," Radio said, picking up a piece of gravel. He wound up and fired the pebble at the church. It ticked off a stained-glass window.

"That's bad luck," Ghost said. "Don't do that."

Radio shouldered his pack and started walking with Ghost. When they crossed the lawn in front of the church, Radio dug another pebble out of his pocket but Ghost was watching him so he did not throw it.

They drove to Hammond, Indiana, where Ghost booked three motel rooms so they could rest and use the swimming pool, and so that Rebecca could make her telephone calls.

On the drive from Des Moines, Rebecca sat in the backseat with Radio. Eventually, he took his headphones off, and they talked. He gave her the name of his school and the address of the cottage; he also gave her the name of the prison where he believed his father to be, then showed her on the map where it was. Last, he showed her the photographs, which she held carefully as the wind swirled around. Ghost followed their progress in the rear-view mirror. He watched Radio allow Rebecca to rest her hands on his backpack as she looked at the materials, and Radio studied Rebecca's hands as carefully as Rebecca studied the photographs.

Standing outside the motel rooms, Radio said to Rebecca, "Are you going swimming with us?"

"Maybe later."

"Why not?"

"She has some telephone calls to make," Ghost said. "Come on, let's go change."

"We can wait if you want," Radio said to Rebecca, without looking at her or Ghost.

"You go ahead," she answered. "Go on in and start changing, I need to talk with Ghost for one minute."

Radio went into the room.

Ghost observed Rebecca watching Radio walk away.

"Careful," Ghost said, "he's like a piece of something that gets stuck between your teeth."

"You could just say that you like him."

"So, did you get anything?"

"Some to start with. But I also have my story to work on, Ghost. I want you to arrange for me to speak with Judge Davis Ely. And then this Dr. Wyndham."

"Have you already tried?"

"Yes. Neither would take the call."

"Judge Ely is old," Ghost said, holding back his irritation. "Why squeeze him?"

"He was your father's closest friend and adviser. I need to talk with him."

"Look, I'll call my secretary and have her set it up. If I call the judge myself he'll want to have a parade meet me in Chicago and I don't want that right now."

"As long as you arrange it."

"I'll do it right now."

She turned the key in the lock to her room.

"Listen," Ghost said, hesitating outside his door, "thanks for being that way with the kid. With Radio."

"I like him, too," she said.

Ghost went inside to change.

Radio had the roll of cash out of his pack and was counting it on the dresser.

"What're you up to?" Ghost asked.

"Two hundred twenty."

"Your status as an amateur athlete is in jeopardy."

"What?"

"Never mind."

"You're a millionaire," Radio said, "aren't you?"

"Why do you want to know about that?"

"I heard them say it on TV once."

"They say a lot of things on TV."

"You are, though, aren't you?"

"I've been lucky."

"What's it like?"

"I guess you don't have to worry so much about having money. Except sometimes it makes you worry about it more, because you're afraid of losing it."

Radio picked the *National Geographic* pages out of his pack, and pointed to a picture of Sun Valley.

"How much is a house here?"

"Like anyplace else, it depends on the house."

"What about *this* house?" he asked, pointing to a large A-frame that was facing Bald Mountain on the banks of Warm Springs Creek.

"I'm not sure about what property costs up there," Ghost said. "Something like that looks pretty expensive. Could be a couple hundred thousand dollars."

"What about if you build a house?" Radio asked, pointing to a meadow along the creek. "Look at all this land."

"It might be less to build."

"If you own the land, you can have a tent on it and camp."

"Maybe you could do that," Ghost replied.

"It'd be good to be right by the creek."

"Yeah, the trout might jump out of the water and into your breakfast fire. They have a lot of trout up there."

"I wonder if my father likes to fish?"

"Oh, I'm sure he does," Ghost said. "So, you're a fisherman?"

"I love fishing."

"Yeah, it's fun."

Radio nodded.

"Where did you learn your fishing?" Ghost asked.

"On TV. Sometimes they have this show on Saturdays where this guy goes fishing and shows everything you're supposed to do. He catches tons of fish. My mom used to watch it sometimes when I was watching it."

"You learned that way?"

"Yeah."

"Once I caught a fish that was bigger than you, almost twice as big as you."

"Really?"

"Sailfish. Huge."

"Where?"

"Mexico. Cabo San Lucas."

"I don't know where that is."

"It's on your map. Just keep going down the California coast right into Mexico. It's down where the whales go to mate. I didn't go to catch a whale. But this was one big fish. Took me almost three hours, I think, to land it. My arms were coming right out of the sockets, like I was trying to pull a truck into the boat. It was real hot there, too. You know, that Mexican sun just pounds down at you. There's noplace to hide because you're in the ocean. They had to keep giving me bottles of water and sandwiches. I don't think I've ever been that exhausted as I was trying to land that fish. But I did it. Next day, of course, I hooked one that was even bigger than the other, probably a world record of some kind. No doubt about it. But it snapped the leader somehow and got away. It was definitely one of the largest fish ever to swim in the waters of planet Earth."

Radio looked at him, and Ghost laughed.

"Hey, what can I say, Radio? All fisherman know that the biggest fish they ever caught is the one they don't land. Or it's the next one they're going to land. Something like that. Tell me about your biggest fish."

"I don't know," Radio said.

"You didn't actually have to have landed it. Just the biggest tug on your line."

"I haven't caught a big fish."

"Well, what's the biggest *small* fish you ever caught?"

"There isn't any."

"There must be."

Radio shook his head.

"I don't get it," Ghost said.

"I never caught a fish."

"What do you mean you haven't caught at least *one* fish. Nobody's luck is that bad."

"I've never been fishing."

"You just got through telling me you learned how to fish from watching Gaddabout Gaddis or somebody on TV, and that you love fishing."

Radio turned his eyes back to the *National Geographic* article and pointed to Warm Springs Creek running in front of the A-frame. "It says you can catch trout right from your porch there. Do you think that's true?"

3

Ghost sent Radio down to the pool. Then he called the office and Miss Dupree answered.

"Mr. Galvin, how are you?"

"Not too bad. Things okay out there?"

"Things are in order," she said. "Would you like your messages?"

"No, hang on to them. But I'd like you to make a call for me. To Judge Ely. I don't want to get into a big thing with him right now, so will you please call him and let him know that a journalist, Rebecca Blesser, will be contacting him for an interview, and I don't mind if he speaks with her. It's the girl Hardin brought to the party the other night. *Life* magazine is doing something on my father."

"I'm familiar with Miss Blesser," Miss Dupree said.

"If he doesn't want to talk to her, that's his business, of course. But I want him to know that as far as I'm concerned it's all right. The thing is, I've asked her to do a favor for me."

"I apologize, Mr. Galvin," she said, her voice dropping in pitch the way it always did when she was angry. "I tried to keep her out of your business. I don't know how she was able to locate you, unless it was someone in Mr. Jamison's office."

"It's all right," he said. "I made a little trade with her."

"I'm sure Mr. Jamison can arrange for her to leave you alone."

"I can handle it."

"It's just aggravating for you to have this reporter tracking you down. And it is hardly appropriate under the circumstances. I'll have her office on the line in two seconds to straighten this out."

"Really, there's nothing to straighten out," he said, holding the receiver away from his face for a moment and frowning at it. "I'd appreciate it if you'd take care of the judge for me."

"Of course."

"Hey," Ghost said, "there's a fellow named Alan Webster who used to work for my father; he's in L.A. now. Ring a bell?"

"I'm not familiar with Mr. Webster."

"He was my father's top aide. I didn't know he had moved to L.A. Anyway, I heard he wracked up in a car the other night and he's in the hospital. Could you find out what hospital he's in and send him some flowers for me?"

"Yes, I'll try and locate him."

"See if you can get a number for me and maybe I'll call and say hello."

"I will take care of that," she said in her monotone.

Miss Dupree replaced the receiver on its base, then picked it right up to order the flowers. She didn't have to track down Alan Webster, because she knew exactly what hospital he was in, having read about the accident in the newspaper.

4

Ghost joined Radio in the pool, and when they were through swimming they went back to their rooms. They heard Rebecca talking on the phone. Ghost changed into his shorts and laced up his basketball shoes. He scribbled a note on the motel stationery, and gave it to Radio, who had changed into shorts and rejoined Ghost.

"Stick this under Rebecca's door," he said to Radio, "then go put on your sneakers."

"Where are we going?"

"We can't leave Hammond without checking out the courts, can we?"

Radio shoved the note under the door to Rebecca's room, grabbed his sneakers, then dashed down to the Galaxy to wait for Ghost.

They drove through the city streets and passed a few school-yards with basketball courts, until finally finding one with players on it. Ghost parked the car across the street from the courts and watched while Radio eased into a game. During a water break, he pitched the other players on a bet, then bounced the ball three times, Ghost's signal to join him.

One of the players Radio had included in the bet was a tall black kid who, by the look of his shooting abilities, had spent plenty of time around the game. He saw Ghost approaching and announced, "The man's too tall, bet's off."

"You can't change the bet," Radio insisted.

"Bullshit I can't," he said.

"You're just chicken."

"And you're full of shit, little man."

The other players drifted off, since no game was materializing.

"All right," Radio said, "how about a game of horse?"

"Now you got the idea," the tall kid said.

"Do or die for first," Radio said, moving to the top of the key to take the shot, which he missed.

The game consisted of a player taking a shot from anywhere on the court. If he made it, then his opponent had to duplicate the shot. If the opponent missed, he gained a letter. First player to spell *horse* lost.

It was decided that Ghost and Radio would play as a team, alternating shots. Leon, their opponent, was on his own.

Leon chose a twenty-foot jump shot from the right baseline for his first effort. It swished through the net.

Radio had to duplicate, or gain a letter. He missed—H.

Next, Leon pumped in a twenty footer from the top of the key.

Ghost's try at duplicating Leon's shot rattled inside the rim and fell out—O.

Leon swept in a twelve-foot left-handed hook shot, but Radio was not strong enough to match it—R.

"Guy's lucky as hell," Radio whispered to Ghost.

"Guy's good," Ghost answered.

Leon went to the free throw line and made a simple fifteen-foot set shot. This time Ghost didn't miss. Leon put in another from the line. Because Ghost had made his last shot, he didn't have to alternate with Radio. He shot again and made it. Another from Leon. And from Ghost.

"Not bad, city," Leon said to Ghost, returning to the line, swishing through another.

Ghost dropped it through.

"War of the worlds," Leon said, stepping back to the free throw line. "War of the worlds."

The stalemate continued for five more shots each. Leon then decided to change the shot, as was his prerogative, to a baseline jumper.

Ghost pumped one in right on top of Leon's.

Next, Leon tried a thirty footer, right side, that went in and out. Now, it was Ghost's turn to establish a new shot. He went to the opposite side of the court and floated a thirty footer. All net.

Leon matched it.

Ghost took five steps back and made another.

Leon missed. Ghost and Radio: HOR, Leon: H.

Following Leon's miss, it was Radio's turn to establish a new shot, and he executed a tight spin hook that surprised all three of them by going in.

Leon missed the follow-up—O.

Daylight was failing, leaving a grainy glow on the horizon. The hoop was becoming difficult to see.

Ghost let loose with a twenty-foot hook that Leon couldn't match, and then the teams traded a miss, a make, and a miss to even out the score at HORS to HORS. One letter to go. Sudden death.

Saving it for the end of the game, Ghost put in a difficult behind-the-backboard shot. Leon duplicated the shot. Then Ghost shifted to a solid eighteen-foot jump shot, the kind he could make all day. Leon matched, and did so five times in a row.

"Okay, Leon," Ghost said, "let's get down to business." He moved to the free throw line.

By now they could barely see the basket.

Ghost and Leon traded twenty-two shots from the line.

Radio stood under the basket to make certain the ball was actually going through the net. On the thirty-fourth try, Ghost missed.

The missed shot meant it was Leon's turn to establish, and he decided to stay at the free throw line. He made his next shot in darkness.

Leon laughed and said to Radio, "It's just you and me now, little man."

Ghost was standing under the basket next to Radio.

"Don't even think about it," Ghost said. "Just walk up and shoot it."

Radio squared himself at the line and bounced the ball twice to put himself in his rhythm. He lofted the shot, and they all waited an awful second in silence. It rattled around the rim and fell through the net.

"Hey, not bad, little man," Leon said, setting up again at the line.

This time he missed.

Radio stepped up to the line, bounced the ball twice, and swished it through.

Now Leon had to make the shot or lose the game. The moment he released his shot he said, "Shit, it's short," and the ball hit the front rim and fell to the pavement.

Radio let out a war whoop.

"I'll collect," Ghost said, giving Radio a hug.

Radio ran for the car, yelling, while Ghost went over to Leon, who was holding out the ten dollars.

"Keep it," Ghost said.

"Your money, man," Leon said.

"Keep the money," Ghost said, and walked away.

Back at the car, Radio was carrying on a celebration.

"I can't believe it," he said as Ghost approached in the darkness. "I can't believe it. I shot it and didn't think about anything. I just shot it and it went in. I can't believe it!"

"Neither can Leon."

"He was good," Radio said.

"You bet he was good."

"But we beat him."

"We beat him but he was good, Radio. Real good."

Ghost sat behind the wheel, waiting.

"Let's go," Radio said. "Let's buy something with the ten bucks."

Ghost didn't say anything. He sat motionless. In the stillness of the summer night he could hear the sound of a basketball hitting the backboard and rim and falling through the net to the ground.

He sat in the darkness listening to Leon practice.

5

"Thought we skipped on you?" Ghost asked Rebecca in the restaurant next door to the motel.

"The note you left was a little cryptic."

"It was great," Radio said. "You wouldn't believe it."

"We got involved in a game," Ghost said.

"Horse," Radio added.

"The kid here can shoot in the dark."

"Is that good?" Rebecca asked.

"You bet that's good."

"Ghost made most of the shots," Radio said. "And the guy we played didn't even know it was Ghost."

"Let's eat something," Ghost said.

"How many in a row did you make?" Radio asked.

"I don't know. Leon made as many."

Radio said, "I made two in the dark."

"Game winners," Ghost said.

The waitress brought them water and menus and waited at the table to take their orders.

During dinner, Radio never stopped talking. He explained the game of horse to Rebecca and described the tricky shots Ghost had made earlier.

When they finished, Ghost said, "We might as well stay here tonight, and drive into Chicago in the morning. You go to bed, Radio. I want to talk with Rebecca."

"I'm not tired," he said.

"You look like you're asleep."

"But I'm not tired."

"Watch television for a while if you can't sleep."

"There's nothing on."

"How do you know? Maybe they've got cable."

"I'm not tired, Ghost."

"Say good night to Rebecca."

Radio got up from his seat but stood by the table.

"Rebecca's trying to help us," Ghost said. "We're trying to find your father, but if you don't let us talk a little, we're not going to be able to do very much."

"When are you coming up?"

"We're going to have coffee and talk and then I'll be up."

"Wake me up," Radio said.

"You're not even close to being asleep and you already want me to wake you up."

"Wake me up when you come up to your room."

"Why? The idea is to sleep."

"Just wake me up. And then I'll go back to sleep."

"This guy never stops negotiating," Ghost said to Rebecca.

"Good night," Rebecca said to Radio.

Radio snatched his pack and went out of the coffee shop and up to the room.

Ghost sighed and dropped his forehead down on the Formica tabletop.

"What?" Rebecca asked.

"What am I *doing* is the question," Ghost said, his head still on the table.

"That's right. What are you doing?"

He lifted his head and said, "No. I mean, what *am* I doing? I'm asking you. I thought maybe you could tell me, because *I* don't know what the hell I'm doing."

"First tell me again what horse is; I couldn't figure out what you guys were talking about."

Ghost laughed. "It's not important. It's a game. It's how Radio makes his living."

"Evidently he does pretty well at it."

"Oh, very well."

"With a little bit of your help."

"Not much."

"Where did you learn to be so good with kids?"

"Easy."

"Why?"

"I never grew up. So I don't know the difference. When you make your living running around in your underwear shooting hoops, it's kind of tough to grow up."

She smiled at him. "I'm serious. You're very good with him."

"Please don't write about that. My reputation will be shot."

"California's most eligible bachelor?"

"They say that, do they?"

"That's what you read in the press."

"Ah."

The busboy served them coffee.

"We're certain Radio is an only child, right?" Rebecca asked.

"That's what he says. I imagine it's true. From the description of his old man, though, who knows? Who knows if he has ever seen Radio, or even knows he's alive?"

Rebecca looked at the clouds of cream as she poured it into her coffee.

"Radio needs to prepare for that," Rebecca said. "He's never met his father, so right now Radio can have his father be anything he wants him to be. But when he goes to meet his father that's going to change, and he might not like it at all."

"He's going to do it anyway. One way or another."

"I know he is."

The waitress came over and refilled Ghost's cup.

"Did you ever want a brother or sister?" Rebecca asked.

"I never thought much about it as a kid. There were always people around, because of my father. I got lots of attention and I liked that. Most of the time, I was playing basketball. I had friends from playing ball. My father traveled all the time, of course, but he'd come to my games and a lot of times he'd come just to watch me practice. I wasn't a lonely kid." He looked straight at her with a simple, truthful expression. "Now I think a bit about being an only child because my family is gone. So in the sense that I'm on my own I think about it. When everybody is gone you have your past and that's it. The past becomes your family; it's what you've got."

"Then why let me be the one asking questions about your family and your past? Unless maybe it's too painful for you to do."

"Please don't start analyzing me," he said, pushing his coffee cup forward on the table, as if he were going to get up.

"I'm not analyzing you. But you didn't show up in my hotel room the other night looking for a date. I know you care very much for Radio, and you want my help, but he wasn't in the picture when you turned up at the Chateau Marmont. Here's what I think. It's easier for you to have someone else ask the questions, because then if you don't like the answers about your father you can look at me and walk away. I want to tell you I don't think it's going to be that easy, Ghost." Rebecca reached across the table and put a hand on his forearm. "I saw the look in your eye the other night when I started asking you about how your father died. It was obvious to me you'd given it plenty of thought before I brought it up. But *I* want to know a lot more. I want to know about how he died, and why he died and what he was doing the last year of his life, and a lot more. A lot more. So maybe I'm not the person you want to have sitting here. You *can* lose your past, you know; I've seen it with adoption research, watching people go back to find this and that, sometimes they're left with *less* than nothing. They were better off simply with nothing, because then they could make up whatever they didn't know. Once they knew something, though, they had to live with it. You'd better know that for you, and you'd better know that for Radio, because when you take him up to that prison he's going to be looking to somebody for a few answers, and I think you're it."

He watched her hand as Rebecca slowly removed it from his forearm. Ghost leaned back in the booth and looked at her.

"I want to know if my father killed himself."

"You think he did?"

"I don't know."

"Obviously, you do."

"He might have."

"And then what?"

"I just want to know."

"Suppose you find out; what good is it going to do?"

"I'm not looking for it to do any 'good.' I just want to find out, so I can stare it in the face."

"Then you're going to want to know why he killed himself."

"I know why."

"Ghost, you really think your father killed himself, if he did, because you took a year off from basketball?"

"I took a year off from *him.*"

"It won't be that simple. I don't even know what happened, but I know it's not going to be as simple as that. Have you asked

132

Judge Ely about this? If he's the person who's supposed to know everything about your father . . ."

"I can't ask him."

"Why?"

"It would hurt him for me to ask him a question like that."

"I don't get it."

"It's not that tough to get, Rebecca," Ghost said, leaning forward again, his voice an urgent whisper. "It would hurt Judge Ely for me to ask him that question, because it would hurt him if he thought that's how I felt about my father. My father was everything to Judge Ely."

"Then he shouldn't mind the question."

"Christ."

"So you can't ask Judge Ely. Just like you couldn't ask your father if he loved you, or whatever you wanted to ask him, so you stopped playing basketball to wait and see if *he* would say something to you. Is that what it was all about? Because it's getting a little late to ask anybody anything."

Her last words sounded angry. Rebecca leaned forward, her face a foot from Ghost's, and found herself speaking in the same emotional whisper that Ghost had been using. She looked at him and felt her eyes closing of their own will. "I'm sorry," she said. "I'm out of line. I'm . . ."

Her eyes remained closed, but Rebecca could feel Ghost's eyes upon her face.

"So why do you care what I find out about my father?"

She released a deep breath; her voice became quiet again, barely audible. "I've spent a lot of time thinking about my past, and like I told you, I've spent a lot of time with other people who are . . . obsessed with their pasts. And I know, I've observed, that there are costs involved. And I just like things to be clear." She avoided telling him about Elizabeth Folger, thinking that she should know more of the truth before revealing any of it to Ghost, but she began to wonder if she did this for his protection, or because she was afraid of losing his cooperation.

"You really didn't answer my question," Ghost said.

They were exhausted. The bright fluorescent light of the coffee shop became unbearable to both of them.

He stood and she followed. They walked across the parking lot and up the stairs to the rooms.

"Listen," Ghost said, standing in the hall as Rebecca opened the door to her room, "get some sleep and I'll see you in the morning."

"Okay."

He paused outside of her door.

"It scares me a little bit to talk with you, but I like talking with you."

"Is there a compliment in there somewhere?"

"I guess there is."

"Then I'm glad. It scares me to talk with you, as well."

"What have you got to be scared about?"

"It's easier for me to do my work if I've just got me to think about."

She closed the door and sat on the end of the bed. Half an hour went by until she took off her clothes and went to sleep.

6

The door to Radio's room was ajar, and Ghost went in to check on him. Radio was asleep on one of the twin beds. All of the lights were on. A horror movie was playing on the television set. He cautiously removed the backpack from Radio's grasp, took off the boy's shoes, and helped him under the covers. He sat on the other bed and snapped off the lights. His thoughts turned to the game they had played with Leon. It was habit for Ghost to think about basketball at night. Prior to games, he'd often lie in bed visualizing his own moves and those of the player he'd be defending against; the professional version of the sport had become big business, and complex. Opponents were studied on film and on computer; endless statistical analysis was conducted to pinpoint what choices certain players made in game situations. Flights and meals were scheduled to correspond to circadian rhythms. The science of sport, the technology of winning, chemical and nutritional superiority: this was the new jargon of general managers and the sports media. Team trainers were no longer short fat guys with rolls of tape bulging in their pockets; now they held Ph.D.s in sports medicine. This is what's waiting for Leon, Ghost thought. He'll find out soon; he's too good not to. If he's lucky, he'll get a scholarship to a school that has a decent coach who can prepare him for the big time. And he hoped that Leon would not forget the reason he is so good at shooting free throws is that he used to practice them in the dark, or some night he would find himself searching for a playground to rediscover answers he'd once known.

The sound of a bouncing ball echoed in Ghost's mind. Free throws in the dark. He could smell the smoke from his father's cigar, and see its orange glow in the distance. He could hear a child's voice, his own—jumbled, muffled words, senseless phrases—counterpoint to the bouncing ball. Ghost then realized the voice was not his own, but Radio's, and pulled himself out of his half sleep. Radio was mumbling and thrashing around under the covers. Formless words spit out of Radio's mouth. Ghost flicked on the light and saw the boy tangled in the blankets, forehead flushed.

"Radio."

The dream continued, the boy's lips were moving.

"Radio." Ghost stood then sat on the edge of Radio's bed.

"Wake up," he said. "Radio, wake up."

The boy sat up but wasn't awake.

"Are you going out?" Radio said.

"No."

"Is it a school day?" Radio asked. His eyes were closed and his lips barely moved when he spoke.

"It's not a school day. You were having a nightmare. Are you okay?"

"Wake me up when you come home."

"I'm right here."

Radio was propped up on one arm.

"Lie down and go back to sleep," Ghost said.

Radio did so. Perspiration shone on his forehead and cheeks.

Ghost went to the bathroom and soaked a face cloth in cold water, then placed the compress on Radio's head.

It took down the color.

Radio reflexively put a hand out toward Ghost and hesitantly Ghost took it. The boy's hand was tiny in Ghost's.

Ghost waited until the hand relaxed and the boy fell back asleep, and then he turned out the light and quietly went to his own room.

7

The doorman at the Whitehall Hotel in Chicago looked suspiciously at the Galaxy and its passengers, but when he recognized Ghost his attitude changed; the Lakers stayed at this hotel on road trips and, anyway, everyone in Chicago knew Ghost Galvin. The doorman notified the manager and concierge, and they were waiting in the lobby to escort Ghost and his party to their twelfth-floor suite of rooms.

Having never been any higher than the third floor of a building, Radio was stunned by the sweeping views from the suite's picture windows. The rooms were designed to be like those of a comfortable urban penthouse rather than hotel rooms, and the furnishings were antiques and fine-quality reproductions. A waiter arrived pushing a cart filled with hot hors d'oeuvres, fresh fruit, and champagne, compliments of the management. After the snack, Ghost ordered a limousine to take the three of them first to Marshall Fields, where Radio was reluctantly outfitted with new clothes, then to a film and a late supper.

In the morning Ghost called room service to order a large breakfast, and when it arrived, he knocked on the door of Rebecca's bedroom.

"Time to eat."

"Didn't we just eat?"

"That was dinner. It's time for breakfast."

"I'm on the phone. I'll be out in a minute."

When she arrived, Ghost put down his *Tribune.*

"You're a professional athlete," Rebecca said, surveying the spread of food on the table. "You can eat like this. I can't eat like this."

"Take what you want."

"Radio still sleeping?"

"Yes."

"He's got to be exhausted. I'm exhausted."

"We had fun yesterday, didn't we? I think Radio had fun."

"It was fun. I just haven't gotten much work done."

She looked at him, and he shrugged. Ghost felt comfortable, sitting at the table in a sweat suit, watching Rebecca prepare her coffee. Driving in from Iowa two days before, they hadn't talked much, but he'd liked the feeling he had with the two of them in the convertible, just driving. Talking with her about his father had felt strange to him, but liberating, because conversations about his father were usually short and polite, with people telling him they remembered the senator and missed him. There was a formula that repeated itself with almost unwavering consistency. "Oh, let me shake your hand; it's so good to meet you. I knew your father and . . ."; a small intimacy followed, the kind created by politicians skilled at making people think the moment spent with them was the most significant part of that politician's day. People remembered those moments. And Ghost had heard thousands of them. But the father he knew was the man who stood in the dark and watched Ghost shoot baskets. That was the person Ghost had talked with Rebecca about, and he found doing this exhilarating and frightening, because it was hard to know what he thought, at times, until he heard himself saying the words. There was something dangerous in talking to Rebecca, the words were irretrievable and she seemed to know whether or not he was telling the truth; he could see it in her eyes.

"Did you call Judge Ely?" Ghost asked.

"I called," she answered. "I left a message that I called and told the housekeeper I would try again. I didn't say I was in Chicago. The housekeeper knew my name."

"What else?"

"I gave the L.A. bureau Radio's name and address. They'll do some legwork and Telex me here. They'll run the criminal record on the father, too. I tried reaching Alan Webster, but he's still in ICU. There's a detective named Ross in Santa Monica who is investigating Webster's accident, and I spoke with him."

"You've been busy."

"They're calling Webster's crash hit-and-run. Ross was able to have a brief conversation with Webster yesterday, and Webster claims a car pulled out at him, which he swerved to avoid. No witnesses and Webster was legally intoxicated, but I guess the skid marks on the scene support Webster's claim. Of course, even if they found the other driver, Webster's testimony would get thrown out of court. Ross says someone definitely left the scene of the accident, and probably caused it. But he thinks that's going to be the end of it."

"What about Webster?"

"He'll recover."

Ghost could see that either Rebecca's thoughts had turned

elsewhere or she was telling only part of what she knew about Webster's situation.

"You know," he said, "I want to trust you. I'm not certain about why or whether I should. But I want to."

"Which means you don't."

"Why won't you tell me what else you're thinking? About Webster."

"That it wasn't an accident."

"Because he was talking to you about my father you think somebody ran him off the road? That sounds like a stretch to me."

"You asked me what I was thinking."

"If the guy was drunk, he probably didn't need any help dumping his car. There's such a thing as coincidence."

"I don't believe in coincidence."

"Will you please—"

"I'm serious. I don't believe in coincidence. Things happen because people do things that cause them to happen. I don't like mysteries."

"Okay. Explain Webster to me."

"I will when I can."

"What does Webster have to say to you about my father that could mean a goddamn to *any*one, other than me? Tell me who to ask and I'll pick up the telephone and call. It's my life and I want to know."

But who does the past belong to? Rebecca wondered. Perhaps part of his past belonged to her, and vice versa. If the senator had fathered another child, and that child had been put up for adoption, then the records were sealed: in that case, as far as the law was concerned, that child's past did not begin until the day it was adopted. The birth parents did not exist, except on a piece of paper buried in a vault (and it would not be uncommon for the senator's name to appear nowhere). If Rebecca could prove nothing, if Elizabeth Folger did not step forward—even then it might be too late to prove conclusively what had happened—what part of the senator's past, or of Ghost's past, could she lay claim to, make her own? She was already invading Ghost's past by asking her questions about his father. Whatever he learned could alter his view of the past and, if it is true that people are shaped by their pasts, then it might alter his future too. Rebecca wondered if she had the right to do that, without certainty of information.

138

Elizabeth Folger had the legal, if not moral, right to do what she did, so perhaps the choice was Elizabeth's. Perhaps the choice was sealed with the records. Or perhaps Rebecca had no choice but to move forward as deeply into the subject as she felt she needed to go. It might not be choice at all, she thought, it might be like blood washing itself in the body, a process that simply has to take place. The moral choice came in how much to tell Ghost, and when. She again wondered if her decision to withhold information was shaded by the fact that she felt good about being with Ghost, and that the information might cut between them. Ghost sat across from her and she looked at him, wondering if she was revealing information to him in layers because she was testing out a relationship that might or might not exist. And, if so, what kind of relationship? Her half-brother, or a man she was attracted to? She shoved the second thought back in her mind.

"Okay," Ghost said, waiting for her to answer, "you think about who I should call. But while you're thinking about it, I think we should all take the day off. Radio has never been here, and I want to show him Chicago. I promised I'd show him where I used to live, and I've planned a couple of surprises."

"Senator Nolan Wells is going to be in town tomorrow to speak at a convention. I've arranged for an interview, and I need to prepare."

"Senator Wells?"

"Yes."

"I didn't even know the man was still alive."

"Very much alive. And still a senator. At one time he and your father were very close."

"We had him up to Nippersink a couple of times."

"There was a falling out of some kind over a banking scandal Wells got into."

"I never paid attention to that stuff. I played ball."

"Some people think your father fanned the flames of that banking thing. Having to do with political clout and the presidential campaign."

"If it's politics, I don't really care. And I don't know about it. Make sure you wear sneakers today, because we're going to be on our feet a lot."

"I'm not kidding about the work I've got to do."

"So work for half a day. I want you to come with us."

Radio entered the room wearing pajamas Ghost had bought

for him at Fields. The bottoms were the new ones, anyway; for a top he was wearing his old sweatshirt.

"Radio," Ghost said, "tell Rebecca you want her to go with us today."

8

"Museum of Science and Industry," Ghost said to the limousine driver, then turned to Radio. "I know it sounds boring, but you have to trust me. I haven't been there in fifteen years, but I used to love it."

They arrived at the steep stone steps leading to the museum. "So what do you think, kid?" Ghost said. "Any chance you could beat me to the top?"

"It's not fair," Radio jumped out of the car and took off in a sprint up the stairs. Ghost loped up the steps after him, but Radio touched him out at the museum's door.

"We'd better wait for Rebecca, since we're supposed to be gentlemen," Ghost said. He led the way into the museum's rotunda. Radio stepped inside and looked around cautiously, as though the massive building was going to swallow him.

"Come on," Ghost said. "It's not a church. We can make noise." He took Radio by the hand and led him to the museum directory; Rebecca joined them there. "Now, the first place we want to go"—he continued, putting his finger on the model of the museum—"is right . . . there."

He led them to a room that had a black floor and ceiling, and white walls; a large incubator, filled with dozens of eggs and newly hatched chicks, was in the center of the room. Color photographs of the chick's development, from embryo to the moment the beak first breaks the membrane of the shell, lined the walls of the room.

Children surrounded the incubator box, which emitted a halo of heat. Radio approached the incubator slowly, almost sneaking up on it. At first, he doubted the eggs were real, even though chicks were stumbling around and chirping for food. Then he focused on a single egg. A tiny pink beak poked through the white shell, battering its way into the world. The moist matted head emerged from the membrane, working its way out of the shell, stunned by its new surroundings of light and noise and other chicks. Radio pressed against the glass casing of the incubator and felt its warmth. He stared at the baby chick as it tottered into consciousness.

Radio felt Ghost's hand on his shoulder.

"We can come back to this later. Ready for the next one?"

He took them next to the coal mine exhibit, then to the tour of the German U-boat that sat in dry dock just outside the museum.

"I feel like eating junk," Ghost said, after the submarine tour. They went to the cafeteria for hot dogs, fries, and milk shakes.

"I can't believe they leave you alone here," Rebecca said to Ghost, looking around the crowded cafeteria.

"People recognize me in places where they pay attention to who's around them. Airports, hotels, restaurants. Not museums."

"Evidently."

"When I used to come here with my father people left him alone. If we'd go to a Bears game or something fans were always stopping him to take a picture, get his autograph, or complain about their taxes. A place like this they'd just leave him alone. When I was a kid I used to beg my father to take me here."

After lunch, it was the farm exhibit and a visit to the nickelodeon theater. It was two o'clock by then. "We've got one more exhibit," Ghost said.

The entrance to The Body Human exhibit was a long, circular corridor lined with neon tubes crisscrossing in intricate patterns, like psychedelic spider webs. There was a disorienting change in scale once the three of them reached the main part of the exhibit. People became tiny travelers in a world of displays depicting the inner and outer workings of the human body. Epidermal layers were a foot thick. There was a giant eye people could look into and see its iris react to a changing light source. A corner of the room was devoted to the brain. They walked into the middle of the brain and saw a network of light filaments demonstrating the electrical impulses that fire by the billions through the brain. Another model of the brain illustrated the roles of the right and left sides; when Ghost touched a portion of the brain, a panel lit up to show what physical or mental function was being stimulated.

All of the displays were hands-on, and Radio missed none of them.

The room's centerpiece was the human heart. It was the first place Radio wanted to go when he entered the room, but Ghost made him save it for last. This model was large enough for someone six feet tall to walk straight through. Its arteries were the size of air-conditioning ducts, its veins like garden hoses. Blood in the form of colored light flowed through the heart, its path charted by tracers, its purposes explained by a voice emerging from hidden speakers. A constant pulse kept pace with the blood flow inside the heart, and reverberated in the body of anyone inside the heart. With Ghost standing behind him, Radio paused in the center of the display, listening to the narrator's voice and the thumping pulse. The changing flow of blood cast shadow patterns upon their faces as they stood there, turning their heads, listening.

The center chamber of the heart led to another tunnel of light and out of the exhibit, but the throbbing pulse followed them down the hall and into the rotunda of the museum.

9

Ghost directed the driver along Lake Shore Drive.

A fresh breeze blew in off Lake Michigan. The blue water was flecked with whitecaps, sailors hoisted spinnakers that became fat with wind.

"It looks like the ocean," Radio said.

"Do you know the five Great Lakes?" Ghost asked him.

"No."

"Neither do I. This is one of them."

Rebecca was looking in the opposite direction from the water. She was looking at the large apartment buildings along Lake Shore Drive, watching for the one where Mrs. Towsley lived, and where Elizabeth Folger used to live.

"Driver," Ghost said, turning toward the buildings, "slow down just a bit, please. Okay, Radio, I'm going to show you exactly where I lived until I was about your age. I'm talking about the school year; now in the summer I was at another place."

"They look like office buildings," Radio said.

"A little imposing, aren't they?" Ghost asked, gazing at the high-rises. "That's the building, right there." He pointed to 3550 Lake Shore Drive.

"I thought your family lived in a town house on Sheridan Road," Rebecca said.

"I thought it was your job to know this stuff. We lived here for nine years. The town house came after that. Okay, driver, let's go."

"No," Rebecca said quickly, stunned that the Galvins had lived this close to where Elizabeth Folger had lived twenty-five years before. "Can you just keep driving slowly for a little bit?" She was pressed up against the window. The building where Elizabeth had lived, and Mrs. Towsley still lived, was two buildings down from 3550. Rebecca recognized the blue-and-white canopy over the entrance.

"You know that building?" Ghost asked, as Rebecca stared.

"An acquaintance of mine lives there. She's lived there a long time."

"Then I probably passed her in my stroller a hundred times. My mother and father used to take me in the stroller along the lake. All the mothers had their kids out every day when the weather was warm enough. It was a traffic jam of strollers."

The sidewalk was crowded with walkers and joggers, and there were several mothers and fathers pushing infants in strollers.

"I learned how to walk right around here. See that stretch of walkway leading to the marina? That's where my father used to take me to see the boats and throw bread to the birds."

Rebecca felt a small sting in her stomach, as she pictured Elizabeth Folger looking down from the eighth-floor window, watching the senator and the senator's son. As the car rolled slowly past the building, Rebecca wondered if Elizabeth had stood in that window, looking down at the senator, knowing she was going to have his child, and knowing she would not keep it. If Elizabeth had loved the senator, Rebecca thought, wouldn't she have wanted to keep his child, to raise her and know her? She looked over at Ghost and felt a wave of jealousy. Maybe Elizabeth didn't keep her child because she was not Ghost. She was not the child that the world would know as the senator's, the child that the senator was proud of and loved. He was the right child.

10

"Have we seen enough?" Ghost asked. " 'Cause we've got places to go. Driver, you know where we're going next."

"Yes, sir. Almost there."

The driver turned off Lake Shore Drive to a harbor entrance, drove through the parking area, and stopped near a dock. Sitting there on a sail box was a husky man with wisps of sandy blond hair blowing around his nearly bald head. He was deeply tanned, and wearing jeans, sneakers, and a blue sweat shirt. An unlit Camel was wedged into a corner of his mouth. He studied the limousine through his tortoiseshell Wayfarer sunglasses.

Ghost pushed a button to roll down a window.

"Skipper, you look kind of fat."

"From catching too many fish."

"You still do that?"

"Now and then."

"We near ready?"

"You bet."

"You're *sure* you still know how to fish?"

"Can give it a try."

"You've got two serious fisherman here," Ghost said.

"I can tell by the car."

Ghost turned to Radio. "Let's go, kid. First we check the boat." Radio was listening to his Walkman. Ghost pulled the wire right out of Radio's ears. "He's got the best fishing rig in the harbor. He knows where the fish are." Ghost turned to Rebecca. "Ahab and I are going to do some fishing. The driver will take you wherever you want."

"I'm not going to do any work now. I'm going with you."

"Good, then let's go."

Ghost and Rebecca got out of the limousine. Radio hesitated, but Ghost grabbed him by the arm and pulled him out to the dock.

"There it is," he said, pointing to a twenty-eight-foot centerhelmed fishing boat. It had a handmade sign hanging from the stern that read Radio's Revenge.

"Captain Bob, this is Rebecca and this is Radio. Guys, he knows where the fish are. At least, he used to."

"Give you a hand, folks?" the skipper said, standing in the boat, reaching out to help Radio aboard. He looked at Rebecca's skirt. "Those aren't the best fishing clothes I've ever seen, miss."

"It'll have to do," Rebecca said, stepping aboard.

"Okay." Ghost hopped in behind them. "Let's get this thing moving."

Radio watched as Ghost cast off, and the skipper piloted the boat away from the dock, through the harbor, and past the breakwater into open waters. Captain Bob Luxem angled the craft through the small chop kicked up by the wind. Ten minutes out of the harbor, he engaged his sonar and got on the two-way.

"*Bahama Mama,* heading over to Blue Cove, anybody there?"

The radio crackled, and a response came over the speaker: "Roger, Bob, *Sadie's Sister,* we're near the cove. Over."

"Read you, Greg, any action? Over."

"Negative, *Bahama Mama.* Quiet all day. Striking over at Lucy's earlier. Over."

"Roger, read you, over."

Captain Bob checked his compass, opened the throttle, and steered a course for Blue Cove. "That son-of-a-bitch is a bad actor," Bob said to Ghost. "They must be hitting."

"Well, let's go get 'em."

"Get up here, Radio," the skipper said.

Steadied by Ghost, Radio picked his way to the helm.

The skipper said, "Just hold on here and keep her steady. See this arrow? Don't let the red line leave the arrow. Yeah, right there. Keep her there. Nice and steady." Radio looked back at Ghost, but Ghost motioned for him to watch the water. The skipper popped open the ice chest and offered beers to Ghost and Rebecca.

"I would have warned you to wear jeans," Ghost said to Rebecca, "but I didn't think you'd want to end up in a fishing boat."

"We haven't caught anything yet."

Sighting *Sadie's Sister* and another craft near Blue Cove, the skipper took the helm.

Ghost cast two of the lines and set them in the trolling rigs.

He let Radio check the third pole. The boy seemed to know his way around the tackle.

"Okay," Ghost said, "give it a nice, slow cast. Keep your eye on the line so you don't take Captain Bob's ear with it." The line went out a fair distance. Ghost showed Radio how to secure the pole in the trolling rig.

The first strike was on Rebecca's line. Smelt. They threw it back. Next, Ghost's pole bent and the line raced out. He knew it was coho. The skipper worked the boat while Ghost battled the fish. Radio watched, enthralled, while Ghost's powerful arms gradually brought the fish into the side of the boat, where the skipper netted it and killed it with a swift strike of the billy club.

Because he was busy examining Ghost's fish, when a coho hit Radio's line he almost lost the pole from the rig. But its awkward jerk helped set the hook. The fight was on.

"You got him, stay with him now," the skipper said, bringing the bow around to keep Radio's line taut. "Just let him do the work for a while."

For twenty minutes, Radio battled the fish, taking instructions from Ghost and the skipper. When his arms began aching, he looked to Ghost, who helped, but returned the pole when he felt the fish beginning to yield. Captain Bob worked the boat into the chop and the current finally exhausted the fish. Ghost got a net under it and brought the salmon aboard.

Rebecca couldn't tell if Radio was flushed with excitement or exhaustion, but she could see Ghost's pleasure.

He billied the fish and removed the hook.

"Well, you're a fisherman, kid," Ghost said, holding the fish out to Radio. Ghost shook his can of beer and sprayed Radio in the face. "And now you smell like one."

Radio was too tired to fight back. He sat down and stared at the salmon.

"Lines back in the water," the skipper said.

"Hey," Ghost said, "we're just warming up."

By sunset, Rebecca had caught a coho, and Radio another. The skipper decided it was time to head back. He set the course and let Radio take the helm. Ghost sat on the bow, the warm evening air and chilly spray from the lake blowing against his face. Rebecca bundled herself in one of the skipper's foul-weather coats.

The twin engines cutting through the chop made the only sound during the cruise to shore.

7

An aide to Senator Nolan Wells woke Rebecca at seven to inform her that the senator's schedule had changed, and that he would be available for a breakfast interview in half an hour in the Whitehall's dining room. Rebecca showered, and reviewed her notes while dressing. She was down in the dining room just as the senator, accompanied by his aides, arrived.

The Democratic senator from Wisconsin, Wells had been in Washington since the late 1950s, and early on had made it clear to the press and his constituency that the presidency was his goal. Ten years ago his candidacy had appeared promising, significantly boosted by a strong showing in the New Hampshire primary. However, *The New York Times* ran a story shortly thereafter that revealed questionable dealings between Wells and an investment banking firm. The source of the leak was never publicly revealed, but Wells attributed it to aides (Alan Webster in particular) of Senator Galvin, one of his primary opponents. Until that rift, Wells and Galvin had been friends, frequently seen golfing together at the Burning Tree Country Club. They became bitter political enemies after that campaign episode, and remained so until the time of Senator Galvin's death.

"This is Miss Blesser," an aide said, presenting Rebecca to the senator.

"Yes, how do you do? I don't believe we've previously met."

"We haven't."

"No. I would have remembered your face."

"I work out of the New York office," she said. "I don't usually cover Washington."

"Well, I'll put that in your plus column." The senator produced a practiced smile. He had the tall, cumbersome body of a former football lineman, but the perfect cut of his gray suit made him look more fit than he was. Wells was sixty-three, and still made occasional comments about running for the presidency, but only in the fashion certain senators always do in order to maintain their media coverage.

They were seated at a corner booth. The aides took a table at a discreet distance from the senator.

A waiter brought coffee and took the breakfast order.

Wells leaned forward, the starched collar of his white shirt cutting into the folds of skin around his neck. "So," he said, "*Life* magazine is doing a piece about Thom Galvin."

"Yes."

"I understand his boy is in the hotel. Someone told me that on the way in."

"I imagine he was in town for his grandmother's funeral."

"Now, I don't suppose *he's* doing an interview for your magazine."

"Not so far."

"I understand he's not fond of the members of your profession."

"Evidently."

"I suppose he has his reasons," Wells said. "The boy has his own life now. He's quite a celebrity, isn't he? So, what is it you want from me? You're not dragging up that goddamned old banking thing in this story, are you? It's ancient history."

"You and the senator were friends before that," Rebecca said.

"You work for Red Hurlburt," Wells said, referring to the magazine's managing editor. "He's my good friend, going back to the days he was a pup reporter on the Hill. If Red hired you, I imagine I can be frank with you. Miss Blesser, I'd just as soon be left out of this story altogether. I'm not fond of retrospectives, and I don't like dragging up the past. So if we're going to talk, it's going to be off the record. Hell, Red is bored with me anyway."

"All I'm looking for is background."

"Well then, fine. I've been sitting here wondering how you can manage to look so pretty this early in the morning. Lord knows I've never been able to do it myself." He laughed, allowing the waiter to serve the breakfast. "Anyway, the late Senator

Thom was a damn fine politicker, not much question in any-body's mind about that. And he might have squeezed into that vice-presidential spot. But if things got put in the oven and started baking, I think he would have had his share of problems, don't you?"

"Why is that?"

"Hell, an awful lot gets thrown in the wash at that point. You know, there are those members of your profession who thought I had a damn good chance at the nomination that year. But it gets very windy the closer you get. People get real hungry. Suppose I just wasn't *mean* enough at the time; I let 'em ride over me pretty good. But, hell, Thom Galvin could have been presi-dent. Sure, why not? He and LBJ were the best boys I've ever seen when it came to putting legislation on the books. Thom could rattle through a bill providing snow removal in Tucson, if he had been inclined to do so. But I think he got about as close to the White House as he was going to get."

"I don't understand."

"Simple. I don't think she would have allowed it, in one fashion or another."

" 'She' being Senator Galvin's wife?"

" 'She' being *she.* Senator Thom liked good food, good wine, Monte Cristo cigars, and he certainly had an eye for beautiful women. Now, that Nicole of his, his wife, was a charming girl, lovely. Hell, I don't think I saw that other girl more than a few times in all those years. And we're going back quite a ways. Back to when Thom was a congressman. But she never went away. I can tell you that because Thom told me that. Some of the boys on the Hill can get a little carried away with the ladies. It's a pressure cooker up there. But ol' Senator Thom bit off more than he could chew with that one. She must have done something right for him now and then because he didn't walk away from her until the end."

"What do you mean by the end?"

"The campaign. The vice-presidential thing. He knew he'd better put a lot of distance between himself and that one if he was planning to go to the White House. Except he and that girl had something like a fifteen-, twenty-year history. I suspect she gave him hell."

"Who was she?"

"Never mentioned her name to me. Senator Thom and I were friends for a long time. And there are some things you don't want your friends to know in case that friend is ever in the position of having to answer an embarrassing question. To a wife or someone like that."

"Can you tell me what she looked like?"

"Dark hair, dark eyes. Pretty. She was no bimbo, if you'll excuse the expression. I never studied her, though. Just met her in passing a couple of times."

"Did she live in Washington? I mean, was this a constant thing with Senator Galvin?"

"Don't know where she lived. I think she'd go in and out of his life."

"And did everyone in Washington know about this?"

"No, ma'am. Thom was a discreet man. He was not one of the boys that made a show of running around with women. I don't expect very many people knew about it. As I said, we were close at one time."

"I wonder if you can clear up one rumor that's gone around about this woman and Senator Galvin. That they had a child."

Wells looked at her with a totally unrevealing gaze. He had been in politics his entire life; no one was going to ask him a question that surprised him.

"I doubt that very much."

Rebecca felt the familiar slow burn in her gut.

"Why do you doubt it? I've heard it from several sources."

"Well, it's a good story. Probably not a true one. What sources?" He seemed geninuely interested.

"People around the scene."

"You hear a lot of things in Washington, as we know."

"So you don't think it's true?"

"No."

"Was her name Elizabeth Folger?"

He gave her the same politician's unrevealing stare.

"Now that I don't know."

"But you said you met her. More than once."

"I don't think Thom even introduced her by name to me. He never referred to her by name."

"I see."

"But, look, from what I saw, this woman was a little crazy. She worked on Thom pretty hard at the end. He looked like shit before he died. I'd seen him upset a few times in the past when he was having problems with that lady. But he rode it through. I don't know what hit him before he died, but something hit him.

National elections make all sorts of funny things happen, don't they? People do things. Things happen. It's very windy territory. And the closer you get to the White House, the windier it gets, doesn't it? I think that whole thing with the woman might have hit him hard when it got close to election time. He just let it go on too long or let her get too close. Something to that effect. But Senator Thom solved it all by having a heart attack. You just don't know from one day to the next."

"If few people knew about the woman, why would it have destroyed a campaign?"

"Sometimes it only takes a few people. But I hope your magazine isn't planning to write a story about that. The man is dead and gone. Thom Galvin was a fine senator. That's what you ought to write about. Nothing else much matters at this point, does it?"

"Then why talk to me?"

"I told you, Miss Blesser, that this was off the record. Thom Galvin had a fine record. It's just if you were going to drag out that tired old banking thing, I wanted you to have some perspective. Hey, Hap," Wells called over to one of his aides, "Miss Blesser here works for Red Hurlburt. Come on over and say hello."

With that, she knew breakfast was over. She thanked the senator and excused herself.

Rebecca went to the desk to check for messages; there was a teletype from the L.A. bureau and several telephone messages, one of which was from Mary Lee Rush, Rebecca's research assistant in New York.

She sat down on the circular sofa in the center of the lobby. It was impossible to penetrate the practiced mask of Senator Wells's face. Whether or not he knew more was irrelevant, because Rebecca knew she'd gotten from him exactly what he would give. And she knew it had been a trade. When Wells had heard of *Life* doing a Thom Galvin piece, he wanted to stay out of it, at least in reference to the banking thing, so he was willing to trade Rebecca information for an unspoken promise to be removed from the story. And she was sure Wells had been delighted that the kind of information she was looking for only made Senator Galvin look bad anyway. She was sure Wells was sitting in the dining room feeling quite pleased with the exchange. If the magazine had been planning to glorify Thom Galvin, maybe there would be some second thoughts.

It was Elizabeth Folger whom Rebecca thought of now. If it was Elizabeth Folger who had lived in a building in Chicago a hundred yards from the building where Senator Galvin had lived, and if it was the same Elizabeth Folger who had been with the senator and conceived a child, and it was *his* child, then clearly this was the Elizabeth Folger who was Rebecca's mother. In her mind this was clear. Clear but not certain. Clear was for the head, certain was for the heart. Certain was being able to go upstairs and talk with Ghost about it, or certain was leaving Chicago and never talking with Ghost about it because maybe it was better for him not to know. Certain was what she was not, and hadn't been since birth.

Rebecca went to one of the public phones in the lobby and called her office in New York.

"Good morning," Rebecca said when Mary Lee answered the phone. "What have you got?"

Mary Lee read a list of messages.

"Nothing exciting. Any mail?"

"The usual pile of adoption letters. Sometimes I think half the people in the country are looking for parents or a kid. I've got a stack of those. Plus I got a teletype from L.A. The stuff you wanted."

"I got a copy."

"Good. You've got three letters here marked personal, so I haven't opened them."

"Open them."

"All right. This one's from Fort Wayne, Indiana, someone named Alicia Coulton . . . says you interviewed her . . ."

"Right, for the adoption story."

"She's saying she's married and pregnant and how happy she is . . ."

"Okay, hold on to it. I'll write her back."

"Next one is postmarked . . . Miami . . . no return address. . . . 'Dear Miss Blessiar'—that's a new spelling—'Would you be available to help me locate my father'—she rattles on about her childhood—'I'm willing to pay a substantial fee for your assistance . . .' The usual stuff."

"You answer that one," Rebecca said. "Tell her I'm writing a book and working for the magazine."

"Right. And this one came in an envelope inside another envelope. Very exciting. Let's see. No return address, of course, postmarked on the outside from San Francisco: 'Dear Rebecca, the letter you wrote months ago finally found its way into my hands, how, I'm not sure, since the post office box you wrote has not been mine for years . . .' Okay, she goes on about moving a lot, then, let's see . . .' The emotions I felt . . .' Blah, blah, blah . . ." Mary Lee fell silent.

"Mary Lee?"

"My god, Rebecca," Mary Lee said quietly.

"Read the letter!"

Mary Lee continued. " 'I'd always hoped your life would be the success that it seems to have become. I'd always hoped for that. I believe it best to keep things the way they are, however. The questions you ask in your letter, I cannot answer. Meeting would not be satisfactory for either of us. You must trust the fact that I know myself in this regard. So please do not pursue me further. Leave me to my life. I accept with regret and responsibility that I cannot be part of yours. My choices were sealed many years ago and I must live the way I am. I have given this letter to a friend in the States to mail for me, as I now live out of the country. I was pleased to hear in your letter that Mrs. Towsley is still well; she is a dear woman. Sincerely, Your Mother.' "

Rebecca leaned against the wooden partition that separated the bank of telephones. She stared at the hotel guests as they casually crossed the lobby on their way to breakfast or off for business meetings. There were at least fifty letters like the one that had just been answered still circulating around the country. Every time Rebecca or her assistant came across a new lead on a Folger, they followed it up with a letter and a telephone call. In a follow-up piece to the *Time* article, *Life* published the story of Rebecca's personal search, and included an open letter from Rebecca to her birth mother, in which she asked for contact. So the letter Mary Lee had just read to Rebecca could have been a reply to the published letter. There was only the San Francisco postmark to go on. And it could be from a crackpot. There had been several letters like that, from people claiming to be Rebecca's birth parents; of course, their stories never checked out. And even when reading those other letters Rebecca didn't get excited, because they felt wrong, fake. It was just an instinct. But right now her stomach was turning over and her hands were sweating and her skin was tingling. The feeling that this letter was real vibrated within her. She knew it. She knew it the way some women know they are pregnant within days of conception.

"Are you okay?"

The telephone line had been humming in their silence.

"I think so."

"Do you want to call me back?"

"No. Stay on the line. Please."

"I'm here."

"I'm standing at a pay phone in the lobby of the Whitehall watching all these people walk by, and they all look so strange to me." She laughed nervously. "I've been trying for ten years to get this woman to acknowledge me and now she's written this letter and I'm shaking, but all these people are walking by and couldn't care less. It's such a weird feeling. I think I expected the world to stop or something if I ever got close . . ." Rebecca turned away from the lobby and leaned her head into the corner of the open phone booth. She was crying.

"Mary Lee?"

"I'm staying right here."

"It's like I expected some great message when I finally heard from her. I expected to find something out. . . . *What,* who knows? And I know better than to expect anything. I wrote the damn book on this and I've seen a hundred letters like this, but I thought *I'd* get something else, not 'nice to hear from you but never want to see you good-bye.' Is it the right handwriting? What does the handwriting look like?"

"It's typed."

"Typed?"

"Neatly. Perfectly. Looks like IBM elite."

"Signature?"

"No signature. Typed. It's all very neat."

"I guess that follows."

"I guess it does."

"Some family, huh?"

Rebecca laughed as she continued crying, and tried keeping her voice down.

"How are you feeling?"

"Angry. Confused. Mostly angry. And I keep wanting to laugh. I think maybe I'm a little unglued." Rebecca searched around in her purse for a Kleenex. "I feel like I'm in *Ben-Hur* and my mother's a leper and she doesn't want me to come into the cave. God, I don't even know what I'm feeling. I guess we'll see in a while."

"Do you want me to send the letter to you?"

"Just send a copy for now. I'll call you later to let you know where to send it. You may be seeing me real soon."

"If I can offer an opinion, I don't think this moment is a good time for you to decide anything."

"I suppose not."

Rebecca took the elevator back up to her room, and opened the drapes. The sky was light blue and clear over the dark blue waters of Lake Michigan. She stood in front of the mirror that was over the dresser, and wondered if Elizabeth had done that, too, after writing the letter. Did she write the letter, then stand in front of a mirror looking for clues about this person she had never known? Or did she do what she always did in Rebecca's dreams: stand by a window and look out at a world that she didn't seem to be part of.

Rebecca walked into the bathroom and removed her earrings and the thin gold necklace she was wearing, then brushed her hair back and tied it into a child's ponytail. She washed her face, scrubbing her skin until the blush and eyeliner and lipstick were completely removed. With her slender fingers she traced the outlines of her face, feeling the bones of her cheeks and the jaw and chin, as though the skin might peel and the features of another person would be revealed.

2

Ghost sat at the table having coffee and reading the morning papers.

"Radio still sleeping?" Rebecca asked, walking into the room with the teletype she'd received from Los Angeles.

"Still sleeping."

"Still recovering from yesterday."

He sensed that she was upset, and assumed it had to do with the teletype she was holding.

The telephone rang.

Ghost picked up the line and the operator told him she had Judge Ely holding.

"Put him through," Ghost said.

The line clicked.

"Thommy? You there?"

"Good morning, Judge."

"Thommy, son, it's me. Now, since when do you slip into Chicago without warning me?"

"It was a little spur-of-the-moment."

"I read in the papers that you left L.A. because you didn't want to talk about the contract thing. There was even a story that you were retiring."

"They write to fill space," Ghost said.

"Well, it's good to hear your voice, son. Everything's been taken care of for Marie, all the way she wanted it. Nothing fancy."

"You were a good friend to her for a long time."

"You know how I feel about the family. You know, after we talked the other night I had this little suspicion that you'd be coming back, coming to Nippersink. I didn't think you'd want to make any decisions about selling the house without coming back to have a look. You are planning to come up, aren't you?"

"Sure. Pretty soon."

"You have a home-cooked meal waiting for you."

"Sounds nice."

"You haven't been out to the lake here in, what, five or six years? It's good weather right now."

"Looking forward to it," Ghost said.

Judge Ely said, "You know, I got a call from your Miss Dupree the other day. About a writer from—"

"Rebecca Blesser."

"Yes."

"Miss Dupree said you okayed it but I didn't know exactly what that was all about."

"She's doing a story on Dad."

"She's called several times in the last few months. But you know how I feel about talking to outsiders about the family."

"Well," Ghost said, hesitating, "she's doing some favors for me."

Judge Ely laughed. "Son, from what I've seen, you don't need any favors from women. Not the Thommy Galvin I know. She can't be that good-looking."

"She's helping a friend of mine."

There was a pause, then he said, "So you know this girl?"

"A little."

"I see."

"Not well," Ghost said.

"I know I'm an old man," Judge Ely said, "and this is none of my business. But I'd watch out for her, son."

"Why?"

"Oh, I don't know. Maybe you should just give an old judge some credit for being able to smell trouble. I don't like her doing you any favors. I can't remember reporters doing favors that didn't end up costing me. I don't believe she's any friend of your father's." Ghost could hear Judge Ely shifting in his chair. "You know, I have to tell you something. When I was watching that seventh game of the play-offs this year, and you made those two free throws down the stretch, *then* you stole the inbound pass; damn it, Thommy, I have to tell you I had tears in my eyes. How's that for being sentimental? I was sitting there with Eleanor with tears in my eyes, because I had to think what your father would have felt watching that game. Do you know how proud he'd be of you, son? With what you've done, he'd be so proud he'd hardly be able to stand it." The wicker chair creaked into the telephone. "You know, that Blesser girl cornered your grandmother at Nippersink."

"She told me."

"See, I don't like that. I've learned it all the hard way with these reporters. They'll tell you anything to get you going, hoping you'll get mad and start giving them a story. They'll tell you anything. Thommy, just because a judge gets old doesn't mean he stops thinking like a judge. You just have to forgive me."

"There's nothing to forgive."

"Your father was a damn good man."

The judge's voice sounded both like an apology and an admonition, rather than the paternal and backslapping tone Ghost was used to. And he knew that Rebecca was the reason for this.

"I'll call when I get out to Nippersink," Ghost said.

"Sooner the better," the judge said. "Sooner the better."

3

Judge Ely put down the phone and looked up at his housekeeper, who had brought his lunch to the gazebo.

"Opry, honey, I've changed my mind about lunch. I want to

take a ride into Nippersink. Save that sandwich for me."

"Why don't you eat something first?"

"Oh, a little later." He pushed himself, groaning, out of the wicker chair.

Opry handed the judge his white hat, and he walked to the garage. His Cadillac was an older model, but he'd kept it in good shape. Its radio was tuned to his favorite station, and music filled the car as soon as he turned on the ignition. But he turned off the radio; he didn't like listening to music when he needed to think. He took the back road from Lake Geneva to Nippersink, a route that cut through farmland. Here a man could gather his thoughts without the distraction of traffic and road signs and, well, people. There were just so many people now, even in Lake Geneva. New developments, condominiums. And they were people he didn't know. In the past, it didn't matter where the judge drove around Lake Geneva or Nippersink or, for that matter, Chicago, people knew him, looked upon him first with recognition, then respect, deference. When he used to walk into Rabar's Coffee Shop in Lake Geneva he'd hear that momentary hush that signaled the importance of his presence; it made people feel good to see a judge that they knew, he was a sign of order and stability. Because of him people's way of life might be preserved in some acceptable manner; there was somebody in charge who, at least, knew what he was doing, knew what was right. Of course, to the new residents of Lake Geneva and Nippersink, the judge was just another retired person looking for a little quiet down the home stretch. The young people looked at him with those tolerant smiles that mean "Isn't it nice you're up and around, but don't stay at the Stop sign too long." So the judge pretty much avoided Lake Geneva now, preferring the back roads, where his thoughts could roll out across the farmland like clouds and he could look at them and know what to do.

Like most mornings, this one had been busy for the judge. He had made telephone calls, answered mail, taken care of business as executor of Senator Galvin's estate. He'd also checked in with the doctors looking after Alan Webster in California, and he'd spoken with his friend in the Chicago FBI office, Matthew Gregs. Gregs had been kind enough to have the Los Angeles FBI office quietly check on Alan Webster's accident. The police report had arrived in this morning's mail, and Judge Ely had read it carefully. He'd then spent twenty minutes talking on the phone

158

with Miss Dupree, Ghost's assistant. No, he had explained to Miss Dupree, there had been no interview as of yet with Rebecca Blesser. Yes, Rebecca was staying at the Whitehall in Ghost's suite, and no, he didn't know what this business with the boy was all about. Miss Dupree was agitated and insistent that the judge put an end to this involvement with Rebecca Blesser. You let me handle it as best as I can, he'd told her several times. After that conversation he called Ghost at the hotel. Then it was time to take a drive into Nippersink.

The judge's old Cadillac rolled across the worn two-lane blacktop, steady as a ship in familiar waters. Friends chided him about keeping the same car for so many years; this one was outdated, with its flaring, pointy fins and its gas-slurping, eight-miles-to-the-gallon V-8. It rides just fine, the judge always told his friends; I like this car: You keep a good car long enough, in fact, and it becomes a classic. Plus, he liked its air-conditioning. Americans might not be able to build efficient or sleek cars, but they can make air-conditioning that will freeze a slab of beef.

Alan Webster was going to recover, the doctors were confident about that; it was too early to ascertain what kind of residual effects the accident might have upon him, however. When the judge first received news of the accident, he thought about Webster's family. Webster was divorced, and his teenage daughter lived with her mother. Still, the judge thought, how awful for them; what an awful telephone call to receive. Webster's life for several days had been little more than a series of electronic blips on the monitoring machinery. The judge could not admit to anyone that when he heard the news about Webster, which came to him in the middle of the night, he'd gone out to his gazebo to settle himself with a glass of cognac and a cigar, and the thought did posit itself that Webster's death, like Marie Galvin's death, would mean one less worry, however private, for the judge. It was the kind of thought he used to have in chambers, when preparing to read his decision in a sentencing matter to the court. Lives were changed by those decisions; he was the chosen architect of the defendant's future; and by doing so he became the final arbiter of the defendant's past. Society had entrusted him with that power—to silence those who should be silenced, and to look after those who should be looked after. As a judge, society had entrusted him to decide what evidence should be allowed in a case, and what should not. What was a person's life if not a series of events, and when life was lived too close to the edge those events became testimony for the record. Alan Webster had been a good and loyal aide to the senator, there was no doubt in the judge's mind about that. But there was nothing to be done for the senator now, other than to preserve his past. And if Alan Webster's death contributed to that end, then it was not a life wasted. The judge knew it was not the kind of thought he could share with someone. But out here on the open road he was alone and, unlike most people, not afraid of his thoughts.

And if Alan Webster was going to live, then God bless him.

4

"This is what they sent from Los Angeles," Rebecca said, pushing the teletype across the table. Then she stood up and walked over to the window.

To: Rebecca Blesser
From: Jamie Kasem, L.A.

Re: William Boone, Jr.; Pamela Boone; William Boone, Sr., aka William Jessup, Jessie Porter, Jessie Hill, Bart Coulter, Tony Adams.

RB, here's what I've got so far:
   William Boone, Jr. . . . age 11 . . . arson suspect in fire at St. Charles Church, North Hollywood, as reported to police by pastor . . . mother: Pamela Boone, deceased . . . father: still checking on William Boone, Sr. . . . attended St. Charles elementary school, North Hollywood . . . nickname "Radio" . . . only child . . . ran away nine days ago from the apartment of Karen Costner . . . last seen, believed Las Vegas, where he was in temporary custody of police before escape.
   Pamela Boone . . . William (Radio) only child . . . she died a month ago . . . age 32 . . . cause of death listed as overdose of heroin, Percodan and alcohol . . . had previously been hospitalized for overdose and

for attempted suicide by barbiturate overdose . . . worked as cocktail waitress at Starlite Lounge, North Hollywood, and at Howard Johnson's Motor Inn, North Hollywood . . . had three arrests and one conviction for prostitution, sentence suspended.

William Boone aka, etc. . . . incarcerated Michigan Fed. Penitentiary . . . still tracking records . . . will teletype later today . . . please advise location for transmittal.

JK.

"I don't think he knows all this about his mother," Ghost said.

"He must know something," Rebecca replied.

Ghost looked at the door to Radio's room and lowered his voice.

"He heard a priest talking to that Karen about the suicide. Radio told me that. But Radio doesn't believe it was suicide."

"Of course not."

"The arrests, the drugs, all that, I don't think he has much of a clue."

"His mother couldn't hide that entirely from him."

"I think she did."

"Not all of it."

"She was his world," Ghost said. "I get the feeling she was good with him. I don't think he knows about all that other stuff. And he doesn't know much at all about his father."

"We don't know if that's the right father, yet," Rebecca said. "And if he is, a man with twenty aliases isn't going to be thrilled to have a kid show up from a past the guy probably never wanted in the first place. He's probably better off not going to that prison."

"Oh, he's going to go. With us or without us. Did you see him yesterday, when he was fishing?"

"I'm sure it was close to the greatest day of his life, if not the greatest."

"But did you see the look on his face?"

"That's what I'm talking about. It was the look of a happy kid."

"There was something else."

"What?"

"He was having a good time. But he had another look, too."

"What look?"

"I hope we didn't . . . I hope I didn't steal something from him."

"Steal what, Ghost?"

"He was thinking about his father. He wanted to be fishing with his father. What was happening maybe wasn't very real to him because it wasn't happening with his father. I mean, he'd been thinking about fishing with his father for a long time. He's talked to me about it."

"Radio had a wonderful time."

Ghost thought about the first time he played in a basketball game after his father had died. It had felt strange to play the game and not talk about it on the telephone with his father; basketball was playing with his father watching, or playing and then talking to his father about it. After his father's death, the game had become something else to Ghost, a promise that couldn't be fulfilled no matter how good the game, no matter how many points he scored.

"He wants to know about his father," Ghost said.

"Really? Do you know how many times I've heard that in the last two years? From people looking for their parents. They have to *know.* Even people who are reasonably happy with their lives—they have good lives, good jobs, good friends, all of that. But they have to know about their parents. It's just that at a certain point you don't turn back, because what you find is what you live with. You look for your past and then you have to live with it. No more thinking about what it might be, or what you want it to be—none of that."

"That didn't stop you from looking."

"I'm my own responsibility. And I'm not saying you're responsible for Radio. But it sounds to me like *you're* saying it. Or feeling it. He's going to have to deal with the police about the arson thing, and he's got to know that."

"He's eleven years old, for chrissake. They're not going to throw him in jail. The church wouldn't bury his mother in a certain cemetery, so I guess he was trying to get even."

"Whatever happened, they've got his name in the legal pipeline and that will take some straightening out. And you'll run into the question of how much are you going to tell him about what you find out? If Radio finds this man Boone, and he is the right guy, what if he tells Radio that his mother was a hooker and a junkie and then Radio wants to find out about *that?* Are you going to be there to sort out the mess?" She pointed to the teletype in Ghost's hands. "That's somebody's past you're holding. And that means it's got their future written all over it. But it's only their past if they know about it."

"I'm not pretending to know what I'm doing."

Rebecca sat down on the ledge by the picture windows. Ghost could see that she was close to tears.

"Listen, I'm sorry. I'm sorry. You're doing fine," Rebecca said, quietly.

"What about you?"

"I spoke with my assistant in New York this morning. A letter arrived from my . . . from the woman I've been looking for. My mother."

"Jesus."

"She said she knows about me and she's proud of me, and doesn't want to see me. No return address, no phone number, no signature. Just—here it is, and good-bye."

Ghost walked to over to where Rebecca was sitting. She folded her arms and seemed uncomfortable that he was standing so close.

"I keep all my emotions about this thing way out of reach, because there are just too many dead ends in the search. Then my assistant comes across this letter in a stack of mail and I feel the emotions jumping off the shelf. Then she reads the letter and I know why I kept the emotions out of reach."

He hugged her but Rebecca did not unfold her arms. It was like trying to hug a child who is unused to being held.

"I wasn't planning on throwing you out the window," Ghost said, stepping back from her.

She looked away from him, afraid of his comfort, afraid of the responsibility that would come with it. The letter did not mean the end of her search. She knew that. But it meant that Ghost was going to be sucked deeper into the search, because his father and his father's past were the last markers on a tenuous map. The doors were not going to open without Ghost, yet she sat there, frozen, still unable to tell him everything she knew. Rebecca was terrified of being wrong, of throwing black paint on a past he was already questioning. During the interview with Senator Wells, she had found herself feeling badly for Ghost; listening to Wells describe this woman in Senator Galvin's life, Rebecca thought not only of what this woman might mean to her, but also of what she could mean to Ghost. If finding out about

Elizabeth Folger would answer questions for Rebecca, it would only open them for Ghost. It was a mistake to get this close to him, she thought. It was a line she didn't want to cross. It was the kind of thing that is easy to recognize once it's too late to do anything about it.

"Let's get out of Chicago," Ghost said. "Let's go to Nippersink."

5

Judge Ely eased his beige Cadillac down the gravel driveway of the Galvins' home at Nippersink. He parked in the willow tree's shade and with weary familiarity looked up at the house.

He went inside and found the house as he'd left it the night Marie died. Her bed was still unmade. Dishes sat unwashed in the sink. The glass he'd used for his gin-and-tonic stood with its withered lime on the kitchen counter. It made him feel tired and sad, as if he hadn't slept in days. He should have had the maids come in and clean, he thought, but he hadn't wanted to until he'd had a chance to look things over. But it wasn't easy for him to look at things the way they were, the way he'd left them. Who would blame him for saving an old woman from a lonely decline in health and memory? No one liked seeing someone they loved rambling on about things that could hurt the living and sully the memory of the dead. No one likes to see that kind of suffering, but few people, he knew, had the courage to do something about it. He knew that from sitting on the bench for almost forty years.

He went from room to room, checking drawers, opening closets, sifting through letters and papers. He sat down at the postmaster's desk next to the dresser in Marie's bedroom. Under the dresser's glass top were photographs of the senator and Nicole and Ghost and the Elys. On top of the desk was a duplicate of the family portrait that Ghost kept over his desk in Los Angeles. Judge Ely examined the contents of each of the desk's drawers. He found bills and bank statements and receipts for things purchased thirty years ago. Then he found a stack of letters and postcards bound by a frayed rubber band that broke when the judge removed a letter. He looked at each letter and card, pausing to read certain ones; he read the ones from Nicole Galvin, post-marked Paris, written to Marie in the years following the sena-tor's death; he read her postcards from Cairo, Singapore, Rio de Janeiro, Manila, and Madrid. There were two letters from Ghost, thanking Marie for birthday presents. He came upon another set of letters written by Nicole Galvin to Marie during the last few months of the senator's life. Judge Ely sat down on the end of Marie's bed and read those letters line by line. They spoke of the distance that had grown between her and her husband, that there was a great weight in his life that he wouldn't share with her, and it was making life on the campaign trail unbearable. She told Marie that Ghost and his father were hardly speaking, and she did not understand what was happening to these two most im-portant men in her life. If not for the campaign, she would go back to France and stay awhile with her family. But that wasn't possible with the reporters and the fund-raisers and other duties required by a campaign. *I have never seen my husband this depressed,* Nicole said in one letter, *and it leaves me feeling useless, shut out of his life. If you can help, you must,* another letter concluded.

When he finished reading, the judge put the letters inside his poplin jacket. The innocuous letters and postcards he rebundled with another rubber band and returned to the drawer.

Then he went to the bedroom that had once been Ghost's. He picked an old boot out of the closet and removed a brown belt from it that he'd put there years ago. It had been the senator's favorite, one he used to wear with everything when he was at Nippersink. It never mattered whether the colors matched. It had reminded him of the simplicity of his life at Nippersink, where it was just his family—fishing and Ghost playing ball. He had always left the belt at Nippersink. Judge Ely had returned it a few weeks after the senator's death, and concealed from Ghost the fact that his father had been wearing the belt with his gray suit when he died. He'd cinched it around his waist without using the loops on his slacks. If the senator had planned to leave for Chi-cago from the lake, the judge had surmised, he wouldn't have worn the belt; it was not something the senator would have taken with him on the campaign trail. Judge Ely had asked Sheriff Baines to remove the belt from the senator's waist and give it to him for safekeeping; the judge didn't ever want Ghost to see a picture of his father, dead, with that belt on him. It should just be hanging in the closet at Nippersink, like always, waiting for the senator. That's the way Ghost should see it and remember it.

Now the judge unrolled the old belt and hung it on a metal hook that was fixed to the back of the door.

The judge locked the front door and followed the fieldstone path back to his car, stopping in the shade of the willow tree to dab at the perspiration on his face. "It's going to be a warm day," he said under his breath, sliding into the front seat. He turned the air-conditioning up full and flicked on the radio, this time welcoming the music that filled the car.

8

Once they left the city, taking the tollways out of Illinois, past Chicago's suburbs and into Wisconsin, the air was redolent of cornfields and farmlands.

"Look down the rows," Ghost said to Radio, turning onto a two-lane blacktop bordered by cornfields. The stalks swept in perfect rows to the horizon. "Look at how even and perfect they are." Rows of green stalks flashed by, row after row upon row. Blackbirds swirled over the green fields, similar to those in the painting that hung over Ghost's mantel in Los Angeles.

"Should we stop?" Ghost asked.

"Yes."

"But you know, then, what that means?" Ghost said, slowing the car. He eased it to the shoulder of the road, careful not to let it settle into the loamy earth near the fields. "We'll have to play assassin."

"That's a new one," Rebecca said.

"Cornfield assassin," Ghost replied. "I thought you grew up in Wisconsin."

"Not in the cornfields," she said.

"Well, since Radio and me are known between here and Las Vegas as skillful athletes, we'll definitely have an advantage at this game. Though, maybe not. Were you a bookworm in school?"

"I put in time in the library, yes."

"If you did a lot of skulking around the rows in the library," he said, "then you could be a natural at this."

"I don't get it."

Radio said, "What's the 'assassin'?"

"Okay," Ghost replied, "here's the deal. We spread out along the edge of the field, fifty yards apart. On my signal we disappear into the cornfield and start moving. You better be moving low and quietly or you're a dead man right from the start. Start skulking around . . . you know what 'skulking' is, Radio? . . . It's like sneaking, but with a slightly evil purpose . . . kind of like this. . . ." Ghost narrowed his eyes, crouched, and moved slowly around the others, boring his eyes into theirs. "That's the idea," he continued. "It's like playing defense in a ball game, when you're guarding a guy one on one, and at the same time you're patrolling for picks . . . that's skulking. Okay, so now you're out in the field skulking for all you're worth, never stopping for a moment. That's rule number one. Can't stop moving. Even a little. If you stop moving you're morally eliminated from the game. How will anyone know if you stop moving? We'll *know*. Movement at all times and at all costs. Okay, you're moving through the cornfield, picking up every scent, listening to every sound, feeling the earth for vibration with your feet, peeking through the rows for signs of motion, and while you're doing this, you have to be watching your step so that you're not making your*self* too obvious. You might step on something that reveals your position, then suddenly you've got two assassins on your trail."

"How do you win the game?" Radio asked.

"By not being too anxious *to* win. You're skulking around the cornfield, slipping in and out of rows. Now you spot somebody. Keep them in your sight. They don't know you're there and you've got them spotted. Now you go from skulking to stalking. You start closing in. If you're smooth, you might pick up a stone and throw it in a direction away from you, a decoy. You stalk him and start pointing at him like your hand is the barrel of a gun, and you bear down on him with your eyes. When you do that, if you have the true stalker's power, the person will eventually turn and look right at you. When they do, and they see your eyes and your finger pointing at them, they're yours. Frozen. Assassinated. They then have to stand right where they are until the game ends. And in this case the game ends when two people are frozen. The winner will know who he, or she, is."

Ghost leaned against the trunk of the Galaxy and removed his shoes.

"We used to play this all summer in the fields in back of our house. Someone would show up and drag me off the court and we'd play in the dark and scare the hell out of ourselves because in the dark you have to touch someone to assassinate them. That's advanced assassin.

"You have to play barefoot," he added.

Radio kicked off his sneakers and ran down the road.

"You can start from the car," Ghost said to Rebecca. "I'll head down the other way."

Rebecca tossed her light pink windbreaker into the car. "That's too much of a target," she explained.

Ghost got himself into position, waved, then shouted, *"Go!"*

He crouched to stay below the top of the stalks. He knew not to drift too deeply into the field and give up the natural boundary of the road. But Rebecca and Radio made the beginner's error of heading directly for the center of the field. As the game started, there were flurries of rustling cornstalks, birds squawking, and muffled sounds when one of the players stepped on a stone. But they grew accustomed to the terrain and found rhythms that allowed movement with silence.

Ghost laced a crossing pattern along the perimeter of the field. The fecund scent of the soil and the coarse texture of stalks were as familiar to him as the smell of a gymnasium and the seams of a leather basketball.

A master of the game could play it with his eyes closed until someone was nearby. His movement was silent and he would pick up the scent of another player long before he could see him. Eyes and sounds deceived; scent never did.

The only girl Ghost had ever kissed without thinking about what he was doing was the first girl he kissed. It occurred in a cornfield at night when they were playing assassin. Christine was English, spending the summer with American relatives at Nippersink. She used to come by the courts to watch Ghost practice, and leave without either of them exchanging words. One day she brought a soccer ball to the courts and kicked it around on a grassy area adjacent to where Ghost was practicing. She asked him if he knew how to play. She showed him how to work the ball with his feet, and he showed her how to shoot baskets. Standing close to her, he found that Christine had a certain scent. It was not perfume, but also not like someone's skin—it was sweeter than skin smells, a sort of musky sweetness that was faint but never left her. When he was with her he felt uncomfortable, as if a knot of heat were shifting around in his body. But it did not feel bad to be that way. One evening he was playing assassin with eight other kids. Their sounds of stifled laughter and rustling stalks carried over the cornfield like spirits. As evening turned to night, the game grew frenzied, hands flashing out to freeze another player. Ghost moved slowly, relying on his ears and nose. And he suddenly became aware of Christine's presence, the familiar scent like a musical note mixing with the sweet smell of corn. In the failed light he could not see her, and thought maybe she wasn't there at all. He wasn't sure why he wanted her to be there, only that he did. "Thomas," her voice whispered, and a hand was upon his shoulder. She was standing like an apparition directly behind him. His muscles felt awkward and charged. Christine leaned forward and kissed him full upon the mouth. Her lips were warm and soft moving across his immobile mouth. She squeezed his hand and disappeared as completely as she had materialized.

Two black birds swooped out of the blue sky, circling a corner of the cornfield. Ghost edged in that direction. Through the stalks he glimpsed Radio's red T-shirt. He saw the excited, frightened expression on the boy's face. Ghost closed the gap between them, positioning himself at the rear of the arc Radio was describing. Radio's steps were short but not tentative. He clearly had a plan and was sticking to it.

Since he started at the northeast corner of the field, he had not considered the possibility of being outflanked.

One of the hovering birds landed in the field twenty yards to Radio's right. Radio had not seen the bird's descent. Ghost lofted a stone in the direction of the bird and sent it flapping into the sky in a fury of black motion. Radio jumped backward, waiting for the sky to settle and for his heart to stop pounding. But when Radio turned to regain his bearings, there was Ghost, five feet away, staring, pointing. The boy's eyes widened and his mouth opened but he didn't emit a sound.

"Now you wait about five minutes, then yell 'Out,' and she'll know it's down to the two of us," Ghost whispered. He quickly disappeared into the field.

Ghost returned to the safety of the perimeter, using the boundary the way a defender uses the baseline in basketball. He cut through the rows, purposely making plenty of noise for a few seconds, then moving silently, decoying his position. Nearing the road he heard movement off his west flank, and crouched low to monitor it. A swish of stalks unsettled a pocket of air above the field, noted by the circling birds. One swooped down for a look, while the others kept their altitude. Ghost edged toward the sound, scarcely displacing a leaf with his movement. He spotted Rebecca's pale yellow blouse twenty yards away. Ghost threw a stone in her direction. She stayed on the same line.

Ghost was starting to feel lightheaded from the heat rising off the fertile ground. He squeezed the warm earth between his toes as he crept along, working himself close enough to see the Lee patch on Rebecca's jeans. It had been twelve or fifteen years since he'd played this game, but its instant familiarity made him think of nothing else, as when he stepped on a basketball court and whatever was happening in his life dissolved into the pure expression of the moment. It was that intoxicating feeling of his senses and instincts being suspended in time, when everything is sensation and action without judgment. He shadowed her pattern from the rear, until there was just one row of corn separating them. At each stride, he closed the gap between them, hearing her feet sink into the earth, smelling the faint fragrance trailing her. Rebecca sensed a presence and slowed. She looked to her left and saw nothing, then whirled to her right, her dark eyes cutting through the green stalks. In that same second Ghost grabbed her from behind and pulled her toward him. He pressed his mouth upon hers and held her there. Rebecca pulled back to put space between them.

Ghost was three feet away looking at her as if he weren't thinking anything, as if he were just *there*. If she could have recaptured the moment seconds before, she would have, but it wasn't possible. The sun was hot, the air heavy and humid. Rebecca felt the presence of Elizabeth Folger between them. She wanted to fall into water and shed it like a second skin. She wanted to be immersed in cool, silent water that would protect her, unburden her, make her weightless.

"Out!" Radio shouted, from a distance. The small cry sliced across the silence of the field. Ghost turned in the direction of Radio's voice.

Ghost yelled back and Radio came running to join them. He took Radio's hand and Radio took Rebecca's hand, and Ghost led them single file out of the field. When they were in the car and driving away, Rebecca looked back and could see the crows swooping down to reclaim the cornfield.

2

Nippersink's entrance was bordered on one side by its golf course, and on the other by the white wooden fence of the Kraft farm, with its red barn and silo—the farm had changed owners several times since the Krafts, but the locals still called it by that name. Ghost slowed the car and pointed out certain trees and areas of rough on the golf course that always yielded lost balls. And he watched for pathways through fenceless yards, gaps in hedges that once served as shortcuts to the lodge; these private paths were now overgrown and gone. Surely, there were new ones, Ghost thought, but it would probably take Radio to recognize them.

The Galvin home at Nippersink sat on a knoll where the road leading to the lodge forked toward back country. There were two other homes atop the knoll sharing a grassy, sloping yard. At the base of the yard was a hedge and a dirt service road separating it from the fields.

It had been five years since Ghost visited the Nippersink house, but things inside were as he expected them to be. His mother frequently redecorated the Chicago apartment and, later, the town house, but the Nippersink home she left alone; he liked knowing the chairs and couches and tables would stay in their same places.

Ghost noticed new drapes in the living room, but everything else looked the same. Judge Ely had sent in a maid from the lodge to clean and air the house, change the beds, and place fresh towels in the bathrooms. Ghost went to his old bedroom and found his father's favorite belt hanging on the back of the door. His father used to wear the belt unlooped around shorts, jeans, or slacks, regardless of their color or style; and he wore the belt only at Nippersink. Nicole, Ghost's mother, tried persuading her husband to abandon the old brown belt for ones appropriate to his clothes; but that was the senator's Nippersink belt. Here, he didn't worry about his constituency or the press; Nippersink was for being with his family, fishing, walking, watching Ghost practice ball. Ghost opened the dresser drawers, where certain of his boyhood clothes survived, weathered and shrunk from a thousand washings, old shirts and shorts that used to hang on the clothesline like ragged flags, signs of summer.

He walked down the hall and into the master bedroom. There was an empty glass on the nightstand, and next to it a copy of an Agatha Christie novel. In the closet Marie Galvin's clothes hung in neat rows. The closet still kept her scent, like the smell of sherry that's been left overnight in a glass. He remembered his mother packing away the senator's clothes the day after he died; the sight and scent of them were too familiar. That day Ghost had grabbed a few of his father's sweaters and kept them. For weeks, the scent of his father had clung to those sweaters, where Ghost hoarded them in a drawer in his room at school, as if everything left unsaid by him and his father could still be settled by pulling a sweater out of a drawer. Finally, the sweaters took on the scent of the room and he no longer cared about them; they became like photographs left out in the sun, and he gave them to a charity.

The orderliness of Marie's room didn't deceive Ghost. He knew she was gone. In the days following his father's death, there had been procedures and processions and speeches. There had been things to do. Friends, colleagues, and acquaintances had offered their respects. Priests and men in suits whom Ghost did not know, their faces practiced masks of authority and knowledge, had guided the rituals, ceremonies, and receptions. For his grandmother, death was simpler. When someone in midlife dies unexpectedly, it is their unlived future more than memories of the past that is mourned. But Marie was old. It was time. She chose cremation. Ghost thought of the thin papers in which Amaretto cookies are wrapped—it was possible to fold the wrapper into a funnel and stand it on end, put a match to it, and watch it burn and float above the table, then disappear. Poof. Old people die quietly, like trees.

"Ghost?" Rebecca called.

He went to the doorway.

"Someone to see you," she said, nodding toward the front door.

He walked through the dining room to the door and saw Mrs. Warren, the Galvins' next-door neighbor for forty years, standing there, holding her Jack Russell terrier in her arms.

"Well, my god, hello," Ghost said, surging forward to greet her.

"Oh, Thomas," she said, pleased by his exuberant greeting, "I know you only just got in, but I was so surprised to see you step out of that car, I thought you might get away before I could say hello."

"It's wonderful to see you," he said. "This is Rebecca Blesser, and that's Radio Boone. Come on in."

"I won't stay. I know you just got in."

She was a tiny woman, with ruddy cheeks and a constant look of surprise on her face. To Ghost, Mrs. Warren looked the same as always, only smaller.

"Don't even think about it," he said, escorting her into the living room. "You look terrific."

"Oh, I look like an old shoe."

"Cold drink?" Rebecca asked.

"No, I'll only be a minute." Mrs. Warren turned to Ghost. "We are all so sorry about Marie. I miss her so."

He nodded.

"She was a dear woman. Like family to me. I just wanted to give you my condolences."

"You were very kind to her."

"Oh, we looked out for each other."

"We'll get together for dinner while I'm here."

"It's so nice to see you back at Nippersink, even for just a day or two. You know, there aren't many of us original folk left. I walk down to the lake some days and don't know a soul. When I walk past your house it's hard for me to imagine Marie not being in there. I'm so forgetful now that I even came up here a couple of days ago to pay a visit. You see what happens when you get older? I'm going to let you get settled in now."

Ghost walked Mrs. Warren outside and down the hill, then retrieved the luggage from the car.

"You're in the master," Ghost told Rebecca, leaving her luggage in the room. "Radio, you're down the hall in my old room. I'll stay in the middle room, to keep you guys from fooling around."

"I've got some calls to make," Rebecca said.

"There's a phone in the master and one in the enclosed porch. Take your pick. I think I'll take Radio on a tour of the neighborhood. Why don't you come?"

"I want to get as much done as I can, before anyone realizes I'm staying at your house."

"It's too late for that. Mrs. Warren has met you. They don't have a newspaper at Nippersink because they don't need one."

"I'll get busy."

"It's nice out on the porch this time of day. You'll get a nice breeze out there."

He watched her walk out to the porch. Rebecca had hardly looked at him since leaving the cornfield. He was sure it was not

174

out of shyness that she kept averting her eyes from his; her mouth had yielded to his when he had kissed her, before she pushed him away. And it felt good to have her here in this house, not strange as he'd thought it would.

3

Rebecca spread her files across the glass-topped table on the porch, selected the file marked Coroner, and opened it. At four o'clock she took a steno pad with her across the street to the clubhouse of Nippersink's golf course.

She had learned that Dr. Thomas Wyndham, the Cook County coroner, owned a weekend home at Nippersink, and every Friday during the summer he left his office in Chicago in time for nine holes of twilight golf.

Rebecca bought a Coke and waited by the practice putting green.

At 4:45 Wyndham's white Cadillac pulled into the parking lot.

He was a tall, thin man in his late fifties; his skin showed the pallor of someone who spends most of his time in artificial light. His silver-framed glasses glinted in the sunlight as he opened his trunk and pulled out his clubs. Rebecca identified herself, and though he was irritated, he did not seem surprised to see her. Wyndham took his golf spikes out of the trunk and began putting them on.

"This is not an appropriate method of handling yourself, Miss Blesser," he said.

"I had no luck reaching you through your office."

"You were furnished with copies of the documents you requested."

Rebecca held up a copy of Senator Galvin's autopsy report, which Wyndham glanced at. "This is your signature, isn't it?"

"Of course it is."

"Isn't it unusual for an individual to die in one county, or in this case, another state, and then be brought to another county for the death report and autopsy?"

"The individual you're referring to wasn't a normal case.

Perhaps if you addressed your questions in the form of a letter my office could—"

"I'm done with that route. Here it is: You and your office could be in serious trouble, and you might save yourself considerable public attention by answering my questions accurately, and right now."

When he turned his head to look at her the sun reflected off his glasses.

Wyndham folded his arms and leaned against his car. "You're rather rude for such a young woman. Do they teach rudeness in journalism school?"

"It's of no interest to me what you think of my manners."

"What's your point, Miss Blesser? Three gentleman are waiting for me."

"Why was Senator Galvin's body brought to Chicago for autopsy?"

"Because he died in a very small town. They wanted top-flight facilities and people. It was done by judicial order."

"What court?"

"I have no idea."

"Let me guess. Judge Ely."

"The instructions could have come from Washington, for all I know. We're talking about a United States senator and a candidate for vice-president. This wasn't a farmer who fell into his threshing machine. There are always special circumstances when a high-ranking official of the government dies."

"You were satisfied that the cause of death was heart failure?"

" 'Satisfied,' " he said, snapping out the esses, "is not a relevant word. The cause of death was myocardiac infarction. It's a biological occurrence, not a guess."

"This man had no history of heart trouble, nor is there a history of heart trouble in his family. His medical records are remarkably clean, except for the fact that the senator had been given a prescription for barbiturates sometime around the beginning of the campaign. Yet you ordered no pathology report." Rebecca held up the death certificate. "This report is incomplete at best."

"That report was witnessed by the senator's personal physician. The entire matter was handled in his presence and in consultation with him. Our decisions were based on fact and experience, two qualities you lack. I suggest you stick to facts. I don't know what story you're writing, but I'm certain the senator's family would prefer you let him rest in peace."

"The only family is his son."

"Then I'm sure that's what his son prefers. This case is closed, as it should be."

Rebecca lowered her notebook. "Perhaps, if I need to get in touch with you again, you'll accept a telephone call."

"I can only repeat what I've just told you."

"That's why you may hear from me," she said.

Wyndham locked his car and walked to the clubhouse. He went downstairs to the men's locker room and picked up the pay phone.

"Davis," Wyndham said, when Judge Ely answered.

"Hello, Wyn," the judge said quietly.

"That Blesser girl was waiting for me in the parking lot at the club. I probably should have just stayed in town, but I'll be damned if I'll . . ."

"Wouldn't have mattered," Judge Ely said.

"Well, I don't see the point in this at all. There's got to be a way of going over her head."

"I think she'll leave you alone now," the judge said. "I don't think you'll be hearing from her." Judge Ely looked at his watch. "You must be about ready to tee it up, Wyn."

"Just about. We'll get in nine holes."

"Sure you will. Get in eighteen as far as that goes."

"You'd think they'd let the man rest in peace," Wyndham said.

"Oh," the judge said, "she's young, I suppose. I don't think you'll hear from her again."

4

After their walk, Ghost drove Radio into Twin Lakes to the supermarket, and they returned with groceries and plans for a barbecue.

Rebecca waved to them from her makeshift office on the porch. She had the phone against her ear and papers spread out on the table in front of her.

Ghost assigned Radio the task of cleaning the grill, while he shucked the corn and marinated the chicken. They set a table on the outside porch, and lit kerosene lamps to keep the mosquitoes away. While he waited for the food to cook, Ghost fixed gin-and-tonics for him and Rebecca, and poured a Coke for Radio; he brought the drinks on a tray to the living room.

"See if you can find me a few coasters in here," he said to Radio.

"What's that?"

"Something to put the glasses on. Look in the tables by the couch."

Ghost stood holding the tray of drinks, while Radio, who still was unsure of what Ghost wanted, emptied the contents of the end tables. Along with playing cards, coasters, and scraps of papers, Radio pulled out the stack of letters Marie Galvin had left there the night she died. Ghost put the tray down and looked at the letter on top of the pile. He recognized his father's handwriting, and saw that there were several letters from his father in the pile.

When Ghost's mother had moved back to France, they'd sold the town house in Chicago, and included in the sale everything but clothes and certain books; what wasn't sold they donated to charity. Ghost had gone through the house with his mother, looking for things he might want to keep, and had decided on a few photographs and the desk that had been in his father's Washington office. But there hadn't been any letters or diaries around the house, at least that Ghost had known about. All of his father's letters had gone to the University of Chicago, where the senator's papers were kept under the trusteeship of Judge Ely. It had not occurred to Ghost to look in the Nippersink house for written remembrances of his father, because he did not consider his grandmother to be a saver, and because she had so little to say about the senator after his death. Ghost couldn't imagine her keeping old letters. Of course, he realized, he had never asked her if she had. Ghost decided he wanted to read them later, when the others had gone to bed.

"Would you put these on the bed in my room?" Ghost asked Radio, handing him the letters.

During dinner, Ghost talked of Nippersink's secret places: the small stream at the northwest corner of Lake Tombeau, where snapping turtles sunned themselves; an abandoned house behind the Kraft farm that was haunted; the pond on the seventh hole of the golf course where bull frogs the size of waffle irons lived; a valley in the fields filled with cow bones; Sandusky's barn, where kids who weren't afraid of bats would go. There were other secret places, he told Radio, but they were too secret to talk about.

"Let's go down to the end of the yard," he said. "I want to show you something you won't see a lot of in North Hollywood."

They found seats in the willow, and waited to see the fireflies Ghost had talked about at dinner.

"There," Ghost said, pointing to a wavering dot of light.

"I didn't see anything," Radio said.

"Keep watching."

Another of the bugs zigzagged in the darkness, fading just in front of the tree.

Radio ran up to the porch and returned with a glass.

"It's bad luck to catch them," Ghost said. "So don't try too hard."

"Why is it bad luck?"

"I'm not sure. Mr. Kane told me that. He was the caretaker at the lodge. He told us if we got lost we could follow the fireflies home. But if we'd catch them we'd end up lost. He probably just didn't want us out in the fields all night catching bugs."

Radio put down the glass.

After a while, Radio grew tired. They went up to the house, and Ghost put Radio to bed, then went to the kitchen to help with the dishes.

The sound of a freight train rolled across the flat land.

"It's been a while since I heard one of those," Ghost said, standing at the sink. "My grandmother said that you didn't have to gossip at Nippersink, all you had to do was sit on your porch at night and it would come to you."

Ghost washed the dishes and handed them to Rebecca, who dried and stacked them in the cupboards.

"My office followed up on Boone," Rebecca said. "They're fairly certain he's the man you want."

"Fairly certain?"

"His name's on Radio's birth certificate. Everything fits in the chronology. Unfortunately, right now he's in his sixth year of an armed robbery conviction, assault with a deadly weapon, and car theft. The list goes on from there. He was denied parole recently."

"How much longer has he got on his sentence?"

"Six years. But with good behavior and the possibility of parole, he could be out in a couple of years. Or he could go the full term."

"Christ," Ghost said.

"It's up to you what we do next. I can contact the warden, probably set up a meeting. I don't know that it's a good idea to let them know my magazine is involved. It makes people nervous."

"I have to take Radio there. I promised him."

"I doubt Mr. Boone, based on his history, is going to be moved by the gesture."

"Anyway you slice it, the kid takes it in the teeth. He's probably better off not going there, but I know that he will."

He handed her the last dish.

She put it away, then leaned against the counter, across the kitchen from Ghost. Rebecca had always heard that if you felt strongly about a man—she didn't risk the word *love*—you liked doing almost anything with him. She thought about her childhood, when in the evenings she sat on the living room floor while her father read the papers and her mother did the books for the charities where she worked. That was Rebecca's fondest memory of the past; not Christmas morning or going to Disneyland or the time her father took her to New York. It was those evenings in the living room. She felt whole then, complete, without questions or doubts.

It felt good to her to stand next to Ghost, taking the clean plates for stacking. She liked listening to him talk about Radio, just as she'd enjoyed listening at dinner when Ghost talked about Nippersink. The words were true and simple and from the heart. Words of love. It felt for a moment like being with her family. But she pulled herself from that moment, just as she had this afternoon when he kissed her, because what was unknown and unsaid about their pasts infected the present. Ever since she knew about adoption she felt her life possessed by a woman she did not know. Rebecca wanted to know where she came from in order to feel free in the moment, unbound. Part of her felt imprisoned by the presence of unknown blood in her veins.

"I'll help with Radio in any way I can," Rebecca said. "But I think I'll have to do it from Manhattan. I should leave."

Ghost felt mystified by Rebecca's sudden statement, and

assumed she was thinking about the afternoon in the cornfield when he had kissed her. It frustrated him and scared him that he could not read her thoughts.

"For chrissakes, Rebecca, I'm not planning on attacking you. Don't you feel good being here right now? I do."

"What I don't feel good about is the fact that I haven't been completely honest with you. About what I'm doing. I haven't been *dis*honest, it's just that I haven't told you everything I know."

He pulled away from her, recalling the judge's warning about Rebecca not being trustworthy. He'd gone on instinct, letting her in as close as he had, and now began to feel weak for having done so. "What haven't you been honest *about?*"

"Your father, and what I'm doing here. I haven't wanted to tell you partial facts, when I can't put the whole story together. I guess in court they call it circumstantial evidence."

Ghost placed his palms flat upon the Formica countertop, leaned forward, and looked sidelong at Rebecca.

"Why don't we bottom-line it, because I've been standing here feeling good about being with you and being with Radio. So if you're going to fuck me around, let's get right to it."

"The woman I believe is my birth mother, whatever you want to call her, could be a woman who was involved with your father for several years, perhaps for a long time."

"Involved?"

"His mistress."

Ghost felt momentary hate for Rebecca and for what she was saying; what he hated most was that she had the power to say something that could change his life, because in his experience anyone with that kind of power only changed your life for the worse. He thought of standing in the dean's office at Stanford, with the light blinking on the telephone, a roomful of people assembled to reveal the senator's death, and all Ghost wanted then was to stare out the window at the eucalyptus tree, feeling unwilling to surrender his father, yet realizing that his father's death removed the matter of choice from the situation.

"This is good," Ghost said darkly. "How long have you known this?"

"I don't *know* it. That's the point. Facts point to it."

The word *facts* sounded hollow the moment it left her lips, a false protection; she was talking about her mother, and about

Ghost's father, and as much as Rebecca hoped to diffuse the situation by stating "facts" she knew her words were cutting to the center of Ghost and herself.

Ghost looked away from Rebecca. "You're telling me my father had a child with this woman?"

"The woman, if I have the right woman, did have a child during the time she was seeing your father. My name is on the birth certificate. There is no father listed. Like I told you, it's circumstantial evidence; I didn't want to dump it into your lap without more proof. But it seemed impossible not to tell you at this point."

"Whatever that means."

"You kissed me and I wanted to kiss you back. That's one reason, isn't it?"

Ghost felt surrounded by deception. He felt tricked by whatever unconsidered emotion allowed him to grab Rebecca in the cornfield and kiss her, and he felt tricked by the contentment he'd felt sitting in the tree with Rebecca and Radio, watching the fireflies slash the darkness with their light. And, finally, though he tried beating this feeling back, he felt tricked by his father, because whatever might have been withheld by him from Ghost was not truly withheld, only postponed.

"This *Life* magazine story about my father's career, that was just to get in the door?"

"No. The magazine *is* doing a piece on your father as part of the special issue I told you about. I wanted the assignment when I found out about this woman. I wanted the access. I'm not denying that. Put yourself in my shoes. But I didn't expect to be getting close to you. Look, I'm not planning on writing about this, but I can't walk away from it either. It's *my* life we're talking about, too. But I don't have to pursue this right in front of you, Ghost."

"It's a little late to change that, isn't it?"

"Don't look at me like that. Really, *don't*. I didn't invent all of this. And *you* called me from Iowa wanting me on the next plane, remember? I'm probably the one person on the planet with some idea of what you're feeling right now, so don't look at me like that. I have no intention of trashing your father or your feelings. I'm just trying to find out where I came from."

"This is just a little hard to take, to stand here and listen to this about my father."

"If you think I used you, then there's nothing I can do about that."

"That's the point, you did use me."

"I didn't know you. I couldn't come to you with this. How would you have reacted?"

"You were in my house. You're in my house now."

"I'll leave."

He didn't want that, but couldn't say it at the moment because the thought felt like a betrayal of his father. Ghost, in fact, felt drawn to the tenacity and honesty he saw in Rebecca's eyes. He thought about the last time he saw his father, when they stood together on the porch a few yards from where Rebecca and Ghost now stood, and his father had looked out the window toward the fields and talked about Ghost's not playing ball. But the words had sounded muted and without passion, as if his father's thoughts had gone elsewhere but he did not know what else to discuss with Ghost. Ghost had never seen his father's eyes look unfocused as they had on that afternoon, and he regretted being unable to penetrate them, to follow his father's gaze to a place of understanding. Ghost suspected Rebecca knew how to do that, that she had a clarity about her emotions and a willingness to meet them that Ghost lacked, and he felt pulled toward her because of it. He looked at her. They stood a few feet apart and let silence surround them, until they shared a moment of recognition: they studied each other's faces, feature by feature, as if they'd met at a high school reunion. He breathed deeply and let out a laugh that sounded like a sigh.

"I keep thinking you're talking about somebody else, like when people come up to me in airports and tell me they knew my father and they've got some wild story that sounds like an entirely different person, and usually is. Why don't you just tell me what you know?"

"I found the hospital where I was born and I traced the name of my birth mother, and published it in *Life*. A woman in Chicago named Mrs. Towsley wrote me that she knew a woman by the same name . . ."

"What name?"

"Elizabeth Folger."

Rebecca watched the name wash past Ghost's eyes without any light of recognition.

"The chronology fit Miss Towsley's story. She and Elizabeth

Folger were neighbors in that building on Lake Shore Drive, just two buildings from where you lived as a child. In any case, I circulated a description of Elizabeth Folger to the *Time* and *Life* people, just on chance. One of the older staffers covered your father in Chicago and later in Washington. And he told me that evidently there was another woman in your father's life. She more or less fit the description of Elizabeth Folger I'd gotten from Mrs. Towsley. Senator Wells confirmed the story for me yesterday. Off the record, of course. No one has said anything about a child. But Elizabeth Folger left Chicago in a hurry about eight months before I was born. I may not be able to come up with final positive proof. We'll see. You know about as much as I do, at this point. And part of me feels like apologizing to you. For what I'm not sure. I mean, I'm just handing this to you and saying 'here it is . . .'" She closed the cupboard and walked across the kitchen, her back to Ghost. "What if I'm right?"

"I don't think you can be."

"I'm right about Elizabeth Folger. That much I know." Rebecca's voice became quiet. "She was in your father's life. I'm sorry to be the one to tell you about it."

"About the child, I mean," Ghost said. "My father wouldn't have done that, had an illegitimate child."

"Illegitimate" sounded ugly and crude to Ghost as he said it, and Rebecca stiffened hearing the word from him.

"Why?" she asked.

"I'm certain he wouldn't have done that," Ghost said, feeling like he was trying to hold on to part of his father that he did not want to share, or violate.

Rebecca hated the word *illegitimate* and felt that people used it for protection, as a way of not feeling responsible; society used to trace bloodlines for the passage of property and wealth, but it was not an absolution. "You told me you thought your father killed himself. Did you think he'd do *that?*"

"Don't play word games with me."

"I'm not. I just know people have lives other than the ones we think we know. If I've learned anything from studying adoption, I've learned that."

"Who did you talk with today? You were on the phone all afternoon."

"Dr. Wyndham. I stopped him over at the golf course. He wouldn't take my calls in Chicago."

"What's he got to do with this?"

"He performed the autopsy on your father," she said, feeling the words bounce in her brain as she said them. Performed the autopsy. It was a phrase she'd used hundreds of times as a reporter, the kind she rattled off like an address. But looking at Ghost made saying the words feel grotesque, a violation, the ways he'd felt when he'd used the word *illegitimate.*

And in his mind Ghost saw the stainless steel table. Scapels. Cold white skin. "What did he tell you?"

"As little as he could. Like everyone else." She walked past him to the enclosed porch and picked up the coroner's file.

"Why do you even want to know about his death? What's that got to do with what you're trying to find out?"

"It's just part of a pattern of the closed camp that surrounded your father. This is Wyndham's report. I'd call it woefully inadequate. Your father was under prescription for barbiturates, yet there was no chemical analysis done at the time of his death. He was supposed to be fishing when he died, yet they found him wearing a business suit. It starts there. There was no investigation to speak of. Sheriff Baines signed off on what he had to, and Wyndham signed this thing and that made it official."

"You're telling me what I told you, that he didn't die of a heart attack. That he probably did it himself. I already told you that."

"What I'm saying is that it's fairly likely that whatever happened didn't end up in Wyndham's report or the police report. Maybe your father did die of a heart attack, he could have taken the wrong combination of the wrong things and that was that. Or maybe he did take his own life. For all we know someone else could be involved. Whatever happened was important enough to somebody that Wyndham got convinced to sign this Mickey Mouse report."

Ghost glanced at the report and put it down.

"Wyndham and my father were not close friends."

"I know that." Rebecca took a packet of newspaper clippings from the file and handed them to Ghost. "The parts highlighted in yellow refer to Davis Ely being instrumental in Wyndham's appointment as coroner eleven years ago."

He scanned the clippings, then walked over to the window, his back to Rebecca. Thoughts of his father and of "the senator" floated from his head and out past the porch where spotlights poured down on the cement steps, and moths beat themselves against the bright bulbs. Growing up with a famous father, Ghost always felt the sensation of people reaching for him, trying to touch him to have a piece of his power and fame, to have their moment with the senator. Ghost had learned early not to compete for his father's attention with the public or the ceaseless stream of people who came around for meetings, interviews, or brief, intense conversations. He looked, instead, for parts of his father the others never saw—the way his father looked when he was watching Ghost play basketball, or when he and his father went bass fishing in Lake Tombeau early in the morning. His father never spoke much then, but his face looked different from when he was doing business, or doing anything else, and Ghost coveted access to that privacy, as silent as it might have been. Whatever that silence was, Ghost felt it belonged to him and his father only. Now, even that was being penetrated by Rebecca, because Ghost felt that his true feelings for his father existed in that silence, and in one sense he held them unexamined because he did not want them to escape. When he saw pain on his father's face that last day at Nippersink, Ghost did not want to pursue it beyond the conversation about basketball because, at least, the pain was between them, and what was private between them was important enough and powerful enough for them both to feel the pain. In that sense the pain felt like a bond with his father. To unlock it might be to lose it, and then what would be there?

"What's next? That this isn't my family's house? Someone else owns it, we're not really in the state of Wisconsin, and Thom and Nicole Galvin really weren't my parents? The shoes I'm wearing belong to someone else and that kid in the other room isn't Radio Boone, he's really a Vatican spy who's going to turn me in for not going to confession in sixteen years. Are you going to dole out bits of information to me like medicine? I want to know what I know."

She walked up to Ghost. "You know what it feels like to me not to know where I come from?" Rebecca took hold of his shirt with both hands and pulled his face to hers, then kissed him on the mouth. "Feels strange now, doesn't it? In a way it feels good, but we can't trust it. We have to think about it. And maybe we're a little repelled by it, suddenly, because we don't know what we are to each other, we don't know where that kiss belongs. We have to think about it. That's what all this feels like to me, Ghost. That's the way my life has been for a long time. I've had those kinds of feelings going through me about a lot of things in life. When I feel good I wonder if it will last. When I feel sick I wonder if I'm getting some disease my birth parents never bothered to tell anybody about. When I get wound up I wonder if madness is starting to work its way up and out. I doubt things that happen to me because I don't have the blueprint of my parents to look at. I want to know who they are so I have a choice about whether to think about them or not think about them. Because I don't know, I think about them all the time. And it feels like that kiss we just had—it's not something you want to have to think about."

Rebecca stood a foot from Ghost, her face uncomfortably close to his. She felt relieved, to have told him what she knew and what she felt. "I can fly to New York in the morning."

5

There was no air conditioner in Ghost's room, so he cranked open the windows and heard the night ringing with crickets. He picked up the pile of letters Radio had found in the table in the living room.

Ghost counted twenty-three letters in all. Ten of them were written by his grandfather, three were thank-you notes written by Ghost as a child, four were from the senator, and the remaining letters were get-well messages from important politicians, received by Marie when she underwent back surgery eleven years before.

Ghost took out the four letters written by his father and put the others on the nightstand.

He had often received notes from his father; invariably, however, they were brief comments, usually scribbled on a news clipping. The comments referred to a game, or an assessment of the statistics presented in a box score. As Ghost scanned these letters he saw they were lengthy, personal; they reminded him of the long walks his father and grandmother used to take. He felt some apprehension as he stacked them for reading, as if he was about to be told something he did not want to hear by someone he didn't know very well. And since Ghost had never received letters like these from his father, it was as if they were from someone else—there had been, until earlier this evening, "the senator" and his father, and now there also was this person Rebecca created when she talked about Elizabeth Folger.

The first letter was dated August 11 in the last year of his father's life:

Dear Mother,

Wish you could have been there for the convention. I don't think they can show on television how really crazy it all is. But it is exciting, *isn't it? Some of my friends advised against my taking the Vice-Presidential nomination, that I'd disappear in the job. But, heck, I'm a young man, and I think it's the next step before The Big Step. So now I'm campaigning again. Seems like I'm always campaigning, doesn't it? California has gone well. I'm even a little surprised by how well I'm thought of out here. You never think you're going to be known out of your home state.*

I'm writing this aboard an airplane, so if the handwriting looks a little funny, it's because the chop is pretty good in places. But my most peaceful moments these days are aboard airplanes, so right now I'm happy. On the way to a fund-raiser in San Francisco. Called Thommy and asked him to come up to dinner. Must be the first summer of his life he's not spending at Nippersink. Some of the press have been asking me about why Thommy's not playing ball for Stanford. It's tough for me to answer, because I don't know *the answer. I tell them that kids have to make up their own minds about things after a certain age. But I don't understand it. When you have a gift, you should use it. That's the only way I know how to go.*

The other thing we talked about when I visited, that I don't understand either. I know you don't approve and feel I made my own bed and have to lie in it, but I appreciate you at least listening to me. During a campaign you can't say anything to anybody. If I didn't have you and Davis, who am I going to sound off to about this? You know what it's like out here. I'm working hard to steady up Nicole, because things have to be that way now, just have to be. I'm still trying to talk sense into the other but that's not the easiest thing to do.

The doctors say you're doing just great; I knew you would come through like a champ.

Much love, Thom

Ghost placed the letter on the bed. He could hear his father's voice in the construction of phrases, but not in the things being said, except for the part about Ghost not playing ball. "The other thing we talked about . . ." Ghost wondered what it was. Trouble, but "I'm still trying to talk sense into the other . . ." referred to someone; the woman, Ghost assumed. Perhaps I don't have the right to read these, he thought; shouldn't a person have privacy even in death? Probably so, unless death leaves doubt. He turned his eyes to the next letter.

Dear Mother,

Small jet headed for Jacksonville. Speech, press conference, meet the local bigwigs. Same stuff. Roar back into Washington for a vote, then back out on the trail. I'm working the South because we need the support there.

Mom, I read your letter. It's great you feel well enough to write. Dr. Kramer says you're stronger every day, and I told him, of course you are. Anyway, I read the letter and don't agree I'm gambling with my family. I've been in the public eye twenty-five years, so in that sense everything I do, no matter what it is, is a gamble. I think I can take care of this and move forward. Think about the years ahead. You always said you wanted to see your son in the White House. Well, we're getting mighty close, Mom. Mighty close. Take care and try not to worry.

Love, Thom

Ghost went on to the next letter.

Dear Mom,

It's raining like hell today. We're trying to get into Cleveland and get on with things, but the weather isn't cooperating.

Out here, you go from plane to car to red carpet, give a speech, talk to the press, then back to the car and in the plane again. The whole drill goes on five or six times a day and your foot never touches the earth. Some business I'm in, right?

I wish to hell Thommy was playing ball: had a shock this morning when a lady in Akron brings me a scrapbook filled with pictures of Thommy. She used to live in Chicago, and followed Thommy's career almost from grammar school right up to Stanford. I'm not kidding, she must have had a hundred fifty pictures of Thommy. Secret Service almost tackled her when she shows up with this box. Well, it kind of shook me up all over again to look at these pictures of Thommy. What's he doing out there in California, Mom? Is everybody in California goofy? I never told him how to run his life. He played ball because he loved to. I've never told him what to do unless he asked me first. On the big things, I mean. Nicole is upset by it, too. But she's upset about everything these days. The campaign is really hard on her. Campaigning in Illinois was hard enough all those years. But going state to state is almost too much for her. I know she's tired of it. But she married me, right, Mom? That's what the whole other thing was about, understanding me, knowing what I go through. I'm not making excuses. Someone just has to know what I go through. The press gets ahold of that and, like Davis said, it's all over before the shooting even starts.

The other day I was thinking it wouldn't be a half bad life just to live at Nippersink and travel to watch Thommy play ball. On the other hand, he doesn't want to play ball these days, so what the hell would I do with myself? If they'd get this plane down, maybe I'd start thinking straight. I'm rattled because the other won't leave me alone, Mom, and I don't know exactly what I can do about it. I'm in the middle of a campaign, on the run dawn to dusk, what am I supposed to do? Once the election is over, things will actually be easier, I'll be protected. I mean, if she had her way right now she'd be dotting the i's and crossing the t's of my life, running the whole show. She'd be making my appointments, screening my calls, and picking out my ties. I've even heard her start talking about Thommy like he's her boy, our boy. Real goofy stuff. But in a campaign, with a planeload of reporters looking for every shoelace that's untied, it's kind of nerve-racking. I know what you're thinking but stick with me, Mom. You always have.

Love, Thom

Rebecca had shown Ghost the chronology of photographs from his father's last year, the same way she'd shown them to Alan Webster. The increasing strain was obvious as the pictures progressed, month by month. Now Ghost could see them in his head, clicking past like slides on a screen, phrases from the letters changing with them: ". . . he doesn't want to play ball, so what would I do with myself?" Is that why you died, Dad, because I wasn't playing and you didn't know what to do with yourself? "I'm rattled . . . the other won't leave me alone . . . I don't know exactly what I can do about it." Was dying what you did about it? Ghost resented his father's private thoughts about "the other," that there was something so important in his father's life that Ghost didn't know about. She was an intruder.

Ghost went to the last letter.

Dear Mom,

On board Air Force plane for London. Meetings on world economic situation, then NATO briefings in Geneva. No sightseeing, this time, Mom. Nicole gets to visit her relatives in France, though. You know me, I can't tell her third cousin from her fourth. Nicole is sleeping right now. She's worn out, and I should be. Want her to stay an extra week or two in Paris. Will do us both good. Give me time to get back to the States and settle the thing once and for all. You don't know what it's like lately. I won't kid you and say it's not bad. Why do people get that way? They wait until they know they can really hurt you. There are no surprises in life except the ones you really don't want. I've heard the dogs bark before, but I'd be lying if I told you it wasn't getting to me. You know I've spent a lifetime building this career. Anyone who thinks it's easy getting elected to the Congress every two years, then landing a seat in the Senate, anyone who thinks that's easy ought to think again before trying it. Just hanging in there in Washington is more than most people could ever really handle. It's hard to explain that but it's so true. And I'm talking about good men. Having a shot at the number-two job and, with a little luck here and there, the door wide open to the top job, well, what more can you want in a career? It's a long way to come, isn't it? And I'm just immodest enough to tell you I really believe we've done some good for people along the way. And I think I can do more. No way to get where I'm at without a few notches in the gunbelt, I admit it. But I look back and see that I've done a few good things along the way. It's been a hell of a lot of work, but I'm a young man, and willing to do more. To think I've come this far, and now someone, to suit her own needs, not mine, wants to see me turn away from it all. That one doesn't understand what's real and what's not. I guess she never did, but that's what I liked for a time. But she doesn't know what's real, and it scares me now. I offered to arrange appropriate finances, but that's got nothing to do with it now. Nothing makes sense to her. I get black in the head thinking about it, black as can be. Really, she wants to take over my life. Davis is afraid she's going to blow the whole thing wide open, and I'm half inclined not to care anymore. If it wasn't for Thommy and Nicole, I probably wouldn't *care. I'd like to make the whole thing evaporate, even if it meant living a quiet life in the country somewhere. But we're way beyond that. It's so difficult trying to explain this, because I think to anyone but Davis and me she's as normal as can be. So can you see me trying to explain obsession to a roomful of reporters? It wouldn't just be me going downstream, I'd be taking the next President and the party and a lot of baggage. It has gone on much too long for me to explain it, or pretend she doesn't exist. She just won't allow it. I don't even want to tell you the rest.*

You know what I want to think about right now? Thommy. I'm thinking about the happiest moments of my life, just watching Thommy playing ball. You know what I'd do sometimes? Did you know that when I'd come back to town I'd have the car take me by the park or school, wherever Thommy was practicing, before he got to be such a big deal, and I'd sneak up and watch him shoot hoops. He was always there longer than the rest of the kids. Hell, we'd have to drag him home. Remember? Heck, he'd shoot hoops in the dark. That's what he was like. You could hear the ball going through the net and you couldn't see it. But you could sure hear it. One after another. Gosh, he always had the eyes of a champion, you know those eyes of his? He could stare a hole in the backboard with those eyes. Sometimes, I wouldn't even tell him I was there watching. I didn't want him to know, break the spell, you know what I mean? Silly, isn't it? And I'll be goddamned and beat to hell if I know why he isn't playing now. He has something pure, this gift, and I guess he doesn't know yet how much that means. I wish I had Thommy to watch because this other thing has me in knots. I know I did this to myself, Mom, but Jesus there's got to be something I'm not thinking of because right now I'm black as can be. I wish I was at Nippersink.

Love to you, Thom

Ghost gathered the letters and stacked them next to the others on the nightstand, then turned out the lamp.

It was hot in the room. Ghost perspired as he lay in the darkness. He gulped for breath; the room's air was humid and stagnant. Rolling out of bed, he paused in the doorway, orienting himself. Drops of sweat trailed his steps as he staggered down the hall, through the dining room and kitchen, and out to the yard.

Outside, the air felt cooler. He lay spread-eagled on his back in the middle of the yard, letting his lungs fill with night air. He grabbed a handful of grass and rubbed it against his face, feeling its coolness and moisture, tasting its bitterness. He rolled to his side and looked at the dark outline of the house, its curved roof giving the appearance of a giant tortoise. As a child at Nippersink, he was usually up before the others, and in the mornings on the first few days of summer he would sit in the yard, plopped like this on the dewy grass, looking at the house, convincing himself that summer was truly here. He would reacquaint himself with friends he hadn't seen in a year. There was a place down at the lake in the cover of willows that only certain of these friends knew about. They would meet to tell each other what had happened in their lives during the school year, what really happened. All agreed this was a place of truth. Here they would tell who had been kissed, who had cheated on a test or stolen something from a store; they would tell of adventures and trouble, and talk about what they were going to do during the summer. It was liberating to have this place where they had to tell the truth (the pact called for impossible burdens if they did not). They felt like different people when in this meeting place, because part of the pact was for their truths never to leave the cover of the willows. And they all believed it never did.

It felt easier for Ghost to think of the letters now that he was outside, where he could breathe and look up at the clear night sky with its explosion of stars. He sent his thoughts into the night to diffuse them, the way the willow leaves absorbed the whispered truths of his friends.

Ghost wondered what his mother knew of the letters' contents. When she died, alone, in an automobile near Val d'Isère in France, had she carried the weight of whatever and whomever his father had written of? After the senator's death, she returned to France to live in the countryside near St. Paul de Vence, where she'd grown up; maybe for her, he thought, that was like his returning to the basketball courts, a way of going back to what she knew and what was safe. Whatever she knew, she carried back to France and away from him, afraid that he wouldn't accept or understand it. People treated him as if his life were confined to the dimensions of the basketball court. Except now Rebecca had sliced to his center; the urgency of her mission demanded the attention of his heart. It was she, he felt, who prepared him to consider those letters; the intensity he saw in her eyes when she discussed her search forced him to think of another's pain. And from that he felt the pain in his father's words as much as his own discomfort in reading them. For Ghost, the price of excellence had always been the ability to narrow the world down to his own field of vision; one did not become great by worrying if you made the janitor late for dinner by practicing long into the night. You practiced. You shot and shot and shot, until the motion of shooting felt as instinctive as shaking a hand. You didn't become great by worrying as you watched dreams drain out of an opponent's eyes when you finished them off in a championship game; somebody else's pain belonged to somebody else. Rebecca held up to him a man that Ghost did not know; Radio asked his help in finding a man neither of them had ever met; and by doing so it seemed to Ghost they were asking him: "Do you know what it feels like to be *me?*" It was the question he wanted to ask his father, and wished his father had asked of him, a question to ask in the cover of willows.

9

Rebecca was having morning coffee in the kitchen when Ghost brought in the letters and handed them to her. A look passed from him to her, the look of children when they admit fear.

"Radio found these in a drawer yesterday. I read them in bed last night."

She sat at the dining room table and read the letters while Ghost fixed scrambled eggs.

When she finished reading, Rebecca bound the letters and then put them on the counter. She'd read hundreds of pages of research on Senator Galvin in the library at the University of Chicago, and had seen the published chronology of a life lived in public: the speeches, legislation, commendations for valor during the Second World War; this man had had an impact on the landscape of American life. In the arena of public service, details of his life were shared with the media, creating this mythic character called "the senator." But to Ghost, as he told Rebecca the night of his party, "the senator" was not a figure from the news, but a father. Those words came back to her as she contemplated the letters on the counter. Within them existed a man unlike the one she knew from what she'd read, and no matter what she learned of him, the weight of his past would fall with fullest force upon Ghost, not upon her. Rebecca had another past, the one with her family, to turn back to; Ghost did not. By handing her these letters, Rebecca felt Ghost was willing to be at risk.

Ghost set a plate of eggs in front of her.

"I heard you walking around last night," she said.

"I went outside for a while after reading the letters."

"And how do you feel about them?"

"I don't know that person. I know the part about me not playing ball. But what he says about this woman and the problems, that's news to me. I never heard my father express thoughts like that. Obviously, he spoke like that to somebody—to my grandmother, anyway. That he had some kind of relationship with this woman makes me feel a little . . . cheated. Not that he had to confide in me, or that I had some special right to know about it. But if it was that much a part of his life, then it *was* a part of my life, whether anybody talked about it or not. And I don't want to guess at things. I want to *know* why my father died, and I want to know what this whole goddamn thing with the letters is about because I don't want to have to guess. Who is anybody fooling with secret lives? I feel cheated if my father was standing over there by that window the last time I saw him and he was thinking about this woman, because I had to *guess,* and maybe I guessed wrong. I was too stupid or too much inside my own head just to ask him. My grandmother kept those letters and never said a word about them to me but obviously she knew I'd get my hands on them at some point, but she's going to let me guess, too. I want to know what my father was thinking and what he was doing. I'm just a little late in the game."

He looked at the plate of eggs in front of Rebecca.

"I really don't want to cook those again. Please eat them."

She picked up her fork.

"I'm not forcing you, Ghost."

"You already have. I just don't want you to be right."

Ghost found the Nippersink telephone directory in a drawer by the counter. "Do you know who Mrs. Conrad is?"

"The name is familiar."

"She's the woman who . . . found my father. He was using her boat when he died. She always let us use her boat for fishing. I'm going to call her and ask if she'll see us this morning."

Ghost walked down the hall to Radio's room.

"I'll help you straighten that bed. Then we'll go down to the lodge."

Radio watched Ghost tuck in the sheet at the head of the bed. "It doesn't go like that." He pulled the sheet out. "You have to get the bottom part even first."

"Oh."

Ghost stood back and let Radio do it.

"Now you do the top part," Radio said.

"I'm out of practice."

"My ·mom made me do it."

They finished with the bed. Radio pointed to a framed photograph on top of the nightstand. "Is that you?"

"It's me holding the dog," Ghost said.

"That's what I thought."

"That's my father and my grandmother," Ghost said. "And that's my mother standing right behind me."

"She's tall."

"So was my father. That's where I get it. They were both tall."

"I think my father's tall."

"You think so?"

"Yeah."

"I couldn't tell from the picture you showed me."

"I think so," Radio replied. "I think he came to see me one time."

"You told me you never met him."

"I think he came to see me one time at school."

"What happened?"

"One day after school I was playing basketball with these guys . . ."

"Earning your lunch money?"

"There was this man watching us," Radio said. "He was standing by a tree outside the schoolyard. At first, I didn't really see him there, because I was, you know, just playing ball and stuff. But after the other guys left I was still there shooting around and I looked over, and this man was watching me. I didn't stare at him because I didn't want to get in trouble, but I looked at him a couple of times and he looked like my father, like in the picture of him. It really looked like him. I think he came to see

me, because he stood there not doing anything while I shot baskets. He smoked a lot of cigarettes, I could tell. He had a cigarette
in his mouth all the time. I kept shooting around trying to make
up my mind about what to do, then I looked over and he wasn't
there anymore. The other guys had seen him, too, so I'm not
making it up."

"I know you're not," Ghost said.

"I was kind of scared because it was almost dark out, but he
wasn't there when I left."

"Did you tell your mom?"

"No."

"Why not?"

"She didn't like to talk about him. She always said it was
better not to talk about him."

"Why?"

"It made her sad. She said he was a bad man."

"Did she tell you why?"

"She just didn't like to talk about him."

"Did you tell anyone you saw him?"

"No."

"How did it make you feel?"

"I was scared but it was kind of neat. He just watched me."

"Maybe you should have told your mom about it, anyway.
Because you were thinking about it."

"She would have got upset."

"Yeah, but you were thinking about it so maybe you should
have told her. Or told somebody."

"I just told you."

3

They brought Radio to the lodge and left him in care of the
lifeguards at the pool.

"Edwina Conrad lives just a couple of minutes from here,"
Ghost said, "right on the lake."

He drove across the tiny bridge separating Lake Tombeau
from its sister, Lake Richardson.

The single-story house needed painting and the surrounding

trees were due for trimming, but the lawns were newly mowed and the gardens full of color.

Ghost pushed the bell. They heard a dull metallic echo.

"I don't think she's home," Rebecca said, thirty seconds after Ghost had pushed the doorbell.

"She's home."

"You think so?"

"I spoke with her half an hour ago."

"I don't hear a thing."

"She's eighty-five, and a little hard of hearing." Ghost pushed the bell again. Another thirty seconds passed, then they heard a faint voice saying, "Coming, coming."

The door rattled, then slowly opened. Mrs. Conrad smiled, her head bobbing from palsy. She looked as though a stiff breeze would blow her right across the lake; only her resolute jaw anchored her to the earth.

"Thomas Galvin," she said. "My goodness."

"Nice to see you, Mrs. Conrad. This is my friend, Rebecca Blesser."

"Oh my." Mrs. Conrad scrutinized Rebecca. "What a lovely girl."

"How do you do?" Rebecca said, taking Mrs. Conrad's outstretched hand, which felt light as a leaf.

She said to Ghost, "You're such a handsome young man, Thomas. Such a handsome young man." Then to Rebecca, "You know, you're a lucky young girl. Now, come in. I've made iced tea. It's on the terrace. I hope you like iced tea."

It took a while for them to reach the terrace at Mrs. Conrad's pace.

She poured the tea, then settled into her chair.

"I see your picture in the papers all the time, Thomas. I don't know a thing about sports but I look at the sports pages to see your picture. I suppose everyone at Nippersink says 'I knew him when.'"

"But you really did."

"I suppose so. Do you remember me honking my horn at you when I'd drive by the ball court where you were always playing?"

"Yes."

"I used to say to Marie, 'That grandson of yours must go through sneakers like nobody's business.' My goodness, sometimes I feel like I'm two hundred years old."

"You look very well."

She waved a hand at him.

"It's so nice to have you here," she said. "You know, I ran into Davis Ely at the lodge yesterday, and he told me you might be coming to Nippersink. And you're just like your father, no matter how busy he was, he always had time to stop by for a visit. When the general died, it was awfully quiet around here. But your father always had time for a visit."

"He was very fond of you."

Mrs. Conrad put her glass down on the table. "We had a little memorial service for Marie, you know. She didn't want anything, but a few of us ladies arranged one just the same. It just doesn't seem right to let someone . . . disappear that way, without a service. We can hardly play our card game because it reminds us all of Marie."

"It was thoughtful of you," Ghost said.

Mrs. Conrad looked at Rebecca. "These days, people simply . . . disappear. At my age, it's upsetting if the newspaper doesn't arrive on time, not to mention one of your friends."

Ghost refilled their glasses with iced tea. "Lately I've been wondering about my father."

"We all miss him, and we talk about him all the time."

"At the time he died," Ghost continued, "everything happened so quickly, it was hard to sort it all out. By the time I got here from California, things were happening awfully fast. Rebecca has been helping me piece it together. I really hate to bother you with this, but I was wondering how much you remember about that morning?"

"Goodness," Mrs. Conrad said, sitting up straight, "that was such a confusing morning. I so wished the general had been alive. He was the one who was a brick in a crisis. An absolute brick."

"May I ask you a few questions?"

"I can't promise this old brain will be of much help."

Rebecca watched Ghost as he began his questions; she read the strain in his eyes, though he kept a pleasant face for Mrs. Conrad.

"Did my father say anything in particular when he came by that morning?"

"We chatted a few minutes. You know, just visiting. Then he went to the boat, like he always did, for a little fishing. Just like you used to do."

"Yes."

"He said he had a busy, busy schedule and wouldn't able to fish for too long."

"Did he seem upset?"

"Well, not upset. I don't remember him being up*set*. He was always so full of the joys of life. It made you feel good just to be around him. I think the senator was very busy just then, because I remember him being particularly quiet that morning, as I sit here thinking about it. He looked tired, Thomas, and I told him so. I told him he was getting run down and that he should spend a few more days at Nippersink. I told him that."

"Then what happened?"

Mrs. Conrad pointed to the rickety wooden dock jutting from the lawn into the lake. "Your father had his tackle with him, and he took the boat from right there. He didn't start the motor. He rowed. It was so quiet that early in the morning I don't think he wanted all the noise, even though it's a tiny motor. He was out there maybe an hour. I had gone inside to have my coffee and the read the *Tribune*. . . I do the same thing every morning. I have my coffee, read the paper, then work in my garden. I think that's what keeps me going. Mr. Hobbs does the real work in the garden, but I like to totter around and work on the flowers. Whenever the senator was fishing, I'd always look out to the lake now and then. And if he'd see me, he'd hold up his string of fish if they were biting that morning. That day I looked out there . . . his boat was only fifty yards offshore . . . you know the spot he liked, Thomas . . . and I saw him sitting kind of funny. He was hunched over like his stomach was hurting. I walked down to the dock and called to him but, Lord knows, my voice doesn't carry five feet. He didn't look right. I thought he'd fallen asleep, because he did seem awfully tired that morning.

"So I went around to the front yard where Mr. Hobbs was weeding, and I sent him out in the canoe to see if the senator was all right or had fallen asleep. Of course, Mr. Hobbs speaks almost no English." She turned to Rebecca. "I can't pronounce his name in Japanese, so I call him Mr. Hobbs and that's fine with him— he's been with me almost thirty years. Mr. Hobbs went in the canoe and returned very frantic. I hardly knew what to do. So of course I went right in and called Judge Ely, because I knew he'd be a brick."

Ghost listened and looked at the lake, where a bass picked off a bug and cut the calm of the water.

"I know this isn't pleasant," Rebecca said, putting a hand on Mrs. Conrad's thin arm, "but you're being very helpful. What did the judge say when you called?"

"That he'd be right over," she said. "He asked if the men from the Secret Service were there, and I said no. Then he said he'd call the sheriff."

"I see."

"Sheriff Baines came right over. Mr. Hobbs took him in the canoe out to the senator. I could see the sheriff reach over to touch the senator on the wrist. Then he tied the fishing boat to the canoe and they brought it in. I had to get out of the way because the paramedics were running across the lawn. The sheriff said something to them. The man checked the senator, and then Sheriff Baines took over. He didn't want anyone near the boat. When Judge Ely arrived he talked with the sheriff and helped me into the house. Everything started happening, then. The Secret Service men who were staying at the lodge came over, there were helicopters and policemen all over to keep the newspaper and television people away."

Rebecca said, "It must have been chaos."

"Well, Judge Ely took control of things. He had the phone in his hand the whole time. He talked with the sheriff and the Secret Service men. There was a lot of talking and men standing around with walkie-talkies. I didn't know who everyone was. The sheriff had a deputy out front of my house for a couple of days afterward, just to keep the press and tourists away. But Judge Ely was a brick. He told the sheriff exactly what he wanted done and, believe me, the sheriff hopped to it."

Ghost watched a boat on the far side of Lake Tombeau. He felt drained of the determination that had carried him to Mrs. Conrad's house. The man he'd read about in the letters had seemed an apparition, a voice new to Ghost, and the voice was unfamiliar enough that he didn't even see his father's face as he read the words. Listening to Mrs. Conrad, however, was different. When he had settled into the chair and looked across the lawn at the path to the pier, a path he had walked with his father hundreds of times, he saw his father's form sharply outlined at the end of the old wooden dock. He knew that form and that man standing there with a fishing pole and a can of Schlitz, telling him to hurry across the lawn and get into the boat before the bass were finished feeding. And as he listened to Mrs. Conrad's description of the events, he had a vivid vision of his father in the boat; when he heard her describe his father slumped over, the image faded, leaving Mr. Hobbs to find an empty boat for the sheriff to tow to shore. He'd had a similar fantasy at his father's funeral, that the flag-covered casket at the foot of the altar was empty. In his mind all those speeches and sermons and mournful songs had been played to an empty coffin, because he felt unwilling to surrender his father to such a public ceremony; they were there for "the senator," not his father.

Rebecca looked at him, then back at Mrs. Conrad.

"Can I ask you to remember something else? The senator was wearing a business suit that day. Didn't you think that was unusual, Mrs. Conrad? Did he ever come over to go fishing like that, wearing a suit?"

"Usually he was in shorts or dungarees. He told me he was on his way back to the city and the campaign and all. So I assumed that was why he had on a suit. When Judge Ely brought me back into the house he sat me down in the kitchen and he put the senator's belt on the table. When something awful happens you think about the silliest things, and I sat there in the kitchen and looked at the belt on my table and wondered why the senator would wear that old brown belt with a nice gray suit? I thought maybe it had something to do with fishing."

"Did the judge remove anything else from the boat?"

"You'd have to ask Sheriff Baines that. I don't think there was much in the boat. Just the senator's fishing tackle and his coffee cup."

"I've seen the photographs of the boat," Rebecca said to Ghost. "There was no coffee cup."

"Well," Mrs. Conrad said, "with my memory you never know. You're much better off asking the judge. He was the brick."

4

They left Mrs. Conrad's and started back to the lodge.

Rebecca sensed Ghost's agitation. "I'm sorry if I pushed her a little at the end. I thought those were things we needed to know."

"What I should have done was read all the papers and ask these things ten years ago when he died."

"You didn't know much about what happened?"

"I didn't read a newspaper or watch the news for three or four months after he died. I didn't talk to my mother about it or the judge or my grandmother. Nobody *wanted* to talk about it. So when I was sitting there listening to Mrs. Conrad, I saw it. I saw my father walk across the lawn and get into the boat. I could see them tow the boat in and all the people running around. It was just so clear. I've never allowed myself to think about that."

"I've read the newspapers from that time. All of them. What's in the papers is much less than what you heard from Mrs. Conrad."

"Maybe Judge Ely kept it from turning into a media circus."

"I think he did that. Evidently, he was very good at that."

"The coffee cup might have had a nip in it. My father wasn't averse to a shot of brandy in his coffee; the judge wouldn't want the press making a big deal about that."

"With the coroner in his pocket, he didn't have much to worry about there."

Ghost steered the Galaxy across the bridge and up the long driveway that led to the lodge. "When are you going to see the judge?"

"I haven't heard from him. I left my office number in New York, assuming he doesn't need to know I'm staying at your house."

"He'll know by today. Nippersink is small."

"How will he feel about that?"

"He won't understand why I let you get close to me. He'll be surprised."

"I'm under the impression that he isn't surprised often."

"He's protective of my father, and of me."

"Are you going with me to see him?"

"With me he'll reminisce, tell stories. The judge likes talking about the past. I haven't seen him much over the last few years, and then it's been for dinner with him and Eleanor and my grandmother. The conversation usually gets around to the old days at Nippersink, and what we used to do. When my father died things just kind of split apart. A lot of lives changed. My grandmother clammed up. My mother went back to France. I spent most of my time on the road playing ball. It was as if a planet had exploded and you had these comets flying all over the place. I think the judge tried as best he could to get things back in orbit. But everything had changed. None of us ever wanted to talk about *what* changed, though. It was as if my father was the *purpose* for all of us, and the judge wanted that not to change. If you sat in on one of those dinners with us, you'd think my father were in the next room, the way the judge talks about him."

They passed through the lodge and stopped on the terrace that overlooked the pool and the lake. Ghost spotted Radio leaning against the wooden railing at the end of the pier.

"This morning Radio told me he thought he saw his father once. There was a man watching him play basketball at the schoolyard and Radio thinks it was his father, recognized him from a picture. He kept telling me he wasn't making it up, which leads me to think that maybe he was. But I'll be damned if I could tell you what difference it makes if he was making it up or not making it up. At least it's something to hold on to."

"Not nearly enough, though."

"No, not nearly enough. And he knows it. That's what gets me about this kid."

5

They ate lunch at the lodge, then Rebecca returned to the house, and Ghost made good on a promise to take Radio bass fishing in Lake Tombeau.

Ghost rowed to the narrow channel separating Lake Tombeau from Lake Richardson, and drifted in toward a tiny island that was thick with trees and undergrowth. The water surrounding the island was laced with weeds that provided shelter for turtles and bass and bullfrogs. Ghost maneuvered the rowboat in the shade on the east side of the island, then opened his small tackle box and examined the lures.

"Some of these have worked for a long time. Anything look good to you?"

Radio chose a large gold jigger, but Ghost suggested it might be snag prone.

"I like this other one, then," Radio said.

"That's a good one. If the bass has bad eyes, this'll look like a little frog."

"What's the biggest bass they have here?" Radio asked, knotting the lure to a leader.

"Right to it, eh? The biggest don't get caught. There are plenty of big ones, though."

"How big?"

Ghost spread his hands a foot and a half apart.

"You ever catch one like that?"

Ghost spread his hands two feet apart.

"Where?"

"Right near here. Casting from shore."

Radio secured his lure to its leader, tied it to the line, and presented it for Ghost's inspection.

"Give it a little cast over there," Ghost said. "You want to put it just on the edge of that weed patch."

Radio jerked the first cast, causing the lure to plop down a few feet from the boat.

"Okay," Ghost said, "now give it a little more air. Put your arm away from yourself a bit . . . out here. Now, nice and smooth, like a free throw." Ghost watched the lure splash down near the weeds. "Goose it a little. Like a frog. Don't race it. Easy. Yes, yes like that. That's a good action. Now, you've got to talk to it just a bit so it knows what you want it to do." Ghost watched the lure. "Come on, honey, do a little dance for me, a nice little bass two-step, looking good for Mr. Bass. . . ."

Radio was laughing. Ghost popped open a beer.

"Hey, this is serious shit. This is bass fishing. You can't laugh."

They worked the sides of the weed patch for half an hour without results. Ghost gently rowed the boat around the island and picked out another patch.

"We're not thinking right. Put yourself in the water and figure them out. They're probably down there and they recognize my voice from their ancestors. They know me. So they moved to this side of the island to hide. But we'll just park ourselves here and give them something to think about."

Fifteen minutes went by, then Radio got a strike from a perch. Immediately after, Ghost landed a small bass, which he released.

"Go tell your pop what nice people we are. Tell him we're not tourists up here."

The next strike was Radio's. The fish jumped, and Ghost said, "It's a wide mouth. Get that hook in there." The fish jumped again, throwing the lure.

Ghost slid the boat in closer to shore.

Another wide mouth hit Radio's lure, and he landed him.

"Now we're fishing. This is what we call fishing. We're starting to smell like bass; we've got beer; we're getting sunburnt. This is good. I like this." After a long silence, Ghost said, "I'm chartering a plane to take us up to Michigan." Radio recast his line and watched it carefully. "We'll head up there tomorrow."

"How far is it?"

"Won't take long by plane."

"How long do you think?"

"Not long. Hour and a half, two hours. The hard part won't be getting there. But we can't just walk in and then walk out with your father. We don't know how's he's going to take this. For one thing, he's been in there awhile, and still has a while to go. This isn't going to be the easiest thing in the world for him to accept."

Radio worked the fake frog across the line of the weed patch. "Do you know how come he's in jail?"

"I guess at one time or another he got himself into plenty of trouble."

"My mother said he robbed something."

"I guess he did. The thing I'm trying to say is I don't want you to have a picture in your head of this thing being easy tomorrow. If you've planned the way it's going to be, you have to be ready for it not to be that way. You've gotten yourself this far and that's great, but . . . look, we'll do the best we can."

"Let's bring one of our fish."

"We may not even get in there, you know. We're going to try."

"Can we bring a fish on the plane?"

"Sure. Why not?"

"We need to catch a big bass to bring on the plane."

Ghost put down his beer. "Then you're going to have to work in even closer to the weeds. Here, I'll give it a cast, then you work it."

Ghost cast the line, then handed the pole to Radio.

6

Ghost and Radio brought their string of bass around the rear of the lodge to the kitchen. A busboy sat with one of the cooks on the back steps; the two of them smoked and played gin.

"Here's where being famous comes in handy for us," Ghost whispered to Radio. "I'll talk to these guys, and while I'm talking to them, you pick up that plastic bucket, rinse it out at the faucet there, fill it with water, dump the fish in, and keep walking. Just pretend it's something you do every day, and don't even pay any attention to me. I'll catch up with you. Got it?"

Radio cast a conspiratorial glance at Ghost.

They approached the back stairs. The cook and the busboy recognized Ghost and stared at him.

"You're showing your cards, guys," Ghost said, smiling. "Little gin game?"

"That's it, man," the busboy said. "That's why he's winning. I'm showing my cards."

"Can't do that," Ghost said, pausing to shake their outstretched hands.

Radio rinsed out the large ice bucket.

"You guys local?"

"Just the summer," the cook said. "Down to Florida for the winter. Too cold up here in the winter, man."

"No shit," Ghost said. "Too cold. Why the hell do you think I live in California?"

The guys laughed.

Radio filled the bucket with water and plopped in the fish.

The cook looked concerned. Ghost caught the direction of the cook's glance.

"You guys make any money on the play-offs? I hope you had a bet on the Lakers."

"Had to go with the Celtics," the busboy said.

"That'll teach you."

Radio started up the path, carrying his rod and the bucket full of bass.

"Got to go catch my nephew," Ghost said, looking at Radio. "My sister will kill me if I lose the little bastard."

"Okay, man," the busboy said, shaking Ghost's hand again.

"What do you think, man," the busboy said to the cook, elbowing him in the ribs. "That was the *Ghost*, how about it? No one's going to believe this shit, right?"

The cook watched them turn the corner and disappear with his bucket.

Ghost and Radio hurried along the path. They knew the guys weren't after them, but it felt good to think they might be.

"I learned that trick from my father," Ghost said. "When he was up here he never kept any money in his pocket, and we'd be down at the lodge and he'd want a newspaper. So we'd walk by the newsstand and he'd start talking to the girl there, while I picked up a *Tribune* and walked away. Never got caught."

Halfway to the house, Ghost stopped in midstep.

"I just thought of something. Let's stash our stuff over there." He pointed to a cluster of evergreen trees on the golf course.

"Someone might take our fish," Radio said.

"We'll hide them good. I've got another trick to show you."

They went to the trees. Ghost put the rods and tackle box up in the branches of the densest tree, and hooked the handle of the bucket high on a broken limb. "It'll all be safe, come on."

It was late afternoon and the trees cast shadows across the fairways. The grass had been mowed earlier in the day and smelled sweet and intoxicating. Golfers were still on the course, so Ghost took a familiar route through the treelines of the fairways, until they reached the par 3 seventh hole. It was 140 yards, with a pond stretching from the green back to the tee. Players had to fly the pond with their shots to reach the putting surface safely.

There was a wooden shelter near the tee, where Ghost and Radio took a seat to watch a foursome of men approach.

"Now, these guys are one hundred percent tourist. Resort golfers. They probably play once a month or so. As soon as they see that pond they're going to be nervous. Even though it's a short shot to the green, they'll get psyched out by the pond. Good golfers don't even see the water. They know the distance to the green and they know what club they need to reach it. Will you bet me a quarter we can make at least two of these guys hit the ball into the water?"

"How can we make them?"

"We stand up by the green so they see us watching."

"That won't do it."

"Bet the quarter."

"Okay."

"Follow me."

He led Radio through the trees to an area in back of the green.

The first player teed his ball.

"Stay in here for now," Ghost said, holding Radio back within the cover of the trees. "Let's let the first two go without seeing us."

The player's swing was awkward, but he managed to muscle the ball over the pond and to the left side of the green.

Next up was a middle-aged man dressed in orange shorts and peach shirt, with a pith helmet protecting his head. His shot went very high and landed just over the pond, short of the green. But dry.

"Now watch," Ghost said, stepping out from the trees in back of the green. Radio followed.

The next man looked toward the green, and saw Ghost and Radio. He waggled his club, took a mighty rip and bladed the ball. It shot into the reed patch.

"That's one," Ghost said.

The last member of the foursome stood tall over the ball and took a series of smooth, impressive practice swings. But when it actually came time to hit the ball, he produced a looping swing that did not resemble his practice strokes. He looked as if he were chopping wood. The ball flew straight up and splashed softly in the pond's mossy muck.

"Never fails," Ghost said. "Let's get out of here. And you owe me a quarter."

7

It was quiet in the house except for the tick of Rebecca's pencil on the glass tabletop. Her files were spread out before her. She thought about the letter that had come from Elizabeth to her New York office. The timing of it bothered her, that it had arrived within a week of her visit to Alan Webster. She recalled his reaction to the mention of Elizabeth Folger's name; he seemed uncomfortable, sad, and she had sensed guilt in his eyes. It had prompted him to talk about "another life, another time," as if he sought absolution. Rebecca searched her notes and found the telephone number of the hospital where Webster had been admitted. She called and was told he'd been released. Next she called Webster's office, and a secretary informed her that Mr. Webster was recuperating "privately" and could not be reached. Directory assistance for Malibu had no listing. Finally, she called the hospital, found an admissions nurse who sounded overworked, and told her she was calling for Dr. So-and-so; the nurse consulted a file and gave Rebecca a telephone number. Just like that.

A girl answered the phone. "Yes?"

"This is Rebecca Blesser and I'm trying to reach Alan."

"My father is recovering from an automobile accident. He's not taking calls."

"I thought he might want to speak with me. I feel awful. I had been in a meeting with him just prior to the accident."

"What's your name again?"

"Rebecca Blesser."

"Rebecca Blesser," the girl said, her voice directed elsewhere in the room.

There was silence, then a distant voice; Rebecca realized that the girl had cupped her hand over the phone and was speaking to someone. Then she spoke again into the mouthpiece.

"My father will speak with you. But you can't talk for very long. He's not well."

Rebecca heard whispers, and blankets rustling.

"Yes?" Alan Webster's voice was weak; it sounded as if speaking hurt him.

"Mr. Webster? Rebecca Blesser."

"Yes."

"I'm very, very sorry about your accident. But I'm pleased to hear you're recuperating."

"They say I'm going to live. Evidently they weren't saying that immediately after the accident."

"I'm sorry it happened at all."

"What did the police tell you?"

"The police?"

"They said they spoke with you."

"Yes. Detective Ross."

"Yeah, Ross."

"Ross told me you might have swerved to avoid another car."

"That's what happened. Did he tell you I was drunk?"

"He asked if you'd been drinking at the Bel Air."

"I'd been drinking. But I wasn't drunk."

"He just asked me what I knew."

"Did you tell him I was drunk?"

"I told him you'd had some drinks."

"A woman tried running me off the road. She *did* run me off the road, for chrissake."

"That's awful."

There was a long pause, then Webster said, "I saw her in the headlights for a couple of seconds. She looked like that woman you were talking about. Look, we both know I had some drinks. The eyes, though. She looked like Elizabeth Folger. She was on my mind, so I don't know . . ."

Rebecca felt her face and hands go cold.

"Did you tell the police?"

"No."

"Why not?"

"What am I going to tell them? They think I was drunk. They're not too interested in what I have to say. Let them find out who it was and then I'll tell them what I think. We shouldn't have talked about her; she was always bad luck."

"What do you mean by that?"

"I don't want you writing about me. This woman is best left alone. For all I know, she's dead anyway. I don't want you quoting me. She was trying to force herself deeper and deeper into the senator's life before he died. It's better to leave all this alone."

"Better for *whom?*" Rebecca asked, incredulous.

"Just everybody. That's why I'm talking to you." He sounded sad and deeply tired; she thought he might be beginning to weep.

"Why are you telling me this now?"

"Because I almost died."

"I need to know whatever you know. I promise it'll stay with me. I'm not going to write about it. You read my article. You know what I want to know."

"Forget about her."

"She sent me a letter."

"Don't lie."

"I'll have a copy sent to you."

"I don't want a copy of anything. Leave her alone."

"I can't do that. Did she and the senator have a child?"

"No."

"She had a child with someone. The senator's dead. You've nothing to protect."

Webster's daughter came back on the line. She was furious. "This isn't good for my father. The doctors don't want him to talk with anybody. How dare you upset him!"

"It's important that I speak with your father again. Tomorrow or the next day, when he is feeling up to it. Please understand that I am not trying to cause problems for you, and I want very much for your father to recover. But it *is* important. Can I leave you a number in New York, for you to let me know when it's a good time?"

"He isn't *well*. . . ."

"I just want you to have the number."

"I don't want the number." The girl slammed down the phone.

Rebecca walked over to the windows. Ghost and Radio were crossing the street, carrying their fishing tackle and the bucket of bass.

If Webster was warning her, who was he warning her from, she wondered. She'd heard the undertone of apology and sadness in Webster's voice that she'd heard when they met in Los Angeles. What for her had begun as a search meant to free heart and mind of boundaries had become a journey into the doubts and deceptions of other people, living and dead; it seemed as if the moment of her birth had been imbued with doubt, and this doubt had spread into others' lives like vines.

Rebecca watched Ghost and Radio cut through the hedge and walk across the lawn toward the house. Radio told Ghost something that made them both laugh. She wanted to enter the moment and float there.

Ghost preceded Radio through the door. "My friend here has something to show."

Radio stepped out from behind Ghost and pulled the string of bass out of the bucket.

"Bravo, Radio!"

"We waited them out," Ghost said. "A good fisherman is dumber than the fish. We sat in the sun in that damned boat for four hours. But we got our fish."

Radio walked toward the kitchen with the fish. Ghost called after him. "Other way. Take them outside for cleaning and see if you remember what I showed you."

Ghost sat down near Rebecca but watched Radio take the fish out to the back lawn.

He slit the belly of the first bass and cleaned out the guts.

"What are you drinking there?" Ghost asked.

"Gin-and-tonic."

"A good summer drink." He went to fix himself one. Ghost saw his father's letters on the table. "I think we had more fun than you did."

"I think you did, too."

"What'd you do?"

"I called L.A. and spoke with Alan Webster."

"What kind of shape is he in?"

"He's home. Not in good shape. But he spoke with me."

"What he said shook you up."

"He talked about his accident. He said he was run off the road, and that he had a lot to drink but wasn't drunk."

"What was his point?"

"He said that for a second he saw the woman who ran him off the road and he thought it was the woman in the letters." She nodded toward the table. "Elizabeth Folger. But then he said because we'd been talking about her she was probably just on his mind. He told me it's better if I leave this alone. I used to think no one wanted to talk about her because they were protecting your father. But now I'm not sure. I read those letters again, and saw how your father was reacting to her. She scared people. I thought about what Webster said; even Senator Wells was edgy when talking about her. I wonder if they're protecting your father, or if they're afraid of this woman."

"He's going to cut himself." Ghost jumped out of his chair and opened the door. "Don't put your hand under the direction of the knife. Keep it on top the way I showed you. You'll slice your hand in half the other way." Radio nodded and continued cleaning the fish, creating a glistening pile of blue, pink, and red fish guts.

Ghost sat down. "Afraid of what? Who was she? I have a hard time thinking of my father as afraid. That was one thing he wasn't."

"Don't get angry at me."

"I'm angry that she had influence over him. He didn't belong to her. That's what I'm angry about, that she had access to him, because I didn't get the chance to find out everything about him that I could have found out, and he didn't find out everything about me that he could have found out. I resent the fact that she thought he belonged to her in any way. My grandmother knew about her, and I'm sure the judge knows about her, Alan Webster knows about her, even this fucking Senator Wells. Probably my mother knew about her. This woman was something in between my mother and me, because when I was a kid my mother used to laugh a lot, we used to sing together in the car driving out to Nippersink, but later on that was gone, too. She went back to France after my father died. Man, the light went out at some point."

"You never talk about her."

"She didn't want to live in America anymore. And by that time we weren't close. I was constantly on the road playing basketball."

"I can't imagine you wanting to be apart from her after your father died."

"We were close when I was a kid, because my father was gone so much of the time. Later on it was different. There was this basketball thing between my father and me, and she couldn't penetrate that. At least I thought that's what it was about. She was living in her own world. Almost like it was painful for us to be together. She sounded happier to me when she moved back to France. We talked on the phone a lot then. In fact, we talked all the time a few months before her accident. It was like we were rediscovering ourselves. We made plans to spend the holidays together. But that was that."

"I read about her accident."

"She fell asleep driving back from skiing. The car slid off the road."

"God," Rebecca said.

Ghost drained his gin-and-tonic. "I don't know Elizabeth Folger but I hate her. I started hating her last night before I read the letters. We were in the kitchen doing the dishes and I *liked* doing the dishes with you." Ghost leaned his head against Rebecca's shoulder. "I took that as a sign from high powers. In fact, I considered cooking something else so we would have more dishes to do. And then you started telling me about Elizabeth Folger and my father, and it was like she came into the room and stood right between us. Then I read the letters and I felt her standing between me and my father. And I hated her. I want to find her and then erase her. I don't want to be standing in my kitchen doing the dishes and be thinking about her."

"She's all I used to think about, when I didn't know anything about her. Now I don't know that I want her. She certainly doesn't want me. You'd think that much would get through my head by now."

Their silence was jarred by Radio knocking on the window. Hands bloody from the work, he held up the cleaned and filleted bass. Behind him, Mrs. Warren's cats had found the pile of guts.

10

The Mitsubishi turbo jet soared into the sky above Wisconsin's farmland. When they flew over Lake Michigan, Ghost pointed to a boat race below. White-hulled ships with spinnakers fat with wind, curtains of color, pulled through the blue water.

The plane put down in Jackson, where a rented station wagon waited to take Radio and Ghost to the Holiday Inn. Ghost ordered a small refrigerator brought up to Radio's room for storing the bass.

He called the penitentiary and identified himself only as Mr. Galvin, as Rebecca had done in the correspondence she'd sent to the prison via Federal Express.

"Visiting hours are between two and four tomorrow, Mr. Galvin," the assistant warden explained. "I'm looking at Mr. Boone's file. It indicates that he has had no visitors during his incarceration here."

"Ever?"

"That's correct. What's your relationship to the inmate? You're aware that only members of the immediate family and legal representatives are allowed to visit Mr. Boone?"

"I'm a friend of the family. I'm bringing Boone's son."

"His file indicates that he is unmarried and has no children."

"He has a son."

"We have no record of that."

"I've seen a copy of the birth certificate. Investigators have confirmed the fact."

"I'll speak with the warden and call you back."

"Thank you."

Ghost looked at his watch—9:30 A.M.—then called Miss Dupree in Los Angeles.

"I may decide to fly, rather than drive back," Ghost said. "Maybe in a day or two. Have Magda set up two of the guest rooms."

There was a brief hitch of silence that Ghost did not expect.

"Everything will be in order."

"Call Jamison and tell him I'm at the Holiday Inn in Jackson, Michigan."

"Fine."

"While I'm thinking of it, call Frank at the lodge and ask him to have the security patrol keep an eye on the Nippersink house. Rebecca Blesser is working there. People know I've been around, and I don't want tourists showing up at the house and annoying her."

"She is still harassing you?"

"I beg your pardon?"

"I just don't think it is appropriate for her to hound you in this way."

"What's the 'appropriate' way to handle my business?"

"I'm sorry. It's just that her reputation—"

"What reputation?"

"She's a reporter, and—"

"I know what her job is."

"Do you really want her there?"

"I don't get this," Ghost said, his voice rising. "And I don't want to talk about it anymore. Any important messages?"

"Mr. Hardin called."

"Ask him if it can wait until I get back to town."

"I'm certain that will be fine."

2

It was an old house and Rebecca knew old houses have their noises. But the sound she heard upon entering Ghost's house did not seem to belong to the house. The sound had ceased the second Rebecca stepped inside, as though someone walking on the wooden floors froze in midstride.

218

"Ghost?"

Leaving the front door open, Rebecca edged into the dining room and stopped.

"Radio?"

She heard a creak in the hallway.

It was seven-thirty in the evening. Dusky golden light poured through the windows from the west side of the house. Rebecca had spent most of the day in the library at Lake Geneva, reviewing microfilm and old newspapers, reading about Judge Ely and Sheriff Baines, and how everybody knew everybody at Nippersink. And now the light changing hue on the wooden floors took on a sepia tone. Without Ghost there, the house seemed more of a mausoleum than a home. The living allow the past to exist, she thought. Her heart pounded and the surface of her skin felt cold. The house made sounds continuously; she'd heard them, she thought, right from the first night. But this creak came with a humanlike weight, similar to those she'd heard the night she went into Ghost's office at the party in L.A.

The sounds in the house ceased, like a living thing holding its breath.

She had the feeling that her research was waking the dead, although many of the people involved were alive—Ghost, Judge Ely, Alan Webster, Elizabeth Folger—their pasts, like spirits, were being summoned to the present, called to complete themselves and free the future of weight.

The floor moaned beneath Rebecca's feet; she heard a sound in another part of the house. She walked outside and paused on the front porch, thinking she was being silly, overreacting, but she went across the street and from the golf clubhouse called Nippersink's security office.

In five minutes one of the guards drove up in a Jeep.

"I'm sorry," Rebecca said. "But will you walk through the house for me? It was locked and I thought I heard something."

"Of course I will," the young man said. He walked whistling into the house.

Rebecca waited in the entry while the guard went from room to room, taking his time.

He checked the bedrooms, then returned to the porch and said he'd have a look in the basement. A couple of minutes later he reappeared. "I think everything's okay. Mr. Galvin keeping any valuables in the house?"

"I don't think so. Not that I know of."

"Antiques . . . collectibles . . . anything like that?"

"I'm not sure. There didn't seem to be. I'll ask him."

"Well, everything seems fine. The tourists at the lodge all find out where Mr. Galvin lives, so don't be surprised if a few show up on the doorstep now and then. But I wouldn't get too concerned. We're able to keep a pretty good eye on things around here. Call us anytime and we'll be right over. No problem."

"Thank you. I'm sorry to trouble you for nothing."

The guard shrugged. "These old houses do their share of talking. And I'd rather be troubled for nothing than for something, if you know what I mean. Just call us."

Rebecca showered and was drying her hair when the telephone rang. The voice at the other end was unfamiliar.

"This must be Miss Blesser."

"Who is this?"

"Davis Ely. I was hoping to have a word with you."

Rebecca grabbed a pen off the counter, checked the wall clock, then wrote the time and date on top of the scratch paper by the telephone. "What can I do for you?"

"Do you think you might come out to the house tomorrow for lunch? I think it would be best if we spoke in person."

"Can't we start now? On the phone?"

"I'm an old man. Telephones are for young people. I still prefer looking someone in the eye when I talk to them."

"Why do you want to speak with me now?"

"Nippersink is a small community. Most of the people who have lived here for any length of time knew the senator and his family, and are fond of them. I certainly am. Since you sincerely seem to believe you have a story worth resurrecting, I think I might provide you with some perspective, rather than you just running around willy-nilly talking to people who probably don't remember things clearly, anyway. You know how people are."

"What about Ghost?"

"I think a conversation just between you and me is in order. I believe Thommy is in Michigan, is he not?" The judge left a small gap of silence, then continued. "I'd prefer you not mention this to Thommy at all, if you can do that."

"Why?"

"We'll have our lunch and talk, then you can make your own decision. About noon would suit me. At my age you eat early."

"I'll be there at noon."

3

Rebecca went to bed just after midnight, but lay awake for over an hour, listening to the drone of the air conditioner. Sleep came wrapped in dreams of dark colors and strange sounds. Images of Ghost rolled through her dreams, as did images of the woman in the window.

The telephone rang, crashing into her dream.

She fumbled in the darkness, searching for the phone, and knocked her notebook and a glass of water off the nightstand. The glass smashed on the floor. Finally, she found the phone and snatched the receiver off its cradle.

Clearing her throat, she said, "Ghost?"

"You're only hurting him," the voice on the other end said. "What you're doing is hurting him."

Again she cleared her throat and searched for the light switch. "Who are you trying to reach?"

"What you're doing is only hurting him," the voice repeated. "Leave him alone."

The caller sounded like a woman, voice muffled by a cloth placed over the mouthpiece. "What you're doing is hurting him and you must stop."

"I don't understand you," Rebecca replied. "I don't understand what you're talking about. You have to tell me more."

The line went dead, then a dial tone returned.

Rebecca set down the phone, and sat on the end of the bed, waiting for her heartbeat to slow. She closed her eyes and held her face in her hands, listening in her mind to the voice. Picking up the notebook, she jotted down what the caller had said, and wrote the date and four A.M. next to the notes.

At the top of the note page was the telephone number of the Holiday Inn where Ghost and Radio were staying in Michigan. Rebecca picked up the phone, then replaced it without dialing.

She turned off the air conditioner so that she could hear the sounds of the house.

4

When Ghost and Radio rolled up to the guard gate at the prison, the officer said, "Do you mind if I take your picture, Mr. Galvin? We thought this might be a hoax, you know. . . ."

The assistant warden had called Ghost to inform him the prisoner did not want to receive visitors. Ghost realized it was useless not to explain that he was Thom Galvin, the basketball player. So he did, and things changed fast.

The guard snapped the photo, then two other guards arrived to escort Ghost and Radio through the security checkpoints. He signed autographs for the guards and they quickly put the pieces of paper in their pockets so the warden wouldn't notice.

They were led to a bare, windowless beige room with three plastic chairs in it. The light fixture was mounted on the ceiling inside metal mesh.

Radio sat in one of the chairs. Ghost paced.

"By God, it *is* you," the warden said, striding into the room. He was a short, meaty man who looked as if he hadn't slept well in years; he had papery skin, as if someone had crumpled it up.

"Thom Galvin," Ghost said, extending his hand.

"That wasn't necessary. Frank Bedrosian, and that *was* necessary. Now you have to know it's a strange sight to have Ghost Galvin standing in my prison. But I'm tickled to meet you. Just tickled."

"Warden, this is . . . Mr. Boone's son. His nickname is Radio."

"Well, Radio, you travel in pretty good company."

Radio shook the man's hand.

Warden Bedrosian sucked in what sounded like all the air in the room. "Mr. Galvin and I are going to have to talk in the next room. Can you wait here for us, Radio?"

"I don't want to leave him alone," Ghost said.

"I'll have one of the men look after him."

Radio sat down and placed his hands on his knees. He wasn't allowed to bring his Walkman or backpack past the second checkpoint. They had packed the Styrofoam chest with ice and brought the bass with them. It was clear to Ghost that the prison was not going to let them stroll in with a heavy chest of anything; but he had looked at Radio back at the hotel, as Radio carefully layered the bass with sheets of plastic and ice, and knew that it was important for this frozen sacrifice to at least make the journey to the front gates. Sitting here in the room, without his pack or Walkman, the boy looked smaller. Radio did have in his back pocket, however, the *National Geographic* pictures of Sun Valley.

"We'll be right back," the warden said to Radio, guiding Ghost to the door.

The room where the warden escorted Ghost was identical to the last, but with a table bolted to the floor. "It's certainly not the Ritz, Mr. Galvin, but it's amazing what you want *out* of a room when you have to sit *in* it with a murderer. Anyway, it's a thrill to meet you."

"I appreciate your seeing us."

"You haven't picked a pillar of society to deal with. Boone I'm talking about."

The warden opened a file and spread it on the table. "You're not supposed to have access to this, but I thought I could make an exception, you being who you are and all. You won't turn me in, will you?" He turned the file to face Ghost, who read the top page, a summation of Boone's criminal and prison history.

"Everything short of murder," the warden said, while Ghost continued reading. "And I'd be surprised if there weren't a couple of those that just slipped through the cracks. The shameful part of it all is that he *could,* in time, be paroled. You never know what a parole board is going to do. You think that what you're reading is sufficient evidence to keep this man out of society. But he knows how to play the game. Respectful of judges and parole boards, keeps mostly to himself around here. Just bides his time. He can play the game until he gets back on the outside."

"Will he see us?"

"He'll see *you,*" the warden said. "Won't acknowledge the kid. Doesn't even want to hear about the kid. But he'll see you because that makes him a big man around here. Cons like that. They'll be talking about William Boone from one block to the next. *Ghost* Galvin coming to visit a con? That's front-page stuff around this place, and it makes Boone feel very, very important. Makes him look good for the parole board. But when you do see him, I wouldn't buy stock in whatever he says."

"I'd still like to talk to him."

"I'll have him brought down. We'll have to go to a visitor's room with a partition. Regulations. With most of these guys, it's a regulation you wouldn't want to change."

"Let me just see Radio a minute first."

"Surely."

They returned to the other room. Ghost asked Radio for the photographs, the one of Radio and his mother, and the one of Boone. Radio had them protected within the pages of the Sun Valley story, and gave them to Ghost.

"First I'm going to talk with him, and then we'll see what's next."

They stayed in the silence of the room, looking at each other. Through the walls they could hear factorylike sounds: metal upon metal, powerful turbines turning, the low rumble of unseen machines. Ghost had no doubt that Radio was a kid, but he had always seen a removed look in the boy's eyes, a sense of mission that was not childlike. When they played the basketball games, it *was* a game, but even then Ghost had noticed the passion of Radio's purpose; he was a kid who knew that being a kid wasn't going to be good enough to get what he wanted. Ghost looked at him inside this steel and cement room, and for the first time since Ghost had known him, Radio really was a child. It was as if Radio knew it had taken everything he had to put himself in this position, and this was as far as he could go on determination and luck and whatever else had happened. There was nothing left but faith, and no one in the room but Ghost. All the layers of resolve had been stripped off Radio, and Ghost saw a child sitting there, scared and expectant, who had an undefined feeling that to be here in this moment, and to be without Ghost, would be to evaporate; the child in him searched for safekeeping.

Ghost had awakened that morning exhausted, having churned and thrashed through a haze of dreams and worry because he felt stripped naked by what he was going to have to do with Radio in the morning. He had sensed there would be this moment, the two of them alone, waiting for Radio's father, souls summoned for review. What can I bring to that moment, Ghost had wondered. Other tests in his life took place on a court with dimensions and rules and a scoreboard; when there were problems in his life off the court, he chose to face them by believing they would be made right by the future. He could go practice until there were holes in his shoes and blood on the court, and at the end of that practice there would be approval for what he'd accomplished, and the other problems would fall away. He could put so much attention on his ability to play ball that no one, including himself, could dwell on anything else.

Driving to the prison Ghost had envisioned meeting Radio's father and being able to craft a few successful moments between father and son, and at the end of the meeting Radio would know that Ghost had given him those moments. But seeing Radio right now, Ghost realized what this child needed wasn't Ghost looking for a personal victory, but for him to be here, now, fully in the moment, sharing whatever Radio was feeling. There was nothing to practice, no goal to focus on, only a moment informed by what had come before and what might come after. Ghost put his hands on Radio's shoulders.

"I'm scared," Ghost said.

"Me, too."

Ghost hugged him.

Radio remained seated as Ghost and the warden again left the room.

Following the warden through the corridors, Ghost felt short of breath, the sense of confinement surrounding him.

"Don't expect anything from Boone," the warden said, without turning around.

"I don't know what I expect."

"I hope it's not much. People walk in here sometimes expecting things. My experience is that it's not a good idea, if you get my drift." The distant whirring, metallic sounds were becoming louder and more distinct as they walked. "I never knew you did this kind of thing. Worked with kids."

"I don't."

"I mean, is this like one of those Big Brother things?"

"No. I just know this kid."

"Usually you get women here. Mothers and wives and sisters, and they're angry most of the time. They come to visit but they're angry. I swear to god. I mean, everybody here is angry, but the women let you see it. I told my assistant that I'd have to see you to believe it."

They entered a room divided down the center by a white counter with a thick glass partition rising to the ceiling. Backless benches were fixed to the floor on either side of the partition.

"Just push this button when you're ready to leave, Mr. Galvin. They'll be bringing Boone down now. And there'll be a guard watching him through a window on the other side, but not listening."

The warden left. A guard entered from the other door, waved to Ghost, then inspected that side of the room. He checked the metal speaking hole in the glass, looking into it with a flashlight. The door opened again, and another guard escorted Boone, handcuffed, into the room. Boone stopped at the bench, said something to the guards that Ghost couldn't hear. The guards left. Boone sat down and looked at Ghost.

"Pretty fucking hard to believe," Boone said.

The man appeared to be much older than Ghost had anticipated, without the rugged handsomeness depicted in the picture. His thinning black hair was slicked back to cover a bald spot. His skin was pale and papery, teeth stained yellow from chain smoking the Camels that were in his shirt pocket. Rather than mean, he looked weary, milky green eyes glazed by what they'd seen.

"Thank you for seeing me," Ghost said.

"How about that?" Boone replied. "Ghost Galvin. Ghost fucking Galvin." He spoke in the manner of people who say what they're planning to say without being particularly interested in the response.

Boone turned and looked in the direction of the observation panel. "What do you think of this shit?" he said to the door. "Ghost Galvin staring me in the face."

Ghost listened to his name being spoken by Boone. To Boone, he was "Ghost Galvin" just as Ghost's father had been "the senator" to the public. There was no sense of Ghost being a real man in Boone's eyes; he was a name brand, like Kodak film. Inside the cocoon of a public persona, Ghost could find safety, because people did not know whom they were dealing with. They knew the basketball player who performed three-sixty spin moves, who did sneaker commercials on television, who appeared twenty feet high on billboards selling Coca-Cola. And because the public's vision of Ghost was manufactured by images on television and in print, they couldn't reach him. Ghost liked that. Looking at Boone, though, he felt unprotected by his fame; what he wanted to express about Radio's desire did not come from the same part of himself that sold sneakers. And looking at Boone, Ghost felt a flash of empathy for his own father, and for whatever demon had been trapped inside his father's head when he wrote the letters Ghost and Rebecca had read. Because Ghost was certain his father, too, had grown used to the protection of public perception— as "the senator," he deflected and controlled problems that came his way. But Elizabeth Folger had pierced that cocoon of control, driving inside "the senator" to the parts of the brain that nobody understands. Maybe he needed her for that, Ghost thought. Maybe she had looked at his father with the same challenge in her eyes that Rebecca had when she looked at Ghost at his party—the kind of look that dismisses what you think you know about yourself.

"Mr. Boone," Ghost said, "what I'm here for is important."

"No shit?" Boone lit one of the Camels. He seemed undistracted by the handcuffs. "How's that?"

"Your son—"

"Hey, I don't know shit about this kid business. They told me about this kid business, and I don't know anything about it. I just wanted to see if they were jerking me around with this Ghost Galvin thing. Pretty fucking hard to believe."

"His mother died recently. Your son is eleven."

"Mister, it's a kick in the ass to meet you, but I don't know anything about this kid business." Boone sucked in the smoke and it remained for what seemed like minutes in his lungs.

Ghost was frightened by the darkness in Boone's eyes; he had the dead-eye stare of a con who had seen enough in his life to narrow the range of emotion he felt from none to worse.

Ghost held up the photograph of Radio and Radio's mother. "That is your son. And I'm sure you recognize the woman."

"Don't mean a goddamned thing to me." Smoke poured out of his nostrils and mouth, swirling around his head.

They both heard the mechanical grind and whir of the prison's factory.

Ghost pressed the picture against the glass. "You recognize her?"

"Nope."

"She had this photograph of you," he said, lifting the other picture from beneath the counter. The resemblance was apparent, though the man sitting opposite Ghost looked twice as old as the man in the photo.

"I was never that pretty. That's a good-looking fella. It ain't me, but he's a good-looking fella."

Ghost unfolded the copy of Radio's birth certificate. "That's your name on that line. William H. Boone."

Boone shook his head and smiled. "There are plenty of Boones walking around. Plenty. Hey, now let me ask you a question. I hear you're a pretty good stickman. What's it like having all that quiff around all the time? All that money and all that quiff?"

"Why don't you talk to me about your son? He's come a long way to see you, and he's here."

Boone stared straight ahead. When Ghost had held up the photograph and the birth certificate, he had seen Boone's eyes go to them, the images had registered and soaked themselves in some part of Boone's brain. But nothing came back out. Just this stare that seemed held by physical effort. Ghost saw that it was a pose. But with Boone it was a pose assumed so often it was set in his face in the form of lines, like his skin had closed in around his thoughts. Instead of being trapped behind the glass separating them, it seemed to Ghost that Boone was protected by it, a shield against whatever Ghost was driving at. Ghost had an impulse to pick up his chair and smash it against the glass, grab Boone and pull him an inch from Ghost's own face, so that he could feel his breath and the heat from his face and the force of the moment. But the glass was thick and unbreakable; it was Boone's own version of fame.

"Wrong guy," Boone said. "I don't know about kids. I want to talk about money and quiff. If I had your money I sure as fuck wouldn't be sitting in the bucket talking to Billy Boone. I'd be in Mexico. I'd be in the sun someplace."

"You have to understand that this kid has come here to see you. His mother is dead and now he wants to meet you."

"Ain't got a kid, Ghost. Hey, when they threw me in this butthole I could still shoot a few hoops. I mean, not bad. Now I'm lucky to fucking button my shirt with these hands."

Boone lit another cigarette. His hands looked like chunks of driftwood.

Ghost said, "I'm not here to cause you any trouble. Perhaps, if you cooperate, I could be in a position to be of some help when you get out of here."

"No shit? Two, five years from now? Hey, just toss off some of that extra quiff I read about."

"If you will talk with your son, and if you are decent with him, I'll be of some help to you. I promise you that."

The stare. The drag on the cigarette. Ghost stared back. In the glass Ghost saw a faint reflection of himself. He saw the set of his eyes and the wide cheekbones, like his father's. Despite what he was feeling, the frustration of trying to shake down Boone's intransigence, Ghost saw little expression in his own face, as if outwardly he was trying to match Boone's passivity. The thought of his father on that last day at Nippersink opened up in his mind, that image of his father standing at the window, staring off toward the fields, occupying a private world. Whatever his father had felt rested in that distant gaze, as if the clouds alone could know it. Ghost wanted to pull those thoughts back from the clouds, return them to his father's mind, then have his father turn to him and say what he was feeling. If it had been Elizabeth his father was thinking about that day, that would have been all right with Ghost because it was true. Ghost looked at Boone and pictured Radio waiting in the other room. Whatever and whoever this man is to the kid, Ghost thought, he shouldn't have to guess. He should know.

"Ghost Galvin is planning to help Billy Boone? Fuck, man."

"I'm making you an offer," Ghost said, the words rushing out of him with an intensity that startled Boone. Ghost had pressed his face close to the glass and locked his eyes into Boone's.

"Look, I don't want any trouble, mister." Boone leaned back, lifted his arms, and spread his palms open, like Ghost was holding a gun at him. "I just want the fuck out of this butthole, get my ass to Mexico. Yeah, you're going to help me. We'll sign a deal and have the warden witness it. And then if things don't work out the way I like, I'll just sue you. I'll just tell everybody that Billy Boone and Ghost Galvin are best friends and have this *deal.* Right? They'll stuff a straitjacket so far up my ass it'll buckle at the ears."

Ghost backed off, but held Boone's eyes, knowing that for the first time Boone was really listening to him.

"My attorney is looking into the matter of guardianship for your son," Ghost said, "at least until the time when you get out of here. Then maybe I'll be able to help. My attorney will arrange the details."

"I haven't *got* any fucking details," Boone said, sucking on his cigarette. "Sitting in this place I don't need details. Hey, that's the difference between your side of the room and mine, pal. You got details. I don't have any fucking details. Leave me out of this kid crap. You picked the wrong guy. If you want the kid you can have the kid, because I ain't got no kid." Boone focused his eyes on Ghost through the smoke and glass. "Just get me fifty thousand dollars and tell them it's my kid and now he's yours. How about it? That's just piss money to you."

"I want you to talk to the boy."

"Why should I?"

"He's your son."

"We been through that. Look, you get a bank account with

my name on it and you put the money into it and have the fucking warden sign so they can't take it back, and I'll tell everyone I have a kid, but he belongs to Ghost Galvin now. They'll fuck me out of the fifty thousand, but I'll keep the bankbook for a souvenir."

"Spend a few minutes with the boy. Don't jerk him around. Then we'll have something to talk about."

He could see Boone thinking it over, thinking *something* over. Ghost tried to find a reason, an explanation for Radio so that they could leave here and forget about Boone and forget about Radio talking with Boone. Make up a story, tell him it *was* the wrong guy, it was a different William Boone, this one was ill and couldn't talk to anybody, he had a disease that made him forget what he knew. The guy couldn't talk and he couldn't remember, but Ghost had read the file and, Radio, your dad was actually a hell of a guy—it's too late to know him now, but at one time was one hell of a guy. What was the point of that, Ghost wondered. So Radio could come back ten years later and find out for himself? Or so somebody could find Radio and tell him that his father was the person who killed somebody he knew? What was the point of that? Right, Ghost thought, he's a kid; he shouldn't have to sit here and look at this man and listen to what he has to say, and hear it with the force of a son listening to his father. What if he hears something he likes, though, what if through all the crap Radio hears one thing through his child's mind that means something to him, that sustains whatever it was within him that got him this far?

Boone wheezed and laughed and lit up another Camel. "Hard to fucking believe," he said. "Ghost Galvin. You think any of these stiffs here are going to believe me? The bulls won't tell them anything. You know that? That's what they'll do to work on me, see; they won't back me up with the guys." Boone turned toward the observation window. "You guys better tell everyone Ghost Galvin came to see Billy Boone. That's what you guys have to do."

"We'll take a picture," Ghost said. He stood and put his hands on the small counter. He sensed where Boone's thoughts were going. "How about that, we'll take a picture together?"

Boone's lips parted in a half smile. "You walk down the line with me, man. How about *that?* You and me walk down the line and say hello to the guys. Now, I'd like that. That might stick with me. We walk down the line and meet the boys. Then I'll talk to the kid."

"I don't know what you mean."

"Just say hello to the guys," Boone said. "With me there."

"If the warden says it's all right, then I'll do it. You talk with your son first."

Exhaling a chestful of smoke from his nostrils, Boone nodded.

"But don't fuck with the kid," Ghost said.

"Yeah, I wouldn't want to get locked up or something."

"Your parole board won't like it if you screw around with your son."

Boone sucked on the cigarette and stared at Ghost.

"I figured he'd pull something like that." The warden stood with Ghost in the corridor outside the room where Radio was waiting.

"Is it possible?"

"It's not a good idea."

"I think it's the only way he's going to cooperate."

"It's not a safety situation. It's just that it gets the men stirred up. We like to keep things very much the same here. Routine."

"He also wanted money. Fifty thousand dollars."

"He won't trust the money, unless it's cash in his hands. He knows better."

"I'll walk with the goddamned guy."

"I must admit, it would make my life easier to say no. But how do I say no to Ghost Galvin? My son would never speak to me again."

"I want to talk with Radio before he goes in."

The warden nodded. "Tell the guards when you're ready. We need some time for the lockdown."

Radio was still sitting in the plastic chair. Ghost returned the photographs to him.

"You have to understand that this is all hard for him to swallow," Ghost said. "He's been sitting in here a long time."

"What'd he say about me?"

"Remember, he hasn't seen you since you were a baby."

"I think he saw me that time at the basketball court."

"He's been in a cell six or seven years, so he's not about to jump up and down about *any*thing. Don't walk in there thinking you're going to grab your father and go fishing. That's all I'm trying to say." Ghost put a hand on Radio's head. "Okay," he said, "let's go."

The guards escorted them to the visiting room. Ghost took Radio's hand, which was cold, and led him into the room. Boone stood with his back to the partition.

"Mr. Boone," Ghost said, speaking loudly into the metal grate, "this is your son, William, Jr."

Boone turned, looking tired and bored.

"His nickname is Radio."

"Lousy place, isn't it, kid?"

He walked over to the bench and sat down.

Radio let go of Ghost's hand.

"So what do you think about this Ghost Galvin? You don't see Ghost Galvin walking around every day. Not around this place."

Ghost said, "I'm going to wait outside. I'll be right by the door in the hall."

"Well, what about it, kid?" Boone asked, the cigarette still in his mouth. "Ghost Galvin. How'd you hook up with him?"

"I met him." Radio sat down on the wooden chair.

"He give you any money?"

"He bought some stuff for me."

"That won't dent him. He should give you some money. He's got plenty of it. I bet he could give you a million dollars and not even know it's gone. That's how much money he's got. I had a million once, you believe that? At one time I had plenty of money. You ask him, he'll probably put cash in your pocket. Where's your ma, kid?"

"She died."

"You just never know from one goddamned day to the next." Boone lit another Camel. The smoke drifted through the grate. "He got a lot of women hanging around?"

"No."

"Go figure it." Boone shook his head. "With that kind of money he's got his pick of the litter. That's why I like Mexico. You been to Mexico?"

Radio shook his head.

"You got money in your pocket in Mexico and you get the pick of the litter. Any one you want. I'll bet the Ghost would put money in your pocket if you ask him. I think you got his number."

"Did you come to see me one time?" Radio asked, shifting around on the bench.

"I don't know if I can help you with that one."

"I thought you came to the basketball court at my school and then you left."

"I don't know about any school."

"In North Hollywood."

"Where the hell is that?"

"California."

"You stick with that Ghost if you want to play basketball. That's the guy you talk basketball with. You ask me about Mexico. I been to Mexico."

Radio had the *National Geographic* pages in his hands. He put them on the counter. They were worn and frayed and smudged.

"What you got there?" Boone looked nervously at the pages.

"It's a story from a magazine."

"Can't read," Boone said.

Radio did not unfold the heavily fingerprinted pages.

"Can't read," Boone repeated, picking a fresh Camel from his pocket.

"It's mostly just pictures."

"Don't like looking at pictures." Boone busied himself with the cigarette.

"They have a lot of fishing there." Radio watched his father light the cigarette and take a huge draw of smoke. Boone took peeks at Radio, avoiding eye contact.

"Mexico," Boone said, "I'm telling you right now, that's the place to be. You don't want to be here. You don't want to be anyplace else. Mexico. You get some money in your pocket and go to Mexico. They leave you alone there."

Boone stood up and and walked over to the observation window, motioning to the guards to let him out. He stood with his back to Radio while the guard opened the door.

The warden looked at Boone. "We're going to make one pass down the line, and I want you to remember that this isn't a Fourth of July parade. I'm not in favor of this, but Mr. Galvin gave you his word, so we're going to do it. Just don't get carried away."

"I want a cigarette."

"No cigarettes on the line."

It took them ten minutes to pass the security lock-offs leading to the main cell block. Boone was silent; he kept looking at Ghost's shoes, the Converse high-tops.

They entered on the lower level of the two-story cell block. Twelve guards had taken up positions around the block.

"Let's go," the warden said.

Two guards walked ahead of Ghost and Boone. Another guard and the warden trailed them, a couple of yards behind.

When they entered the main floor, a steel door closed behind them. But the metallic whir of the prison factory still vibrated through the walls.

"These are the boys," Boone said to Ghost. "A real butthole, ain't it? All the boys just sitting in there. I don't like the niggers much. I don't like them and they don't like me."

Inmates in the first few cells stood and leaned against the bars. They started talking.

"Look at that, man," one of them said. "That's the Ghost, man."

"No shit," Boone said to him. "And he ain't here to see you."

"Fuck, man, that's the Ghost. That's the *Ghost.*"

Word ricocheted throughout the cell block, and in seconds all three hundred inmates were on their feet.

Ghost walked slowly. He saw eyes, and hands gripping the steel bars.

"It's the fucking Ghost, man, it's the fucking Ghost!" Inmates shouted from both levels of the block, voices bouncing off metal walls.

Boone turned his head back and forth, smiling. When they reached the middle of the cell block, Boone stopped.

"Keep it moving," the warden said.

"Put your arm around me," Boone said to Ghost. "Put your arm around your pal, Billy Boone. Come on, man."

Ghost put a hand on Boone's shoulder. The inmates cheered.

"That's my pal," Boone said.

The word *Ghost* rippled up and down the rows of cells.

And then it became a chant. An entire section of inmates chanted in deep, raw voices, "Ghost . . . *Ghost* . . . GHOST!" The rhythm of the chant was picked up by other inmates, and in seconds the entire cell block was chanting, "GHOST . . . GHOST

. . . GHOST . . ." The chant filled the metal and steel cell block, a sound so loud that Radio, waiting in the warden's office, could hear it.

On the way back to the warden's office, Ghost asked to use a rest room.

"There's one across from my office. I'll get you the key. You need a key for everything around here."

The warden returned with the key and opened the door. The inside of the rest room was white tile and gray steel. Like everywhere else in the prison, a deep mechanical hum vibrated in the room. Every square inch of the bathroom had been scrubbed clean, until the whiteness was unbearably bright.

The chanting had stopped but Ghost could still hear it, a raw, pounding rhythm that pulsed in his head. He'd heard his name chanted hundreds of times during games and after games, but that was a different sound, a different feeling. Those chants in arenas were curtain calls, and with a wave of his arm he could control the crowds. Hearing his name chanted by the inmates he felt stripped of control; they were controlling him. Inside these walls, feelings were weaknesses to be bargained with, like cigarettes and drugs. Boone smelled the opening and went to it like a jackal after wounded game; he paraded Ghost like a new car through the neighborhood. And now Ghost wanted to step out of the skin of "the Ghost," shed it inside these sterile white walls, and leave it powerless on the floor.

He splashed water on his face, wet a paper towel, and held it on the back of his neck. With his eyes closed, he felt the cold water on his skin. When he returned to the warden's office, he saw the secretary looking at him with shy recognition.

"You're the Ghost, aren't you?"

He extended his hand to her. "Thom Galvin, how do you do?"

The guards returned Radio's pack, while Ghost spoke with the warden, who then told Radio he would do his best to see that his father got the bass.

Ghost stopped the station wagon a block from the prison and parked it in the shade of an overhanging willow tree. Radio fiddled with the buckles on his pack. Ghost sat and stared at the boy until, finally, Radio looked at him.

"How did it go for you?" Ghost asked.

The boy considered the question.

"I wish they didn't have that glass."

"That's part of their rules."

"It was like a cage."

"Rules."

"He knew me."

"Did he say that?"

"No. He wouldn't look at me for very long. I could tell he knew me. He kept looking away."

"What did he say?"

"He talked about Mexico."

"I guess Mexico sounds better than where he is."

"He was the same guy who watched me play basketball that time."

"You think so?"

"Yeah."

"Then he probably was."

"He was. He looked like that."

Ghost nodded.

"How did you feel . . . seeing him and all?"

"I hated him."

"You did?"

"I hated him at first, anyway."

"Why?"

"Because of my mom. Because he made my mom sad."

"Did you tell him that?"

"No."

"What did you tell him?"

"I told him I saw him when he came to watch me play basketball. And I said something about fishing. He kept talking about Mexico. I didn't know what he was talking about Mexico for."

"He probably didn't know either. He was nervous, too. Scared."

"Yeah. He kept looking away."

Radio was whispering, his head bowed over his pack. Ghost knew he was crying and trying not to show it.

"That's how I feel, too," Ghost said. He put a hand on Radio's shoulder. "You've got a lot of guts, I'm telling you that right now. I know guys I bang heads with in the NBA who don't have the guts you do. I'm telling you the truth. I'm proud of you."

236

Radio was crying but held the sound back. He pressed his face into the pack.

Ghost rubbed the boy's back.

"Just let it out," Ghost said. "You're starting to be my hero, man."

11

Following Opry down the stone path that led to the gazebo, Rebecca saw the judge through the gray screen; his white shirt, white trousers, and white hair were outlined against the dark lake in the distance. If he heard Rebecca and Opry approaching, Judge Ely made no motion of acknowledgment until Opry opened the screened door.

"Well," he said, "come in and sit down. I thought we would enjoy lunch outside, sun or no sun."

"Lunch isn't necessary."

"Then we'll set it out in front of you and see what Opry's cooking does for your appetite." The judge patted his stomach. "You can see what it's done for mine. How about a lemonade? Fresh made this morning."

"That would be fine, thank you."

He turned back toward the lake. "I've been looking at this lake for forty years, and I never grow tired of it. Believe me, I've made quite a study of it. The lake itself changes little. It's the shoreline that changes. And quite a bit. My wife and I are active in efforts to preserve the shoreline from further development. I suppose you could say we were environmentalists before it became a fashionable pursuit. Naturally, the new developers are not fond of me. But . . ." He shrugged.

"It's a nice view from here."

"Best on the lake. I sat here for a month until finally choosing the exact spot where I wanted this gazebo built. And now I spend as much time here as in the house. You value a view such as this at my age—the fact that it is there for you and it doesn't change.

I've made it my mission to see that this view remains. I've raised hell about it. Nobody wants you to stand in the way of progress, but I have my own ideas about what progress is."

Opry returned with a tray of food. She served tuna salad, sliced watermelon, and fresh corn bread.

"I love that smell." The judge folded back the linen napkin covering the the corn bread. "I don't think a week goes by that I don't ask Opry to make her corn bread. Of course, she won't tell anyone how she makes it. That's one of the reasons it's so good."

Judge Ely bit into a piece, then dabbed at his lips with his napkin. He looked up at Rebecca as though a thought had suddenly occurred to him.

"You've been a busy young woman. Very busy."

"In what sense?"

"Well, you seem to bump into a lot of people with whom I'm acquainted."

"You have a long list of acquaintances." She picked at pieces of the watermelon.

"A man can't spend forty years in a community and not make a few friends, and some enemies."

He refilled their glasses with lemonade.

"It's the friends that I like to think about. And, of course, it was Senator Galvin I was closest to. Since the senator's own father died when Thom was fifteen or sixteen, I suppose I filled in a gap or two. Now, Ghost was a bit older . . . what? . . . nineteen . . . when the senator died. So I've been close to three generations of Galvins. There's something to be said for that in and of itself, isn't there? The way people live now, the way people pick up and move." He reached for another piece of corn bread. "You've struck up quite a friendship with my Thommy."

Rebecca began to reply but the judge held up a hand.

"No one has to tell me that Thommy's a terrific boy. I've known since his diaper days that he was special; I've always felt something particular for him, especially after his father died. Which is why, I must tell you, it made me a little sick to read in the sports pages that Thommy was thinking of quitting basketball, that he didn't want to sign a new contract with the Lakers. Thommy's a good businessman, but I know he wouldn't be using a story like that to up his price. So I've been looking forward to him arriving at Nippersink so that the two of us could talk it out.

"Basketball is in the boy's blood, Miss Blesser. Now, I recall him going through this sort of thing once before. He quit playing for a year in college." Judge Ely shook his head. "Greatest college player in the country and he didn't want to play any longer. Just broke our hearts, in a way. We just didn't think *not* playing made Thommy any happier. If not playing had made him happy, so be it. Somehow I knew that wasn't the case, however.

"And now there he is this season, winning the world championship. Most Valuable Player, too. Thommy's father would be the proudest man in the world about that. And Thommy should be the proudest kid, having the senator for his father. I wouldn't ever want that to change."

Rebecca watched the judge's small eyes fix upon her; they were dark gray. She sensed anxiousness, discomfort at her presence, beneath the judge's reminiscences of the Galvin family. She discerned this not from his eyes, but from his steady stream of words, the busy hands around the food. It was as though the discomfort was beneath the level of conscious thought, because what was coming to her from his eyes was controlled, unrevealing; he was studying her. But the hands were busy and he kept talking, as if his body was relieving itself of tension. She recalled Alan Webster's anxiety, which had been masked less successfully.

Rebecca said, "And why would Ghost's feelings about his father change?"

"I was wondering if, perhaps, you could shed some light on that subject. You see, it"—the judge looked out at the lake, searching for his word—"dis*tresses* me that since you've been digging around in Thommy's life, he seems to be losing interest in it. Not wanting to play ball. Not having come out yet for a visit. To an outside observer, Miss Blesser, it might appear that you've worked your way into someone's life, and not for the better."

"Ghost is capable of making decisions about his own life," Rebecca said. "And I'll make decisions about what I'm doing." She picked up her glass of lemonade and sipped from it.

"Oh, he's capable. And I'm sure that you are as well. It's just that these kinds of decisions carry consequences. So you can't just think about yourself, can you? Knowing the senator as I did, and Thommy as I do, I believe you are on a path that is damaging to one's past and the other's future. If you *do* have personal feelings for Thommy, you'll consider what I'm saying."

"Then tell me what you are saying."

Opry reentered the gazebo to clear the dishes. Judge Ely sat in silence as she did so, but never took his eyes off Rebecca.

When Opry left, Judge Ely removed a Monte Cristo cigar from his linen jacket. Rebecca noted a white envelope that was in the same pocket.

"My wife has limited my cigar smoking to the confines of this gazebo and to my study." He lit the thick cigar. "I hope you don't mind. At this point in my life, the simplest pleasures are the most meaningful."

He puffed for a few moments, then spread his hands. "You see me as sort of a corrupt old humbug, don't you?"

For the first time she saw a flicker of feeling in the back of his eyes. Was it remorse? She didn't trust it; he had seen enough remorse in his courtroom to know what it looked like and, perhaps, to summon it. And remorse for what? It was a trap she'd fallen into in the past, when pursuing the truth about her birth. She often found guilt in people's eyes when she questioned them about the past, about links with birth certificates, adoption agencies, and birth parents, as if instinctively people knew it was beyond the bounds of right to withhold truths about someone else's birth. Rebecca looked at the judge and was sure he was not feeling remorse for her, but for himself, and for some private burden he had taken upon himself.

When Rebecca didn't answer, the judge continued. "I just want it known that I have no illusions of how you view my position. What I've invited you here for today is to discuss a different perspective. You can accept or reject what I say, but I at least ask you for careful consideration. I take strong interest in what is dear to me, and I take strong interest in whatever would tarnish what I value. This is not an abstract matter to me, the people involved are very real and have been much a part of my life. You've pressed Thommy into interrogating elderly Mrs. Conrad. You've ambushed Dr. Wyndham at his golf club. Alan Webster has had a visit from you that he will not forget. You've sought out that son-of-a-bitch Senator Wells. And I understand you are attempting to interrupt the vacation of Sheriff Baines at Nippersink. Ask me what you want to know."

"Let's start with why you covered up circumstances surrounding Senator Galvin's death."

"Covered up." He repeated the words slowly, punctuating them with a puff of smoke.

Rebecca continued. "The press did not fully report the circumstances involved with the senator's death, evidently because they had little access to information. Details disappeared—a belt the senator was wearing, a coffee cup that was in the rowboat. The autopsy report was perfunctory, at best. And every time I push at the edge of these details, I find your fingerprints. To what end, I'm not yet certain."

"You've interested Thommy in your theories?"

"It's obvious to me that he thinks he's responsible in some way for his father's death. He can't forgive himself for being estranged from his father during that last year, and he equates that fact with the senator's death. The senator had been using barbiturates to sleep, he'd been drinking much more than he ever had in his life. Was it a heart attack, or was it something else? I think Ghost needs to know. For starters."

"All this is for Thommy's benefit? What beneficial effect is your research going to have on Thommy? Isn't that the question here? Or are you making decisions on his behalf? Perhaps you've already decided what is beneficial for him to know and what is not. That is quite a responsibility you've assumed. If you truly have Thommy's interest in mind, I might actually be of help to you."

"This isn't a hearing on my integrity," she said, raising her voice.

"It is." Judge Ely removed the cigar from his mouth. "That's it, exactly." He pushed himself away from the table. "Let's walk down to the lake and talk about what you're really after."

She followed him down the fieldstone path to the dock. He hadn't turned to see if she was there, he simply started walking.

He sat down on the dock box. "I move like a dinosaur. I wish someone could tell me something good about getting older. I can't think of a damn thing. Well, in any case, the reason you are here, Miss Blesser, is not to listen to my complaints." He removed the envelope Rebecca had seen earlier, and held it out in front of him. "This is a letter Senator Galvin wrote to me. It's quite brief. I want you to read it." The judge handed the letter to Rebecca, then turned his attention toward the lake.

She opened the single handwritten page.

Davis,

I'm on the way back to Chicago. Since I'm in a black mood the thought occurred to me that one of these planes might go down sometime, or something else might happen. You never know. If so,

I'd hope you could keep things square with Thommy, and I hope you could keep E. level. I count on you to help with that for Thommy's sake. You're the only one who can protect him. I'll see you.

T.G.

" 'E' being Elizabeth," Rebecca said. "I know about her."

"Of course you do." He watched two fisherman work a weed patch for bass fifty yards down the shoreline. "Have you discussed this with Thommy?"

"He read the letters."

The judge turned and looked at Rebecca. His facial expressions revealed themselves so slowly, that at first Rebecca thought the judge was reacting with great anger to what she had just said; but as she watched, she realized it was not anger overtaking his face but surprise, and sadness. His eyes seemed to recede into his head, and there was a weariness in the way his lower lip fell open, exposing tiny, tobacco-stained teeth.

"Tell me. What letters are those?"

"Written by the senator to his mother. During the campaign. He doesn't mention Elizabeth Folger by name, but he talks about the problems he was having; or, at least, their effect upon him."

"And you're certain these letters were actually written by the senator?"

Games, she thought, considering his question, mind games. She had studied the senator's handwriting and signature enough to know it; the letters were real.

"Ghost had no doubt about it."

"And in them the senator talks about this 'woman'?"

"Elizabeth Folger."

"He mentions her name?"

"I told you he didn't. It is obvious who he is writing about."

"Sometimes things are obvious because you want them to be."

"We're not going to play puzzles right now." Yet, the color of doubt flowed momentarily through her thoughts. Could the senator have been writing about something else? Something entirely different from what Rebecca had led Ghost to believe? It was the kind of thought that usually came to her in the night; because her search for her birth parents had been informed by assumptions, it was her task to replace incomplete birth certificates and adoption records with specifics. She locked her eyes on his, unwilling to yield what he was searching her for, the areas

243

of doubt in her mind. He looked for them in the same way he looked for truth and lies in the eyes of a defendant testifying before him.

Judge Ely puffed on his cigar and returned his attention to the fisherman down the shoreline. "It's unfortunate things have progressed this way. I planned to talk with Thommy about this matter. I decided I would have to, with you stirring things up the way you have."

"Don't you think I have a right to stir things up?"

The judge continued talking, without looking at Rebecca, as though speaking to himself. "I would explain that anything that might have happened with that woman was unfortunate but, finally, not fundamental in terms of his memory of his father. Leave it at that. I think Thommy would accept that from me, and the issue would be diffused. His life could continue as it should. And mine, as well. Memories in their proper place."

"And I'm supposed to disappear? I'm not going to. Elizabeth Folger was the senator's mistress. She had a child at the time when they were most frequently seeing each other. I am that child, and I'm not going to go away."

"No." Judge Ely shook his head slowly; his voice was quiet, tolerant, like that of a teacher responding to a student's misinformed comments.

"Don't dismiss me. I have been looking for this woman for years. It's obviously not my doing that she was involved with Senator Galvin."

He continued shaking his head, and spread his arms, as if trying to gather her words and keep them within the span of his grasp. "Thommy did not have to know about this woman."

"He does, so forget about that. Will you look at me for a moment and forget about Ghost and forget about the senator? This woman is my mother and I have a right to know about her."

"I've seen the documents you've seen. I've spoken to the people you've spoken with. You're assuming much too much. The senator was not your father." The judge finally focused his eyes upon her.

"I don't believe you."

"You *should* believe me. You should leave things as they are. Obviously, Elizabeth Folger does not want to be a party to you, as she rather completely removed herself from your life. You should view that fact as providential."

"Tell me the truth."

The judge turned away from her, and seemed to address an unseen spot far out over the lake.

"What I'm telling you is truth; though I do sympathize with your reluctance to accept it."

Rebecca found the weariness that had overtaken the judge's voice oppressive, and raised her tone to shake him. "I *don't* accept it. Elizabeth Folger was blackmailing the senator at the end of his life. That was made absolutely clear in the letters the senator wrote. He was being blackmailed by her."

"Yes."

"Why?"

"She was an obsessive woman." The judge's voice rolled out over the lake. Watching him, Rebecca knew he was picturing Elizabeth, suspending her out there in the distance. And in the tone of his voice, Rebecca heard an accusation, but one aimed against Elizabeth: What have you done to *me?* At that moment, Rebecca sensed that the judge's sadness and anger came from the intangible power this woman held over him, as though she was the cruelest joke in life. He had spent his life taking control, giving order to things, deciding in his courtroom what could be placed in evidence when determining a right versus a wrong, even determining when lunch was over and it was time to walk down to the dock. Yet after more than half a century of being a fulcrum in people's lives, the judge, too, had been forced by Elizabeth Folger to surrender power. Rebecca watched thoughts churn through the judge's eyes and suspected he, like she, felt in some way imprisoned by Elizabeth.

"But what was she blackmailing him *with* that would ruin his campaign, and his life?" She asked the question, but prepared to give him the answer.

"He was the object of her obsessions. Through all the years that the senator was not . . . seeing her—and there were many at the end—one would have thought her attachments would have diminished. They did not. In fact, the opposite was true. In the middle of the campaign she demanded the senator divorce Nicole and marry her. That, of course, was ludicrous. She became an extreme irritant. That was her blackmail."

"No, she was blackmailing him with me, wasn't she?"

"That's your invention. It serves no purpose to aggravate me, Miss Blesser. You must trust me when I tell you that."

"I don't trust you."

"Then why are you here?"

"I'm here be*cause* of you. You had me followed in Los Angeles. I had a threatening call last night. If I was so wrong about this, those things would not be happening."

The judge removed the cigar from his mouth. Again, he turned to look at her.

"Who followed you?"

"Stop this game."

"I did not have you followed." He looked at her intently. "And I did not telephone you last night. You can be certain of that."

"Then you'd better tell me more. Who else would do that?"

"You should leave this to me."

"Leave what to you?"

"This entire matter."

"I can't do that."

"You should."

"You're not giving me answers. Elizabeth Folger demanding the senator divorce his wife would not be enough to make the man kill himself. I don't believe that."

"You're making assumptions, and I don't like assumptions. You look at the records, and you'll see that your assumptions are not borne out. He did not kill himself."

"Damn the records," she said, her voice cutting across the dock. "If you're so concerned about Ghost, you're going to have to convince *him* that his father didn't kill himself, because it's eating him up. And if you're so concerned for Ghost maybe you'll decide to help me, because he wanted to make love to me the other night, and I wanted to make love to him, but that's just not possible at the moment, is it?"

Judge Ely rose slowly from the dock box, as if the bulk of his body was impossibly heavy. Rebecca thought he was preparing to leave.

"I want your cooperation," Rebecca said, "or I'll publish the whole story and let it sort itself out."

"Not if you care, as you say you do, for Thommy. The only matter of importance in life for me at this point is Senator Galvin's memory—that it is properly preserved for history and for his son. Having done the research you have, undoubtedly you're aware of the interest I took in assisting Thomas Galvin win his congressional seat, then his place in the Senate, and we had a perfectly workable strategy for the White House. Those memories are very much a part of me. You see, I don't have children, Miss Blesser, so my legacy rests in a man's memory and his son's belief in that memory. And now you seem to want to explain to that son that his father killed himself over this woman, Elizabeth Folger. And this is something you do not know. In fact, there are records that dispute your position. You, above all, should know about the importance of records. You of such a solid upbringing on Radison Avenue in Milwaukee, with a hardworking banker for a father, and a mother who tirelessly involves herself in civic issues. Solid, straightforward people who created a wonderful path for you in life. And now I see this obsession of yours, and wonder how your parents feel, after the life they've provided for you. You've become famous for writing about adoption and its emotional rigors, yet you're one of the lucky ones who've lived a good family life. But I am not responsible for whatever void you feel, and Thom Galvin, Jr., is not responsible, either, for that void. Neither, in fact, is Senator Galvin." Rebecca returned the judge's stare, but some of the force she'd felt earlier had drained from her eyes. The mention of the specifics of her life, where she lived, what her parents did, chilled her. Judge Ely looked at her with a knowing that weakened her. And the way he was talking about Senator Galvin, it was as if the man were standing in the house waiting for the judge to join him for a game of gin. "It is not a surprise to me that you are standing here. I want you to understand that. I fully expected to hear from you in some form. But you've entered an arena that does not belong to you, and will never belong to you. I know this, but am having trouble making you believe it. What you must believe is that all of this is best left in my hands. If you cannot trust me, I want you to give me time. I know what's best for Thommy. This situation must remain with me. You will allow that if you care for Thommy. I don't want Thommy dragged into this."

"I *have* the birth certificate. I want to know who the father is."

"I have no idea. I'm asking you to forget your search and live your life. I know that's a difficult thing I'm asking. But I have my reasons."

"You'd better share them with me right now."

"I can't do that."

"Elizabeth Folger is alive. I want to see her. I want to talk to her, and I'm certain you can arrange that."

"She's alive and the senator is not, which is not the way I

would have it. But I want her out of Thommy's life. She's volatile and dangerous and you are going to inflame her by pushing Ghost away from her."

"He never heard of her until I told him."

"Leave this to me."

Rebecca shouted at him. "Help me!"

"Check the records of that hospital again. Forget about Elizabeth Folger. I don't want your magazine crawling all over the senator's grave. Nor do I want you trampling a son's image of his father."

"I've checked the records. I found the birth certificate. And I'm not about to hand my life over to you for safekeeping." Rebecca turned to leave.

Judge Ely took a step after her. "The senator left his life and his son's life in my hands, not yours. You should believe that I know what I'm doing. This is not a matter to be left for fate. I'm exhausted by fate. This woman is dangerous."

"And you're not?"

Rebecca hurried up to the stone path to the driveway and her car.

Removing his cigar, the judge studied it a moment, then dropped it in the lake. It hit the water, hissed, then sank into the dark silt. He looked across the lake at the old Porter estate. Alice Porter died last year, leaving six heirs who wanted to subdivide the estate and build thirty condominiums. Alice left no stipulation in her will about the disposition of the estate, but if she knew, the judge thought, what her heirs wanted to do, she would have stopped them. And he was not about to go to his grave having to look at thirty condos where the Porter mansion used to be. He'd already filed suit.

12

The boat race whose qualifying runs Ghost and Radio had seen from the air on the way to Michigan was an annual event sponsored by the Lake Shore Yacht Club. During its decade of existence the race had grown in size and popularity, to the point where it was now tradition for people to picnic at the shoreline to witness the finish. Mrs. Towsley was among this year's spectators; the finish buoy was opposite the building where she lived. She wore a white sweater over her pink dress, keeping one hand close to her sun hat, which fluttered in the breeze. Spectators stood three deep along the sidewalk; Mrs. Towsley found a spot without a crowd around her. She, like most older people, did not like crowds.

Three boats approached the finish within seconds of one another. The crowd cheered their favorites. The Wrigley-sponsored craft crossed the line in first position. Mrs. Towsley clapped her hands and cheered; Wrigley was a name she knew, a good Chicago name.

The crowd slowly dispersed, while Mrs. Towsley stayed in place, waiting for the commotion to settle before she started to the crosswalk.

There was a cement bench facing the lake a few yards from the crosswalk and as she approached it, Mrs. Towsley saw the profile of a woman who was sitting on the bench, arms folded, calmly looking out toward the lake. The woman was wearing a charcoal-gray dress and black blazer, as if unaware of the humid summer day; she seemed perfectly comfortable. Her hair was tied back, and her skin appeared pale in the afternoon sunlight.

Mrs. Towsley stopped ten feet from the bench, looking at the woman. The way the hair was pulled back from the face and the chin jutted slightly looked familiar, as did her steady gaze toward the water. This woman looked to Mrs. Towsley like an older version of Elizabeth Folger; the nose and the area around the eyes didn't seem exactly right, but the posture and the gaze, and the unrevealing hint of a smile on her lips—those traits belonged to Elizabeth.

Rebecca had called the other day to say that she was in Chicago, and if she had time would stop by to say hello; that was sweet of her, Mrs. Towsley thought, young people don't usually think about those things. So maybe, she thought, just talking to Rebecca brought Elizabeth to her mind. But that image was of Elizabeth as Mrs. Towsley had known her twenty-five years ago. This was a mature woman sitting on the bench, yet Mrs. Towsley felt as if she knew her, and recalled the way Elizabeth used to sit by the window, camera on the sill, gazing out at the water with those dark eyes that in an instant could become distant.

Mrs. Towsley approached the bench. The woman turned and looked deeply into her eyes. There was surprise and recognition in the look, yet immeasurable distance.

A fresh breeze blew in from lake, and Mrs. Towsley had a hard time standing still in it.

Elizabeth was looking at her, and Mrs. Towsley thought, I must look a hundred years old by now, she may not even recognize me.

"Elizabeth?"

The woman on the bench did not change her expression, nor did she respond.

Mrs. Towsley stepped closer.

"Oh, my eyes," Mrs. Towsley said, "my eyes are so bad. You look like someone I knew."

"How are you?" Elizabeth asked.

"My lord, my lord, it is you!"

"How are you?" Elizabeth asked again.

"Well, I'm fine. Oh, I'm so flustered. I can't believe it's you. I just had a call from . . . my lord, I can't believe it's you."

"Who called you?"

Elizabeth's expression didn't change when Mrs. Towsley sat on the bench next to her. Mrs. Towsley took Elizabeth's hands in hers. "Elizabeth Folger, I can't believe I'm sitting next to you."

"That's not my name anymore. Who called you?"

"Well, a young woman, Rebecca. Do you know about that? My lord, she'll be so happy. Have you spoken with her? Oh, my lord, I'm so flustered. I have to get a hold of myself."

"When did she call you?"

"Three days ago. She was in Chicago. When I saw her last she was looking for you."

Elizabeth cut her off. "Yes, I know."

"Have you spoken with her? She'd be so excited. She's a wonderful girl. I don't even know what to say. Elizabeth Folger. My lord."

"I'm not her mother."

Up close, Mrs. Towsley could see Elizabeth's eyes. What she saw scared her. There was distance—she'd seen that before—but any suggestion of softness was gone. Whether it had been youth or simply different times, Elizabeth once had areas of softness in her eyes, even with that secretive look. Mrs. Towsley had always thought that somewhere inside of Elizabeth there was a belief in promises to come and promises to be kept; Elizabeth's solitude *had* to be sustained by some belief. Mrs. Towsley saw hollowness in those eyes now, however; it unnerved her to return Elizabeth's gaze, as if Elizabeth had submerged herself in a secret life for so long that the glint of self Mrs. Towsley once recognized had disappeared.

"Rebecca brought all this research to my apartment several months ago and was so anxious to try and locate you. You see, I didn't know anything about this, because of course we haven't seen each other in years and I could only tell her that you lived across from me and all." Mrs. Towsley was speaking rapidly and hardly hearing what she was saying. She was scared. Her heart was pounding. "There was the magazine article and all of that . . . Well, I just don't know what to say."

"She's not my daughter."

"I have this telephone number for Rebecca's office in New York. Maybe you'd like to call—I have it upstairs."

Elizabeth turned toward the water again and did not say anything for a while. Mrs. Towsley anxiously retied the scarf she was wearing.

Then Elizabeth turned to her and said, "This is where the senator and his son used to walk, isn't it?"

Mrs. Towsley felt quite confused. "I'm sorry?"

"The senator used to take his son for walks here, along the water." Elizabeth stood and looked down at Mrs. Towsley. "I'd prefer it that you not tell anyone we've seen each other. I have a different life now."

Mrs. Towsley wanted to ask her what she meant, but Elizabeth began walking away, and Mrs. Towsley was too old to catch her. She watched her walk away. Elizabeth looked out of place walking the breakwater in her charcoal skirt and black jacket, unaware of the people passing her, a figure from another time.

"Are you all right?"

A young woman pushing a stroller stopped and looked at Mrs. Towsley.

Mrs. Towsley did not respond.

"Ma'am, excuse me, but are you all right?"

"Oh. Well, yes. No. Yes, I'll be fine. I just need to sit for a minute. I'll be fine. I've had quite a start."

"Can I help you?"

"No. You're so kind. I just have to rest. I live across the street. I'm going to go home in a moment and rest."

2

Rebecca took a beer from the refrigerator and went for a walk in the fields. The evening sun was near the horizon, slicing wild grass shadows across dirt roads that smelled of oil. She found a place where the fields converged in a knoll, went to its top, and sat there in a nest of wild grass and weeds. The air above the fields vibrated with the sounds of grasshoppers and crickets. Fireflies drew crooked lines in the growing darkness, while the dome of the night sky revealed pinpoints of starlight. Rebecca lay on her back looking at this light. The starlight she saw was ancient. How far up the beam of light did one have to travel, she wondered, until ancient light gave way to the future? Is there a place in space similar to where a great river meets the sea and the composition of water changes from fresh to salt, and the life forms existing therein change also? Is there a point in those streaks of light emitted by stars where past and future blend? That would be a place of peace, she thought, a place of truth. A burning light in the vacuum of space, where light is absolutely pure—the past, the future, and the present merge in celestial harmony. Isn't that what everyone wanted in life, she wondered. To be free of boundaries created by the past, unburdened of future demands, and to live fully in moments of timeless clarity? She lay there thinking that the origins of her blood, like starlight, came from a past that, because it *was* the past, felt as unreachable as an exploded star; the light remained, the source was gone. In this clear night sky Rebecca saw a shooting star streak to the horizon. We chase the light, she thought. We pack ourselves in rockets and launch into space, released from the earth's gravity, chasing ancient planets so that we can study their composition to learn about our past. We send sensor probes out to the edges of the universe, out to where the light predates our planet, hoping that in our pursuit of the past the future will be illuminated. We look back to see forward.

The judge seemed to see himself as the caretaker of the senator and the senator's son. It was obvious to Rebecca that he saw her as he would a witness who might disrupt the "proper" outcome of a trial; the lawyers had met in chambers and worked out the deal, but here was a witness with testimony that hadn't turned up in depositions. Her presence pricked the judge's sense of potency and purpose. It was as though the past were a piece of music, and Rebecca was refusing to play her part. She had listened to the judge talk about the senator and Ghost and Elizabeth Folger, and it had not sounded as if he were talking about *people;* she felt as if he were trying to hold on to a vision, a canvas of his own creation that validated his existence as protector of a private pantheon. In fact, Rebecca felt she understood his thinking. She'd lived for a dozen years with the image of the woman at the window in her dreams. This was her birth mother. To Rebecca, this woman's existence was a completion of her own; this woman was never a real person—she was an answer to the riddle of Rebecca's life. Whatever Rebecca felt was missing from her life, when this woman arrived she would suffuse Rebecca's darkness with light. Whenever fears and doubts pursued Rebecca in the night, she attributed them to the absence of this woman. But now she had disappeared from Rebecca's dreams. This woman frightened people. Maybe the idea is not to go to her, Rebecca thought, but rather to let her go.

Rebecca felt drowsy, drugged, and closed her eyes to sleep. She dreamed that the judge stood above her on the grassy knoll. He opened his arms as if conducting a symphony and held mirrors in his palms and in the lining of his coat; suddenly he was covered with mirrors and he used them to bend the starlight in every direction, from mirror to mirror, like a web of lasers. She heard music, deep bass sounds that vibrated until she felt the veins in her body being plucked like strings, tiny high-pitched notes atop the deafening bass that increased in intensity as the judge raised his arms to the night sky, tangling the light and sound into a cacophony.

3

When she awoke it was after ten o'clock. She returned to the house. Rebecca heard the telephone ringing as she walked uphill to the porch. The ringing stopped by the time she reached the phone, but fifteen minutes later the ringing resumed. Rebecca counted the rings. Ten of them. Fifteen minutes later, again, the phone rang. Ten times. If it was the judge calling, she didn't want to talk to him right now; if it was the voice from last night, she didn't want that either. But it could be Ghost calling. In five minutes it started again, and this time she picked up the receiver.

"Hello?"

"Rebecca?"

Rebecca relaxed; it was her assistant, Mary Lee.

"Did you just call?"

"No, I tried a few hours ago, that was it. Everything all right?"

"I think so. What's up?"

"You got a call this afternoon from that woman you interviewed in Chicago—Towsley?"

"Yes."

"Right, well, she called looking for you and in between all the apologies for not wanting to bother you, I squeezed out of her what she wanted to say. She saw Elizabeth Folger."

Rebecca felt wary, rather than elated, since she did not believe in coincidence. Moments ago in the fields she had dropped the dream of Elizabeth. But maybe it was too late for that; Elizabeth was making herself visible. But who for?

"Where did she see her? And when?"

"In Chicago today around lunchtime. Across the street from the building where Mrs. Towsley lives."

"I'll call her right now."

"She was a little upset."

"Why?"

"She said the woman acted strangely. Mrs. Towsley didn't really want to get into it with me. I didn't want to push her. She sounded shaken up."

"I'll call you later. Thanks."

Rebecca pulled Mrs. Towsley's file and looked up the telephone number. She found herself glancing around the house and out the windows. It was dark outside, so all she could see was her reflection. She saw fear. She stood alone, and outside, in this house and place she did not know. There were signs of the senator's life all around the house: photographs, bar glasses engraved with his initials, old clothes. A voice in the night, sounding like an unsettled spirit, had admonished Rebecca for pursuing her search, for being here at all.

Rebecca picked up the phone to call Mrs. Towsley, glancing at her watch as she did. She hung up the phone. It was almost eleven-thirty, and she did not want to shake the woman out of her sleep.

Instead, she dialed Ghost at his hotel.

"We just packed it in," Ghost said. "I can hear the television on in Radio's room, of course. You miss me?"

"Yes, I do."

He heard the edge in Rebecca's voice. "You all right?"

"I'm frightened."

"What's wrong?"

"I went to see the judge this afternoon. He's very upset with what I'm doing."

"We expected that."

"He's upset about Elizabeth Folger. He told me she's dangerous."

"He said he knows her?"

"He wanted me to think so."

"What's he talking about?"

"He wouldn't tell me everything he knows, and he didn't want me to tell you anything. He thinks he's protecting you."

"From what?"

"From her, from me—I don't know. He admits that Elizabeth

Folger was your father's mistress, but denies that they had a child. He was surprised that you had those letters; I don't think he knew anything about them. He said the blackmail had to do with this woman wanting your father to divorce your mother and marry her. I'm sure he's holding something back, I could feel it. It doesn't make sense that Elizabeth was in your father's life, disappears for a short time, during which she had me, then reappears, and I'm not supposed to have a father. If I had another father, the judge would know that. He would have the man's name, rank, and serial number. Ghost, he knew about my family, my parents, where they live, what my parents do. That didn't make me feel too wonderful. He sits out in that backyard of his and acts like he runs the world from there."

Ghost knew the yard well, with its gazebo, lawns, and dock. A funny image came to his mind; it was of the judge urging his portly figure around the back lawn, chasing the dogs who lived next door. Last time Ghost had been there, five years before, the judge had complained about two ill-mannered retrievers who sneaked through his hedge every day to do their business on his lawn. They did it at night, when he sat outside to smoke his cigar. Ghost remembered that as a child he'd heard the judge complain about dogs dumping on his lawn. He remembered a particular tirade the judge delivered to him and his father one afternoon on the subject of loose dogs. So the next day the senator rented a pickup truck and borrowed the dog of every family he knew in Nippersink. Just after dinner, the senator and Ghost rolled the truck into the judge's yard, waited for him to walk out the back door toward the gazebo, then let the dogs loose, and hid in the bushes to watch the show. Of course, Ghost and his father spent a good part of the night rounding up the dogs. At least up until that moment in their lives, Ghost considered his father's dog stunt the greatest thing he'd ever seen a human being do.

"It's hard for me to see the man you're talking about," Ghost said. "I guess he still sees me as a kid, and I still see him as my father's friend."

"I got a phone call last night, someone saying that what I was doing was hurting you."

"Why didn't you tell me this? For chrissake, Rebecca. . . ."

"It was in the middle of night. I didn't want to call you."

"Of course you should have called me. Was it a man or a woman who called you?"

"It was a woman masking her voice."

"Did she threaten you?"

"She kept saying I was hurting you."

"I really don't get it."

"That woman I told you about, Mrs. Towsley in Chicago? She talked with Elizabeth Folger today. In Chicago. She called my assistant to tell her. I don't know much about it because I haven't been able to speak with Mrs. Towsley myself."

"I'm calling the judge right now to find out what the hell is happening. This is a bad dream."

"Don't do that," Rebecca said quickly. "Not tonight."

"Why?"

"I'm scared."

"I'm coming back then. I'll see if I can get a plane tonight." He thought for a moment. "They'll never take off from this little strip here at night."

"I'm going to go down to the lodge and stay there tonight."

"I'll call and arrange it. But I want to know what's happening. And I want to know what the fuck it is with this Elizabeth Folger. I'm going to get the goddamn judge out of bed and find out what's going on. I'll drive out there tomorrow and talk to him."

"I've been looking for her for twelve years, Ghost. And now I think she's looking for me. That's why I'm scared. Alan Webster told me she was obsessed with your father. It's obvious from the letters. Maybe for some reason she doesn't want me near you. For whatever reason, she's coming out into the open. I had this whole fantasy that when I found her she'd be this wonderful person who gave me up for a noble cause. This isn't it."

"Go to the lodge and call me from there. The plane is scheduled to take us back at seven, so we'll be in early. But call me when you get to the lodge."

"You haven't told me about Radio. How is he? How did it go?"

"We saw Boone. I talked to him alone, then Radio talked to him. This guy is so far gone I don't what the hell to tell you. The kid handled it goddamn well. Better than I did. We'll talk about it when I get back." Ghost reached over and turned out the lamp on the nightstand. "I don't understand what's happening there, but we're going to handle it. I wish I was there right now . . . which is a coward's way of trying to tell you how I feel about you."

"You're not a coward. And I wish you were here, too."

"Call me from the lodge."

Rebecca went into the bathroom to wash her face and brush her teeth. She then sat at the vanity table in the bedroom and packed some cosmetics to take with her to the lodge. The vanity had numerous photographs under its glass surface—pictures of Ghost and the senator, Nicole Galvin and Ghost's grandmother, the judge sitting on the porch with the senator. There was one photograph that Rebecca particularly liked. It was of Ghost and his father standing on the pier at Lake Tombeau. Ghost was holding a fishing pole and a string of fish. He looked tan and young with his crew-cut hair and preadolescent body. The senator was relaxed, leaning against the wooden guardrail. He kept one hand on Ghost's back and waved to the camera with the other. The picture caught them, father and son, in a moment of contentment, a place, Rebecca thought, where starlight is ancient and new.

4

Rebecca packed clothes to take to the lodge, then began turning out the lights in the house. When she turned out the lights in the rooms where Radio and Ghost had slept, the hallway went dark, and she hurried out of it; the darkness felt cold behind her. She went to the screened-in porch and heard the soft slapping of moths against the screens. Then she heard sounds coming from the back bedrooms. Creaking floors and the crack of contracting glass. Rebecca felt her pulse start pumping. The light in her bedroom was still on, as were the lights in the kitchen and bathroom. She turned off the bedroom and bathroom lights, but left the kitchen light on because it cast a glow across the dining room and into the living room, giving the appearance of someone being home. She picked up her overnight bag and started for the front door. The light from the kitchen reflected off the windows in the dining room and living room, enough for her not to be able to see outside; she could see the faint image of her reflection, and felt the chill of eyes upon her. It was a pressure, a pressing against her skin, like being in the sea and feeling the weight of the water all around her. Eyes, she thought, someone is watching. The front door was unlocked. She searched her purse for the key, then she locked the door and walked down the path to the parking area. Just before she reached the car, she heard a sound from below the house, from the basement. It was the sound of something crashing and breaking on cement, like a clay pot. The basement was dug into the hill, with a door at the bottom of the yard. She looked back at the house. The single light in the kitchen glowed faintly through the windows. The door to the basement was a few yards from where she stood, so she walked tentatively toward it.

Rebecca did not consider herself brave, yet she found herself propelled forward. Adrenaline pumped through her body. She carefully put her overnight bag on the ground, then reached for the door. She thought of something Ghost had said the other morning prior to visiting Mrs. Conrad: whatever it was between his father and Elizabeth Folger, and whatever caused his father to die, Ghost wanted to find out what it was and stare it in the face. At the time Rebecca had thought it was a naïve thing to say, a macho athlete thing to say. But now as she put her hand on the metal knob of the basement's door, she wanted to stare into Elizabeth Folger's eyes, confront her, look as far into her as she could and pull out of her eyes what part of Rebecca's soul Elizabeth possessed. The door was open, and Rebecca's touch on the knob pushed it further so. She reached inside and felt for a switch. Her fingers found the plastic cover plate, then she flicked the switch. Light sprayed across the room from the bare bulb. There was a screech as something leaped from a shelf to Rebecca's right. She fell against the wall and put up her arms, trying to take in the flurry of movement. There was another screech from the back of the basement and a pure white animal shot into the air. Then there was a frozen moment when the two animals stopped and stared at Rebecca, their backs arched, fur standing up. Rebecca recognized Mrs. Warren's cats. The cats meowed with fright, then trotted silently past Rebecca and out the door, moaning louder when they reached the lawn, as if to scold her for interrupting their nocturnal explorations.

She leaned against the wall, breathing hard, perspiration sliding down the sides of her body.

Let her go, Rebecca thought. Elizabeth's appearance, after twenty-six years of silence, meant only this: Elizabeth wanted questions stopped, not answered. And in this idea rested a lie of the mind, Rebecca thought, that the past belongs to someone, as if it were a piece of land that one could hold title to. And for the first time Rebecca began to think that perhaps she was not given away by her birth mother, but set free from her.

She heard another sound. Above her, coming from the house. There was a pattern to the sound, like footsteps. Rebecca turned off the light and hurried to her car, feeling that if she did not leave now those sounds would be in her head forever.

5

The airport where Ghost and Radio landed was fifteen miles from Nippersink. Rebecca had left the lodge an hour and a half early to wait for them.

"You look like you missed us," Ghost said, tossing his bag in the backseat of the car.

She hugged Ghost and Radio. "Of course I did."

"You all right?"

"I'm all right. I fell asleep right after I called you from the lodge."

"No other calls last night?"

"Not at the lodge."

Rebecca and Ghost hugged again.

He had told her little of the visit to the prison, but she saw that the trip had changed him; he looked tired but strong.

"I want to take the back way to Nippersink." He pulled the car out of the gravel parking lot and headed south on the two-lane blacktop.

Rebecca noticed a blue pickup truck backing out of the parking lot, fifty yards behind them.

Ghost came to an intersection and looked around.

"I think we go this way," he said, turning left.

The road took them through farm country. Ghost knew his way by the location of old homes and barns.

The morning air was moist with humidity and carried upon it the smell of pigs and cattle and corn.

Rebecca turned and saw that the blue pickup was still behind them, keep a fifty-yard cushion. "I'm not really looking forward to going back to the house," she said.

"After I talk with the judge, we can leave. There's no other reason to stay. I've explained to our friend in the backseat that the best thing we can do right now is go back to L.A. and get things straightened out there. But first I'm going to see Judge Ely and get him to lay this Elizabeth Folger crap on the line."

"He's not going to like the fact that I told you about my conversation with him. He already believes I brought the devil into your life."

"He sees me as the senator's son and as this basketball wonder. I don't think we ever had a conversation outside of those two areas. It's time we do."

They came to another intersection. There was a large farmhouse just west of them. "I remember that door." Ghost pointed to the faded yellow farmhouse and its red front door. "You always turn left at the red door."

Rebecca watched to see if the truck made the turn.

"What do you see?" Ghost glanced at Rebecca. "You keep turning around."

"That truck back there. It's been following us since the airport."

He looked in the rearview mirror.

"So?"

"I haven't seen any other cars. Just that one. Is this a common road?"

"It's common if you live on one of these farms, or you know the shortcut to Nippersink."

"It's just that they pulled out right after us at the airport and they've stayed right there."

"He really scared you yesterday." Ghost turned the car east and picked up speed.

"He scared me because I don't think he's telling the truth. He kept warning me about Elizabeth Folger. Alan Webster warned me, too. What I'm not certain of is if it's me that makes the judge and Webster nervous, or if it's her. I've come around to thinking all of this 'let's preserve the memory of Senator Galvin' as a lot of self-defense that these people have cemented into their minds. It's a cover-up by all of them. The judge, Webster, Wyndham. Somewhere down the line there was a screwup, and I don't know who made it, but I'm getting the idea that I'm the result. People only get this uneasy when they've done something wrong." She looked back at the truck.

Ghost thought of Boone sitting in the prison, blowing out

enough cigarette smoke to shroud San Francisco. Boone had known about Radio; Ghost smelled that from the second he walked into the cell. But Boone had his own problems, he may even have thought he was doing Radio a favor by not acknowledging him. After all, what could he offer the boy? "I'm your father, and I'll be spending the next five years in this prison, and after that I'll be doing something that'll land me in here again. Nice to meet you, son." Maybe Radio was absolutely right, and it was his father who came to the schoolyard that day to have a look at him. And maybe it was in a moment of perverse compassion that Boone slipped away before having to confront his son. But he's not doing a favor for the boy in avoiding him, Ghost thought; it's Boone doing a favor to himself; it's Boone bullshitting himself into thinking he has nothing to offer the boy, so he won't saddle him with acknowledgment. Who was Boone kidding, Ghost wondered. Not Radio.

Then Ghost thought of the senator standing on the porch that last day at Nippersink. If his father had been thinking about Elizabeth Folger, but protected Ghost and himself from those thoughts by rehashing the argument about Ghost not playing ball, it was the most damaging kind of evasion, because what was said took on the tone and meaning of what was actually troubling the senator, coloring the words with a darkness they did not deserve, but one Ghost had absorbed. After sitting in the cell with Boone, Ghost decided that what people withhold is at least as important as what they share, because whatever is withheld informs what is shared, shapes it like bones shape skin. Ghost thought of thousands and thousands of free throws he practiced after his father's death, each shot an apology for whatever had been withheld between them.

"What do you think they've done wrong, the judge and Webster?" Ghost asked.

"I don't know. Elizabeth Folger knows." The truck still tailed them.

"You think maybe she's in the pickup truck? Let's stop and say hello." He put on the brakes and stopped the car in the middle of the road so as to block passage around it. "Look, as fond as I am of you, I'd be delighted to find out you're not my sister. Really delighted for the right reasons. I'm done playing 'the senator's son' or Ghost Galvin for the judge, or for myself or anyone else. Let's just see who is in the truck."

The morning sun was strong, and the chrome grill of the

pickup truck shimmered and wavered in the heat that rose from the blacktop. Ghost waited by the Galaxy's trunk as the truck approached. It stopped twenty yards from Ghost, who walked toward it. Two startled teenage boys sat in the cab, frozen by Ghost's approach.

"Morning, guys."

Neither looked older than seventeen. Both wore white T-shirts and faded blue jeans. Their faces and arms were sunburnt, farmer tans.

"Hi," the driver said quietly.

"Hi," the other boy said in a squeaky voice.

"Didn't mean to startle you, but I had this weird feeling that I was being followed."

"Uh, we saw you at the airport. My brother's a mechanic there."

"We dropped him off," the one in the passenger seat said. "He told us you were landing there in a plane this morning and we thought he was kidding."

"I guess your brother isn't a kidder. I'm on the way home with my friends up there. Is there something I can do for you?"

"You got out of the airport kind of fast. We were hoping to have you sign this, Ghost." The driver pulled a basketball out from behind the seat. "We were just hoping to get your autog₄aph."

He recognized the familiar look of fans.

"Listen, I'll sign it if you want. But I'd rather just shake your hands and say it's nice to meet you." Ghost extended his hand through the window, and the first boy took it. "Thom Galvin," Ghost said.

"Bill. Uh. Bill Epps."

The other boy quickly extended his hand.

"Gary Bird."

"As in Larry?"

"No relation."

"Well, I'm Thom Galvin, and it's good to know you, Gary." They shook hands.

"Jesus, I never thought I'd meet somebody great," Gary said.

"I wouldn't spend too much time thinking about that, if I were you."

"We'd really like you to sign the ball," Bill said.

"You know what? I'm not going to sign it, because then you won't use it. You're better off using it."

"It'd be great to have proof, though, you know, that we met you."

"You got all the proof you need," Ghost said, slapping the car door. "See you guys."

Ghost returned to the Galaxy and started back down the road.

6

"You sealed this place like a tomb," Ghost said to Rebecca, who stood in the kitchen cutting cantaloupes for breakfast. "We'll roast in here." He opened windows on the enclosed porch, then went to his room and opened windows there. Outside, Radio took the basketball from the trunk of the car, and Ghost watched him head for the courts. Ghost turned to leave the room then stopped. Both nightstand drawers were open. He walked over and looked in one, then the other. In the left one he saw the flashlight and Bible and box of buttons that had been there before. The drawer to the other nightstand, where he had put the pile of letters, was empty.

He called Rebecca.

She found him standing by the empty drawer.

"I put the other letters back in the shoe box and left them in the drawer," he said. "Did you take them out?"

She shook her head. "I never saw them. I only saw the letters you gave me. They're on the table out on the porch. That's where I left them."

"You're sure you didn't take them out? Because they're not here. . . ."

"I didn't touch them."

"I remember putting them back. Right in there."

"Don't look at me like that."

She saw the flash of uncertainty in his eyes, and felt the power Elizabeth now had over both of them, the power of doubt.

Ghost said, "If you're not honest with me, the cut's going to be so clean I won't even feel it at first."

He saw that he'd hurt her, and put out his hands to touch her. "I'm sorry. I think I realized that you can hurt me, and I'm not used to that. I'm sorry. I'm freaked that someone's been in here."

She thought of the noises she'd heard while she was down in the basement.

Ghost moved closer to her.

Rebecca spun around and hurried out of the room. Ghost trotted after her. She went straight to the porch and stopped at the table she'd been using as a desk. Most of her notes and files were gone. "My god." She scrambled through the remaining papers, trying to determine what had been taken. "Everything's gone. My notes, the transcripts, the newspaper clippings." She dumped the contents of a folding file case out on the glass tabletop. A few scraps of paper fell on the table. "That's where the letters were."

Her eyes were wild and unfocused when she looked up at Ghost. She ran to her bedroom and pulled open the drawer where she'd kept her tape recorder and tapes from telephone interviews. The tape recorder was there but the tapes were gone.

"It's either the judge or her or both of them," Rebecca said to Ghost, who was standing in the doorway.

He went to her and held her. "I'm going to the police. I'm not going to screw around with this. It's gotten out of hand."

"I don't think you should waste your time with the local police," she said.

Ghost felt Rebecca's body suddenly go rigid. She was leaning against his left shoulder, but out of one eye she saw the vanity table. Rebecca stepped away from Ghost and went to the table. The Galvin family photographs she had studied the night before were gone from under the glass. All of them except for one: Ghost and his father standing on the pier at Lake Tombeau. That one had been moved to the center of the table.

"What are you looking at?"

She spread her hands over the vanity. "All those pictures, the photographs, they're all gone. I was sitting here looking at them last night before I left for the lodge." Rebecca was frightened, but even with her fear she saw a perverse clarity at work; Elizabeth, or someone, actually thought they could possess the past by stealing it.

She sat down on the end of the bed.

"Pack your stuff," Ghost said. "I'm going to get Radio and then we're getting out of here. We're going to go see the judge, then we're getting on a plane and flying to Los Angeles. If I have to hire my own police to find out what the fuck's going on, that's what I'll do."

Ghost picked up the phone and dialed his office in Los Angeles. The answering machine reponded. He looked at his watch. It was nine A.M. in L.A. It was Miss Dupree's habit to be in by eight. He called the house number, and Magda answered.

"It's me. I just called the office and the machine was on."

"She's been sick for two days."

Ghost couldn't recall Miss Dupree ever having missed a day of work.

"What's wrong with her?"

"I don't know. She just leave a message here."

"I'm coming back tonight with two guests. Let's have lots of fresh flowers."

He then called the number at Miss Dupree's Beverly Hills apartment; an answering machine was on there as well. He spoke, thinking she would answer. "This is me, trying to get a hold of you for a few things. Magda told me you've been out ill. . . . I hope you're all right. . . . Anyway, you're not picking up so I'll assume you're not there. Talk to you later."

7

It was humid and hot as Ghost walked toward the basketball courts where he had so often played. Heat bounced and rolled off the cracked and buckled sidewalk and pressed against his legs. He took the shortcut across the back side of the eighteenth hole of the golf course. From there he could see the court. He stopped by a tree and watched. Radio was going one-on-one with another kid, while two boys shot around at the hoop on the other end of the court. Ghost moved down to another group of trees, twenty-five yards from the court.

"Radio, let's go!"

Radio looked over and saw him, but did not wave or leave the court.

It was a tough match for Radio because he was six inches shorter than his opponent. But Radio's quickness equalized the size difference. The two of them traded four or five hoops, then

Radio stole the ball and knocked off three baskets in a row. His opponent was frustrated by Radio's speed, and gave up at the end. Radio canned two shots and the game was over. Ghost saw money change hands. The boy rejoined his friends at the other end of the court; they conferred, then sent another player down to Radio. Words were exchanged. The two shook hands and the game began. This boy, a more skilled player than the last, reeled off three quick hoops. But even from a distance, Ghost saw the familiar intensity in Radio's form. The pressure of the past few days poured out of Radio as he pounded the the ball on the pavement; on defense he reached and grabbed and body-checked the other boy. There's going to be a fight if he keeps it up, Ghost thought.

But he studied the game and wondered if Radio noticed that every time the boy prepared to take a shot, he dribbled twice to the right to find a comfortable rhythm.

The boy scored again to take a four-nothing lead. He dribbled, looking for an opening between Radio and the basket. But now Radio overplayed the boy's right side, preventing him from stepping into his shooting rhythm. Each time the boy tried his two-bounce, pull up rhythm, Radio lunged in at the boy's right leg, and forced him left. The boy missed the next shot and Radio pulled down the rebound. Take him to the left, Ghost thought, he's got no first step to the left. Radio faked a move to the right, then spun to his left, charging down the left lane for an uncontested lay-in. He missed his next shot, but stuck with his defensive plan of overplaying the boy's right side, and forced a turnover.

A few minutes later, Radio closed out the game, 8–4. More money went into Radio's pocket.

Radio walked to center court and spoke with the three boys. Ghost watched the discussion and waited for the nod in his direction. But it never came. The two boys who had already played Radio walked back with him to the court.

Radio had agreed to play them one on two.

The new game began. Ghost moved out of the shade, closer to the court. This time, Ghost observed, Radio had overreached. The two boys swarmed over Radio on defense, and when on offense spread themselves cross-court, forcing Radio to wear himself out running back and forth.

Ghost realized he was standing in the same spot where his father had often stood to watch him practice.

The action on the court grew frenzied. Both boys played better together against Radio than they had individually; Radio made a game of it, but couldn't contend with his opponents' advantage.

"Practice," the senator used to say to Ghost when he watched at this court, "don't just run around, practice." And Ghost would practice, hundreds of lay-ins, dribbling drills, free throws, jump shots. Even with the endlessly repetitive drills, Ghost would look over at his father and see the intensity of his father's concentration. He was with me, Ghost thought. And the fact that he felt his father's attention made him do the drills properly; in practice he never tossed a shot or made a move without a purpose, and this freed him in actual games to rely on instinct, and the instinct was usually right. When playing poorly, Ghost had only to picture his father standing on the knoll to elevate his performance. If there was a failure between us, Ghost thought, it was that the game should have been the beginning of a conversation, and not the conversation itself.

Ghost heard a horn sound, and turned to see a Cadillac come around the corner and stop. Its door opened and Judge Ely labored out, white hat in one hand and a cigar in the other.

"Wouldn't I know it?" Judge Ely walked slowly up the knoll to where Ghost was standing. "Wouldn't I know it?"

Ghost went to greet him.

"Wouldn't I know I'd find Thommy Galvin at the basketball courts at Nippersink," he said, opening his arms to Ghost. "Would I look anyplace else?"

They embraced. Ghost felt momentarily drained of will. Seeing the judge, the familiar scent of his cigar—the same brand his father had smoked—being here at the Nippersink courts, caused Ghost to wish the clock turned back twenty years. Then he heard a shout coming from the court. Ghost turned. Radio had shoved one of players, who shoved back. They squared off and swore at each other.

Ghost called to them. "Knock it off. Play or don't play, but knock off the crap."

The boys didn't recognize Ghost from the distance, but they responded to his strong voice, and resumed their game.

He turned back to the judge. "I should have been over to see you and Eleanor days ago, but I've been running around all over the place with my friend there."

"So you have. So you have."

"He's the runaway I told you about. I've got to get him back to California to straighten out his legal situation. They're looking for him for an arson thing."

"Parents no good?"

"The mother is dead. His father is in jail up in Michigan. We went there, but the guy really doesn't want to have anything to do with the kid. The guy's a deadbeat."

"Maybe we can force him to shape up a little. I've got contacts in Michigan. We can put a little pressure on the prisoner. You shouldn't be afraid to call me about something like that. I can help."

"Jamison is working on it. And I don't want to mess around with the kid's head. Radio's seen his father, spoken with him, he should form his own judgments. I won't do anything behind his back."

"Now I didn't mean that." The judge's face fell, and he studied Ghost. "I just meant help."

"I appreciate it." Ghost touched the judge on the shoulder; he knew what he said had hurt the judge. "It shook me up, visiting the prison."

"I can understand that. My god, you look fine. You look well and strong."

"So do you."

It was as if they both were putting off what they were there to talk about, knowing their relationship would change once they did. Ghost knew it had already. And, looking at the judge, he felt the judge knew it, too.

The judge smiled. "Come on now, son. You can't bullshit me. They're getting ready to send me out to pasture any minute. Maybe they've done it already and haven't told me. I have to stay one step ahead of them or they'll put me out of my misery."

"How's Eleanor?"

"She'll bury me, there's not much doubt about that. She's anxious to see you. Opry can't wait to put on the dog for you with a home-cooked spread."

"I'll have to put that off for a while. I need to get Radio back to California and deal with his situation. Plus we've had some trouble at the house here."

The sense of Rebecca now fell between them.

"What kind of trouble?"

"Things were stolen. Someone came into the house and took things."

The judge appeared surprised and wary. "What things? When?"

"Notes, letters, photographs. Research materials that belong to Rebecca Blesser. Research. Evidently they came in last night or early this morning. It happened when I was up in Michigan."

"Have you called the sheriff?"

"Not yet."

"You should. Right away. What photographs and letters?"

"Family stuff. Pictures from my grandmother's room. Letters my father wrote."

The judge's shoulders sagged and he tilted his head forward, as if a weight had shifted within his brain.

"I'd read the letters," Ghost said. "I think Rebecca told you that."

"Yes, she did."

"Who would want to steal this stuff?"

The judge looked troubled. Then he brightened.

"You've always handled the press beautifully, Thommy. You haven't let them into your life. You've kept yourself free of all that, and I think showed a wisdom in that regard far beyond your years. Truthfully, I don't know why you'd want to change that. Rebecca Blesser may be a very nice young lady; in fact, I'm sure she is. I visited with her yesterday, wanting to get the measure of her, and she is a nice young lady. She has the credentials and all. I listened to her story and I listened to her theories. But you and me, Thommy, we loved your father, we respected your father, and we respect his memory and his record. That's something she cannot understand, because she's not one of us."

Ghost watched the judge's eyes withdrawing into a private place, but he didn't want to go there with him; he wanted to bring him back to the present moment. "Who would want to take those family things from the house?"

"Perhaps Miss Blesser has her reasons. I'm sure she's very nice, but I warned you about her. She'll tell you anything for her own purposes and won't worry about the consequences. I've seen this kind of thing for years. But your father doesn't belong to her. He belongs to us."

Ghost wondered if this distant look in the judge's eyes had always been there, but he couldn't remember seeing it when he was a child. He wanted to reach into that private place and retrieve the judge, as he'd been unable to do with his father on their last day together at Nippersink.

"I want you to understand something." Ghost put his hands on the judge's shoulders. "My father doesn't be*long* to anyone, and his life was not a buffet for us to pick and choose from. You loved my father, and I loved my father. But there are things about his life that I have to know. I don't believe Rebecca's out to get me and get you and get my father. What for? A story? The world will keep spinning no matter what anybody writes about Dad. She's shown me her research, she's told me what she knows about Elizabeth Folger, and I read the letters my father wrote before he died. Rebecca believes my father and this Elizabeth Folger had a child, and she's it. That deserves an answer."

"It's not true."

"Then show her it's not true. Show *me.* Who was Elizabeth Folger?"

"Someone who chased your father like a lot of people chased your father."

"It was a hell of lot more than that from what I can see. Those letters—"

"He was blowing off steam. This woman just wouldn't let up. He was in the middle of a tough campaign."

"She wanted Dad to divorce Mom and marry her."

"Rebecca Blesser shouldn't have put all of this in your head. She's trying to make you see your father in a light that simply isn't true."

"How long did they know each other?"

"Mostly it was this woman trying to work her way into your father's life; she made a career out of it. Your father loved your mother and he loved you, especially. That's what's important, Thommy. Anybody can pick things out of someone's past and invent stories around what they find. And it's not right, just not right at all."

"There's nothing to protect me from." Ghost bent down to regain eye contact with the judge, who was looking past Ghost, across the courts to the golf course and blue sky. "I'm going to ask you something and I need the truth. Did my father kill himself?"

The judge pulled himself back from the place of the distant gaze, and looked at Ghost. "That's something he would never do. He would be hurt if you thought that."

The judge's response felt like a punch in the gut to Ghost. But he kept his eyes on the judge.

The judge saw what was in Ghost's eyes.

"Your father's death was not your fault."

"No one stopped me from thinking the world revolved around me in those days. So why wouldn't I think his death was my fault, too?"

"His heart gave out, son. What Rebecca told you about me running around telling people what to do, telling Wyndham what to do, that was just me looking after your father. No one knows what happened out in that boat, and I didn't want the whole thing turned topsy-turvy. You know what the press is like. They would have made their own conclusions before anybody really knew anything. And I didn't want to see your father's life end that way. I wasn't about to let his memory be thrown to the sharks."

"What happened in the boat?"

"I don't know."

"Was he drinking? Taking pills?"

"He was bone tired. I talked with him that morning."

"You've never told me that." Ghost wiped the sweat away from his face and let out a deep breath. "You spoke with him that morning?"

"Briefly." The judge's voice dropped to a whisper. He looked exhausted.

"What about? What did he say?" Ghost's tone rose, and he felt tears in his eyes.

"He said he hadn't slept. He had a flight to Denver, but first he was going into the city to have it out with Elizabeth, to try, once again, to convince her to leave him alone. So he decided to go fishing very early. And he had himself a heart attack."

"Then why did you go to the boat and take out the coffee cup and the belt?"

"I didn't want that belt returned to you in a plastic bag with a tag on it. You know the way he was about that belt at Nippersink. Your father told me he'd taken sleeping pills the night before, and they hadn't helped. He wasn't against taking a nip to take the chill off the morning. I didn't know what was in that coffee cup, but I didn't want to leave it for somebody else. All I knew was that your father was dead, and that wasn't going to change. He never talked about killing himself. It wasn't in his makeup to talk about it, or to do it. But when you're running against the clock, not sleeping, taking pills, and having a drink to calm the nerves, bad things can happen. And *did* happen. He died.

It was an accident. I know that, and I didn't want it to look like anything but that. There's the truth."

"When you spoke with him that morning, did he say anything about me?"

"Just that you went back to school."

"He didn't talk about me not playing?"

"Not that morning, Thommy."

"But we argued about it the day before. That's all he talked about with me."

"He knew you'd come around. He knew what kind of kid you were. Sure, he wanted to see you play ball. We both did. But we knew you'd come around in time. He never doubted that. If he bellyached about it, it was because it took his mind off things."

"You don't understand something, Judge. . . . I thought it was me. I thought he died because of *me*. I should have talked to him. He just stared out the window and asked why I didn't want to play ball anymore. And I didn't have an answer for him. I wish I could have put my arm around him and just have told him I loved him, said anything to cut through it all. I didn't know how."

"You loved him, Thommy. He knew that."

"I should have said it and watched him see me say it. Why didn't you tell me you talked to him that morning?"

"His . . . passing . . . was enough for you at the time. You were a kid."

"But I felt like I'd *done* it."

"There was no reason in the world for you to feel that."

"*I* didn't know that. And I didn't know about this woman, and I'd never read letters like the ones he wrote to my grandmother."

The judge spread his arms and spoke to Ghost as if he were speaking to the sky, to some larger purpose, rather than the person who stood before him. "None of that was what your father was about. I've tried to make damn sure people knew then and remember now what he was about. What you think of your father means everything to me. It's poison that you even know about this Folger woman. I don't want you to think of your father in the wrong way. I've never wanted you to know about this business, because it's got nothing to do with you and your father. And whatever I've done was for that reason."

"Whatever you've done like what?"

"I've tried to keep that woman to her own world, tried to keep a lid on her because she's a liar."

"If she's not Rebecca's mother, and I can't believe you'd ever look me in the eye and tell me that if it weren't true, then what's she got to do with my life now?"

"She'd poison your father's memory. She'd poison it for you and for the world. She hates me. She believes I kept her away from your father, that I advised him to stay away from her. This is a woman living with delusions and obsessions, and I had hoped that after your father passed on she would never be heard from again." The judge looked away from Ghost, as if Ghost's proximity now made him uncomfortable. "I just wanted your father's memory to live on for you as it should."

"Elizabeth Folger is in Chicago. Is that where she lives?"

"What do you mean?"

"A friend of Rebecca's saw her yesterday in Chicago."

Judge Ely shook his head and looked beaten. "I told . . . I suggested to Rebecca that she leave this to me, that she not push any further."

The more Judge Ely spoke, the further from him Ghost felt, as if the judge had become a stranger. And the judge acted similarly, as though the man he stood next to were unknown to him. He was not the senator's son and he was not Ghost Galvin; the judge looked away to search for familiarity, as if he might find it in the sky.

"I think she has a right to push."

"Your father had one child. That is you. Rebecca should leave this to me. I won't have your memories poisoned."

"I'll be fine," Ghost said quietly, fighting an urge to grab the judge and shake loose the look of absolute right. "You're talking as if memories are photographs that someone can just pour ink over. Or steal."

"The past is worth preserving, Thommy. You'll learn that when you get older."

"What past? Something made up? I was afraid of the past because I thought it was pointing a finger at me, and then only because I thought the whole fucking world *was* me. I'm only afraid of what I regret, and what I regret is not having had this conversation with my father. And we're not going to end this conversation because I truly believe you care about me."

They heard shouting and scuffling coming from the court, and turned toward the noise.

Radio and the two boys were fighting, dragging one another off the court to the grass. One of the boys yelled, "You lost, you lost, so just pay!"

Swinging his arms wildly, Radio yelled back. "You cheated! You fouled on every play, you asshole!" Arms and fists were flying, entangled in a flurry of limbs and curses.

"Hey!" Ghost ran to the pile of players and plucked Radio out of the middle. "What's going on?"

Radio, face red with fury and tears, tried walking away, but Ghost held him.

"He lost and he doesn't want to pay the money."

Radio turned his back to all of them, so they couldn't see his tears.

"They cheated."

"What do you mean they cheated?"

"They fouled on every play."

"We did not. He just lost."

Ghost looked at the boys.

"What happened?"

"He lost. It was fair and he knows it."

"Pay them the money, Radio. You made the bet, and you lost. So pay them the money."

Radio folded his arms and wouldn't turn around.

Ghost stuck his head in Radio's face.

"I hope you're not waiting for me to pay the money, because I'm not. I saw the game. Everybody hacked everybody. But you lost. You weren't going to win that one if there had been ten referees. Just pay the money."

The two boys realized they were next to Ghost Galvin. They stood, brushed themselves off, and stared.

Radio dug into his pocket and pulled out the ten bucks he owed them. He tried handing it to Ghost, who stepped back.

"Pay them."

He handed the money to one of the boys.

"Everybody shake hands."

They limply complied, then the two boys walked away.

Ghost signaled to the judge that he'd be a minute, then squatted down to Radio's eye level.

The judge stood on the grassy knoll, cigar in his mouth, watching Ghost talk with Radio.

"You hacked them every bit as good as they were hacking you. I was watching."

"They cheated."

"They *didn't*."

"They . . ."

"There were two of them, they weren't all that good, but there were two of them, and together they were good enough to win. You play enough to know that *you* weren't going to win that bet."

"Who's that man?"

"He was my father's best friend."

Radio knelt down and picked up some stones from the grass and rolled them around his hands. He threw one at the metal pole that held the backboard.

"Don't do that."

Radio looked down at his hands, scraped from fighting.

Ghost said, "It was a bad bet and you lost it. You played hard. Forget about it."

"I could've beat those guys."

"Maybe if one of them had a seizure and the other one passed out you could have beaten them. Look, it's done, you lost. If you make them all life-and-death you're going to die a lot."

"You made him see me, didn't you?"

"What?"

"My father didn't want to see me, did he?"

"He was nervous about it."

"You made him."

"I didn't make him."

"He didn't want to."

"I don't know what he wanted. But I didn't make him. I couldn't."

"I could tell he didn't want to see me."

"He was scared. I don't think he wanted to let himself feel too much. He knew that no matter what he felt he was going right back to his cell. I don't know what that feels like, but I know it's bad. Do you understand what I'm saying?"

Radio rolled the rocks between his fingers.

"If he told you he loved you he'd still have to go back to his cell and I'm sure that's a lot more than he was ready to handle. He's been in there too long to think about loving anybody."

"He doesn't love me."

"He doesn't know you."

276

"He doesn't even want to."

"Maybe he doesn't know how. Maybe he never learned to do that. You're lucky your mother loved you, you're lucky right there, aren't you?"

"Yes."

"Well, you've got that going for you. So maybe you'll have to teach your father. But don't blame him for something he doesn't know how to do. If you know how to do it, then *you* do it. I don't know what else to tell you."

"Can we go back there?"

"I promised I'd take you back."

"When?"

"When we get some things taken care of in L.A. Then we'll come back. Come on, I want you to meet that man over there. But clean off your face."

Radio started wiping his face with his filthy T-shirt.

"Use this," Ghost said, pulling out his own shirttails, which were clean.

They walked toward the knoll, but the judge was heading for his car. He opened the door of his Cadillac and waited there for Ghost and Radio. He looked lost.

"This is Radio Boone, Judge. Radio, Judge Ely."

They shook hands.

The judge looked at Ghost.

"I have things to do. I need time."

"I need you to help Rebecca."

"I'm going to help Rebecca. I'll deal with Elizabeth Folger, and I'll show Rebecca she's not right about what she thinks. I'm going to make this right, son. I'll speak to you in California."

"Then we'll talk tomorrow."

"Tomorrow," the judge said. "Thommy, your father was a good man."

"I know that. But right now we're not talking about my father. We're talking about Rebecca. Her life."

The judge nodded and shut his door. "How do those courts up there look to you?"

"Familiar."

"You know, kids come around and want to shoot there because they know that's where you used to practice. The lodge was going to put a plaque there, but they were afraid someone would steal it. Even at Nippersink."

"I'm planning to sell the house, Judge. I should tell you that. There's no reason now to keep it."

"Be a shame for it to sit empty, I suppose. Hard for me to think of strangers there though. I'd drive into Nippersink another way so I wouldn't have to see it. You get that way when you get old."

PART III

13

Opry went into the den to pour Judge Ely's cognac. Already it was after ten o'clock, so she knew the judge would be home soon. Mrs. Ely had gone to bed. He shouldn't be out this late anyway, Opry thought, looking the way he does lately, not sleeping and on the telephone all hours. She poured a finger of cognac into the snifter and placed it on the silver tray. The judge had called from Nippersink earlier in the day and told Opry he wouldn't be home for dinner, that he was going to dine with Sheriff Baines in Twin Lakes. It wasn't like the judge to do things spur of the moment, she thought; he liked his day to be organized, planned out. "Oh well," she said, reaching for the cognac bottle again. Opry poured another finger into the snifter. "Calm his nerves."

This being the height of the bug season, Opry didn't turn on the lights when she carried the tray outside. She'd walked this path thousands of times and knew the texture of every stone. The lake lapped against the dock; crickets sawed steadily. She placed the tray on the table next to the judge's rattan chair, cleaned the glass ashtray, and removed the plastic bag from the trash can. Opry surveyed the gazebo. Moonlight, reflected from the lake, illuminated the dock and gardens and gazebo. The cement floor of the gazebo had been swept clean earlier in the day. She understood why the judge liked it out here. The glow of light from the house was distant but close enough to be comfortable; standing out here one could feel separated from the world, protected by the screens from the mosquitoes, but with a view of the lake, which in the night looked dark and endless, and the faint, twinkling lights from homes on the other side. She made a last check of the gazebo—the judge always wanted to find his chair and table and ashtray just where he'd left them—then started back toward the house.

Opry heard a sound in the bushes, and she stopped halfway up the stone path. Sometimes, the neighbors' dogs made nocturnal visits.

"Shoo!"

The crickets went silent.

"Shoo!" she said, waiting for another sound. Seconds passed, then the crickets resumed. The lake lapped behind her as she went inside and shut the door to the night.

2

The limousine carrying Ghost, Rebecca, and Radio turned off Sunset Boulevard and onto Roxbury Drive. Pine trees cast long shadows across the lawn and driveway of Ghost's estate, as the iron gates opened to receive the car. The sweet scent of jasmine permeated the air.

Magda came down the steps to greet them. Ghost introduced Radio and Rebecca to her, and they followed her into the house.

"I have supper ready for you. I set the table on the terrace."

"We'll get ourselves settled. Then a little supper sounds great. I thought Miss Dupree would be here to check in on us."

"She left a message on the service. Yesterday and today, she's not feeling well."

"Did she leave any messages for me?"

"No, sir. Just a message each day that she's not coming in."

Ghost told the maid to show Rebecca and Radio to their rooms, then went into the kitchen and phoned Miss Dupree at home. Her machine answered.

During the flight home, while Radio and Rebecca slept, Ghost had made a list of things that needed to be done. He planned to meet with Norman Jamison and Miss Dupree and give them the list: He was ready to hire whoever could do the job, above the table or beneath, to dig into the adoption records that Rebecca had been unable to obtain. He wanted Jamison to approach the police and the social agencies on Radio's behalf, and planned to have Miss Dupree find a competent psychologist to give him some advice on handling Radio now that they were back home. These were the kinds of things Miss Dupree could organize within hours. And he could not recall her having been sick once during the two years she'd worked as his personal assistant; she ran the details of his life with such precision that he relied on her not to be.

3

Judge Ely felt exhausted as he pulled his Cadillac into the garage. He groaned, rolled himself out of the car and walked into the house, where he found Opry finishing the dishes. He shook his head. "You really didn't have to do those dishes, did you? You're just waiting up for me. I'm seventy-five years old, and I should be allowed to stay out late once in a while, shouldn't I? Now you get to bed."

"You're the one needs his sleep."

"So that's how it is, is it? Now I've got *two* women telling me what to do—you and Eleanor. I spend twenty years as a lawyer and thirty years on the bench, and I end up with two women telling me what to do. What a hell of a thing!"

"You know I'm right, Judge."

"I can't sleep in this heat."

"Air-conditioning works fine. Maybe you should have a little hot chocolate, like Mrs. Ely does."

"So now you're telling me I can't have my cognac? I plan to have my cognac and a cigar. And don't start on me about the cigars, either. You get to bed."

"You don't look well, if I may say so."

"I don't feel well. I'm still going to have my cognac and cigar."

He went to his den and selected a cigar to take with him outside.

The humid air surrounded him as he walked down the stone path to the gazebo; with each step Judge Ely grimaced at the gout in his left knee. Sighing as he sank into his chair, he dipped the butt of the cigar into cognac, then lit it. From the kitchen, Opry saw the flame from the match, then went to her room, thinking of the two occasions during the last month when he actually fell asleep out there; she decided to set her alarm for one hour so she could check on him.

"Well," he said, settling into the chair, cigar in one hand, snifter of cognac in the other. He took a long draw of mellow smoke, and watched the smoke drift around him and out into the night. Moonlight reflected off the water and outlined the trees bordering the shoreline; he could discern the shapes of his sculpted bushes and of the wooden benches by the boat house; streaks of light from across the lake rippled on the surface of the water. "Thom," he said, to hear himself say the senator's name. He thought of the hundreds of times the senator had sat with him in this gazebo, puffing on a cigar and sipping a cold beer on a hot summer afternoon. "It gets away from us, Thom, doesn't it?" During the last year of the senator's life, he'd visited the judge here on several occasions, and after discussion about Ghost and Nicole and politics, their conversation always worked itself around to Elizabeth Folger, about how the senator might extricate himself from her, even though it was years too late to do that. There is one thing a man does not say to another man concerning women, the judge decided, and that is "You should have thought of it then." They weren't going to change Elizabeth, the judge was certain of that—contain, perhaps, but not change.

The judge became aware of a form in the darkness beyond the gazebo; it moved slowly across the lawn between him and the lake, blocking out the distant lights as it passed them. Judge Ely sat up in his chair and strained to see in the moonlight. It could be one of the damned retrievers from next door, he thought, but even as the thought came to him he knew it wasn't true. "Opry," the judge said, irritated, "you're wandering around here like a cat." The screen door opened. He started to get out of the chair.

"Stay in the chair."

He could not make out the face but the voice was familiar.

The judge fell back into his wicker chair, aware of his own weight. "You shouldn't be here."

"What have you done?" Her voice was even, emotionless.

"Why are you here?"

"She's with him. You shouldn't have allowed that."

He recalled hours, days of useless conversations with her, when he tried convincing her to stay out of the senator's life.

Always the monotone voice. He'd grown to hate it. "I allowed nothing."

"She's with him in California."

"Of course she's with him. Do you think Rebecca Blesser is going to disappear just because I ask her to? Do you think I like the idea that she's made friends with Thommy? I couldn't control that. It was the last thing I thought he'd do. I thought if he ever got into a situation where Rebecca came looking for him he'd come straight to me, and I'd be able to take care of it. He didn't do that."

"They should not be together in Los Angeles. I couldn't stay there."

"You should not have gone to Los Angeles in the first place, and you should have stayed completely away from Thommy. But since you were unable to do that, you should have disappeared the first moment Rebecca Blesser turned up in the magazine. You should have disappeared and left Thommy alone, left Rebecca Blesser alone, and left me to my life." The judge put the cigar back in his mouth and closed his eyes. He knew nothing he could say in the way of reason would matter to her. The only thing that would matter was a conversation he'd had earlier in the day with Alan Webster, and he decided to wait to see how far she would push before he told her about it. Judge Ely lifted the snifter and took a solid slug of cognac.

"I am good for Thomas," she said.

He waved his cigar but did not respond. In the darkness the judge could see only Elizabeth's form blocking the door. It would serve no purpose to see her eyes, anyway, he knew. Those eyes were impenetrable, locked away in a world of her own making; he'd seen eyes like that hundreds of times in people who had stood before him in court.

"Don't tell me you are good for Thomas," he said. "I don't want to hear that from you."

"I'm good for him," she repeated. "And I was good for his father."

"I don't plan to sit here listening to this." He felt the weight of his flesh upon his bones and braced his arms against the crush of the past. A man became memory after his death, the judge believed, and the memories of a life led in public were shaped by the records left behind. This woman was not part of those public records, and existed now only as a vague mention to the few who connected her with the senator; in time those mentions, too, would fade like light with no destination. It was as if Elizabeth knew that, and needed Ghost to be a mirror to give her life. It was the judge and now, too, Rebecca Blesser who could prevent that.

"What has Rebecca Blesser told Thomas?"

"That you were his father's mistress. That she is your daughter. Someone at her magazine who was around in the old days put her onto you. Senator Wells decided to speak with her. She even found a former neighbor of yours in Chicago. And, unfortunately, all of this comes at a time when Thommy is ready to talk to somebody about his father." The judge felt his heart palpitating, perspiration fell from his forehead. "I told Rebecca that she was not your daughter, but I didn't tell her why. I want time to provide her with an acceptable answer. Something that will allow her to get on with her life. But you can be sure she'll investigate whatever I tell her. And since Rebecca is your invention, the truth about her birth simply makes the senator appear to have participated in a most undesirable activity. Which is not a legacy I want left for Thommy. I won't be in much of a position to defend the senator to his son, because my credibility will be down someplace equal to yours. That is not a position I want to find myself in, and I've yet to decide how to resolve it. The truth is bad for both of us, isn't it? But Rebecca Blesser is not going to go away."

"I'm not interested in Rebecca Blesser. She's not my daughter."

"On paper you did an excellent job of making it appear that she is. I'm forced to explain this to Thommy, because he is *with* Rebecca. Do you understand what I am saying?"

"I won't allow that to happen."

"You don't have any choice. Thommy isn't a fifteen-year-old kid shooting baskets anymore. When I saw him this afternoon I was talking to someone I didn't really know. He's outgrown us. I never wanted you in Thommy's life, and sitting here I hate myself for not stopping you two years ago. You got yourself that job knowing damn well it was insane for you to work for Thommy, and knowing damn well I'd stop it when I could. I protected you because I had to protect Thommy. I've allowed you to live out your madness while I've tried to think of a way to put an end to it. But Rebecca Blesser's done that for me. All I can do for the senator at this point in my life is provide the truth to his son in the most acceptable form that I can. What else is there for me to do? I can't protect you any longer, and you certainly can't protect me. So I want you to disappear, again, and completely. I'll help you. And you know I'm the only person in the world who would have any interest in helping you, and then only because I don't want to see you again."

The judge finished off the cognac and put the snifter down on the table.

"I'm not going to leave him. I am good for Thomas."

"Are you listening to me? I am going to meet with Thommy and I am going to tell him what happened, because I don't have a better choice at the moment. Rebecca won't let go of this, and neither will Thommy. And *I* won't leave them in anyone's hands but mine. I'll deal with the devil when I die but I'll do what I have to do while I've still got the chance. What you can do is disappear. People do it successfully all the time. Thommy knows nothing about you. If you simply disappear it will make it easier for him. He won't have to know you were ever in his life."

"I won't leave him. He is my son."

"That I *won't* listen to!"

Judge Ely tried rising from his chair, but his heart pounded and his legs were weak; he felt sharp pains in his head and chest, and he fought to take a full breath. Elizabeth had started in the final months before the senator's death to refer to Ghost as her son. She had said this to the senator and when the senator sent the judge to deal with her, she repeated it again and again to him. The frustration of those final months flooded the judge's brain as he sat trapped by his weak body. Elizabeth had demanded the senator leave his wife, threatening that she would go to the press with Rebecca's birth certificate. God knows what she would have told the press, the judge thought, and even with a shred of truth she could be convincing. The campaign would have been over. After the senator's death Elizabeth disappeared for some months from the judge's life, then he began hearing from her by telephone, calling him to say that Ghost was her son. That was when he began to see the depth of her madness. For eight years she was silent. Then two years ago she resurfaced, and this time in Ghost's life.

"You should have simply stayed away," the judge said. "I have reasons for doing what I've done. You don't. I can't crawl into your head and figure out what you're thinking, because I've sat in courtrooms long enough to know that sometimes that simply isn't possible. And if your reasons aren't comprehensible to me, then you simply don't have reasons. That's the way the law works. You leave, and I'll help. You don't, and I'll stop you."

"You will tell Thomas nothing, and you will do nothing." Elizabeth spoke in her monotone, as if there was a voice in her head that spoke and her body was merely a vehicle for sound.

"I'm not that foolish."

"I'm the one who's good for Thomas. How long is he going to believe Rebecca? She'll leave."

Pain swept through the judge's head, then centered itself in the center of his brain. Perspiration dripped from every pore of his body.

"The madness is over. You'd better understand that. It's out of my hands and I certainly wouldn't leave it in yours. I've taken steps to ensure that Thommy knows what's true, regardless of me."

"Now you're lying."

"I don't have to lie." He began to say something else, but his words came out slurred. He tried to stand, and managed to get himself halfway up before falling back and blacking out.

Elizabeth reached for the snifter, then realized her reason for doing so did not exist, if what the judge had just told her was true. In fact, at the moment she could not think of a reason to exist at all.

Opry heard the gazebo's screen door slam shut, and waited the usual thirty seconds for the judge to open the kitchen door. When a minute passed, she sat up in bed. When two minutes passed, she put on her robe and went outside to look for him.

4

"Here's where we are," Ghost said, pointing to a spot on the map that was spread across the bed in Radio's room. "Now let me get a more detailed map." Ghost returned with a Thomas Guide and a bag. He put the bag on the floor next to the bed.

"Okay," Ghost said, "show me on the map where you used to live and where your school is."

Radio found Acama Street and pointed it out to Ghost, then found the junior high school that he attended.

"I'm pretty sure it was my father watching me play basketball after school that day."

"It could have been."

"I'm pretty sure."

Ghost nodded.

"I'm going to ask him again."

"You'll get a chance."

"And I want to show him the pictures of where I want to go."

"From the magazine?"

"Yes." Radio reached into his pack and pulled out the *National Geographic* pages.

"I've got a little present for you."

"What?"

Ghost brought the bag up to the bed and handed Radio a brightly wrapped box. "For you."

Radio tore the paper off and opened the box.

It was a camera.

"Man, that's great!" Radio said.

"It's got the flash and all that, so you can take pictures inside, outside, anywhere. You like pictures so much I thought you should have a camera and take some of your own."

"God, it's great. Thanks. Do you know how to work it?"

"It's a no-brainer. Everything's automatic. We'll fool around with it in the morning. Right now you should go to sleep. Let's put this back in the box."

They repacked the camera in its Styrofoam casing and set it on the nightstand.

Ghost began to pick up the map books, but Radio put his hands on them.

"Can I look at these?"

"How about in the morning? It's late."

"Just for a couple of minutes."

"Okay. Three minutes and turn your own light out. It's after midnight already."

"Are you going out?"

"Tonight?"

Radio nodded.

"No," Ghost said. "I'm going to bed. My room's on the floor above you. If you need me just come up the stairs. The hall light's always on."

Radio pointed to Acama Street on the map. "How far is it to there?"

"Twenty minutes by car."

"All my stuff is there."

"We'll look into that."

"They won't let me stay at my house, will they?"

"I don't know what the situation is going to be about your house. You can't stay there on your own."

"But all my stuff's there."

"We can get your stuff."

"Can we go tomorrow?"

"We'll try and go there tomorrow if you want to. We can get whatever you want. Just remember, going to that place isn't going to be the same without your mom there. In fact, you might not like it at all."

"I have this clock that I want to get. And a sweatshirt."

"We'll get them."

Radio looked again at the map. He pointed to a tiny green area. "I think that's where my mom is. That's the place where she's buried. I just know where the place is but I don't know where they buried her. They don't let you watch."

"We can take some flowers to her grave, if you like. You think about it."

Ghost couldn't recall what his father's grave looked like. His mother's was in a cemetery in France near St. Paul de Vence. His father's was in a small cemetery near Nippersink, where there was a Galvin family plot. Ghost had gone there once after the funeral but had felt frozen in thought and feeling as he stood by the grave, unable to think of what he wanted to say.

"I'm going to get into trouble for that church," Radio said, bringing Ghost back from his thoughts of his father.

"We're going to have to talk to the police, or the juvenile authority, or whatever they call it. We're going to have to do something about it."

"That priest was a liar. He said my mother killed herself, and so they couldn't bury her in the place where Karen wanted her to be buried. He didn't even know my mother and he was talking about her. That's what I hated. He didn't even know her."

"You don't have to worry about what he says."

"I hated him."

"I can tell your mother was good from watching you, so don't worry about the priest."

"Is he going to arrest me?"

"I don't think it's going to be that. We'll work something out. Get some sleep."

Ghost touched Radio on the head, then left the room.

Radio fell asleep with the light on and maps spread like blankets across his bed.

5

Elizabeth stopped the car on the small bridge at Nippersink that separated Lake Tombeau from Lake Richardson. She parked and stood against the railing facing Lake Tombeau and Nippersink's lodge. The lake looked dark in the pre-dawn light. Once, during the single summer she worked here thirty years ago, they attempted a drop-line measuring of the lake, but ran out of line at six hundred feet. A thin mist rose from the lake and blended with the first signs of sunlight. Busboys emerged from the lodge to begin setting the patio above the pool for breakfast. The fans above the kitchen started whirring. Elizabeth watched the busboys crank open the umbrellas over the tables. Other than new paint, the lodge looked the same to her now as it had thirty years ago. She expected it to, because she viewed her photographs of it often, and believed once a place was photographed, some part of it was permanently hers—she possessed it and controlled it by holding the image in her hands. She recalled sitting as a child in the attic of the home where she lived with her foster parents. On a shelf above the dormer window she kept a metal box she had found there, filled with faded black-and-white photographs of her real parents, given to the foster parents along with the child. One afternoon she found the photographs, and brought one to show her mother, telling her she'd found it in the pages of a book. Her mother explained to Elizabeth who the woman in the photograph was—Elizabeth was two years old when she was turned over to the foster parents—and Elizabeth never told her mother she had the entire box. Standing on the bridge at Nippersink, looking out at the dark, deep lake, Elizabeth tried remembering why she hated her foster parents. But she could not. In fact, she could hardly remember them at all. She thought of them standing together in the kitchen of their house, but they were faceless. When she disappeared from home, at fifteen, she took only a few clothes and the box of photographs. She never tried to find her real parents and felt no desire to know them; she was more interested in the photographs, and spent nights in her room spreading the photos across her bed and falling into a trancelike state in which she lived another life with the people in the pictures. They were captives of her mind and heart and never escaped the bounds of their metal box.

Across the lake, a fisherman cranked his small outboard. But in the silence of the early morning the sound carried across the lake. Elizabeth saw the speck of a boat leave its dock and head in her direction. She heard the slap of sandals on wood as a young fisherman walked out on the wooden pier that jutted from the beach below the lodge. He set his tackle box on a chair, uncorked his hook, and baited it with a bread ball. The boy cast his line and the weights plunked down in the water, supported by the red-and-white plastic bobber. Elizabeth thought about the photograph of Ghost and the senator that she'd moved to the center of the vanity table in the Nippersink house, the picture that showed them standing at the end of this pier with their fishing poles and a string of bass. That was the picture she liked, the two of them. And she saw herself in the picture, a presence binding father and son; she was their center, their animator; this was what she believed.

She knew that by now Judge Ely would be dead. I've killed him, she thought, and he believed that he was killing me. However, he'd arranged for Ghost and Rebecca to get the information he wanted them to have; she knew that would be his method of killing her, by removing her from Ghost's life. For two years she'd spent every day in Ghost's house, making his appointments, screening calls, organizing parties, booking travel, decorating his rooms—possessing him while keeping the judge at arm's length. It would be impossible to work there now, or to see him; the judge said he had taken care of that, and she believed him. But she would not surrender Ghost to Rebecca Blesser or to anyone, nor would she surrender his father. I will inhabit them, she thought, opening her purse and removing a note pad and pen. Elizabeth wrote a brief note in her precise script, and addressed the envelope to Ghost at his Beverly Hills home. She pulled a single key from her purse, folded the note around it, and slid it into the envelope. Before getting into her car, she removed her wallet, containing credit cards and driver's license, and dropped it into Lake Tombeau.

She drove to the lodge and bought a stamp from the machine next to the gift shop and dropped the envelope in the slot; she wanted Nippersink's distinctive postmark across the stamp.

Elizabeth next went to the Galvins' home. Her heels clicked on the stone steps as she walked to the front door; she had a key. The recently vacated house still had the sense of Ghost, Rebecca, and Radio about it. Objects were imbued with the afterglow of their presence: a cushiony chair retained the shape of its last visitor, Rebecca; two glass tumblers on a coffee table suggested a conversation between Rebecca and Ghost, comic pages left crumpled on the dining table belonged to Radio. Elizabeth picked through the implied patterns of activity, then began to straighten the house. She fluffed cushions on the chair and couch, brought the glasses into the kitchen, and threw away the newspaper. Chair by chair, she arranged the dining room set to give it symmetry. Wetting a rag, she wiped off the kitchen counter and dropped half-full juice bottles in the trash. Radio's room was in good order, the bed made, curtains drawn, closet closed. Scattered across the top of his dresser were several flat, smooth stones he'd found at the lake; Elizabeth stacked the stones and brushed away the residue.

Ghost's room was disheveled, the nightstand drawers pulled out and left on top of the bed, dresser drawers open, hangers lying on the floor of the closet. She took pleasure in cleaning it, putting it right. When she finished, she stood in the doorway and surveyed her work for several seconds, then went to the master bedroom. A hint of Rebecca's perfume remained in the room; Elizabeth cranked open the window and let the morning breeze float through the screen. Marie Galvin's dresses still hung like old flags in a corner of the closet; Elizabeth pushed them tightly together. Then she sat on the wood-and-wicker chair that faced the vanity and, as she'd done two nights before, carefully slid the glass top from the table and placed it on the bed. She opened her purse and removed the pile of photographs that she had stolen. Elizabeth glanced at the photograph on the table, the one of Ghost and the senator standing on the pier with their fishing poles; she straightened it, then turned to the pile of pictures in her lap. The first showed the senator and Nicole sitting on the back patio of the house flanked by Judge Ely and his wife, with a ten-year-old Ghost perched on the stone wall behind them, basketball in hand. She took a small pair of scissors from her purse and began cutting the photograph. She cut precisely around the senator and around Ghost until the images of the judge, Eleanor, and Nicole, with a final quick snip, fell to the floor. Then she placed the photograph on the table above and to the right of the central one. Next came the family portrait, the one with the senator and Nicole, Marie and Ghost and Ghost's collie; this one required minutes of careful cutting to prepare for the table; Nicole and Marie fell to the floor with the other scraps. In all, she cut seven photographs, arranging them in orbit around the first one. She set the glass down on top of them.

Elizabeth went into the kitchen and drew a glass of water. The house, now more orderly than when she arrived, felt if not comfortable then acceptable. With the chairs straightened, pillows fluffed, glasses washed, stones stacked, the rooms now had the character of theatrical sets before actors bring life to them. She had decorated Ghost's home in Beverly Hills with sparse simplicity, so that she could inhabit the space with her imagination, rather than being confronted by personal objects. Only photographs appealed to her; she believed that they mirrored imagination, and their tangibleness validated what the imagination conceived. She believed that as you photographed someone you snatched from them a part of their soul, and if you photographed them enough you could erase them and re-create them in your own imagination. What is a person if not what you see in him? How can he be anything else to you? For Judge Ely to talk to her about Ghost being a different person from the one they both knew, a new person, was not possible. The judge did not understand that Ghost could only be what she perceived him to be. And if the judge insisted on rupturing her access to him, thus destroying her image, then she would make her vision of him and his father immortal, before anything could be changed.

Taking the glass of water with her, she returned to the bedroom, sat in front of the vanity, and removed a plastic bottle of Percodan from her purse. She swallowed three tablets, then sat motionless, staring at the photographs under the glass. She swallowed three more tablets. The senator smiled at her from the central photograph of the collage. She had last seen him two days before he died. Elizabeth recalled the way he persisted in explaining why he could no longer see her or have any contact with her, and told her that Judge Ely would see that she was taken care of financially. She refused the explanation and the senator had grown angry. She tried telling him that it was not possible for her to leave his life, because he did not exist without her, that in fact he would disappear without her presence. He had not understood that. He understood politics, so she patiently described the disruption in his political life that would result from his abandoning her. The day ended badly, but he said he would talk with her again in two days, before leaving for Denver and the campaign. When he died at Nippersink of a heart attack she was not at all surprised. He disappeared, she thought at the time, as I told him he would.

Elizabeth poured ten Percodan tablets out on the glass tabletop, and took five of them. Her head felt compressed and heavy, as if the fluids in her body were coagulating.

She put the scissors on the table next to the bottle of Percodan. They were sharp stainless steel German scissors that glinted as shafts of sunlight came through the window.

The senator and Ghost, their expressions frozen by the camera, offered their souls to Elizabeth from the circle of photographs, and she centered their images deep within herself, feeling them imprinting themselves on her cells. They existed there and only there and she would keep them free from any other vision.

She took the scissors and punched a hole in the top of her left hand. The pain felt distant, the kind of pain you can watch. Blood dripped from the wound onto the wood floor, landing with a soft splat. Elizabeth took the five remaining pills from the table and swallowed them, then poured a fistful of pills from the bottle into her palm. Dropping them in the glass she drank the pills with the water, and felt herself sinking into a stupor. Images of Ghost and the senator filled her being and she felt herself becoming them, being their breath and their blood, making herself and them immortal. Looking down a last time at the collage of photographs, she lifted the scissors with both hands, the point turned toward her face. Her skin felt like lifeless meat as she ran the sharp point down her forehead, then hovered it over her left eye. She closed her eyes and bit into her lower lip until she tasted blood in her mouth. Elizabeth pressed the point against her eyelid, summoned her strength, and pushed as hard as she could.

14

Steam rose from the brick patio surrounding the pool as water from the lawn sprinklers spilled onto it. Ghost sat on the terrace, reading the paper and keeping an eye on Radio, who was splashing around in the shallow end of the pool.

"Mr. Jamison for you, Mr. Thomas," Magda said, bringing out a tray with coffee and fruit.

"On the phone?"

"No, sir. I just opened the gate for him."

Ghost put down the newspaper and looked at his watch.

Norman Jamison was already walking out to the terrace.

Ghost stood to greet him. "Am I still in the wrong time zone, or are you an hour and a half early?"

"I'm sorry I didn't call," Jamison said. "I did try the office line but the service is on. I wanted to come over in person."

"What's wrong?" Ghost asked, looking at Jamison's strained expression.

Jamison sat down. "I'm sorry to be the one to have to tell you that Davis Ely died last night."

"Norman . . ."

"At his home in Lake Geneva."

Ghost looked at Jamison, staring at him as though the news could not be true.

Jamison nodded his head.

"I saw him yesterday morning."

"He passed away last night. I'm deeply sorry, Ghost. I know what he was in your life."

"Christ, Norman," Ghost said, staring straight ahead.

"A Sheriff Baines reached me through our service half an hour ago. Evidently, he's a friend of the family . . ."

"Yes."

"They tried reaching you earlier but the service picked up." The phone had been ringing since six in the morning, but Ghost left it to the service, waiting for Miss Dupree to come in and handle the messages.

"I don't see this happening. I don't see it."

"I should tell you that there is a coroner's investigation," Jamison said. "A Detective Shepherd called the office to ask for your number. There seems to be some confusion as to whether the judge suffered a heart attack or stroke or what. They want to rule out the possibility that he took his own life. As you said, you spoke with the judge yesterday morning, and they wanted to talk to you about that. I don't have all the facts. Baines called me again just before I came over here and told me he would handle things directly with you. He said he would call you."

"Suicide?" Ghost didn't believe it; he did not want to consider such a betrayal by the judge.

"They're checking it out."

"Was there a note?"

"Baines didn't say if there was."

"He wouldn't commit suicide, Norman. It wasn't in him."

"I'm sure not."

"I'm telling you."

"I believe you."

He stood and walked over to the terrace wall and sat on it. The lawn glistened from the soaking. Ghost had dreamed about Judge Ely the previous night. In the dream they were at Nippersink in the lodge's dining room. Ghost sat with Rebecca and Radio, the judge was at another table with Eleanor and several people Ghost did not recognize. They were all there enjoying the Friday-night fish fry. But it was as if the judge and Ghost hardly knew each other. There was brief eye contact, and then just an awareness of the other's presence. The dream had faded into another dream, but when Ghost awoke he thought of Judge Ely and the dream and felt again the strangeness of it, the detachment, as though the judge had purposely separated himself from Ghost, become someone else, the way people do when they know they are going to die.

Magda arrived with a tray of coffee.

"A family friend of Mr. Galvin passed away yesterday," Jamison told her quietly.

She set the tray down and blessed herself.

"Will you get Miss Dupree on the phone for me, Magda?" Ghost said. "I have to start making arrangements."

Magda went to the kitchen to place the call. When she returned she said apologetically, "The machine answers."

"Jesus, Norman," Ghost said, "she's missed work once in two years, now I can't get her on the phone. We haven't heard from her in days."

"Where does she live?"

"Right here in Beverly Hills. On Charleville, just down the street from Jimmy's Restaurant."

"I'll call Lee Davidson at the police department, and he'll have a couple of the guys over there in two minutes."

Ghost waved a hand. "Don't start with the police or I'll have the press calling me five minutes later."

"You stay put," Jamison said, "and I'll ride over there myself. In the meantime, I'll have one of our secretaries here in ten minutes to handle things for you."

"Magda will give you Miss Dupree's address."

They shook hands, then Jamison left. Ghost stood stunned, thinking of the expression on the judge's face when they had talked yesterday; the judge kept looking past Ghost to the horizon with sad, weary eyes, as if he saw his own death written on the sky. The eyes had looked like those of his father on that last day at Nippersink.

2

Jamison arrived at the ivy-covered, two-story apartment building where Miss Dupree lived. The Spanish-style building had a cobblestone courtyard with a wishing well in the center. He knocked on 2B and tried the buzzer. No answer. He located the manager's apartment and received no response. As he walked down the stairs and through the courtyard, Jamison spotted an elderly woman working in the garden. Short and fleshy, she wore a turquoise-colored terry-cloth sunsuit and purple-lensed sunglasses the size of saucers.

"Would you know where I could find the building's manager?" Jamison asked her.

She adjusted the enormous straw hat that shaded her from the sun. "My husband's the manager. He's out at the moment."

Jamison presented his card and explained the situation. He asked if she would open the apartment.

"Under the circumstances, I suppose I should," she said. "Although, I must tell you, Mr. Jamison, that Miss Dupree left a few days ago and I haven't seen her since. I was working right here in the garden when she left. I'm the only one in the building she talks to, I think. And I'm sure I'm the only one who knows she works for the basketball player. He must pay her well. The rent isn't cheap here."

"Did she say where she was going?"

"No. It wouldn't be like her to tell me that. I'm always out in the garden, and our conversations are usually brief. She had a suitcase; it was obvious she was going someplace. Miss Dupree isn't one to travel, either."

Jamison said, "May we have a look in the apartment anyway?"

"Well, you're an attorney. I suppose if you say it's all right, then it's all right."

The woman went to her own apartment for the key and met Jamison at the door of 2B.

"I'm sure everything's in order," the woman said, unlocking the door. "It's a furnished one-bedroom. We couldn't ask for a better tenant. Always pays her rent early and in cash. She's always dressed so neatly, any time of day or night."

They walked through the living room into the kitchen. Morning light poured through the greenhouse window and reflected off the white counter tiles. Folded dish towels hung from a rack next to the spotless sink.

"I don't think this kitchen has ever been used," Jamison said.

"Oh, that's the way she is. She's had me over for coffee once or twice. She always keeps the place like this."

"Really?"

"Oh, yes. Neat as a pin. She gets more mail than any of the tenants. Lots of newspapers and magazines, dozens of them. But every Saturday morning when the recycling truck comes by she has them stacked and bound with twine, ready to go. No mess."

"She's a reader?"

"She clips them. I've seen the stacks when they're out there for the recyclers. All the papers and magazines have been clipped. I assumed it has something to do with her job."

The manager's wife followed Jamison to the bedroom.

He stopped at the foot of the bed and surveyed the room. Each nightstand supported a lamp. There was a clock radio on one side, a telephone on the other. The dresser top was clear except for a brush and mirror set and two crystal perfume bottles, both empty. Jamison opened the closet and saw suits and dresses, all in dark colors, hung in neat succession.

"Does she really live here?"

"Of course she does, Mr. Jamison."

"What's strange is that I don't smell anything. Perfume, air freshener, clean clothes, dirty clothes, food, *some*thing. This place has no scent. I don't *smell* anything."

"Well, she's just very clean, I suppose."

"What about friends? Does she have many visitors?"

The manager's wife, still busy inspecting the room, stopped to consider the question. "I don't recall her having visitors, no. She keeps very long hours with her job. He must pay her well."

3

Mrs. Warren, the Galvins' Nippersink neighbor, learned about Judge Ely's death early in the morning from Edwina Conrad, who had heard about it at the lodge.

"Do you think Thomas knows?" Mrs. Conrad asked.

"Well, I've no idea. I think he's still here. There's a car in the driveway. I'm looking out the window right at it. I didn't see them last night though."

Mrs. Warren was shaken by the news and forgot she had water boiling for eggs. The pan frothed over, and she told Edwina she would have to call her back. She cleaned up the stove top while answering the phone, which rang constantly as the news spread around Nippersink.

Shortly after noon, she decided to walk next door to see Ghost and share condolences.

"Ian," she called, summoning her Jack Russell from his nap. The terrier raced to the front door and waited there, tail wagging.

"Don't go running off," she said, opening the door. "We're just going next door, and then coming home." The dog bolted down the path, up the lawn shared by the Galvins, then back to Mrs. Warren. She walked up the Galvins' driveway to the front of the house. Her cats followed Ian at a safe distance.

Mrs. Warren reached the Galvins' door, and pushed the bell, even though the door was slightly open.

The ring echoed in the house.

"Anyone there?" she asked, leaning her head to the opening.

Ian bounced up behind her, then shot between her legs into the house.

"Damn, Ian! Come *here!*"

She heard the dog scrambling around on the hardwood floor, so she pushed open the front door and went in after him.

"Thomas? It's Mrs. Warren from next door. Anyone home?"

All she heard was the ticking of Ian's nails on the wooden floors.

"Ian, come here this instant," she commanded. But the dog had already gone into the hallway; he barked, then went silent.

Mrs. Warren called again and again, but the dog did not respond. She poked her head in the hallway, then heard Ian sniffing around in the master bedroom. Reluctantly she went in to retrieve him.

Ian, his stub tail sticking straight up, sniffed the dead form of Elizabeth Folger, who lay at the foot of the vanity table, her face covered in a glutinous paste of blood, flesh, and pieces of eye.

4

Ghost brought Rebecca to the downstairs den, sat on a corner of the old mahogany desk that had belonged to his father, and told her about Judge Ely's death. Rebecca leaned against Ghost and wrapped her arms around him.

She felt surprised and scared. "How did he die?"

"They don't know if it was a stroke or heart attack or what. They haven't ruled out suicide."

"My god, I'm sorry. I'm very sorry." Rebecca backed away and sat down on the leather couch.

"Right now I don't feel sorry," Ghost said loudly. "I feel angry. Fucking angry."

"I pushed too hard. I shouldn't have pushed everyone so hard."

"You asked questions. I asked the judge the same questions and a few questions of my own. That's not pushing anybody. He looked me in the eye and told me my father didn't kill himself, and he told me my father had nothing to do with you being born. And as much as I believe him, I keep thinking about how he looked past me to the sky, like he was planning to carry some secret to the grave. He may have been thinking about something entirely different than my father dying and this crap with Elizabeth Folger, but that's what we were talking about and that's what I think was in his head when he was looking past me. So that's what sticks in my head right now. The last time I talked with my father we talked about basketball and me not playing, but the judge told me my dad was thinking about his problems with this fucking woman and not about me at all. But I don't know that. How the fuck am I supposed to know that? If my father or the judge had something they didn't want me to know about, if they thought they were carrying something to the grave, they were so goddamned wrong it makes me want to spit blood. You carry nothing to the grave; you're just leaving whatever it is for somebody else to clean up." He stalked across the room and stood by the window. "This is bad form, right? I'm supposed to be in tears, and I'm sure sooner or later that'll happen. But damn, god*damn* it, I'm angry."

The gate buzzer sounded. Jamison was back from Miss Dupree's apartment. Magda brought him to the den.

"Rebecca, Norman Jamison," Ghost said, not moving from his position at the window.

"We met briefly at the party," Jamison said, shaking Rebecca's hand.

"So what did you find?" Ghost asked.

"Nothing."

"She wasn't there?"

"No. She's gone. The apartment manager's wife said Miss Dupree left with a suitcase early in the morning a few days ago."

"That doesn't make sense."

"That's what the woman told me."

"She called in sick."

"What about a vacation?"

"She doesn't take vacations. I've given her tickets to take vacations but she won't use them."

"Well, she's gone. The woman I spoke with seemed to know Dupree. I took a walk through the apartment. Actually, it didn't look like anyone ever lived there, the place was so neat. There were clothes in the closet and things like that, but it looked like a showroom."

Ghost buzzed for Magda, who appeared moments later in the doorway.

"Did Miss Dupree leave us *any* notes or messages?"

"Just the message on the service that she wasn't feeling well."

"But you didn't actually speak with her?"

"No."

"Mr. Jamison just came back from her apartment and says that she's out of town."

"I don't know." Magda absently touched the silver crucifix she wore around her neck.

Jamison asked Ghost, "You've never had a problem with her?"

"You know I haven't, Norman. She runs the place like it's hers; she takes care of everything for me."

"What about money?"

"What about it?"

"Did she handle any money for you?"

"Just the household account. Petty cash."

"Then I give up. I had Gail read the file to me—she's my office manager, and she's the one who hired Dupree. Gail said the employment references all signed off fine during the screening process. Does she have some friends we can call?"

"I wouldn't know who they are."

"The manager's wife told me Dupree didn't have visitors that she knew of."

Rebecca sat forward on the couch, listening to Jamison and Ghost talk about Miss Dupree, and felt the chill of recollection. She thought of Mrs. Towsley describing Elizabeth Folger's spotless apartment, the lack of visitors.

Ghost walked back to the desk and sat on the edge. "I don't know what she did or who she saw when she walked out of here. She worked long hours and that was that."

"Evidently she liked newspapers and magazines. The lady told me Dupree subscribes to dozens of them, and keeps clippings, like a hobby."

"No idea what that's about."

Rebecca stood and moved to the bay window, where Ghost had been. She pictured the piles of clipped newspapers and magazines that Mrs. Towsley described Elizabeth dumping down the garbage chute. The similarity between that and the person Jamison was describing made Rebecca feel sick.

Radio bounded into the room, spinning a basketball on one finger. Magda was close behind. "You come with me now. Mr. Thomas is busy."

"Do you want to shoot around?"

"Maybe later we can," Ghost said.

Magda tugged at Radio's T-shirt and pulled him out of the room.

"Could you have a copy of Dupree's file sent here?" Rebecca asked Jamison, who looked to Ghost for approval, which came as a nod.

"I'll have it sent right over," Jamison said. "I don't know what else to tell you at this point. We really don't have a reason to go to the police."

"For chrissake," Ghost said, shaking his head and letting his voice trail off.

The temporary secretary sent over from Jamison's office knocked on the den door. Jamison looked at her, displeased at the interruption.

"I'm sorry," she said, "but I have a Sheriff Baines from Nippersink calling and he says it's urgent that he speak with you or Mr. Galvin."

"Be my guest," Ghost said to Jamison.

"I'll take it in the living room."

Rebecca joined Ghost at the desk once Jamison had left the room.

"When he was describing Dupree he was describing Elizabeth Folger," Rebecca said. Her tone did not sound speculative.

Ghost's mind felt clogged with thoughts of the judge and with Dupree's disappearance, but the mention of Elizabeth Folger cut to the center of him and summoned his deepest feelings of frustration; she seemed rooted at the epicenter of his doubt about his father and the judge, and though he saw no connection between her and Dupree, Rebecca's mention of them in the same sentence disturbed him.

"What do you mean?"

"That was the way Mrs. Towsley described Elizabeth Folger to me—the apartment, no friends, the newspapers and the clippings—it was the same kind of person. I'm not trying to be ridiculous. It just kind of scares me."

"What are we talking about here?"

"What do you know about her?"

"Jamison's office found her. They sent three women for me to talk to, and I liked Dupree because she didn't say much and she's older; I figured she'd keep her mind on business. And I was right. It's been a fucked-up day but you're going off the building with this Elizabeth Folger stuff. Dupree used to take all my calls, she talked with the judge plenty of times. You don't think he'd know it if I had fucking whoever-she-is working for me?"

"What if he did know," Rebecca asked, "and didn't tell you about it?"

5

"Want me to show you something?" Radio asked Magda, as she walked him out to the terrace.

"What's that?"

"I'll show you right over here."

"Mr. Thomas wants you to go play your baskets."

"I will, but look at this."

He took her around to the side of the house where he opened a box that contained the controls for the automatic water system.

"You don't play with that. That's not for you."

"I looked at this when the sprinklers went on this morning. I know how it works."

She hadn't known the box was there. "That's not something for you."

He looked at the cluster of dials in the control box. "It looks like the airplane I was in."

"The gardener, he's working with men in the front yard. He

doesn't want you playing with this. Go play your baskets now."

"I think you move that to make it work." Radio pushed a button labeled Master Reset, then turned a timer labeled Front for ten minutes.

"Don't touch that. You come with me now." She grabbed him by the T-shirt and pulled him back to the yard. "You're like my grandchildren, you have to be touching everything."

"Want me to show you something else?"

"You want to get me in trouble is what you're going to do."

"I saw all the little TVs," Radio said, standing by the pool. "Mr. Thomas has lots of TVs. He never watches them."

"We're on TV right now."

Radio pointed to a small video camera mounted on a corner of the house, aimed at the terrace.

"That's for the security," Magda said.

"There's one, too," Radio answered, pointing to another camera, locked onto the fence by the tennis court. "I walked around this morning. There're cameras all over the place."

"They use them for the security."

"I know where they go."

"You don't touch them or Mr. Thomas is going to be very mad with you."

"I didn't touch them, but I know where they go."

Magda looked at him warily, wondering what he'd been up to. "Did you play with those cameras?"

"No. I promise. But I'll show you where they go."

The security system was Miss Dupree's province; Magda left it to her and the guard who came by at night.

Radio walked up the steps of the guest house and went inside. The temporary secretary had gone into the main house to see Jamison and Ghost, so Miss Dupree's office was empty. Magda caught up with Radio, then stopped at the threshold of the office; it was her practice not to go into Miss Dupree's office, and the conversations between Miss Dupree and Magda tended to be limited to household business.

"I think you should come out of there," Magda said to Radio.

"Okay, but look . . ." He sat down in the chair behind the desk and nodded toward the cabinets to the right of the desk. "That's where they are."

"You've been snooping. She don't like it if she find you here."

He hopped out of the chair and pushed open the cabinet,

306

sensing that he had Magda's curiosity overriding her irritation. There were four monitors, each changing pictures every ten seconds. The cameras covered the front gate, all entrances to the house, the yards, surrounding walls, and the garden area off Ghost's office in the back of the guest house. "You can push these buttons and change the pictures," Radio said, pushing a bank of buttons on the desk.

Magda had no idea that the security system so completely covered the home's exterior and grounds, like wide-angle windows.

"Now I know where you were when I looked for you for breakfast," Magda said.

Radio pushed a button that stopped one of the monitors on the front yard. They could see four men working in the gardens and on the lawns. Then all the men jumped, as if they'd heard a loud sound, and began running.

Magda stepped forward and stared at the monitor. "What's happening there?"

"They're getting wet," Radio said. He grabbed his basketball off the desk and started for the door.

She looked at the monitor, on which the men were just running out of frame, their shirts soaking from the sprinklers. Magda stifled a laugh and called after Radio. "Don't let *her* catch you in here!"

"Who?" he said, running outside to the safety of the basketball court.

6

The story of the suicide at Ghost Galvin's house in Nippersink broke nationally minutes after Jamison took the call from Sheriff Baines. The identity of the woman remained unknown for a couple of hours, until the rental car in the driveway was traced to Miss Dupree, and the fingerprints from Dupree's employment file were matched with those of the body. Dupree's next of kin, listed as an aunt in San Francisco, appeared to be, so far as the San Francisco authorities could ascertain, a fabrication. No police record existed for Miss Dupree, not even a traffic ticket. Los Angeles detectives, working in cooperation with Wisconsin police, turned up little on her, other than two modest bank accounts and copies of income tax returns. A check on her home telephone revealed only calls to restaurants and businesses, all of which appeared to be made on Ghost's behalf.

Packs of reporters and camera crews clustered outside the gates of the Galvin estate, waiting for Ghost to make a statement about the apparent suicide of his secretary; the gruesome circumstances of her death had not yet been revealed to the press, only that she died of a Percodan overdose. The police were also making no comment about a possible link between the deaths of Dupree and Judge Ely, pending further investigation.

Ghost spent most of the afternoon on the telephone with the police, though he didn't have much to say to them. He answered questions about Dupree but did not provide them with any suggestion of a motive. A detective questioned Ghost about his relationship with Rebecca Blesser, who they knew had been with him at Nippersink, and theorized that perhaps Dupree harbored secret romantic attachments to Ghost and found Rebecca a threat. The detective said he'd seen such scenarios before. "I have no idea," was Ghost's response to the theory.

Ghost had asked Rebecca to listen in on the conversations with the police, and when the detective described the pile of cuttings from photographs found in the bedroom, Rebecca closed her eyes and quietly replaced the phone on its cradle. She thought of her last night at Nippersink when she'd heard noises and had gone into the basement, hoping to come face to face with Elizabeth—to confront her and take whatever would come. But Rebecca felt that if she could have looked Elizabeth in the eye that night at Nippersink she could have undertood her, and whatever Rebecca feared to find in Elizabeth could be dispelled by understanding. Elizabeth avoided that confrontation, Rebecca thought, and erased herself, leaving behind no discernible past, only a body with the eyes torn out.

"What would we tell if we tell them anything?" Ghost asked, sitting with Rebecca in the open-air gazebo near the tennis court. "That we think my father's mistress changed her name and worked as my secretary for two years? Both people who could answer the question are dead. I want to wake up from this nightmare."

"I think it was Elizabeth, and I think she killed the judge because he was going to help us. If that's what he was going to do."

"Then why did she kill herself?" Ghost felt numb from the events of the day, but looking across the lawn he had no desire to go into the house. It was not that the house contained objects that reminded him of the judge or his family or of Miss Dupree; the lack of personal things was what bothered him now. Miss Dupree had decorated the house simply, like a nice hotel. The anonymity of it reminded him of her anonymity, the way she had entered his life silently and moved through it with quiet efficiency, all the while watching him with a head full of thoughts Ghost hadn't known about. He sat in the gazebo thinking that if he sold this house he'd take his clothes, his father's desk, and the painting of the cornfield that hung in the living room—those were the only things he felt belonged to him.

"Why didn't she just disappear the way she did after my father died?" Ghost continued. "Or why didn't she show up here like she had nothing to do with anything. If she was crazy enough to kill the judge, then she was crazy enough to turn up here again."

"I don't expect to follow her reasoning," Rebecca replied, remembering the detective's description of the way the family photographs had been clipped. On the floor they'd found the parts of the photographs containing the senator's wife and mother, as well as cutouts of the judge. "I always wanted to find my mother and have her reveal a secret about my future, just by seeing who she was and what she was like," Rebecca said. "What's always scared me is the idea of finding my mother and discovering madness, or seeing the worst part of me full blown. And now it seems that that's what I'd have to look forward to."

"You're jumping from doubt right to the worst case."

"Anything's better than living with doubt."

"Are you talking about us, or yourself?"

"Both."

"I won't accept doubt," Ghost said. "If Elizabeth Folger thought by killing herself that every time I'd think of my father I'd also think of her, she was wrong. I'm sure she thought I'd close up and push you as far away as possible, but that's not what's going to happen. In that sense she underestimated me; from what she knew of me, I'm not surprised."

7

At ten-thirty Jamison emerged from the guest house and sat with Ghost and Rebecca in the gazebo.

"Thank you, Norman," Ghost said, offering him his hand. "You got us through today."

They could hear the ball bouncing on the court where Radio was practicing.

"I'll be back about eight. You should get some sleep if you can. Don't stay up all night."

"We'll get some sleep."

"There's a couple of things I need to mention, because I have to deal with them first thing tomorrow. As I've told you, the police find absolutely no next of kin, or anybody, for Dupree. The state will handle her burial unless . . ."

"I'll pay for it. Arrange something in Chicago."

"It'll be taken care of. The other thing I wanted to talk to you about is the boy, Radio. I wish that it could wait but I've been pushing ahead with the guardianship issue so the authorities know that he's here and they want to talk to him."

"Who wants to talk to him?"

"The police need to talk to him about the church fire. The social worker assigned to the case and the guy from the juvenile authority want to talk to him."

Ghost turned his head toward the darkened part of the yard, thinking he heard something.

"Can it wait until after the funeral?" he then said to Jamison. "I don't want to drag Radio back to Chicago for that, but I don't like the idea of them messing with him when I'm not here."

"I'll be here to handle it. I've been trying to push everything along, so when what happened today hits the eleven o'clock news tonight, I know I'll have a call from the social worker first thing in the morning. We have to be absolutely cooperative with them to get what we want."

"They're not going to come here and want to haul the kid off someplace, are they? I mean, I'll take him with me if I have to."

"That wouldn't be a good idea; I think it's best if I deal with them right now."

"Okay."

Ghost turned in the other direction, closed his eyes, and listened.

"What's wrong?" Rebecca asked.

Ghost realized what he heard was not a sound but lack of sound; Radio had stopped shooting baskets.

"Radio?"

"Yeah," Radio replied, from somewhere out on the lawn.

"Come here, will ya?"

Radio appeared out of the darkness and Ghost pulled him over to the couch and sat him down.

"Don't be sneaking around. It gives me the creeps."

"I was just going into the house."

"Well, wait for us. We're all going now."

They walked Jamison to his car, then went inside, though none of them felt like sleeping.

15

Nobody in Chicago wanted to leave his air-conditioned home or office on that burning July day, but Holy Name Cathedral was packed for Judge Ely's funeral. Though the services were scheduled for nine A.M., the arrival and seating of an overflow crowd delayed the start by forty-five minutes. By then the temperature was ninety-six degrees, and the humidity, too, hit the nineties. Outside, dozens of photographers and news crews recorded the notable mourners. A video cameraman passed out. Portable fans were dispersed throughout the church; the fans droned beneath the solemn dirge coming from the pipe organ. Programs with pages of hymns and recitations were distributed to the mourners upon entering the cathedral. From the loft, choir members watched hundreds of the white programs waving back and forth in the pews below.

Cardinal Flannery entered the sanctuary preceded by two dozen monsignors and priests and a dozen altar boys—a phalanx of vestments and folded hands that fanned out across the altar. He beckoned the congregation to be seated, and wisely suggested they remain seated throughout the ceremony.

The prayers, hymns, and blessings commenced, directed toward the flag-draped casket at the foot of the altar. Thick incense floated from the altar, down to the first few pews, then up to the cathedral's great arches, carrying words from the succession of speakers who addressed the congregation. Finally, the cardinal spoke.

The Cardinal looked old and angry, his voice deep and sure, the voice of a man used to being listened to.

"If a man's earthly life is measured in terms of those lives he has touched, then Davis Ely achieved temporal greatness, for he touched many lives, helped many people, and your presence here today confirms the magnitude of his works. He devoted the majority of his life to public service, spending more than thirty years on the bench in vigilance over the rights and freedoms of the citizens of this state. He was a judge. It was his duty to listen to the facts, to weigh evidence, and then to make decisions. That, in and of itself, is a courageous act, because it is God who is the final judge, who has the final word, and the judgments we make on earth will be reflected when we seek our ultimate peace, cradled in the hands of the Lord. It takes immense courage to be a judge, because some decisions will be popular and others unpopular, yet the good judge must not be swayed by momentary passions or personal opinions. Passions and opinions are testing grounds for us mortals. Society selects certain people and asks them to pass judgment on matters most of us, if we privately examine ourselves, would rather leave to others to decide. A judge shapes futures by designating what information juries are allowed to consider. That is a burden and responsibility few want to carry in life. Davis Ely lived such a life. And so with his passing we are forced to consider *our* futures, *our* judgments. As we live our lives, what will our individual consciences record permanantly on our souls? We have been forgiven our sinful pasts by God, and in his doing so he gives us freedom. And because we have that freedom, we have the obligation to forgive those who have sinned against us. Our earthly judgments should emanate from God's law, lest we play havoc with our immortal souls. It is with and in this spirit that the life of Davis Ely . . ."

Ghost sat with Rebecca in the second pew and listened to the language of death. Sonorous, steady, sure, the cardinal spoke on, enraptured by the correctness of his own words. The same cardinal had spoken at the funeral of Ghost's father, summoning a similarly unswerving tone, eyes aflame as he danced with death: The righteous have nothing to fear. . . . Sinners beware. . . . Be clean in heart and mind and deed, so that death does not catch you carrying unshed sins. At his father's funeral, Ghost had heard the words but had silently sent them back to the speakers. The cardinal and the succession of dignitaries who had spoken that day talked about "the senator," of his accomplishments, the bills, laws, and speeches that would become a part of the American record. One of the speakers had looked directly at Ghost and said,

"What pride a son can take in knowing his father leaves a legacy that covers an entire country and even reaches, due to his support of NASA funding, into space." Ghost had never expected to hear the word *funding* at his father's funeral. During the speeches that day, as the list of the senator's accomplishments accumulated, Ghost had thought of an afternoon at Nippersink when he was young and his father had taken him fishing in Lake Tombeau. His father had hooked the biggest bass of the day, but had handed the pole to Ghost for the fight and the landing; Ghost recalled the feeling of that pole passing from his father's hands to his, like wrestling lightning to the ground, and when they netted the bass they didn't think about whose fish it was.

Fund that, Ghost thought, hearing the music begin as the judge's funeral came to an end.

2

During the hour and a half drive from the cathedral to the cemetery, Ghost and Rebecca watched the city and its outlying industrial areas gradually give way to the Wisconsin farmland. Thunderheads gathered on the northern horizon, joined by humidity in promise of rain.

Their limousine pulled into a small cemetery located a few miles outside of Nippersink. The cemetery was surrounded by a vine-wrapped wrought-iron fence; a row of trees shielded it from the two-lane road. Its gravestones and tombs were old and weather worn. Shadows cast by the gravestones on the freshly cut grass disappeared as thunderheads moved in from the north.

Only family and a few close friends attended the burial ceremony. Ghost and Rebecca walked to the gravesite, where two dozen other mourners were positioned. The priest from the Elys' local church conducted this ceremony, which was quite brief. Afterward, Ghost paid his respects to Eleanor Ely, then rejoined Rebecca at the car. He stopped and looked across the cemetery to a far corner, where his father and paternal grandparents were buried in the Galvin family plot. An extension of wrought-iron fence separated the Galvin plot from the rest of the cemetery, and a large willow tree shaded most of it.

"There's someone there," he said quietly, staring.

Rebecca turned and looked in the direction of Ghost's gaze.

"My father's buried over there. Somebody's standing under the tree."

She saw the man also. He stood fifty yards from them, inside the fence surrounding the Galvin plot. He appeared to be supporting himself with the assistance of canes.

Ghost walked toward the plot.

Halfway there he felt Rebecca take his arm. "That's Alan Webster."

For two days Rebecca and Ghost had been trying to reach Alan Webster by telephone. They had decided not to think further about approaching the police with the story of Elizabeth Folger unless they could convince Webster to come to Chicago and look at Dupree's corpse and make an identification. His office took messages without promising Webster would check in for them; the home answering service gave the same response.

Webster watched from the cover of a willow tree as Rebecca and Ghost approached. When they were ten yards away, he said, "Thommy. You won't remember me looking like this." Webster wore a neck brace, a cast on his left wrist, and through his shirt and jacket they could see the outline of a back brace. Ghost pushed open the metal gate and followed Rebecca into the plot. "Hello, Rebecca," Webster said, his voice weak and scratchy.

The Galvin family gravestones were made of gray marble and set flat into the ground. Rebecca and Ghost had to step around them to reach Webster.

"I'm not adept at shaking hands at the moment."

They smelled the peppermint freshener on Webster's breath, and the gin beneath it.

"It's been a few years, Alan," Ghost said.

"Yes, it has. I lived in London up until a few months ago, when I decided to give the States another shot. Washington had me pretty well burned out. After your father, there wasn't anyone I wanted to work for. I read the American papers, so of course I knew how well you were doing."

"I didn't see you at the judge's funeral. I looked for you."

"I'm not up to seeing a lot of people. It's not easy getting around at the moment."

"I'm sorry about your accident. I didn't even know you were in Los Angeles."

"I'd planned to give you a call once my life was in better

order. The past ten years it's been kind of a wreck."

"I'm sorry to hear that."

"Right. Well, lately I've had plenty of time to think. Almost dying has a way of clarifying one's thoughts."

Rebecca recalled the last telephone conversation she'd had with Webster, when he'd sounded contrite and burdened. Now she stepped closer to Ghost so that Webster would look at her.

"What do you know, Alan?" she asked him. "Why are you here?"

He leaned against the fence to relieve weight from his legs.

"I went to the morgue yesterday. When I heard the news about the judge and about Ghost's secretary, I wanted to see for myself who they were burying. So I looked at the body, which I can tell you isn't something I'll forget, but I looked at it and knew it was Elizabeth Folger. They had something over her eyes, because from what I understand she tore them out. But it was her."

Rebecca felt a knot in her stomach; her name was still on the birth certificate. "Why are you sure?"

"I looked at her and I knew who it was."

"Did you go to the police?" Ghost asked.

"Dr. Wyndham got me into the morgue. The police don't know about Elizabeth Folger. It wouldn't make much difference if they did. They wouldn't find out much. Elizabeth wasn't one to leave tracks. They'd just be changing the name on the death certificate. Not much else would change."

"She left a birth certificate with my name on it," Rebecca said.

Webster pushed on his canes and straightened himself up. He closed his eyes for a few seconds, then opened them and looked at Rebecca. "I don't know who your mother was, but I can tell you it was not Elizabeth Folger. I promise you that. And I promise you that Senator Galvin is not your father."

Rebecca returned Webster's stare with a cynical expression that masked the hopefulness she felt listening to his words. There had been that moment when she stood alone in the basement of the Galvins' house, when she'd heard the sounds above, and wanted only to let Elizabeth Folger go, release her and be released by her. But to show belief or hope to Webster as he spoke, she felt, would be to arm him, to empower him. And though she sensed Webster was made uncomfortable by the disdain he saw in her face, he did not look away, and he did not look like a man who was lying.

"Alan," Ghost said, "we heard this from the judge. But there's nothing to protect. I tried explaining that to Judge Ely. I've seen a copy of the birth certificate with Elizabeth Folger's name on it and Rebecca's name on it, and if my father was involved, so be it. We have a right to know that." He said the words hoping to free Webster from any lingering obligation, but burned to believe him, standing these few inches from his father's grave.

"I've seen the birth certificate, too," Webster replied. "But it was Elizabeth's doing." He turned toward Ghost. "And she did it to get at me and the judge, and your father. I spoke with Judge Ely a few days ago, right after he saw you, Ghost. He called me the day he spoke with you and he was worried about Elizabeth, who he thought might be in Chicago, and told me that if anything happened to him to find you and tell you what I knew. I would have done that anyway. After my accident, when I was laid up and didn't have a chance to do anything but think, I decided I was going to find Rebecca and tell her what happened and try to explain why we did what we did. It was wrong, what we did. This was twenty-six years ago, and sometimes when you're in Washington and you're young and in a position of power you don't think you can do anything wrong, you—"

"Tell me what happened," Rebecca demanded.

Webster rolled his head back and forth, and when he resumed speaking Rebecca wondered just how drunk he was.

"Elizabeth became pregnant by the senator and wanted to have the child. The senator confided in Judge Ely and myself and we convinced him that for Elizabeth to have his child was absolutely intolerable. It was politically impossible. Now this was the late nineteen fifties and abortion wasn't what it is today. It wasn't talked about openly. We had to be very cautious. Elizabeth didn't want to hear about it at first, but if it came down to having the child or losing the senator, she was prepared to have an abortion, at least that's what she told the senator. In any case, that became moot because she miscarried. We arranged to have her taken to a private hospital in Virginia, a place where unwed mothers had their babies and put them up for adoption. It was very discreet, and we felt we could control Elizabeth's . . . medical records there. Those were different times than today. Elizabeth was in that hospital for two weeks and took it upon herself to learn the adoption system. She befriended one of the nurses and one of the girls, and what surfaced a year later was a birth certificate with Elizabeth's name on it, and yours.

"We thought she'd gone absolutely mad, but she managed to convince the senator it was something she did out of emotional distress. Of course, the paper trail had been created, the child"— Webster looked at Rebecca—"had been adopted through a reputable agency, and we had to be cautious about looking into the matter. The senator's name was not on any of the documents, of course, but we couldn't just go in there and demand an investigation to clean it all up. Elizabeth had been very clever. This hospital was discreet. There were admittance records, but these records did not indicate what the patient was being admitted for. This anonymity had cost us a great deal of money. But anyone backtracking over the events would find Elizabeth Folger being admitted to a hospital known as a center for unwed expectant mothers; they could find a birth certificate with Elizabeth's name and the name of the child. It would look exactly as if Elizabeth Folger had had a child, and would be possible to find out through which agency the child's adoption had been handled. These are sealed documents, but they exist, as Rebecca knows. We considered our options. We had used an assumed name for Elizabeth when dealing with the hospital. It wasn't until a year later that we found out she had convinced the nurse to keep the records in her real name. She knew exactly what she was doing, step by step. She found a woman who was more than happy to have absolutely no record of having had a child. I have no idea who that woman was, but I suppose her name is there somewhere in the hospital's file. Once we found out what we did, we stayed far away from those records, feeling that the more time that went by the better. After all, the senator's name was not on them, and the adoption records were sealed.

"Against my wishes and the judge's wishes, your father continued to see Elizabeth on and off over the years. When he accepted the vice-presidential nomination, we knew the relationship had to be completely severed. The senator finally tried breaking it off, and Elizabeth became more and more . . . demented. She threatened to bring up the whole child thing again. And now we were no longer in the realm of Illinois politics. We were talking about a man who could be once removed from the president of the United States. We could have fought the issue head on, but Senator Nolan Wells would have added enough fuel to the fire to end Senator Galvin's candidacy.

"Of course, the senator died, so there was nothing more to be done. I moved to England. I knew nothing about Elizabeth Folger changing her name and working her way into your life, Thommy. I did not know one thing about that until Judge Ely told me on the phone a few days ago."

"Why did he, my father's great friend, let me sit there with that woman in my house every day for two years?"

"The judge told me he didn't know it was her until months after she was working for you; he said he usually only spoke with you when you were in Chicago with the team. He wanted to get her out, but he was being cautious. He didn't know what she would do. You see, at the end of your father's life Elizabeth was truly going mad. She was calling the judge and saying you were her son and that she wanted you back. Things that were beyond comprehension. Frightening. But she would appear perfectly normal to people. She could fool anyone. The judge hoped he could get her out without having to drag you into the past, Thommy. I'm not defending what he did. I think at this point I would have handled it much differently. But that was the way he was. You knew him."

"What about *me*," Rebecca said, hurling the word *me* at Webster. She wrapped her arms around herself to control her body, which shook with anger. She had stood motionless listening to the apologies and the explanations, and heard her name come up only as a by-product of somebody's lie. "You're telling me all of this was done to protect a man's reputation?" She looked over at Ghost. "And your father *allowed* this to happen?" Rebecca turned to Webster and screamed, "What about *me!*"

"It was politics," Webster answered, unable to return Rebecca's glare.

"That's pathetic!"

"We were wrong."

"You were *cruel.*"

"We investigated the agency that handled your adoption. Though they had a policy of not releasing information to adoptees, the judge was able to find out where you went. Evidently, to a very good family. Frankly, we never thought we'd see you or hear from you. When the magazine article came out, and then you called me, I told the judge this was going to hit us in the face, that we should do something about it. I didn't want it over my head any longer. I never felt *good* about it. It was something we did in the line of duty, the way men do things in the army they wouldn't think about doing otherwise.

"The judge didn't tell me, when I called him about your article, that Elizabeth had worked her way into Thommy's life. As far as I knew, she had dropped off the face of the earth, which was exactly what I wanted to believe. The judge told me he wanted time to think about the article and what Rebecca was doing. He didn't want me to talk to you, as I told you."

"Then why did you?" Rebecca asked.

"I knew it would get back to him somehow. I guess I didn't want to live with what I knew. I didn't have the courage to come out and start saying things, not to the press. I wouldn't do that to Thommy. I didn't take the judge's calls after my accident, until I spoke with him the other day."

The sky had clouded over with thunderheads, and the air smelled steely and ready for rain.

Rebecca pointed in the direction of Judge Ely's gravesite. "Goddamn him. Goddamn him to hell."

"He didn't put your name on that birth certificate," Webster said.

"How do I know that's true? Because you're telling me? You're telling me what the judge told you to say, and I don't have any reason to believe you." She searched his eyes for any hint of deception.

"And I don't have any reason to lie to you. I didn't go look at the corpse yesterday so I could come here and lie to you. I'm doing this for me, because I don't want to die with it all on my head. I don't have enough faith for that."

Webster looked tired and pale.

"I don't understand why my father allowed himself to be involved in what you're describing," Ghost said. "I find it hard to believe."

"I never understood his relationship with her. That was an area of him that was not accessible to me."

"But what did he tell you about her? There must have been a reason for the attraction. He must have talked to you about her."

"He didn't."

Looking at Webster, Ghost believed him. What he had read in the letters from his father to his grandmother, what Senator Wells had told Rebecca, as well as what the judge had said, all seemed plausible to Ghost. He knew what Webster was saying could somehow be checked out, and he planned to do so. But as Rebecca wondered at the composition of her genes, Ghost wondered about the parts of his father that went unshared, that went into this attraction to Elizabeth and an inability to extricate himself from it; those parts of his father had been withheld, Ghost felt, but shared in the form of doubt, because if his father felt compelled to live part of his life on the dark side of the moon, Ghost wondered what ticked inside of his own mind that might take him there also. And Ghost wondered what was lacking in his relationship with his father, and in the relationship between his father and mother, and his father and the judge, that left a need for Elizabeth. So what had been withheld, Ghost knew, had not been unshared, and at this moment there could be no secrets between father and son, only things withheld.

"That absolves no one," Rebecca said to Webster. "Because the senator didn't talk to you about her absolves you of absolutely nothing. You still allowed this deceit to exist." She pointed to Senator Galvin's gravestone. "And it absolves him of nothing. He was party to this."

Ghost whirled toward Rebecca. "I'm not ready to condemn my father. If you are, you do it when I'm not around. What he did was wrong. But he's dead, isn't he? He's not preventing you from doing anything, which is something I can say to you, because I've been saying it to myself."

3

The day of Judge Ely's funeral Norman Jamison arrived at Ghost's Beverly Hills home at eight-thirty in the morning. A social worker assigned to Radio's case, and a priest from the parish where Radio lived, were scheduled to arrive within the hour. Jamison had persuaded the police to wait until the social worker made an assessment of the case before questioning Radio about burning the church. He parked his Jaguar and walked around the back of the house, expecting to find Radio on the basketball court. Jamison had dropped by the previous day to prepare Radio for the visit from the social worker and the priest. Radio hadn't said much; he shot free throws and listened while Jamison talked.

Magda brought a tray with coffee and juice and sweet rolls to the terrace and greeted Jamison.

"Mr. William is having a shower to get ready for the visitors."

"Good."

"I'll tell him you're here."

Radio had solved the mysteries of Ghost's music system, and had directed rock-and-roll from the upstairs den to the auxiliary speakers in the guest rooms. Magda covered her ears with her hands and went into Radio's room. She knocked on the bathroom door and called his name. The music was hopelessly loud and she had no idea how to turn it down. She opened the door a crack and felt the rush of steam from the shower.

"Mr. Jamison is outside waiting for you. You get dressed and come downstairs now."

She went to the terrace. "I hate that music he plays. It makes your ears bad. I told him to get dressed."

When Radio didn't appear on the terrace in fifteen minutes, Magda went back upstairs. First, she went to Ghost's den and started pushing buttons, and kept pushing them until the music stopped. Then she went into Radio's room and pushed open the bathroom door. A blanket of steam surrounded her. Magda opened the window and looked in the shower and saw that Radio was not there. She called his name and waited for a response. When none came, she walked to the hallway and said loudly, "Mr. William, Mr. Jamison is going to be very upset if you are not dressed for his meeting. And Mr. Thomas is going to be very upset with me."

She searched room to room and finally went outside and asked Jamison to help her look.

The social worker and the priest arrived and joined in the search.

4

The Learjet carrying Ghost and Rebecca shot up from the runway and climbed into the night sky. Rebecca closed her eyes and felt the pull of earth's gravity.

She was thinking of a lecture about the myths of origins given by an anthropology professor when she was in college. Passed down from generation to generation by shamans, rabbis, priests, and storytellers, myths of origins crossed cultural and ethnic lines, and supplied the common need to know of the beginnings of humanity. Entire cultures, it seemed, craved maps to ground zero. Rebecca remembered her bible classes in which she was given a past that could be traced to the beginning of time. Religion gave people a devil so they wouldn't doubt the demons in themselves, and it also gave them angels so that no one had to face the demons unarmed. Most cultures, the professor had said, provided its members with a past—mythic or otherwise—that served as a view to the future and as a force for stabilizing the present. These myths were prototype plans for the continuity of a culture or, in religion, direction for a spiritual life. Still, to her, they felt less potent than what passed between a parent and child. She thought of Alan Webster standing in the graveyard talking about the senator and Elizabeth Folger, while she and Ghost stood, like supplicants in an ancient rite, summoning the spirits of the dead. Rebecca knew she should feel freed of the weight of Elizabeth Folger's sins, but for a time this had become the known past; it was the devil she knew, as opposed to the one she did not. And Webster's story meant that her mother not only was willing to give her up for adoption, but also found solace in not having her name attached to a birth certificate at all.

She looked over at Ghost. His head was turned to the window on the other side of the plane.

"What are you thinking?" she asked him.

"I'm wondering if we're doing what they did by not going to the police—Webster and the judge and my father. They thought they were leaving well enough alone."

"At this point, as Webster said, I don't know what going to the police is going to change, other than to give the papers something to write about your father for a week or two while they dig into the story and won't find enough to keep going."

"I was thinking about Radio. He'll keep poking around about his father and, I'm sure, his mother. The other night he sat there on the bed looking at the maps of where he used to live, showing me where his house and school and all that was, and I know he's going to want to go back there. He's going to talk to people, hear things. At some point he'll want to know more about how his mother died, or *why* his mother died. Maybe he'll ask that lady who took care of him, or some friend of his will have kept an article from the paper about his mom. Maybe he'll just ask me to find out. Then what do I do? Already he told me his mother wasn't buried in the Catholic cemetery because a priest said she killed herself, which I guess is against some church law. Of course, Radio doesn't believe that about his mother, at least he's telling himself that he doesn't. But the thought is there. And if he asks you or me about it, do we tell him the whole story, right down to the drugs and the tricks? Where do you cut it off? I'm sure there are things that should be unsaid, it's just that after today it seems foolish to think so."

"I'm sorry if I attacked your father this afternoon," Rebecca said. "I was pretty busy feeling sorry for myself and kept going back and forth emotionally. I want to believe what Webster said, but part of me felt disappointed with what he was saying, because even if it's a past you want to erase, you feel drawn to it, like it's a tool that you can use to make things with. I could learn something from Radio. He walks around with those pictures of Sun Valley in his pack; he wants to make something out of *them*, and he believes that he can."

"Webster was telling the truth, whether it sounded good or ugly, and I know that because when I was with the judge the other day he looked at me differently than he had in the past. I think it made him sad that I wasn't just a kid out there shooting hoops. I was asking him if my father killed himself, and about Elizabeth Folger and you. He was looking at somebody he hadn't seen before, but I got the feeling he wanted to make peace with what I was talking about. He didn't know how to do it on the spot. But I had the feeling he wanted to. And I believe he called Alan Webster and told him to speak with us, in case he didn't get the chance to work it out. Rebecca, the judge knew he couldn't lie to me about you once we'd met, once he knew that I wasn't about to push you out of my life. I already knew about Elizabeth Folger, so he was going to have to make it clear to me about you. If he had continued to try and cover that up, it would have been more of a betrayal of my father than anything the judge could have invented, because he knew that if I thought my father had another child then *I'd* feel betrayed. That was the one thing I don't think the judge wanted me to feel. That's what I believe."

"I think I probably believed that before you did," she said. "I felt it one evening when you were in Michigan with Radio, and I sat out in the fields by myself. I just had this feeling that I was not connected to her, but with the kind of research I've been doing feelings get kind of risky and hard to trust. Sometimes you hang on to something that's wrong just to hang on to something."

Rebecca extended her hand across the aisle and Ghost took it. They listened to the engines and felt the exhaustion of unslept hours. One of the pilots woke them when it was time for the approach into Los Angeles.

16

Ghost knew something was wrong when Magda came rushing out the front door to meet his limousine. And since it was after ten P.M. he was surprised to see Jamison's Jaguar still parked near the garages.

Magda was in tears when Ghost got out of the car. "We can't find the boy."

"When did you see him last?"

"This morning. We've been looking all day. I woke him for his shower to meet with Mr. Jamison and then I don't know where he went. We've been looking all day. A priest and a lady were here to see him. They helped us look, too. I checked everywhere, Mr. Thomas. I hadn't taken my eye off him since you left."

Rebecca asked, "Did he take his things?"

She nodded. "I didn't take my eye off him. He just went in to take a shower."

Ghost shook his head wearily. "It's not your fault. In the back of my head I knew he might do something like this." Ghost checked his watch. "Magda, could you put some coffee in a Thermos? I'm going to take the Jeep and have a look around where he used to live."

Rebecca grabbed her shoulder bag out of the limousine. "You're exhausted. I'm going with you."

Ghost found a Thomas Guide in the kitchen, while Magda prepared coffee and packed sandwiches for them.

He backed the Jeep out of the driveway and started for

Coldwater Canyon, the road that cut through the hills to the San Fernando Valley.

Ghost slapped the dashboard. "Being gone two days doesn't mean I'm selling him down the river. You'd think he'd know that. I called him yesterday. Today we were busy with the funeral. I don't know what else I could have told him."

"Probably nothing."

"If he needed something he could have picked up the phone and found us in Chicago. He didn't have to disappear if he wanted our attention."

"Wherever he is probably has more to do with his mother or father than with us."

They reached the top of Coldwater, and Ghost turned east on Mulholland Drive, the two-lane road that splits the spine of the hills between the valley and the West Side. He turned left on Laurel Canyon and started down into the valley. Rebecca gave directions from the map to the street in North Hollywood where Radio had lived with his mother.

They found the street and Ghost started looking at numbers. "What's the address again?"

"11348."

He switched on the Jeep's high beams. "It's a house with a shack behind it."

The street was lined with old homes and newer apartment houses, none of them too well cared for. Ghost found 11348, a two-story imitation Tudor home that was painted a mustard color. There was a yellow bug light on the front porch. The curtains were drawn, and some of the windows were blocked out by aluminum foil.

Ghost knocked on the door. He heard dull, throbbing music coming from somewhere in the house.

He knocked again. The music pumped away.

He went back to the Jeep and got a flashlight from the tool kit.

"I'd be careful," she said.

"I just want a look at the cottage."

"Be careful," she repeated, watching Ghost walk down the driveway into the darkness.

There were two cars parked in the driveway. A 1972 Cadillac convertible, and a Volkswagen Beetle convertible. The Beetle's top was down. Ghost ran the beam of his light across the car's dash. The ashtray overflowed with cigarette butts. He edged through the narrow space between the cars and the house and reached a gate that was not locked; the latch clinked when Ghost pulled the string. The windows in the back of the main house were blocked out by aluminum foil. A cement patio separated the main house from the cottage, which had its own small garden by the front door. Ghost aimed the beam at the cottage. The wooden siding needed painting and repair.

"I'll shoot you if you turn around," a man said, his high-pitched voice edgy and persistent.

Ghost froze. From the sound of the voice, Ghost figured the man was ten feet away.

"And I will," the man insisted. "Keep your hands out from your sides."

"I'm not a burglar. I knocked at the door and no one answered."

"What do you want?"

He could be on speed, Ghost thought, listening to the voice. "I came looking for the people who live in the cottage."

"Nobody lives in the cottage."

"Are you the landlord?"

"I'm one of them."

"I was looking for Pamela Boone."

"She's not here."

"Where is she?"

"We've got nothing to do with her. She just rented this place."

"Do you know where she is?"

"Who are you?"

"Just a friend."

"If you were a friend you'd know she's not here anymore."

"I haven't seen her in a while."

"Stay right where you are. I've already called the cops."

"That's all right. That's fine with me. Is the boy here?"

"Who?"

"Pamela Boone's son."

"He's gone. They're both gone. What do you want here? They just rented this place."

"What kind of trouble were they in?"

"She's dead. You can't be that good of a friend or you'd know that. The place is cleared out. Someone else is moving in next week."

"Is it all right if I have a look? I'm just looking for the boy. I'm a friend of the family."

"What's in your hand?"

"A flashlight."

"Put it down. Slowly. Very slowly. I'll shoot you right in the back. I don't give a shit."

"I'm putting it down. It's a flashlight. Don't do anything."

"Just put it down."

"Here it goes."

He set the flashlight down on the cement.

"Now walk with your hands out back down the driveway, and get the hell out of here."

"Have you seen the boy? That's all I want to know."

"She owe you money?"

"No."

"Are you a cop?"

"No."

"If you're a cop you'd better tell me right now. It's the law you have to tell me if I ask you."

"I'm not a cop. I'm trying to find the boy. He ran away."

"The boy isn't here. The lady is dead. That's all I know. I'm sick of people coming here looking for her. She owed people money for her goddamned shit. I'm not her banker. I didn't even know her. She owes us four hundred dollars in back rent. So maybe if you're a goddamn friend of hers you'll pay the money."

"Can you tell me where the boy is? Have you seen him?"

"You going to pay me the money?"

"How do I know she owed you four hundred dollars?"

"Three hundred dollars. The rest is interest."

"You want me to reach for my wallet?"

"Where's your wallet?"

"Back pocket."

"Go slow."

Ghost removed his wallet and found four one-hundred-dollar bills.

"Drop them on the ground and move over by the cars," the man said.

Ghost did, while the man slowly circled to where he could stand over the money.

Money in hand, the man's mood improved. "The boy came by this afternoon looking for his things. But we already cleaned out the place. It was a mess. We put their things in boxes and left them at the church. It took two days to clean this place. You know what we found underneath the kitchen counter, stuffed up against the wall? About fifty pair of panty hose tied up in knots, all balled up. It was all dusty and dirty under there. The boy must have known his mother was a hooker and thought he could keep her home by hiding her panty hose." The man laughed nervously.

Ghost felt his stomach turning.

"Did you talk to the boy this afternoon?"

"I told him we didn't have his stuff. The church has it. We're not running a storage bin. She owed us all that rent."

"Was the boy all right?"

The man laughed nervously again. "He took pictures."

"What?"

"He wanted to take pictures. I let him. I didn't give a shit."

"Where did he go?"

"He just left. It was none of my business. He didn't seem in any big hurry."

"The kid's mother is dead and he shows up here alone. I guess it didn't occur to you to ask where he was going."

"None of my business. I've got nothing to do with her, man. I told you that. She had her own shit."

"Can I leave you a number to call if you see the kid again?"

"This is none of my business, friend. There's nothing for the kid here. I told him that. I told him to go see the church if he wanted his stuff. He was worried about a clock."

"A clock?"

"Some little wall clock from Disneyland. I told him we put it in the box with the rest of the stuff. This isn't a storage bin."

"If you see him tell him to call Ghost."

"Ghost. That's cute."

"Just tell him. You've got my four hundred."

"She owed it to me. Now get out of here. Ghost."

He walked slowly down the driveway to the Jeep. The man followed at a safe distance.

"I thought you called the police," Ghost said.

"I did. They'll come by sooner or later. They don't like this neighborhood."

The man stopped halfway down the driveway, turned off his flashlight, and waited for Ghost to reach the Jeep.

Ghost opened the door on the passenger side.

"You drive," he told Rebecca.

It was past midnight when they found the church in Radio's neighborhood. Rebecca parked the Jeep in front of the rectory, next door to the church. Street lamps illuminated scaffolding and tarps that covered the fire damage; the scaffolding reached to the dome above the sanctuary, and made the church look like a dry-docked ship under repair.

Ghost pushed the rectory's doorbell. "I guess it's kind of late to be doing this."

"I'm sure they get plenty of night visitors. That's the business they're in."

An old woman answered the ring. She wore layers of dark blue cotton and looked tired.

"The fathers are sleeping," she said. "Are you troubled?"

Ghost smiled at her. "I'm sorry to be disturbing you at this hour, but I'm looking for a runaway boy. His name is William Boone and his nickname is Radio. His mother was Pamela Boone and I believe she went to church here."

The woman showed no recognition at the mention of the names. But she gestured for them to enter, and directed them to a receiving room.

"If you'll wait here I'll speak to the father." She closed the door when she left. The room was plain and filled with worn furniture. There was a painting of Christ the Redeemer on the wall above the couch, and a crucifix surrounded by votive candles sat on one of the end tables. The room smelled of disinfectant.

The old woman returned carrying a tray with mugs of coffee.

Ghost wondered how she opened the door and still carried the tray.

"Father Crowley is on his way down." She set the tray on the table. "Would you care for coffee?"

"Thank you," Rebecca said.

They heard the scrape of slippers on the wooden floors of the hallway, and Father Crowley appeared at the door, as the old woman walked past him and out of the room. The father looked to be in his middle sixties, short and fat, with a skin condition that gave him a permanent flush. He wore black pants and a black shirt without the white collar.

"I'm Father Crowley. How can I help you?" He shook hands with Ghost and Rebecca, motioned for them to sit on the couch, then dropped two sugar cubes into his mug of coffee. The priest tilted his head back and looked at Ghost. "You're quite famous, aren't you?"

"I play ball for the Lakers."

"Yes, you do. I've seen you. I read in the papers that you don't plan to play anymore."

"I've changed my mind about that. I'll be playing again this season, if they'll have me." The words came unplanned from Ghost's mouth.

"Not much doubt about that. You lay off the game for a while?"

"No, I've been playing some the past few weeks. Just pick-up games with a friend."

"Well, I'm glad to hear you'll be back."

"We're looking for William Boone. Radio. He's a runaway and we thought he might have come here, or you might have seen him."

"May I ask your connection to the boy?"

"Friends."

"Of the mother or of the son?"

"Of Radio. We didn't know his mother."

"You know of her passing, of course?"

"Yes."

"The police have asked me about William. I haven't seen him since the day of his mother's funeral. Mrs. Boone's landlord left some things here, boxes of personal objects. We've tried contacting Miss Costner, the guardian, but haven't reached her."

"We thought he might come around looking for his belongings. Today he evidently went to the cottage where he used to live, looking for his things. I thought this might be his next stop."

"Not as of yet."

Ghost thought of his conversation on the airplane with Rebecca, when he wondered how much to tell Radio, if Radio asked, about his mother's death. "There was a problem with Mrs. Boone's funeral," Ghost said. "Something about where she was buried?"

Father Crowley blessed himself. "We pray for the everlasting salvation of her soul."

Ghost felt he had asked a direct question, and was irritated by the response. "What does that mean?"

Rebecca put down her mug of coffee. "I think what Mr. Galvin is saying, Father, is that we're aware of the fact that Radio's mother took her own life."

"Yes."

"And because of that she couldn't be buried in a particular cemetery. Due to church law."

Ghost nodded. "That's what I was getting at."

Father Crowley opened his palms and spread his arms. "Certain procedural guidelines are involved in the burial rite, when we're speaking of a cemetery blessed by the Church. It may seem archaic, but change comes slowly to the Church. Mrs. Boone's taking of her own life was a mortal sin. God will forgive her if she believed in God's forgiveness. But the earthly church has laws of its own. . . ."

"He heard you talking about it," Ghost said, standing to walk to a corner of the room, near the painting of Christ the Redeemer.

His muscles twitched from the flight and the driving. Something in the room was making his eyes burn; he realized it was the disinfectant. The smell of it reminded him of his father's closet the day after his father had died; his mother packed the clothes for the Goodwill, and Ghost saved the sweaters he wanted. The maid gave the closet a good scrubbing. When she finished, Ghost had gone into the closet to see if there were any other things he wanted to take with him back to Stanford. The pungent disinfectant had burned his eyes, and the odor remained in his memory.

"The thing is, Father, Radio heard you talking about the funeral and where his mother could be buried. You were at Miss Costner's house and, I guess, you both thought he was asleep. But he wasn't and he heard you."

"I regret that. I sincerely do."

"He heard you talk about suicide. And he knew that her being buried in that particular cemetery meant that she'd done something wrong, or that there was something wrong *with* her. Why would you do that? She was dead. Is that to punish her, bury her in the wrong cemetery? That punishes her son."

"That's no one's intent. Certainly not the intent of the church."

"If you're going to stick her in the wrong ground you've got to tell him that's what you're going to do and why you're doing it." Ghost's voice boomed in the small room.

"We felt he was not of an age for such an explanation." Father Crowley looked unperturbed. "He is a child."

"Look, I know you didn't write the law. I'm just saying he's going to drive by that cemetery for the rest of his life and know his mother is in the wrong ground. He may think she's the greatest mother who ever walked the planet, but he'll know something was wrong when she died. He may look into what happened, and he may not, but I think you have to tell the kid the truth as best you can, because he's going to *feel* something's wrong."

"The church doesn't plan to abandon the child. We would see that he is visited, talked to. It's an ongoing process."

"Then don't whisper when you think he's asleep. So what if she killed herself? She must have done something right with this kid because I see how he's turned out. He's good. So why not bury his mother in the right place just so *he'll* feel better? Forget what she did wrong—she's dead. Do something for him. You know what? The kid knew his mother went out at night and came home unhappy. He knew it. The landlord told me they found knotted nylons under the kitchen counter where Radio used to live. Radio hid them knowing that whenever his mother put on the nylons, she was going out at night. We know about the mother and the drugs and all that. But the kid turned out okay. And he loved her; I know it from spending time with him. Burying her in the wrong place made him feel like his mother was being taken from him twice. Do you see that, Father? I'm sorry for what Radio did to your church, and we'll see that it's made right. I'm sorry for whatever Radio's mother did that got her dumped wherever they dumped her. Rebecca"—Ghost walked behind the priest and looked directly at her; Father Crowley did not turn around—"I'm sorry for whatever my father did, or didn't do. I'm sorry, I'm sorry, I am sorry."

3

Morning came hot, still, and bright. Glare coming off the pool blinded Rebecca as she walked out on the terrace. Ghost sat at the table with the temporary secretary from Jamison's office, sorting through a mound of mail. When Rebecca arrived, Magda served breakfast, and the secretary returned to the guest house.

Ghost had been up since seven, having slept only two unrestful hours. The skin beneath his eyes was puffy.

Rebecca put a hand on his arm. "You look like you slept about as well as I did."

"I didn't sleep much."

"I'd fall asleep, then wake myself up because I kept having nightmares about Elizabeth Folger."

"I had a nightmare about Father Crowley drowning me in a bathtub full of Holy Water, you know, for yelling at him."

"You did take him by surprise."

"Then after all that I couldn't believe he asked to hear my confession. Can you believe he wanted to hear my confession? I must look like a sinner."

"You look capable of sinning."

"Then I haven't lost my edge. Actually, I felt bad for unloading on him. I don't think he knew what the hell I was saying to him, any more than Judge Ely did the other day."

Ghost thumbed through the mail left by the secretary.

The automatic sprinklers popped out of the lawn and sent mist into the morning air. "You said something last night that I wanted to hear," Rebecca said, "and I didn't know it until you said it."

"What's that?"

"You said 'I'm sorry.' I guess I wanted to hear that from someone. I've been chasing my mother feeling that I want to apologize to *her* for being the wrong child. But when you said 'I'm sorry' it felt good."

"I said it three times. Maybe more."

"I know."

"I'll say it all day if it makes you think about me instead of her." Ghost dropped a few more letters, unopened, on to the table. "I've spoken with Jamison twice this morning. He's got a judge and a lawyer and a private investigator going in Virginia, and he promises me they are going to get into those records."

He noticed a Nippersink postmark on one of the letters. Then he recognized Miss Dupree's handwriting. He felt the weight of the letter from the key inside, and let it drop to the table where it landed with a muffled thud. "What in Christ's name do you suppose that is?"

"What?"

"That's from Miss Dupree, or Elizabeth Folger, or whatever we're calling her this morning. I recognize the handwriting. Look at the postmark."

Rebecca picked up the letter and saw that it was postmarked

from Nippersink on the day Elizabeth and the judge died. She felt a metal object in the envelope.

"What the hell else does she want from me?" Ghost asked. "Whatever it is I'm sure I don't want it. But be my guest . . ."

She cleaned a butter knife and slit open the envelope. There was a slip of paper in with the key.

PUBLIC STORAGE
10706 Vanowen
Burbank
Bin 47

Rebecca handed the note to Ghost, who read it, then tossed it on top of the newspaper. "Did she think I'd be touched to get a gift from the grave?"

"I doubt that anyone will ever know what was going on inside her head."

"It makes me a little sick to say it, but I think the judge and Elizabeth may have had more in common than I want to know about. They had an image of my father that meant something to them that I'm never going to understand. I don't know that I need to." He picked up the note again and reread it. "Christ."

Magda ran out to the terrace, snapping out a string of Spanish words. Rebecca and Ghost looked at her, then saw who she was yelling at. Radio was walking around the perimeter of the back lawn, dodging the sprinkler spray.

All three of them hurried down the steps to meet him. Magda reached him first; she hugged him but let him know in Spanish what she thought of his disappearance.

Radio put his pack down and looked at them, bewildered by their expressions.

"Hi," he said.

Rebecca gave him a hug and held on to him. "You scared the hell out of us. We've been all over town looking for you."

"I didn't know you were back."

"We were just gone two days," Ghost said. "Magda was here the entire time. You apologize to her. And you knew we were coming back."

"I'm sorry. I had some things to do for my father."

"Then you tell somebody first," Ghost said. "You can't just disappear. None of us slept last night."

"I'm sorry."

Radio's words caught up to Ghost. "What do you mean, 'things to do for your father'?"

"I went to do some stuff."

"Like what stuff?"

"I used the camera you gave me. I took a lot of pictures of where I lived and the school, and I took pictures of that basketball court where he came and watched me play. I'm going to send the pictures to my father before we go back there next time."

"We'll *help* you take pictures," Ghost said. "I'll help you get the things done you want to get done, but talk to me, okay? Ask me things. You've got to let me know what you're thinking, instead of just disappearing and doing things and then showing up like nothing's wrong."

"I wanted to get my stuff."

"We talked about the stuff. I said I'd help. I had to go back to Chicago. But when was the last time I broke a promise to you? You should have told me. Now, come here." Ghost took him by the hand and walked up the steps. The four of them went to the garage, where Ghost had stacked the five boxes of belongings he'd talked Father Crowley into giving them.

"We don't know if this is everything, Radio," Rebecca said, "but that's what the landlord left at the church."

Radio was amazed to see the boxes. He poked through the top two boxes, and pulled out the Disneyland wall clock his mother had given him many years before.

"This is great," Radio said, turning the clock over in his hands with care. He began pulling things out of the boxes— blankets, clothes, dishes, books, tapes. Radio set it all down with care on the cement floor of the garage. He looked at Ghost and Rebecca, surprised and appreciative as he stood amid his belongings. "This is great!"

"So talk to me," Ghost said.

4

After lunch they drove to a one-hour photo processing store and dropped off Radio's film, then continued into Burbank and found the storage facility indicated on Miss Dupree's note. The storage bins were like tiny garages, with corrugated aluminum sliding doors.

"We're doing what she wants us to do," Ghost said.

Rebecca frowned. "We don't have to go in there. I'll go in if you want."

"Screw it. Let's get it over with."

He parked the Jeep in front of number 47 and used the key to open the padlock. In the center of the small storage room were eight cardboard boxes the size of wine cases, which were separated into stacks of four and sealed with brown tape. Ghost cut open the top box, using his key to break the seal. The box bulged with yellowed newspaper articles, neatly clipped and dated. He handed Rebecca a pile of clippings, and sorted through a pile himself, stopping occasionally to scan a story. Most were from *The Washington Post, The New York Times,* and *The Chicago Tribune,* all pertaining to Senator Galvin, some dating back thirty years. Sections of several articles had been blacked out with ink.

Ghost cut open another box and uncovered more clippings; these were ten to fifteen years old, with voluminous coverage of the Senator's vice-presidential campaign. Many of the photographs accompanying the articles had been cut to remove Nicole Galvin from the image, a pattern that repeated itself, picture after picture.

He sliced open another carton and found more of the same.

Ghost turned to Rebecca. "I never once had a conversation with Dupree about my father or my family. Not once. She wouldn't have known who I was talking about, because this isn't my father. Do you think she really believed by cutting my mother out of pictures and crossing out things in print she didn't want to read, that those things didn't exist?"

"I don't know what she believed. It's fairly clear from these pictures what she didn't *want* to believe."

"She sent me this key so I'd look at this stuff and see her in all of it. See her in the gaps. But I don't. I see articles and pictures with holes in them."

Another carton contained clippings about Ghost's career, dating back to the year he resumed basketball at Stanford and continuing through this year's NBA championship. Pictures of Ghost from the celebrity sections of newspapers and magazines, where he had been photographed in the company of various dates, had been clipped to remove the women from the pictures.

The bottom boxes were full of photographs. Black-and-white glossies, some blown up to eight-by-ten. Most had been taken with a telephoto lens, showing the senator on the steps of the Capitol, at podiums delivering speeches, catching him as he walked out of buildings. Others, faded and yellowed, were shots of the senator walking with Ghost, who looked about four or five at the time of the shots, both of them bundled up against Chicago's winds. Those, Rebecca realized, were taken from the window of Elizabeth's apartment, across the hall from Mrs. Towsley. Certain of these pictures, too, had been trimmed by precisely worked scissors.

Rebecca sifted through a stack of photographs and thought of Elizabeth trying to capture light and images from the past to shape with scissors, as if trying to construct a soul. And Rebecca recalled the dream about Judge Ely she'd had in the fields, his arms full of mirrors that reflected ancient light falling from the stars; he juggled and bent the light as if he were in a carnival act, as if to shape the past by shaping its light.

In trying to possess the past, Elizabeth and the judge had become benders of light, and Rebecca believed that the past could no more be possessed than it could be completely shed. The past clings to us, she thought, like the scent of our skin. We chase the lost light of whatever we need or think we lack, seeking permission from the past to live in the present. Yet now, standing in the storeroom of Elizabeth's boxes, Rebecca wanted only to breathe fresh air, and guard against forfeiting herself, and Ghost, in a search for lost light.

"I've seen enough," Ghost said, dropping a pile of photographs to the floor. "I don't need to see any more of this."

Rebecca followed him to the Jeep, where Radio had amused himself by playing with his new camera. Ghost looked in the rearview mirror and realized that Radio had given up the Walkman.

5

In the late afternoon, Jamison stopped by the house and Rebecca prepared a file for him to give to the attorney and investigator hired to pursue the records of the Virginia hospital where Rebecca was born.

Ghost asked Jamison to stay for dinner, but he declined; like all of them, he was exhausted from the past few days.

Ghost had given Magda the rest of the weekend off, so he busied himself with preparations for a barbecued chicken dinner, which he served on the terrace. It was the first time in several days the three of them had been together, other than the trip to the storage bin, without the presence of others, and it felt like a reunion.

After dinner they shared the task of clearing the table and doing the dishes; then Radio wanted to show his photographs to Ghost and Rebecca. He brought the packet of pictures to the living room, sat on the floor with Rebecca and Ghost, and passed them around. He had taken photographs of the cottage, outside and inside, of the school yard where he played ball, with its cracked backboard and rusted rim, and of the weathered red sign of the Starlite Lounge, where his mother had worked as a waitress. There were pictures of a Ralph's grocery store, a bus stop, and a tilted, out-of-focus self-portrait. The last pictures in the pile were of a cemetery, with two overexposed close-ups of a white grave marker.

As he passed around the photographs, Radio talked about them: the basket shown in the schoolyard was one of several, but this was the one he was shooting at when his father came to see him; the Starlite Lounge was a few blocks from the cottage, and he'd gone in there during the day, before they opened, and the bartender let him shoot pool and play the jukebox; he described the layout of the cottage, and pointed out a lamp in the picture that belonged to him and that he planned to retrieve.

Radio told them he wanted to label the backs of the photographs, then send them with a note to his father. He asked for their help with writing the note.

When they were finished with the photographs, Radio went outside to shoot baskets. Ghost and Rebecca returned to the kitchen to put away the dishes. Because of the windscreen around the court, Ghost couldn't see Radio from the kitchen, but saw the ball arching toward the basket.

"I have a boxful of letters like the one Radio wants to write," Rebecca said to Ghost. "I used to sit for hours and write long letters to my mother, telling her things about my life that I never told anyone, not even my parents. I suppose I did that because

I knew I had no place to send them. Then when I got really serious about finding my mother, and had Elizabeth Folger's name, the letters I sent were always brief; I was afraid of saying something that would scare her away. If I revealed too much she'd know everything about me and I'd know nothing about her, and that thought frightened me.

"Now I'd like to find my mother to give her all those old letters. I might not want to know her, and she might not want to know me. But I'd like for her just to read the letters, and have some idea who I am. I think that's all I want from her at this point." That, she thought, and to feel free to follow my instincts, to never second-guess emotions by wondering if at the source of them there existed a genetic flaw.

Ghost put down the plates he'd pulled from the dishwasher. "And what do you want from me?"

His eyes followed the ball as it rose to the basket. Rebecca felt a sense of peace and strength coming from him when he turned and faced her. She believed he had visited the core of his feelings about his father, and found there what he wanted to keep and what he did not. She knew this from watching him with Radio.

"What you've been giving me. Your friendship. Affection."

"That's too polite."

"It's quite a lot."

"I don't want you to go back to New York." Ghost reached over and brushed some hair away from her forehead.

"I have a job, and a life."

"We've been together practically every minute for the past two weeks, and I feel like I don't want that to stop."

"Nothing has to *stop*. . . ."

"Then stay here. *Life* and *Time* have bureaus in Los Angeles, I'm sure."

"Ghost, we've become close, but the circumstances have been a little unusual. I think we're both wrung out and could use some time . . ."

"Screw being wrung out. How do you feel about me?"

"Good."

"Good sounds like how you feel about a new car. I'm in love with you."

Rebecca set down the dish she was drying, and faced him. Her voice became quiet. "I feel the same, but I'm just learning to trust it. I haven't wanted to let it sink in, because we didn't know what our relationship was to each other."

"I have enough faith in my father to believe Webster told us the truth. The lawyer and investigator I've hired are for you, not for me."

"I know that."

"So, are you afraid to touch me?"

"No."

"I can tell you that I'm not afraid to touch you. See . . ." He took her by the shoulders and pulled her in close, the way he had in the cornfield. "There's something good about this," he said.

"I know there is."

"So let's keep it." He kissed her forehead.

She looked up at him. "I'm not fighting you. Do you think I'm fighting you?"

"You're not exactly jumping into my arms."

"Those arms have been jumped into a lot, I understand."

"Is that what this is about?"

She felt embarrassed for having said that, and leaned her head down against his chest. "I haven't been serious about somebody in a long time. I forget what it feels like."

"What does it feel like?"

"Scary."

"Tell me why."

"Have you ever been serious about anybody?"

"No."

"That's what's scary."

"What about you?"

"I dated someone seriously about a year ago. God, that sounds so grim. What I'm saying is that we were close."

"And what happened?"

"I never let myself get close enough to him to find out. I resisted it."

"Like you're resisting me?"

"This is different."

"How?"

"The circumstances are different."

"We're going to get rid of the circumstances. I'm telling you that. Do you trust me?"

"Yes, I do."

"Then?"

"We need to talk about our lives, Ghost."

"I shoot baskets and they pay me. Once you get past that,

342

you've got the rest of me, and that's what I think about when I'm with you."

"You've also taken on a lot with Radio."

"Well, I'm not turning him over to some foster home, unless that's what he wants. And I don't think that's what he wants."

"Of course that's not what he wants. But you're going to be up against a system that might not look well upon somebody who is single and travels as much as you do."

"I travel a lot, but my trips tend to be short. The kid is more independent than you or me. And if you were here, I think he'd feel very comfortable about that. He's crazy about you."

"You can't present that scenario to a social worker, that I'll be out here sometimes and you'll be here sometimes. That's pretty much what they don't want to hear. We have to give ourselves time to find out what we mean to each other."

"That's not going to happen with you in New York and me sitting here."

"You've made a decision about Radio, and you're going to fight for him. I'll help in any way I can. But you've got to sort that out first. It's important for him to get that settled, and I know what it means to you. If I'm just camping out here, and things don't work, for whatever reasons, then I'm one more person who was in his life who won't be anymore. I need to find out who my parents are, at least trace my mother, and close that chapter of my life. Until I do, I won't feel like I have all of myself to give."

"That's why I've got Jamison working on the case. I knew you were going to say that to me. I just don't want to be following you around the country unless you want me to be."

"Is that what you're going to be doing?"

"If I don't see you here enough, that's what I'm going to be doing."

Rebecca put her hands around the back of his neck, pulled his face down to hers, and kissed him.

It had grown dark outside, and Ghost saw that Radio had turned on the lights of the basketball court.

"When you are going back to New York?" Ghost asked Rebecca, who was still leaning against him.

"In a couple of days. I've got to meet with Jamison tomorrow, then fly to New York the next day to catch up on business. And then I'm going to Virginia to meet the attorney and the investigator Jamison hired."

"I'm going to miss you."

"I'll miss you, too. Both of you."

"But I won't miss you for long," Ghost said, "because Radio's never been to New York, so we might be paying you a visit soon."

"I'd like that very much. We'd have a wonderful time in the city."

"And when you come out next time I want you to help me look for a house, because I've decided to sell this place."

"You might want to think about that."

"I thought about it. I told Jamison that I'm going to sell it. I want to look out around Pacific Palisades. Or maybe one of those ranches in the mountains near Malibu. The air is much better out there, and there's room for a kid like Radio to run around and be a kid. I want you to help me look."

"All right."

"I think I'll go outside and check on Jack Kerouac. Want to come?"

"You go."

They left the kitchen and walked to the terrace.

"Ghost," Rebecca said, "I've been wondering if at some point you're going to resent me for dragging you into all this business about your father."

"You didn't drag me into it. I was there. The thing is, I feel better about my father now than I did before, because I'm not afraid to think about him; it doesn't feel like a weight when I do. If he walked into the living room right now, I might have plenty to say, things to ask him, but mostly I'd just be happy to see him. I'd probably ask him if he wanted to go fishing. That was something we did well together."

6

Ghost walked quietly to the court and stood behind Radio. He started talking with the urgency of a sports announcer: "Boone is on the line, the entire arena is deathly quiet, sixteen thousand fans know the entire game rests on the next few seconds. He settles in at the free throw line and stares down the rim, just fifteen feet away. A distance so close, yet so far when an athlete knows the fate of his team and the fate of the free world is resting on the next two shots. Boone deliberately dribbles the ball once, twice, three times, finding his rhythm, shaking off the nerves that surely are jangling in his body.

"But, boy, he doesn't show it, he looks as calm as can be. Setting his sights, he raises the ball, and there *goes* the shot, it's up, a beautiful rainbow arch, and it's good! The fans are going absolutely crazy here in the Galvin Memorial Arena. Sixteen thousand people standing and yelling. But quickly, they gather themselves, they know Boone has to make one more shot to bring off this miracle victory. The first one was an absolute must. But now that it's on the scoreboard it's ancient history, and Boone has to do it all over again. The young superstar works a dribble once again, trying to put himself back into the rhythm that will pro-duce history. The fans are standing, not making a sound. I'm telling you, folks, it's an eerie feeling to be in an arena of this size, surrounded by sixteen thousand fans, and suddenly have them go silent. It's like they're frozen, unable to move, their destiny controlled by the moves of the young man standing at the free throw line. Young Radio Boone, who appears ready with his next, crucial shot."

Radio aimed and lofted the shot. It dropped in a perfect arch toward the hoop, but caught the back of the rim, rattled back and forth, and popped out of the basket. Ghost, still talking, swooped under the boards.

"The shot is in-and-out but Galvin comes out of nowhere, knifes his way between two opponents and snatches the re-bound. The clock is clicking down. Galvin fires the ball back to Boone who is streaking down the lane."

Ghost nodded and Radio came charging toward the basket to receive Ghost's pass.

"Boone takes the brilliant feed from Galvin, soars over Larry Bird and Robert Parrish, and lays the ball in at the buzzer. It's good! It counts! The Lakers are the world champions. And the fans are mobbing the court and surrounding the players. They've got Boone in the air. I've never seen anything like it!"

Ghost snatched Radio from the ground, tossed him up by the rim, and caught him at the waist.

Rebecca could see them from where she stood in the living room. She had been thumbing through Radio's photographs again, and looking at them made her cry. She watched Ghost throw Radio in the air, and saw the fright and joy on Radio's face when Ghost caught him. Rebecca turned and looked at the painting above the mantel; it was the cornfield with golden green stalks beneath a bright blue sky. It was the one thing in the house that reminded her of Ghost.

Outside, Ghost said to Radio, "Now, it's time for you to hit the sack."

"Okay, but one thing," Radio said, running over to the control box. "Remember when we played that guy in the dark?" He turned a dial and the lights surrounding the court went out. Radio dribbled the ball to the free throw line, set himself, then sent his shot toward the hoop. There was a second of silence, then the sound of the ball swishing through the net in the darkness.

Radio laughed. "Remember?"

PART IV

17

The social workers assigned to Radio's case were not convinced that Ghost would be the best guardian for the boy, saying that the frequent travel required by Ghost's profession, combined with the fact that he was unmarried, indicated an unstable home environment. They questioned Ghost about his reputation for being a ladies' man, and with the help of a psychologist, theorized what effects might come from moving Radio from a life-style just above poverty to one of wealth. Ghost, upon advice of his counsel, took the position that his means would offer Radio an otherwise unreachable opportunity for an outstanding academic education, and Ghost offered to employ a full-time tutor, who would be responsible for Radio's getting his work done when Ghost was on the road. In response to the questions about his personal life, Ghost informed the panel that he was involved with only one person, Rebecca Blesser, and she would make herself available to the social workers if they wished to meet her. Both Radio and Ghost were interviewed extensively by psychologists.

The child welfare office took the case under review, and allowed Radio to remain in Ghost's custody while further research was conducted. The social workers continued, unsuccessfully, to search for relatives of Pamela Boone, and records indicated that William Boone, Sr., had an older brother, whom no one could locate; Boone maintained that he hadn't seen his brother since they were teen-agers, and wouldn't know him if he saw him.

When the hearings and meetings finally ended, Ghost and

Radio went to visit Rebecca in New York, and spent a week with her there.

Upon returning to Los Angeles, Ghost learned that he had been granted temporary custody of Radio, subject to frequent review by the social worker assigned to the case. Ghost celebrated by taking Radio on a fishing trip to Cabo San Lucas in Mexico; Rebecca was unable to join them because of a trip to Virginia, but Radio promised to take dozens of photographs to send her.

2

Norman Jamison, guided by Rebecca's expertise, directed the renewed search for Rebecca's mother. The project took four months, during which Rebecca made half a dozen trips to California to visit Ghost and Radio.

With the cooperation of powerful attorneys in Washington, Jamison was able to have a judge issue an order requiring the hospital where Rebecca was born to cooperate with the investigation. Matching admittance records with adoption agency transactions, Rebecca narrowed the potential birth mothers down to two. Private investigators spent seven weeks tracing them. One of the women, a member of a prestigious New York family, cooperated with the investigators, through her attorneys, once complete confidence was promised in writing. She met with the investigator and confirmed the fact that she had been admitted to the hospital, but not to give birth. She, like Elizabeth Folger, went there for observation and recuperation following a miscarriage. The woman was seventeen years old at the time of the pregnancy.

The other woman, Arlynn Hogan, proved more difficult to trace. Rebecca received frequent reports from the investigators as they uncovered information about the woman. After the emotional swings she'd felt during the search for Elizabeth Folger, Rebecca felt a sense of detachment as the reports came in about Arlynn Hogan. Rebecca spoke daily with Ghost, and spent time with him every few weeks, and this made her feel less vulnerable to the news about her birth mother, which was not uplifting.

Rebecca reached Ghost by phone in Sacramento—the Lakers

were in town for an exhibition game—one night in October, to tell him the investigators had located Arlynn Hogan, now Arlynn Kaufman, in West Palm Beach, Florida, where she lived with her fourth husband, a wealthy restaurateur. Prior to that, she had lived in Newport News, Atlanta, Miami, New Orleans, and Houston. Her previous husbands tended to be significantly older, and wealthier, than she.

"The investigator approached her in front of the town house where she lives," Rebecca told Ghost. "Evidently, she was cool and simply denied the entire thing. First, she denied ever having been in that hospital, but our guy had fingerprints, so she got angry and told him she was going inside to call the police."

"Did she?"

"No. He approached her again a couple of days later, and when she realized that the guy wasn't going to disappear, she admitted being in the hospital, told him all the records were private, and she would sue if the matter were pursued. When he suggested the matter of a deal with Elizabeth Folger and a nurse, she totally denied it and said they had the wrong woman. Her family in Newport News was kind of on the fringes of local society, so my guess is that it would have been quite a disgrace for her to have an illegitimate child. From the husbands she's gone through, all of whom she separated from some of their money, she sounds capable of it. She doesn't have any other children. Ghost, I've taken it this far, I just want to know, and then end it."

Concurrent with investigation of Arlynn Hogan, another private investigator traced the nurse who Alan Webster claimed had participated with Elizabeth Folger in the falsification of records. They found her in Phoenix working at an extended care facility. When confronted with the information by the investigator, the woman, now in her middle fifties, admitted her role in the matter. She did not remember the name of Arlynn Hogan, however, only that the birth mother was putting the child up for adoption, and Elizabeth Folger's persuasiveness had convinced her to be involved in something she later deeply regretted. The nurse offered to write a letter of apology to Rebecca, if there was a promise of no legal action against her.

With the written admission of the nurse, the investigators approached Arlynn Hogan-Kaufman again. She then retained an attorney. The Washington attorneys hired by Jamison met with the woman's attorney and convinced him that they wanted confirmation for medical and psychological reasons. Mrs. Hogan-Kaufman, who had worked her way into the lower levels of Palm Beach society, wanted only anonymity, and expressed concern that Rebecca might write about the matter and cause severe embarrassment; she contended that the revelation could ruin her marriage. Sufficiently assured that the matter would be kept confidential, Mrs. Hogan-Kaufman confirmed Alan Webster's story, insisting that she had been a distraught minor at the time and not responsible for her actions. Rebecca requested a one-on-one meeting with her birth mother, which the woman at first refused, but then agreed to if it meant no further contact. The woman decided that she would meet Rebecca briefly in a lounge at Atlanta Airport; Mrs. Hogan-Kaufman set the meeting for three-thirty one afternoon in November, and informed Rebecca's attorneys that she had a four o'clock departure booked.

3

The Lakers played in Boston the night prior to Rebecca's scheduled meeting with her birth mother. In the morning Ghost flew to Atlanta and met Rebecca at the hotel where she was staying. They had lunch in the room. They spoke about Radio and his schoolwork, and Ghost had brought brochures of some of the homes his realtor had submitted for consideration. During her last trip to the coast, Rebecca had spent a day with Ghost looking at houses.

After lunch, Ghost took a nap, and Rebecca lay awake in his arms. All day she'd felt a strong sense of disappointment and hollowness, thinking about her upcoming meeting, and took comfort in Ghost's presence. When the meeting had been arranged, Rebecca dug out the letters she'd written as a younger woman to her unknown mother. She reread them all and shared them with Ghost, then decided not to bring them to Atlanta.

At two-thirty, she dressed in black slacks, a bulky black wool sweater, and brought an overcoat against the cold day.

On the way to the airport, Ghost gave her a small souvenir leprechaun doll he'd bought in Boston. "If you don't like your mother, you just stick pins in this and she'll have a headache she won't believe."

Rebecca smiled and put the doll in her purse.

"At one time I thought this would be a happy day," she said, looking out at the gray weather over Atlanta.

"Maybe it'll be all right."

"I can't say I'm worried about it."

"What do you feel, then?"

"There's really nothing I want from her now. I used to think I'd want an explanation. Or it would be like a reunion and it would be magical and warm. What I'm thinking about now is that I'm anxious to get back to California and spend time with you guys. It's freezing in New York, and I don't like Atlanta. I feel like I'm going to see somebody who died. When my grandmother died I went to the funeral and the casket was open, and I looked at her but didn't feel anything; it wasn't her, it was just this . . . thing, like wax."

"Just go and meet this lady and let it be whatever it is. It doesn't have to *be* anything in particular."

"That's just it, it doesn't *have* to be anything. It doesn't even have to be at all. I used to think it did, that I *had* to meet my mother, and that it *had* to be a certain way, like she had my soul in her pocket and I had to get it back. I don't feel that way anymore."

The limousine reached the airport. Ghost had his luggage with him, because he was flying to Philadelphia to rejoin the Lakers for a game against the Sixers the next day. "I'll wait for you in the American lounge," he said, leaning over to kiss her. The driver opened the door and Rebecca got out, then she leaned back into the car, kissed Ghost, and said, "Thank you for flying down here."

"You didn't have to say that."

"I know. But thank you."

He waited, to avoid any commotion, until she was well inside the terminal before leaving the car.

Rebecca arrived at the Eastern terminal fifteen minutes early for the meeting. She stood outside the VIP lounge, as agreed upon, and watched travelers walk by, lives rushing past her on the way to flights, meetings, vacations—people in transit. Arlynn Kaufman had set the ground rules for this introduction, choosing the location, time, and conditions, as if to prevent Rebecca from springing some kind of trap. Rebecca looked upon the meeting as both an introduction and farewell, because she felt certain she would not see this woman again.

At three-thirty she saw Arlynn Kaufman, accompanied by two men, walk toward her from down the corridor—Rebecca recognized her from the photographs the investigator provided. Kaufman was short and chunky, with too much makeup and a stack of hair that looked too black to be natural. Her eyes were concealed by large, circular sunglasses; she wore silver and pearl earrings the size of Ping-Pong balls. According to hospital records, Arlynn Kaufman was forty-six years old, but her clothes and the makeup made her look older than that. She stopped about twenty yards from Rebecca and spoke with the two men. One of the men was short, fat, and wore a baseball cap and windbreaker that he could not successfully zip over his belly. The other man, dressed in a beige suit and pale yellow tie, carried a valise. After a brief conversation with Kaufman, the man in the suit approached Rebecca; the other man stayed with Kaufman and appeared to be extremely bored.

"Miss Blesser?" the man in the suit asked.

"Yes."

"I'm Jacob Meyers, Mrs. Kaufman's attorney for this matter. How do you do?"

They shook hands.

Meyers turned and nodded toward Mrs. Kaufman, who then approached, followed by the fat man.

Rebecca recalled the hundreds of dreams about the woman in the window, with her Victorian dresses and distant, dark eyes that revealed nothing and promised only, she now realized, what Rebecca had wanted them to promise. The power of those dreams came from Rebecca's need to know this woman, and not from the woman herself. Rebecca was relieved that the power was in her need and not in the person, as Arlynn Kaufman stood in front of her and said, "I'm sorry you felt this was necessary. I didn't. But here I am. I'm Arlynn Kaufman, and you met my attorney, Mr. Meyers." No one bothered to introduce the fat man, who looked at Rebecca with a moment's curiosity, then turned his attention back to the rack of newspapers that was across the corridor.

"I wanted to meet you," Rebecca said, wondering if her mother planned on removing the large sunglasses.

She did not.

"Well," Arlynn Kaufman said, looking Rebecca up and

down, "you're certainly a pretty girl." From the tone of her voice, Kaufman seemed irritated by Rebecca's good looks. "Listen, honey," Kaufman continued, as if to preempt Rebecca's questions, "this all happened a long time ago. I was a stupid kid and my family had a lot of pressure on me, and I didn't know what the hell I was doing. I was a stupid kid."

"I didn't come here to criticize you. I just wanted to meet you once." Rebecca tried to find a connection with her birth mother in voice, looks, or any subliminal feeling that might pass between them. But she kept thinking of her grandmother's funeral, peeking into the open casket and seeing that waxy figure that had evoked a lack of feeling, rather than emotion.

"Mr. Meyers tells me you don't want money. That was my thought when all this started, that you were after my money. It's my husband's money, anyway. I don't have any money."

"Who was my father?" She looked into Arlynn Kaufman's sunglasses and saw only reflections of the fluorescent lights in the corridor.

"That's a sore subject, honey."

"What was his name?"

"It's a sore subject. Forget about it. I lived in Newport News in those days. That's a Navy town. Do I have to tell you anything else?" Kaufman looked over at Meyers, who stood a couple of yards away, checking his return ticket. The fat man squinted his eyes to read the headlines and kept shifting back and forth, searching for a way to distribute his weight comfortably.

"What was his name?" Rebecca asked.

"I don't remember, honey. I only saw him once or twice. Do you get the picture?" Kaufman took a step toward Rebecca, and leaned down, as if to confide something. "I have a pretty good life now, and it hasn't always been that way. To tell you the truth, life has been a hell of a bitch to me. It's finally turning around a little bit, so can we leave it at that? Mr. Meyers tells me you're a successful writer and have a nice family and all. So can we just leave it at that?"

"Yes."

"I wish I had your looks, honey," Kaufman said, more angry than envious.

The fat man wore one of those digital watches that require a press of a button to reveal the time; he struggled with his thick finger to activate the tiny button, and when finally he did, he looked alarmed. He held his wrist in Meyers's face.

"Mrs. Kaufman?" Meyers said.

"Right, right. Honey," she said, turning back toward Rebecca, "we've got a plane."

"I understand," Rebecca replied, as relieved as her birth mother that the meeting was over.

She extended a hand to her mother, who touched it quickly and said, "You've got your looks." Then the woman followed the fat man, who used his bulk to create a path for her.

Meyers smiled politely and shook Rebecca's hand. "My client can consider the matter closed, I take it?"

Rebecca nodded and left to find Ghost. As she walked down the corridor, she thought that she might feel something had been cut out of her when her mother had left to fly back to Florida. But instead, she felt light, buoyant about being unbound from her birth mother, along with a certain sadness that her birth mother had not been someone else; however, she knew the sadness would dissipate because she did not deny the truth of her disappointment. Ghost's flight was not scheduled to leave for forty minutes, and Rebecca was glad for that.

18

In February of the following year, Ghost was in Chicago for a game against the Bulls, and Rebecca had flown in to join him. The Lakers had a day off prior to the game, so Ghost rented a car and drove with Rebecca to Nippersink. The Nippersink house had been sold the previous fall and the lodge was closed for the winter; they did not stop at either of those places. Ghost drove to the cemetery where his father was buried.

The trees surrounding the cemetery were bare and stark against the snow. A cold breeze blew from the north, and Ghost felt the sting of it when he stepped outside; Rebecca waited in the car. He slogged through the knee-deep snow, and found the Galvin plot only because it was surrounded by its own small fence. Using his feet, he pushed away snow from the spot where he remembered his father's grave to be, and uncovered the gray marble marker.

"Since I never visit here, you probably think this is a strange time to come," Ghost said, his words trailing across the empty landscape beyond the cemetery. "I guess the reason I never visited here is that I wasn't sure of what to say. It sounds kind of stupid, doesn't it? But that's the truth. I just always went blank when I thought about coming here. But I want to tell you that I sold our Nippersink house. It was time to do that." Ghost looked around, squinting into the wind. The sky was clouded over but not dark. A few flakes of snow were falling. He shifted back and forth in an effort to stay warm. "I'm told the house was bought by a young Chicago couple with two or three kids. I like that idea. It'll be good for the house to have kids running around in it.

"We've got a game against the Bulls tomorrow. I'm having a good season. I know that the year after winning the championship there's usually a letdown, but the team is playing well and, actually, I'm having more fun playing this year than I can remember in a long while. I've been wanting to thank you for watching me play ball all the time. I know I didn't play at all for a stretch; I guess I wanted to see if you'd watch me whether I was playing ball or not playing ball. I should have just talked to you about it. I know you liked watching me play, and that turned me into a good player. Whenever I walk out on the court I think about you. It's like you're there, and that feels good to me now, a way of having you with me.

"So the other thing I wanted to tell you is that I'm finally getting married. Can you believe it? I suppose it would have been better to meet Rebecca under other circumstances, obviously, but we've been seeing each other since last summer and, guess what, it's working out. I wanted you to know about that. Nobody knows about it right now except for me and you and Rebecca, and our friend Radio.

"Anyway, I know you and Mom always wanted me to get married at Nippersink, but that wouldn't serve much purpose at this point. So I'm getting married this summer in Sun Valley, Idaho, for reasons I'll explain another time." Ghost let out a deep breath, and he could see his breath blowing away on the breeze. "It feels good to talk like this," he said. "We should do it every day."

The snow began falling harder than before, and Ghost watched the large, light flakes fall through the branches of the bare trees. He walked back to the car thinking that he had never been to a place that was so quiet.